Praise for the Novels of

DONNA KAUFFMAN

THE BIG BAD WOLF TELLS ALL

"For a story that will touch your heart,
tickle your funny bone and leave you begging for more,
I highly recommend *The Big Bad Wolf Tells All*."
—*Romance Reviews Today*

"Women everywhere will be taking *Big Bad Wolf* to bed
with them. Donna Kauffman writes smart and sexy, with
sizzle to spare . . . and no batteries required!"
—Janet Evanovich

"Deftly spun . . . with a zippy style." —*Kirkus Reviews*

"Entertaining . . . sure to find an audience with the
beach-reading crowd." —*Booklist*

"Humor and suspense . . . Fans of Laura Zigman will
enjoy this book." —*Library Journal*

"This is one sheepish tale that stands out
from the flock of chick-lit patter with a unique zest
and fire all its own." —*BookPage*

THE CHARM STONE

THE ROYAL HUNTER

YOUR WISH IS MY COMMAND

LEGEND OF THE SORCERER

THE LEGEND MACKINNON

"Intricately woven together . . . This one kept me spellbound.
A terrific read." —*Rendezvous*

"*The Legend MacKinnon* is a uniquely exciting, captivating
and sensational read. . . . A marvelous new novel."
—*Romantic Times* [4 stars, Top Pick]

"Sensuous love stories that will heat up the atmosphere
wherever you are and some laughs to tickle your fancy. Excellent
writing by an author who has mastered the craft of creating
characters to die for." —*The Belles and Beaux of Romance*

The

Cinderella
Rules

Donna Kauffman

Bantam Books

THE CINDERELLA RULES
A Bantam Book / January 2004

Published by Bantam Dell
A Division of Random House, Inc.
New York, New York

This is a work of fiction. Names, characters, places,
and incidents either are the product of the author's imagination
or are used fictitiously. Any resemblance to actual persons,
living or dead, events, or locales is entirely coincidental.

Book design by Laurie Jewell

LIBRARY OF CONGRESS CATALOGING-IN-PUBLICATION DATA
Kauffman, Donna.
The Cinderella rules / Donna Kauffman.
p. cm.
ISBN 0-553-38234-9
1. Triangles (Interpersonal relations)—Fiction. 2. Washington (D.C.)—Fiction.
3. Women ranchers—Fiction. 4. Montana—Fiction. I. Title.

PS3561.A816C56 2004
813'.6—dc21   2003056273

Manufactured in the United States of America
Published simultaneously in Canada

RRH 10 9 8 7 6 5 4

This is dedicated

to my own fairy godmothers . . .

Liz, Karen, and Nita.

Cinderella Rule #1

*W*hile life occasionally makes it appear otherwise, no one has control over your life ... but you. Make decisions with care, because in the end, you have only yourself to blame for the outcome.

—MERCEDES BROWNING, COFOUNDER
GLASS SLIPPER, INC.

Chapter 1

*D*o *not* tell me you had Tugger stop me in the middle of playing midwife to a first-time mother because you're stuck somewhere and need me to bail you out. Again."

Darby Landon didn't wait for a response, but tucked the cell phone under one arm so she could pull off her bicep-length rubber gloves, glaring at Tugger Jack, her ranch manager and all-around right hand. "I'll deal with you later," she told him as she squeezed by.

He shrugged and quickly ducked into the horse stall to take over where she'd left off. "Said it was a matter of life and death," she heard him mutter as the stall door clicked shut. "Don't pay me enough to listen to a woman cry."

"I don't pay *me* enough to have to put up with any of this," Darby grumbled. She wiped the phone off on the tail of her overalls and shifted it back to her ear, as her baby sister continued her latest version of Rescue Me. Baby being the key word. Despite the fact that Pepper had recently turned twenty-three.

Darby stalked out of the barn and across the back stretch of grass to the farmhouse situated on the rise about twenty yards away. Of course, anyone who was old enough to vote and still went by her childhood nickname had serious issues anyway. Not that her only sister did anything as important as vote, unless it was a *People* magazine poll on the world's sexiest bachelor.

Darby knocked her boots against the frame as her sister continued to whine in her ear, then pushed through the screen door to the back porch and went straight to the fridge she kept in the outside corner. That way she didn't have to track barn crud into the house more often than she managed to anyway. To be fair, of course, if she'd stayed back East, she'd likely be a thirty-year-old, politically conscious, *Town & Country* subscribing BiBi or Dinky herself by now.

Okay, sure, technically speaking, Darby was a nickname, too. But the alternative had been so heinous—Darmilla Beatrice? Who did that to their own kid?—that certainly no one, save her father, the man who'd dredged up that horrific tidbit of Landon family ancestry, could blame her for sticking with her maternal grandfather's alternative.

And, as nicknames went, at least Darby sounded like a real name. As opposed to a condiment. Or a lap dancer.

She popped the top on a can of soda and took a long gulp, then rolled it across her sweaty forehead, ignoring the resulting smear of grime, and used her sleeve to wipe off the wet left from the can. "You can't keep doing stuff like this, Pepper," she said, finally interrupting the steady chatter she'd let flow in one ear and out the other.

"But I didn't *do* anything. I can't help it if I'm needed elsewhere. It's not like I'm asking you to come down here. I just need one teensy little favor. I'm sure Daddy won't mind, as long as one of us shows up."

Striving for a calm she definitely didn't feel, Darby spoke slowly, through clenched teeth. "When Dad hears you're not keeping your word—again—he's going to have a cat. And a cow." She broke off, swearing under her breath when she heard her sister's first little sniffle. "You know, he's *this* close to cutting you off permanently, and I don't blame him. After the last stunt you pulled at the regatta in Monaco, he—"

"I know," Pepper wailed. "But it wasn't my fault the ropes got all tangled. I had no idea they were important. You gotta help me out, DarDar."

"And half the reason you didn't worry about literally running a million-dollar sailboat aground in a coral reef is because you knew Dad or I would bail you out. Well, he finally wised up. Maybe it's time I did, too."

"But—"

"And if you value your trust fund, you'll never—ever—call me DarDar again. It makes me feel like an extra on *Star Wars*."

There was dead silence on the other end of the long-distance call, then a snuffle, a little hiccup. And, as always, Darby felt the burden of responsibility begin to creep in. Dammit. "You've got plenty of time to hightail it back home," she said firmly. She wouldn't cave. Not this time. "I'm sure there's an airport within spitting distance of wherever you are." Pepper wasn't much for roughing it.

"But, Dar . . . there's something else. Or should I say someone."

"Isn't there always?"

"But it's different with Paolo, Dar, I swear—"

"Paolo?" Darby squeezed the bridge of her nose as the throbbing in her forehead increased. "Where the hell are you calling me from, anyway?"

In a tiny voice, her sister said, "Brazil."

"BRAZIL?" she shouted. No amount of nose-pinching was going to stave off this latest Pepper-induced migraine. Pinching her sister's head off at the neck, maybe. "You said you were out of town, not off the damn continent."

"Darby, you should see this place Paolo brought me to," she gushed, switching effortlessly from tears to excitement and conveniently ignoring her sister's tirade. A patented Pepper Landon trademark. "It's huge, done totally in white marble, with fountains, an indoor pool—"

"I'm not big on hotels. You're the five-star princess. I had enough room service to last me a lifetime before I hit first grade." Even when they'd been at home, it had still felt like room service.

"It's not a hotel. It's his house," Pepper bubbled.

Bubbles. Now there was a missed nickname opportunity, Darby thought, trying and failing to summon the patience that talking to Pepper required. "I really don't have time for—"

"He's a world famous soccer star." Pepper lowered her voice. "Speaking of which, my God, Dar, you should see the man's legs. Serious flex action, and hamstrings that could probably crack coconuts. And speaking of nuts, he's amazingly well—"

"I get the picture," Darby broke in, trying like hell not to visualize a Brazilian guy with brown stringy coconut balls hanging between his legs. Her sister's love affairs were always of legendary proportions . . . as were the men she had them with. Of course, they usually lasted about as long as the standard hotel-sized bottle of shampoo. "And we both know you'll be back home, heartbroken and depressed, in a matter of weeks. So why not save yourself the trauma and fly home now. That way you can fulfill your promise, and if this big deal goes well—and we both know this business partner of Dad's doesn't stand a chance with you playing stand-in escort—you might even get access to your trust fund again. Sometime before the next Ice Age, even."

"You can afford to joke," Pepper said petulantly. "You don't care about anything but that stupid ranch of Grandpa's."

"It's my ranch now. And you're right. I don't care about jet-setting

hot spots, Dad's money, or working my way through every international power-broker playboy in the Northern Hemisphere."

"I'm in the Southern Hemisphere," Pepper interjected grudgingly.
"And Paolo's not a playboy, he's a professional athlete."

"*There's* a distinction," Darby said dryly.

Pepper huffed. "You're being unfair. I wouldn't ask if it weren't
important. I do everything for Daddy, and we both know how impossible he is. When was the last time you—"

"June fifteenth. Nineteen-ninety-nine. I showed up for your graduation. I'm due at least another decade or so before I have to descend
into the snake pit of Washington power movers and shakers again."

"For Christ's sake, you make it sound like the Animal Kingdom or
something."

"Exactly. Watching the food chain in action is a perfect analogy.
The powerful feasting on the weak." Darby sighed as the silence spun
out. "Listen, you know I've always wanted what was best for you. And
I know it's partly my fault for not pushing you to deal with things—"

"And I've told you a million times that you don't have to play
mommy to me anymore."

Well, then, grow up, Darby wanted to tell her. And it didn't matter how often Pepper told her she didn't need a mother figure. She
did. Hell, they both probably did. Their real mother had died when
Darby was eight and Pepper was barely out of the crib. Of course
Darby felt responsible for her baby sister. It didn't help matters any
that at the age of eleven, Darby had basically run away from home—
or away from their father, to be exact. A man who measured a person's
value by their net worth. In the case of his two daughters, that trans-
lated to parlaying the family name into brokering a decent merger—
what other folks called marriage—to another, equally powerful family
name.

On that scale, they'd both been dismal failures. Darby could care less, but Pepper had to deal with that reality—and him—on a daily basis.

"I know Dad isn't the easiest man to live with," Darby began, ignoring Pepper's snort. "But you've managed to do what I never could have done. I wouldn't last two minutes in that world. You've found a way to thrive in it."

Another little sniff. "I do like the way I live. And the way I see it, Dad shouldn't hold this kind of thing against me. Part of the reason I do these things is because of the way he raised me. I'm merely a product of my environment," she announced with a pitiful sigh.

Darby laughed. It was that or rap the phone repeatedly against the wall. Or her forehead. "Yes, well, you might actually have a point. But we both know the best thing I can do to help you is to stop bailing you out. Besides, it's the end of foaling season. I can't just waltz two thousand miles away and play stand-in for you. I've got horses to feed, stalls to muck—"

"And all three of Tugger's grandsons coming to Montana for the whole summer to help you out."

"Still," Darby said flatly, stalwart to the very end, "I don't have the polish, much less the stomach, to pull off the whole Washington hostess thing. I ride horses. You're the one who rides senators."

"Oh, har, har," Pepper shot back, not remotely offended. "And Morton was a delegate to the House of Representatives, not a senator."

"Which is exactly my point. I wouldn't know a delegate from a horse's ass."

"Actually, they're very similar," Pepper said with a dry laugh. "Or in the case of Morton, an elephant's ass. He's a Republican," Pepper clarified when Darby didn't laugh. "Elephant and donkey?"

"Yeah, I get it, a real party animal." Darby drew dirty circles on the table with the sweat from her soda can, wishing like hell she could just be mad at Pepper and not love her and worry about her all at the same time. "You're the one who needs to get it. Even if I was willing—which I'm not—you really don't want to be counting on me to keep this guy happy until Dad shows up. I'm good with animals, not people."

"But I'm not relying solely on you. I mean, not entirely. I have help all lined up, in fact." She said that last part brightly. Too brightly.

Darby propped open the screen door with her boot and stared unseeingly at the Big Belt Mountains that pitched up just beyond the boundaries of her land, an ominous feeling gathering in the pit of her stomach. "Meaning what, exactly? What have you done now?"

"Well . . ."

"Penelope Pernell Landon—"

"I'll never call you DarDar again, I swear."

Darby didn't smile. "And I'll use the hated full name again and again until you tell me what you've gotten me into now."

There was a pause, then a slight clearing of throat, then, in a perky voice that would put even Reese Witherspoon to shame, she asked, "Did you see that feature article in *People* magazine? About that company that does makeovers? And I don't mean just beauty makeovers, but, like, entire life makeovers. Glass Slipper, Incorporated?"

"Tell me I am *not* hearing what I think I'm hearing. I like movies as much as the next guy, probably more, given the social life—or lack of one—in Big Bend, Montana. But I don't want to read about the people who act in them. You're the one who cares who Ben Affleck is screwing, not me."

"I know. You only care who your horses are screwing. It's sad, Darby." She sighed, deeply disappointed. "I guess I should be happy you know who Ben Affleck is."

"Satellite dishes are a wonderful thing."

"Well, you should keep up more. Ben and I might make an excellent match. We both come from the East Coast, we both believe in having a good time." She laughed. "And we both have a deep and abiding interest in his money."

"Then phone Ben. Because I swear to God, Pepper, if you've—"

"Now don't get your chaps in a knot," she said, dropping the perky persona. "Just hear me out. Besides, it certainly wouldn't hurt you any to do this. I'm actually doing you a favor when you think about it. In return for the one you're doing for me," she added hastily when Darby growled. "Think of it as a vacation. And a chance to improve your marriage options."

"My *what?* Did you just say *improve my marriage options?* I'm not shopping for a goddamn husband."

"I know you don't like to talk about this, but the big three-oh has arrived, Dar. And with language like that, it's no wonder they're not exactly beating down your door. Or stall, as the case may be."

"Very funny," Darby said darkly. "This is not about me. This is your harebrained idea. Your problem. And I refuse to be the solution, but thanks for calling. Please let me know when you've found the mind you obviously lost somewhere in the Brazilian jungle."

"Wait! Don't hang up on me, Dar, please?" Pepper resorted to her little-girl wheedling voice, which went a lot further with men—any age, any tax bracket, didn't matter—than it did with Darby. But it was effective enough to keep her from clicking the OFF button. "You know I wouldn't ask if this wasn't absolutely my last possible chance at happiness."

Darby snorted.

"Okay, okay. I know I've been a bit fickle with men." She sighed, deeply and with the kind of palpable emotion that could have made her a star on Broadway. "But he could be the one."

"Pressing the OFF button."

"No! Okay, okay, no more bullshit, I promise." She blew out a sigh and finally gave up all the finagling and pretense. "Bottom-lining it, I have to be in two places at the same time, on opposite continents. We both know I can't do that."

"We both know you have plenty of time to fly home, handle this hostess job you promised Dad, and fly back to Paolo the Magnificently Coco-Nutted Soccer Boy."

Pepper snickered before she could stop herself, but quickly rebounded. "You don't understand. Paolo has a big match this weekend. He has to have me there." A smug little smile came into her voice. "He says I'm his good-luck charm. He's the goalkeeper and he hasn't been scored on once since we've been together."

"I assume you only mean by other soccer players."

"Darby." She sighed, then in a knowing tone, added, "But honest to God, Dar, he is an animal in bed. I mean, the way he can make me scream when he—"

"Way too much information here," Darby cautioned. Not that she was a prude. Anyone who'd put stallions to stud as part of her daily routine couldn't afford to be at all squeamish when it came to sexual anything. But this was her baby sister. And, okay, maybe a teeny tiny part of her was a teeny tiny bit jealous. Not of Paolo. She went more for the tall, blond and earnest, if not particularly bright type. They were more appreciative and less demanding that way. But the screaming? Well . . . it had been a while.

"It's only a week," Pepper cajoled. "And you get a spa vacation."

"Spa vacation. You mean, makeover hell. I've been out here almost twenty years. It's going to take a lot more than a new hairdo and pair of heels to make me believable as a Washington socialite. This guy I'm supposed to drag all over town and impress for Dad will take one look at me and be on the first plane back to his homeland."

"Which is precisely why Glass Slipper is perfect. That's exactly what they do. They can help get a person past whatever obstacles are in her way to getting what she wants. Whether it's a new job, a new location, a new man, a new life—they'll help give you the tools you need to succeed."

"I'm already a success," Darby stated, but she knew she was wavering. Not because she had even the remotest interest in being pampered, plucked, and waxed. She shuddered down to her DNA at the mere thought. One perk of working on a ranch was that shaving was optional. Horses didn't care. And neither did Tugger. But Pepper actually sounded happy, excited, when for too long she'd sounded bored and restless.

Darby worried about her most during those times. She'd tried to steer her younger sister toward a career, charity work, anything that would give her the sense of self-fulfillment she so desperately needed. Pepper usually ended up letting men fill her, instead. And, in that respect, nothing had changed. But at least this time the guy wasn't old enough to be her father. And he was wealthy enough, apparently, to support her sister's tastes since Daddy had cut her off.

Pepper pressed her advantage. "It's a week. And only three days of actual society stuff. There are only a few events scheduled that you have to schlep him to. It's very important that you show him a good time—"

"Whoa, whoa, hang on right there."

"Not *that* kind of good time."

Darby wondered if her sister would draw the line there. Though even their dad wouldn't expect his princess to go that far. Of course, if it did happen to go in that direction, and helped close the deal, Darby was sure her father would show his appreciation. With a new car, or something sparkly. Which was a big reason why Darby and her father didn't get along. She didn't show proper enthusiasm for the perks of being an offspring of the mighty Paul Landon III. She would have settled for a hug. He was more comfortable expressing his emotions with an American Express card.

"Dad needs this deal to go through. It's important."

Aren't they all? Darby and her father had long ago agreed to disagree. Or, more realistically, she agreed to ignore him and he agreed to pretend he only had one daughter. "What's it about?" she asked, hating herself for even asking. "The deal, I mean."

There was a pause. "It's all kind of complicated."

Meaning Pepper probably didn't know. "Wouldn't it help to have something to talk to this potential business partner about?"

Pepper paused, then said, "Something to do with gemstones. From Africa, I think. Or maybe it was Australia. Or Asia."

Darby visualized the unconcerned shrug that accompanied Pepper's light laugh. "One of those A continents anyway," Darby said dryly, then found herself shaking her head, smiling herself. Her sister was hopeless, but then, so was she when it came to denying her anything. "So this guy is African? Or Australian?"

"Scandinavian, actually. Swedish, I think. His name is Stefan Bjornsen; he's coming in from Amsterdam. Dad was supposed to fly in, schmooze him at all the regular haunts while they talked business, and close the deal. But he got hung up with a deal in Belgium. Or Brussels."

"Some B country?"

Pepper didn't take the bait. She was too close to closing her own deal. And Pepper was nothing if not focused when it came to getting what she wanted. Darby absently wondered what her sister could have accomplished if she'd dedicated herself to following in their father's capitalistic footsteps. Given her people skills, she could be ruling the free world by the time she turned thirty.

"All Dad needs is for someone to play hostess until he can fly in and take over. Stefan is flying into Reagan next Thursday at one. I booked you on a flight into Dulles, arriving Saturday afternoon. I know it's not as close to home as flying into D.C., but it was the only direct flight I could get out of Bozeman and I know how you are about—"

Darby groaned. "God, I hadn't even thought about—"

"There will be a car from Glass Slipper waiting at the main terminal," Pepper rushed on. "You'll be with them through Thursday morning. Then you can pick up Stefan and get settled in at the house. I've already alerted the staff, so everything will be ready."

"You've thought of everything," Darby murmured, still not quite believing she was actually going to go through with this. Twenty minutes ago she'd been shoulder-deep up a mare's birth canal. And perfectly content with her life. Now? She thought about what she was going to face and knew she'd feel a lot scuzzier after twenty minutes back in Washington than she would later tonight, when her newest foal finally came into the world.

"There's a charity event Thursday night, then the rest of the weekend is easy. You're expected on Friday at the annual Belmont Stakes party at Four Stones. Daddy's supposed to fly in Sunday and meet you out there by midday. You can cut out then. All in all, you'll only be gone a week. It's a breeze, really."

Darby was only half-listening. It had been so long since she'd had to fly—since 1999 to be exact—that she'd forgotten all about how much she hated everything there was about it. The very idea of stepping foot in a plane, much less living back under her father's roof—no matter the duration or that he wasn't there—dredged up emotions she wasn't prepared to deal with. "You're asking a lot more of me than a week of my time, you know that," she said quietly.

To her sister's credit, she responded with dead earnestness. "I know." She paused, then said, "I know I lean on you way too much. And I know you worry about me. But, honestly, DarDar, I'm going to be okay. I know it doesn't sound like it now, but I'm really going to turn things around. You'll see." She laughed lightly. "It's funny, how different we are, but you know, we're both where we want to be. Me, in D.C., dealing with Dad, and you handling the ranch. Sometimes it's hard to believe we came from the same two parents. Mom was probably more like you, seeing as she came from that life."

Darby supposed Pepper was right. Their mother hadn't been born to the silver spoon like Dad had. Nor had the former Laurel Stockton been all that pretentious about the lifestyle she'd been sucked into when the great Paul Landon III had shocked everyone by falling in love with his guide during a Montana riding-and-fishing expedition. By a very young age, Darby figured out that her mother was the only real thing in a world filled with phonies and hidden agendas. At least, it always felt that way to her. Her mother was the only one who understood how out of place Darby felt, with her tomboy tendencies. She'd tried to help her understand that being different wasn't such a bad thing. And provided that all-important barrier between Darby and her father, who didn't understand any of that, despite marrying her mother.

She'd felt completely abandoned after her mother's death, which came only a precious few months after she was diagnosed with breast cancer. Her dad had climbed into a cocoon of grief. He didn't even try to understand her. No one did. Except Grandpa Stockton. Grieving himself, he'd reached out to the one real reminder he had of his only child—the grandchild who was so like her. He offered a home and hearth unlike Darby had ever known. Best of all, it was far away from the unending parade of nannies, private lessons, and strict lectures on decorum and expected performance.

But, even at age eleven, leaving Pepper behind hadn't been easy. In fact, it was the hardest thing she'd ever done. It had been a matter of survival for her then, but as she'd grown up, she'd been determined to be there for her sister the way Mom had been there for her, and should have been there for both of them.

"I am changing, Darby. I know you don't see that yet, but I am. I hate it when you and Dad are both mad at me." She sighed, then with absolute sincerity, said, "I swear, Darby, this is the last time."

Darby laughed, trying to ignore the sick feeling in the pit of her stomach. "That is so not true."

Pepper laughed, too, then sighed. "Probably not. But I want it to be. And I know I owe you big. Bigger for this than anything ever," she added hurriedly when Darby snorted. "Anywhere, anytime, I swear it, you name it and if I can do it, it'll get done."

Darby couldn't possibly imagine ever collecting on that debt. Not because she wasn't willing to put Pepper to the test. It would probably do her a world of good if she did. It was just that, looking out back at the paddocks, indoor and outdoor rings, she couldn't possibly envision her sister doing anything particularly helpful, much less anything else actually work-related. Getting dirt beneath her nails was as foreign a concept to Pepper as painting her nails was to Darby.

But she couldn't resist torturing her just a little. After all, it was probably the only amusement she'd get out of the deal. "Great. I'll be sure to call you come next foaling season."

It was almost worth the whole thing to hear her sister audibly choke, then force herself to say, "Sure. Just, ah, let me know."

"I just might," Darby warned, liking the idea of her sister getting far more than dirt beneath her nails.

So, she had three whole days to get everything settled, then make the trip East. She only had one question. Okay, she had a ton of questions, but only one that Pepper could answer. "Who's funding this little Glass Slipper escapade?"

"Paolo," Pepper said. Then, with a little laugh, added, "He considers it an investment in his team's chances for the playoffs." Then she heard a man's deep voice in the background, sexy and cajoling. Then her sister's stifled squeal, the muffled sound of the phone being covered, then Pepper's breathless, "I have to go. Thanks, Darby!"

Darby shook her head, but couldn't help smiling. Pepper was very likely smiling, too, and would be for some time if that deep voice held the kind of promise Darby thought it did. She sighed in envy. "And they said sporting victories couldn't be bought."

Darby fought to maintain that smile as she headed back to the stables, to finish bringing that new foal into the world ... and to talk with Tugger about her upcoming absence.

〜〜⌒〜

*A*ny ability to smile was long gone by the time she exited the plane, white-knuckled and pasty-faced, some three days and five hours later. She more than hated flying. She despised it. Had forgotten just how much she despised it until the plane had pulled away from the earth ... and her guts had pulled away from the rest of her insides and twisted into a knot. She had wished the worst South American disease known to mankind on her sister as she'd upchucked horrible airline food into a paper bag at thirty thousand feet. After all, it was only fair.

"Vacation, my ass," she grumbled under her breath, ignoring the wide berth her fellow passengers were giving her as they were corralled into the midfield terminal transport. So she'd been a little vocal when they'd hit the turbulence. Surely everyone got a little loud when they got nervous. Didn't they?

She exited the crowded car into the main terminal, crunching peppermint Lifesavers, but still feeling shaky and clammy. She wanted a bathroom. She needed to splash water on her face. Brush her teeth. Again. She'd spent the entire flight sweaty and chilled by turns. Between putting her head between her knees and burying it under a too-small airline pillow, the braided rope of hair hanging down her back probably looked like an entire flock of birds had made their home in it. God only knows what the rest of her looked like.

She was itchy, grouchy, rumpled, and restless from being boxed up in an aluminum tube for five hours. And sick to death of the taste of peppermint. She needed fresh, unpressurized air. Wide-open spaces. She hated crowds. And, goddamn, could they stuff any more people into this airport? How did people deal with this on a daily basis? Rush hours, smoggy air, banging elbows just to walk down the street.

She collided with more people in the five minutes it took her to navigate her way to Baggage Claim than she'd bumped into in the past year and a half at home. If she hadn't already sworn to walk all the way back to Montana rather than ever set foot inside an airplane again, she'd have hopped on the next plane to Brazil and personally kicked her sister's sorry, soccer-humping ass all the way to Washington.

So the very last thing she needed to see, the capper on a very long day, and the one thing guaranteed to make her feel every yucky inch of herself ... was the man wearing a crisp black-and-white driver's uniform, standing with a sign bearing her last name in one hand.

And a glass slipper in the other.

Cinderella Rule #2

*L*ife offers very few do-overs. A good first impression is critical. Don't waste yours unnecessarily. 12-Hour Mascara can be just as valuable as a master's degree. An 18-Hour Bra might serve you even better.

—Vivian dePalma, cofounder
Glass Slipper, Inc.

Chapter 2

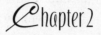

Shane Morgan had been a very bad boy. Well, actually, that depended a great deal on who you asked.

He stepped off the curb in front of Dulles International and was about to sling his heavy duffel bag into the trunk of the Washington Flyer, when he spied a chauffeur with a glass slipper in one hand, and opening a limousine door for an extremely unhealthy-looking woman with the other. He had no idea what was going on with the woman, but he knew exactly where that glass slipper had come from.

Mama Mercedes.

He grinned, knowing she'd hate that name, but for the first time since he'd gotten word about his grandmother's unfortunate demise, he was happy to be back home. Of course, *how* unfortunate Alexandra Morgan's death was, also depended a great deal on who you asked.

He tossed an apologetic smile toward the cabbie, grabbed his duffel, and loped easily across the blacktop, darting around people, and weaving easily through traffic, despite the heavy load on his back.

His many colorful careers did come in handy on occasion. Stamina was never going to be an issue. Physical stamina, anyway. Psychological stamina? Well, now that he was home, that was about to be put to the test, wasn't it?

"Hold up," Shane called out to the driver as he handed the slipper to the woman and closed the door to the limo. He wondered what her story was. A woman more desperately in need of the inimitable services of Mercedes and her two fairy-godmother cohorts, Aurora and Vivian, he'd never seen.

The driver turned then, and took in Shane's travel-weary appearance with a small sniff. "May I be of some service to you, sir?"

"Mercedes always did believe the snootier the better." Shane's grin widened at the driver's stunned expression. "One of the few things she had in common with Big Al."

"Big . . . Al, sir?" He said it like it left a bad taste in his mouth.

"Private joke." Probably best not to share it, even with the Glass Slipper hired help. If it got back to Mama M, she'd rap his knuckles. The fact that he was well past knuckle-rapping age wouldn't matter much where his former headmistress of a godmother was concerned.

She and Alexandra had been students together at the elite Hedgely School for Young Ladies in New Hampshire. Mercedes had gone on to run the school, which made her the obvious choice for ringleader of the makeover empire trio. And, just as obviously, her spare-the-rod-and-spoil-the-debutante background had been a blueprint for Glass Slipper's employee-training manual.

His grandmother had married industrialist Grayson Morgan, taking over his empire after he died at age forty-five. Some said the heart attack had something to do with the dancer who'd accidentally discovered his body—in her own bed. Shane had never known the man, but he did know Alexandra, and had a hard time condemning his grandfather for finding a little comfort somewhere.

Shane supposed he should count himself lucky Mercedes had had a soft spot for Alexandra's only child, Francine Morgan-Lovelle—his mother, and another Hedgely alumna. So much so, that she'd kept tabs on her favorite pupil's only child after Francine and her husband, Chad Lovelle (of the New England Lovelles), had been killed in an avalanche while skiing in the Italian Alps. Shane had just finished up his first year at a boarding school in Switzerland. And while he wouldn't exactly call his godmother an affectionate woman, he'd been grateful more times than he could count to have Mercedes Browning on his side.

After the death of his parents, Alexandra had been intent on turning him into a little empire-building clone. She'd never forgiven him, the last in line to inherit the Morgan family dictatorship, for rebelling. She simply didn't understand that not everyone was excited by the prospect of collecting corporations like other people collected stamps. He wasn't opposed to being successful—he just defined it differently than she did. She'd also never forgiven Mercedes for championing Shane's desire to chart his own course the instant he was old enough to do so.

Okay, so maybe he'd hightailed it out of Washington a bit shy of his eighteenth birthday, but he'd been to boarding schools in three countries before he'd had his first kiss. He knew how to get around. Mercedes had apparently agreed, because she had been the one who'd funded his first foray into the real world, sans trust fund. It had been the start of a life filled with absolute freedom and adventure. One he was still enjoying to the fullest, some thirteen years later.

He held out his hand, which the gloved, liveried driver inspected with distaste—or would have if his impeccable training had permitted it. And, admittedly, Shane's hands had been put through a wringer or two. He liked to think of them as hands with character; the various shiny patches, calluses, and not-quite-straight pinky finger were badges of merit, of a life lived to the fullest. No pampered, buffed, manicured hands for him, thanks. "Mind if I hitch a ride back to Fairy Godmother Central?"

"I beg your pardon, sir?"

"One of them is actually my real godmother," he explained. "Mercedes Browning." The man didn't blink. "She was a close friend, or as close a friend as she was capable of having, to Alexandra Morgan. My grandmother."

Recognition dawned in the older man's eyes. Followed swiftly by a brief flash of unmitigated curiosity, along with a healthy dose of dismay. Apparently, the last of the Morgan lineage hadn't been forgotten in the happy little shark pond that was the Washington corporate elite. "I'll be glad to ride in front. Your client will never know I exist."

Another brief flash, this one of disbelief.

So, his rather storied reputation had also preceded him. Great. So much for sneaking into town, pawning off his inheritance, then hightailing it back to ... well, anywhere but here, before tongues started to wag.

"I'll keep quiet as a lamb," he promised, raising his hand in the universal gesture of faith. Not that he expected the old guy to have any. Which wasn't all that annoying. He'd learned a long time ago to have enough faith in himself so that it didn't matter what anyone else thought. "Go ahead and radio in. But I'm sure my godmother won't mind."

The chauffeur said nothing, but moved stiffly around the limousine, to slide into the driver's seat. Shane thought he was going to close the door and drive off, leaving him standing there with all of his worldly possessions slung over his shoulder. "Well, it wouldn't be the first time," he murmured, even as he held his confident smile.

The old man stared ahead for a moment longer, then glanced at Shane and finally reached for the small cell phone. Shane shifted his bag off his shoulder and hiked to the back end of the mile-long car.

While he waited for the driver to pop the trunk, he tilted his head back and closed his eyes. Home again.

For thirteen years he'd done his best to be anywhere else in the world. And he'd done a damn fine job of it, too. Now he was back. With a whole lot more shit to deal with than he wanted to acknowledge. He couldn't help but wonder if his luck had just run out.

Well, at least the sun felt good on his face.

The trunk clicked and Shane hoisted his bag in, glancing at the battered leather satchel and Army-issue canvas duffel already residing in the cavernous interior. Not the usual set of matched luggage that Glass Slipper, Inc.'s clientele used to tote their designer clothes around. Sure, his godmother's business was helping people improve their lot in life, but someone had to pay the tab. He grinned and snapped the lid down. Probably Aurora's doing, the old softy. Because while Mercedes firmly believed in helping those who were willing to help themselves, she expected to be well compensated for her services.

He was moving alongside the car when the rear window eased down . . . and the woman inside let her cheek rest on the open frame.

He stopped. "Are you okay?"

Apparently she hadn't seen him approach, because she let out a little yelping noise and snapped her head up, then immediately growled and pressed the heel of her hand to her forehead. "First the glass slipper, now what?" she muttered, before gingerly looking up at him. The sun at his back had her squinting. "Who in the hell are you supposed to be? Prince Charming?"

Cranky and not afraid to share it. Shane grinned, liking her already. "Well, I've been called a lot of things, but generally that one doesn't even make the extended list. I'm just hitching a ride in, for a visit with my godmother."

"Isn't this taking the whole fairy-tale thing just a tad too far?

You're a grown man, for God's sake. I mean, it's just a glorified charm school, isn't it?"

He chuckled. "Oh, I think they'd take exception to that description. And please, say you'll let me be there when you share that with the group. But, for the record, I'm not a client. Mercedes Browning really is my godmother. Nothing fey about her in the least, trust me."

"Jesus," she said, then blew out a long sigh and leaned her head back inside the car, closing her eyes. "Just shoot me now. And don't worry, no court would convict you. It would be a total mercy killing." She opened one eye. "Honestly, though, I'm sorry. I didn't mean any offense."

He didn't hold it against her. She looked like hell. Her long, thick hair, a heavily sun-streaked dark blonde, had wrestled half-free of the braid she'd bound it in. Her eyes were an interesting shade of green-flecked hazel and looked huge, probably due to her otherwise wan complexion. Her arms were a deep, golden tan, however, the soft hair on them bleached blonde and a light sprinkling of freckles that matched the ones scattered across her nose and cheeks.

He stuck his hand out. "Shane Morgan."

She did nothing for a moment, then warily took his hand. Hers was clammy, which wasn't a total surprise. What was a surprise were the calluses and the strength of her grip, which came through despite the brevity of contact. So, she had hands with character, too. How intriguing.

He lifted her hand, then bowed at the waist before releasing it. "Black sheep of the East Coast Morgans, at your service, madam," he added, then ruined the whole effect by shooting her a wink. "Although I'm definitely more Dark Knight than Prince Charming, so I give fair warning to accept any services with caution." He nodded at the glass slipper lying neglected on the seat next to her. "You must be Cinderella-In-Training."

"Darby Landon," she replied evenly. "Black sheep of the East

Coast Landons, feeling more like a science project than Rookie Cinderella."

"You don't sound too optimistic about making it to the major leagues." He nodded to the sleek limo she sat in. "I guess that's why you signed up for this ride. Well, trust me, while Mercedes, Aurora, and Viv have no magic powers, they have been known to work a miracle or two."

She arched an eyebrow. "Thank you. I think."

"Hey, I didn't mean to imply that—"

"Yes, you did, but it's okay." She gestured to herself. "Who could blame you? But I didn't sign up for anything. I'm here under duress. The only miracle I need is the one that'll keep me from hitching the first train back to Montana."

He gave her a considering look. "Husband or boyfriend?"

She looked nonplussed for a moment. "As in, who coerced me into this? It's not so simple as that. I could have said no to either of them."

"Have one of each, do you?"

"I'm beginning to realize the depth of my error with that Prince Charming crack. I was obviously blinded by the smile and the blue eyes. But then, I suppose you're well aware of your impact on the fairer sex."

"Now there's a rather backhanded compliment if I ever heard one."

She lifted one shoulder. "Fair's fair. Besides, something tells me you've heard more than your share of those, too."

Rather than be turned off by her sarcasm, he was intrigued. He let a smile be his answer. "So, if it wasn't the hubby or the boyfriend, who got you into this mess? I sense you're not generally pushed around a lot."

"Generally, you would be correct," she said, somewhat warily.

Could it be that she wasn't used to having someone pay such close attention to her? The intrigue continued to grow.

"Sibling guilt," she said reluctantly. "Which makes it my own damn fault."

"Ah. I wouldn't know much about that. My parents wisely gave up reproduction after I popped out."

For the first time, the slightest quirk tugged at the corners of her mouth. A mouth he was just now noticing. And what a mouth it was, too. It was wider than the norm, with a clearly defined upper lip, but a generously fuller bottom one. It was the kind of mouth he could sink tongue, teeth, and heart into. He angled his head, curious about the rest of the package.

The driver popped up and looked over the roof of the car. "Sir?"

Shane acted impulsively. Some things, after all, never change. He opened the side door of the limo. "Your guest has invited me to ride in the back, to keep her company."

The driver shot him a dubious look. Shane wasn't sure if he simply doubted Cinderella would be interested in sharing a ride with a guy like him, or if he was worried that Shane would somehow corrupt her on the drive in. Probably a little of both. *Smart man.*

"Very smooth," she said as he settled himself across from her. The expanse of carpet was wide enough for both of them to stretch out their legs. Which was a good thing, because hers were easily as long as his. And he topped six feet by a few inches. He openly sized her up and decided she was flirting with the six-foot mark herself. Amazon Cinderella. He took in the rest of her. Those strong, tanned arms, the white T-shirt that he'd bet was more likely to sport a Fruit of the Loom label than Calvin's or Ralph's. Her lanky legs were covered in loose jeans that had to have acquired their battered look honestly. Equally well-worn Western boots completed the ensemble. All she lacked was the sweat-stained Stetson and a bandana around her neck. And he'd bet there was at least one of each back in Montana.

And damn if that didn't turn him on. She was the complete

Cinderella-In-Chaps fantasy. He'd never even realized he had one of those. But now that he did . . .

"Assessment through?" she asked. "In case you're wondering, I had to change when I got off the plane. These are my carry-on clothes." That smile teased the corner of her mouth again. "Which, amazingly, look a lot like my what-I-wear-on-airplanes clothes."

He finished his once-over then lifted his gaze to hers, not remotely abashed at being caught staring. He noticed their verbal sparring had brought the color back to her cheeks. "Not much on flying, huh?"

"Gee, what gave me away?"

Despite the deadpan humor, he noted a slight twinge of discomfort. He wasn't sure if it was real embarrassment over her appearance, or unease at what lay at the other end of the limo ride. He could identify with the latter part. His attention drifted out the window as they tooled down the access road, drawing him closer to his fate. He hated admitting he might have finally gotten himself into a jam that would require more than a little charm and a dash of sex appeal to get himself out of.

"Something wrong?" she asked, somewhat grudgingly.

He realized now how unsettling it was to have someone paying close attention. It had been a while for him, too. He managed a smile. "Let's just say you're not the only one here under duress."

"Really." She folded her arms, never once glancing at the crystal slipper she'd tossed on the seat next to her. Cinderella-In-Chaps, indeed.

"My grandmother passed away a few weeks ago. I had to come back, to settle the estate."

She immediately looked contrite. "I'm so sorry."

For some reason, he liked her better when she was snarky. "Don't be," he said, working to smooth the edge sharpening inside him with every mile that passed. "We weren't close. And she wasn't that nice of a lady."

Her lips threatened to curve all the way into a smile, albeit a dry one. "Unlike her grandson, I take it."

"Oh, definitely. Her grandson is engaging, amusing. Hell of a guy."

"She had more than one grandchild, then?"

He relaxed back into his seat, willing to put off the inevitable for as long as he could keep her dry wit engaged. "Nope, just the one."

"Ah. Funny how I missed all that, then."

"The smile probably blinded you to the rest of my shining attributes."

"Oh, something blinded me, all right."

He laughed. "I'm glad I met you, Darby Landon of the East Coast Landons. I've been dreading this trip for seven days, fifteen hours, and"—he checked his diving watch—"twenty-three minutes."

"And I thought I had it bad with three days, six hours, and"—she checked her own nonexistent watch—"four freckles past the hair."

"Not much on schedules, I take it?"

"I run a horse ranch. So my schedule is usually ruled by sunup, sundown, and how many hours I get between the two. Everything else sort of comes along at its own pace."

"My kind of schedule."

She said nothing, letting her gaze travel over him instead. And she made no effort to hide the fact that she was checking him out.

"Conclusions?" he asked, after she finished her casual perusal. And damn if that didn't make him stir a bit, too. He wished he had a Stetson of his own at that moment. For his lap, not his head. He made do with casually propping one ankle on the opposite knee. It occurred to him that his hiking boots had seen as much wear and tear as her Western ones.

"Not sure," she replied. "I read horses better than I do people."

"It's been my experience that horses read people better than people read people."

"You ride?" she asked, obviously surprised.

He could have told her that Morgans were to the saddle born. Only said saddle was generally on the back of a polo pony. He'd tried polo. Unlike his forebears, he'd never been much for it. He'd had a lot more fun the two seasons he'd spent on the bronc-busting circuit. As a rodeo clown. "Let's just say I know which end of a horse to steer clear of."

"That would be both ends, on occasion. The trick is knowing which end to avoid at which time."

"Yeah. I figured that out early on. That, and that being under the horse at any time is always a no-no."

"Hey, you do learn fast."

"I try."

"I bet," she said, half under her breath.

He just smiled. "So, how many siblings are there in the East Coast Landon clan? Was it an older one or a younger one that put the bamboo shoots under your nails?" He held up a hand. "Wait, let me guess. The only people older than you who can wrack you with guilt are usually your parents. So I'm guessing younger."

"I only have one sibling. And yes, you'd be right. She's younger."

"Oh, baby sisters. Say no more."

"You speak with great authority, O single child."

"No, I speak with great authority as a single male who has dated his fair share of both younger and older sisters."

She arched a brow. Natural, unwaxed, and unsculpted—and he'd seen enough to know the difference. Hers were all the sexier because of it. "Who lived under the same roof?" she asked.

"Of course not." He grinned. "They had their own places by then."

She rolled her eyes, but he saw the telltale twitch of the lips.

"So what has baby sister conned you into?"

She didn't answer right off. Finally, she sighed and said, "Playing chauffeur, hostess, and all-around ego-booster to a Swedish financier. He's doing some deal with my father and I have to make nice."

Shane's brows lifted. "Sounds like—"

"As much fun as having skin peeled off my body in tiny strips."

"Wow, that bad."

The corner of her mouth lifted. "We all have our personal hells."

"So why put yourself through it?"

"Baby sis needs her trust fund back and is currently out of the country. I'm helping her out of a jam." She lifted her hands, then let them fall in her lap. "I shouldn't. I rescue her too often. But I can't seem to say no."

Shane grinned. "A handy piece of information to have."

She gave him a "you wish" look.

The car slowed as it pulled into a long, semicircular drive.

"Looks like we're here." He glanced out the window at the aging Victorian mansion that Aurora's state's-attorney husband had left her when he died, some twenty years back. Shane had assumed, back when the three women started this venture, that they'd eventually move when the going got good. Something big and glitzy. But now that he looked at the place, with the ornate shutters, turrets and balustrades, all in a fresh coat of white, the deep front porch cloaked in a lush jungle of azaleas, the immaculate grounds, sweeping old oaks and aging hickory trees ... he realized that this *was* Glass Slipper, Inc. And it suited his godmothers better than any pile of chrome and glass ever would.

An unexpected wave of longing washed over him, surprising him. Suddenly he was dying to see them, to let them cluck over him, take him to task for his renegade ways. To be enveloped by their elegant perfumes and bountiful bosoms—well, Vivian's anyway—and made to feel ... well, welcome. He didn't realize how much that was going to mean to him. But it did. Because this was likely the only home-coming he was going to get.

Darby's rustling pulled his attention back. "You can always skip the makeover," he told her. "I'm sure the Swede will be suitably impressed with you, as is." Hell, she'd blown him away, hadn't she?

"Thanks for the vote of confidence, however sorely misplaced." She stared out the window. "And you're right, I could walk away. But the God's honest truth is, I'm not sure I can pull this off. I've been gone from this world a long time."

"So?"

She looked back to him. "So, I'm missing the gene that makes me care about who the 'in' designer is this fall, or which interior decorator is hot, or why I need a party planner for a dinner with only six people attending. Not to mention I could give a flying flip about Buffy's new club committee, Tad's latest foray into golf therapy, or why I'm not a valid human being unless my day clutch matches this week's hair color. It's like playing dress-up in some Psycho Barbie dreamworld." She shook her head. "I don't relate."

Shane chuckled. "I have a harder time trying to make sincere conversation with people who are only making nice because they want access to my corporate investment capital."

"You're an investment capitalist?"

"You look so surprised." He grinned. "Thank you. And no, the last thing I invested in was new nets for the pearl divers in Pulau. Of whom I was one, so it wasn't an entirely altruistic gesture."

"You're big on altruism?"

He shrugged. "I'm big on enjoying life. And if the people around me are enjoying it, too, so much the better. I just don't happen to equate personal happiness with amassing wealth for the sake of having more stuff than the other guys."

Her mouth curved in a wry smile. "So I take it you don't come to D.C. often, then."

He laughed outright. "Not when I can avoid it, no." He folded his arms and sighed a little. "But I couldn't this go-around."

"No, I guess not. I probably should have, but it's important."

"There's something for you in this big deal?"

She shook her head. "For my sister. And she's a big deal to me. I've always been responsible for her, a pseudomother figure, you might say, albeit not the best one, I'm sure. But I'm all she's got."

"Your dad—"

"Is an emotionally distant ass." She shrugged. "I'm okay with that."

Shane raised an eyebrow, which almost earned him a smile.

"Let's just say I'd rather be with people who don't believe in bartering possessions for love. And he's happier when I'm not around, pointing out that he wouldn't know an honest human value if it bit him on the—"

"I think I get it," he said with an easy smile. "Your sister, does she live here, or with you?"

"Here." She paused, then shrugged. "She and Dad don't have it smooth, by any means, but she pushes him to deal with her. I guess I have to give her credit for at least trying to make him be a parent to her."

"And the playing dress-up part?"

Now her expression grew distinctly affectionate and warm. "Oh, she was born to the role. She runs rings around the Washington society set. I think she sees it as some kind of grand game."

Shane thought he detected a slight shudder, and smiled. So they were both escapees of their respective upbringings, albeit for entirely different reasons. His grandmother had tried to mold him into a heartless, greedy mogul, and her father wanted a malleable Barbie doll instead of a real woman with real needs. Kindred spirits, of sorts.

"I still say you could knock them on their asses, just like you are."

"Only if you mean that literally," she said dryly. "I figure I'm better off taking all the help I can get."

Maybe it was the hint of vulnerability mixed up with all that tough talking, but it was at that moment that he knew he was going to do something rash. And here she'd made it all the way to the driveway uncorrupted, too. Shane slid off his seat and angled his body onto the seat next to her.

She raised her eyebrows at the move, but didn't react otherwise.

"I've always been a firm believer in having no regrets," he told her. "Which is why I'm going to apologize up front."

"For what?"

"Kissing you."

Her eyes widened, but her lips twisted in a wry smile. "Oh, really?"

"Oh, yeah, definitely."

"So why bother to apologize? You're clearly not going to be sorry."

"I don't believe so, no."

Her eyes flashed, and where he'd expected to see perhaps some sort of distaste or discomfort that would make him back off . . . he saw interest. Blatant, direct interest. "Does any woman say no to you?" she asked.

"About kissing? Or generally speaking?"

"Anytime speaking."

"Not usually. No."

"Did you ever think maybe it was time a woman did?"

"Long past time, definitely." He smiled. "Don't look so surprised. Women aren't the only ones who get by for far too long on good looks and a bit of charm."

"So why don't you stop allowing it to happen?"

"I find that life tends to be easier when I go with what works."

She shook her head with a sigh. "It's hard to argue with success, right?"

"Something like that. So, are you saying no, then?"

"I don't recall being asked," she said, then grinned and shook her head with a little laugh. "You know, this has got to be the strangest conversation I've ever had."

He couldn't respond. He was still basking in the sunlight of her full, unadulterated smile. It truly was a wondrous thing. "If I said you were absolutely stunning when you smiled, would you—"

"Be flattered?" She surprised him by appearing a bit wistful.

It did something to his insides, something he, even with his experience, wasn't all that familiar with. And wasn't sure he liked. "I was going to say *punch me*. But *flattered* would be much better."

"Well, I'll hate myself for admitting it, but given how I felt when I climbed in here . . . probably, yes." She gave him a look. "Charm wins again."

He shifted closer. "Does it?"

Now she snorted. "Don't push it."

He reached out and pushed a stray knotted strand of hair away from her face. To his surprise, she didn't pull away. Or knee him in the balls. "You *are* stunning, you know," he said. "Smiling or not."

"Now you're definitely pushing it. Or just full of it. Or both."

"It's my greatest downfall." He stroked his fingers along her cheek. "Pushing it, I mean." He trailed his finger across her lips. "Although some would say it's both." He pressed at the lush center of her lower lip, pushed his finger just the slightest bit between her lips. Thinking she'd most likely bite him, he was surprised when she inhaled with the slightest of gasps. His body tightened almost painfully. "I'm dying to taste you," he murmured, and thought it was highly probable he'd never been more sincere about anything in his entire life.

"Then I suppose you'd better just take your chances," she said, her voice the tiniest bit shaky. "You can tell me later if you regret it."

The driver killed the engine. And he knew their time together was over. "Definitely no regrets," he said, and lowered his mouth to hers.

Cinderella Rule #3

*F*ailing that last rule, regroup quickly and put your best foot forward. Take care to keep your mouth closed while doing so. Better to bite your tongue ... than risk swallowing your foot. And darlings, a bright smile covers a multitude of believed sins.

—AURORA FAVREAUX, COFOUNDER
GLASS SLIPPER, INC.

Chapter 3

His lips were . . . well, as perfect as the rest of him. And he definitely knew his way around a woman's mouth. She tried—okay, for about two seconds—to just absorb the kiss without responding, determined not to react, just to see what he'd do. He was far too used to women swooning and sighing over him, and for some perverse reason, she wanted to be the one who didn't. Except his kiss was as natural as his charm.

And it undeniably went a long way toward taking the edge off the ugly stepsister vibe she'd been carrying around since the moment she saw that glass slipper. Okay, maybe for a while longer than that.

His hand came up, slid beneath her heavy braid, and cupped the back of her head as he moved to take the kiss deeper. Now was the time to casually pull away, show him her studied indifference, maybe a little shrug when he lifted those charismatic brows of his, surprised at her lack of response. But who was she kidding? It had been a long time since she'd been kissed like this. Actually, it had probably been . . . never.

So she let him past her lips, into her mouth, and grudgingly accepted that about the best she could hope for in terms of studied indifference was refraining from moaning wildly and ripping his clothes off. It wasn't much of an edge, but she clung to it.

And then he was lifting his head, taking his mouth from hers. "Cinderella packs quite a punch, glass slippers or no," Shane said. The gravelly edge to his voice sent a hot thrill straight through her.

"No regrets, then," she managed, her own voice a shade rougher than she'd have liked.

He held her gaze so steadily, she forgot where she was, what she was supposed to be doing, even her own name.

"Only one."

She lifted her eyebrows in question, but he was already reaching for her. And this time when he took her mouth, there was nothing light or casual about it. This was no preliminary exploration, no assuaging of curiosity. If she thought she'd felt his hunger before, now she felt as if she were being consumed. Devoured, even.

Her fingers found their way into his hair. Someone moaned, someone growled. Then he was pulling all five feet eleven inches of her across his lap as effortlessly as if she were . . . well, Pepper. It was a rather defining moment for Darby, yet she couldn't stop to examine it. She was much too busy being insatiable.

Unfortunately, being insatiable completely blocked out the sounds of the limo door being opened. More disappointing still, it wasn't enough to block out the trio of gasps that followed it. And most mortifying of all, it was Shane who had to end their wrestling match.

"Hi, Mama Mercedes," he said, his smile as congenial as if he always greeted his godmother with a highly aroused, panting-for-air woman sprawled across his lap. Of course, for all she knew, maybe he did. "It's been a long time."

"Not as long in some ways as others," came the steady reply.

Darby winced. That autocratic tone of disapproval had to belong to no other than Mercedes Browning, head fairy godmother of Glass Slipper, Inc., according to the brochure Pepper had had overnighted to her, along with her plane tickets. Lovely first impression she was making on the former headmistress, too.

You're not being raised on a farm, Darby. Close the front door. Wash your face and hands. Do something with that rat's nest of hair. And for God's sake, try and look like something more respectable than a stable hand when you come down for dinner. Why can't you be more like your mother, God rest her soul? She understood that appropriate attire and be-havior must be suitable to the occasion. In this house, that means you act and dress like a lady, even if we both know otherwise. Is that so hard?

The familiar childhood scolding, delivered as only Paul Landon III could deliver it, echoed through her mind. God knew she'd heard it often enough to commit every syllable to eternal memory, though it had been years since it had surfaced.

She swallowed a sigh, but the hint of a rebellious smile swiftly fol-lowed. Because she had, in fact, spent the second half of her for-mative years being raised on a farm. And she knew with absolute certainty she was a better person for it.

Grasping on to that sliver of hard-earned pride, she acknowledged that there was no graceful way to extricate herself from the current situation. And no way to simply dissolve and disappear, either. So, as calmly as possible, she slid her body to the seat across from where they'd been tangled up in each other, and took a moment to pull her-self together before turning to face her hostesses for the next five days. That is, if they didn't bounce her out on her ass. Which, had she thought of it ahead of time, would have been a great strategy in getting out of the whole thing.

Unfortunately, they were masters of the infernal, if-I-don't-acknowledge-it-then-it-didn't-happen facial expression. Even worse was realizing that almost two decades on the ranch hadn't totally obliterated all of the snooty social skills that had been pounded into her, beginning at birth. She smoothly extended her hand to the driver when he offered to help her out, and just as smoothly ignored the women's shared look of relieved approval before they introduced themselves.

"I'm Mercedes Browning," said the tallest one. She wasn't quite on par with Darby's height, but her attitude more than made up for their slight difference in altitude. "Welcome to Glass Slipper."

Darby took in her tailored navy-blue suit, her no-nonsense string of pearls, and ruthlessly coifed silver hair, then accepted the hand she extended, approving of the firm handshake. Even at a young age, Darby had detested those limp, helpless little society handshakes somebody had dictated that women must use in polite company. That "somebody" most likely being a man, of course. *How easily threatened they must be,* was all she could remember thinking at the time. Her opinion hadn't changed much over the years. Although Shane had certainly rattled it a little.

"I'm Aurora Favreaux," said the second woman, the shortest of the three and easily the most accessible in demeanor. Plumper, and swathed in the sort of drapy chiffon scarf-type thing that made her look fragile and a bit ethereal, her hair was a soft golden halo around her exquisitely made-up face. Her eyebrows alone were works of art. Literally. Darby was pretty sure there was no actual facial hair involved. The wealthy Southern belle, she recalled from the brochure, who'd married into more wealth, along with Washington politics, at a young age and had become quite the society doyenne by the time she was widowed in her late forties. The elegant sprawling Victorian behind them had originally been her home.

Aurora's hands were spidered with blue veins, but whereas Mercedes' hands had been somewhat rawboned, with short, buffed nails, Aurora's were much smaller, softer, heavily jeweled, with what could only be called dragon-lady nails tipping each delicate end. The fact that they were painted a warm shade of peach did little to dispel the notion that, if riled, she could quite easily draw first blood. But her smile was warm, and her gray eyes twinkly. If any of them had an ounce of real fairy in them, it would be this one, Darby caught herself thinking.

"Hello, I'm Darby Landon," she responded, squeezing both of the hands that had been offered her, but easing up a bit on the pressure. More to keep from getting puncture wounds than because she thought the woman couldn't handle it.

"And I'm Vivian dePalma," announced the last, and by far the most startling, of the three. What Mercedes lacked in flash and Aurora lacked in stature, Vivian more than made up for in both. She was the former Hollywood wardrobe fashionista, who dressed the stars and created the trends others tried to emulate. Which explained the outrageous shade of red hair and matching lipstick, but not the boldly colored caftan—in which not one of the swirly colors matched the tone of her hair, yet seemed an oddly perfect accompaniment to it—that ended abruptly just above the knee. The ensemble was completed by black hose and spindly high heels that Darby decided must have steel reinforcements. Because while the septuagenarian sported admittedly killer legs, from the hips up she was built like a fireplug.

"Darby Landon," she repeated as she shook the woman's hand.

Vivian had the firmest grip of the three—more a measuring squeeze than a real shake—and gave Darby a sharp looking-over before gazing quite directly into her eyes. "Welcome to Glass Slipper, sweetheart," she said, her tone more closely resembling that of a diner waitress than a partner in a high-gloss business that had built its reputation on the ability to polish the tarnish off the less favored. Her exquisitely painted lips curved wickedly, and a bit of the devil lit her eyes. "Although I see Shane has already made you feel right at home."

"Ms. Landon," Mercedes politely—mercifully—interrupted, "are these your only bags?"

Darby turned to find the impeccably liveried driver holding her two pieces of quite unimpeccable luggage. She supposed she had Shane to thank for being beyond embarrassment at this point. "Yep, that's it."

Their plucked, painted, and ruthlessly tweezed eyebrows lifted a mere fraction in response to her less than cultured reply, but she noted the mild disapproval nonetheless. *Up again, down again,* she thought. Well, her snooty-tooty training had only gone so far. If she didn't need fine-tuning, she wouldn't be here now, would she? Although she was pretty sure it would take more than these three to stamp out the stable hand in her. Lord knows, many had tried. Most of them employed by her father. All had failed.

"You okay?" came a warm voice, just behind her left ear.

She'd almost forgotten about Shane. Almost. But he obviously hadn't forgotten about her. Out of their line of vision, he traced a single, blunt-tipped finger down her spine, making her work very, very hard at not visibly shivering at his touch. Rebel, indeed. She was way out of her league when compared with Shane Morgan, who was likely a veritable master of mischievousness. It probably wasn't wise, but she envied him that skill.

"That was the one thing," he murmured so only she could hear. "My only regret. The embarrassment. But it was my only chance. And I figured you could handle it."

To both of their surprise, she laughed. "It was definitely a risk well worth taking," she said, leaving it at that.

He grinned. "Glad to hear it, Cinderella."

"I'm not—"

But he was already being swept up in a hug by Aurora, being subjected to a very blatant once-over by Vivian, and was on the receiving end of a disapproving glare by Mercedes, who nonetheless hugged him tightly when it was her turn. *Ah,* Darby thought, unsurprised, *his charm really does know no boundaries.*

She almost choked when Vivian's hug ended with a little fanny pat.

She caught Darby's reaction and winked. "I've been patting this little tushie since it was in diapers. I see no reason to stop now."

Darby could only nod in complete understanding. It *was* quite the tushie, she agreed, now that she'd gotten a good gander at it. And if the welcoming committee had taken just a few minutes longer in getting out to the limo, she might have gotten her hands on it, too.

Two young men, both wearing matching coral blazers, and a young woman in cool lemon linen, stepped off the shadowed veranda and came down the wide front steps, drawing the attention of the three Glass Slipper founders. Darby took the moment to study the trio, thinking that college surely bred some strange lifelong friendships, then ignored the tiny little twinge of regret that she'd turned down the opportunity to forge her own oddball sorority bonds. She smiled, thinking the menagerie she had back home was quite odd enough. And more to her liking, anyway.

"Quite the troupe," he commented, noting her gaze.

Darby turned back, only to find herself momentarily alone with him, the driver having disappeared with their bags.

"Yes, quite. The whole place is ..." She glanced back at the house, the grounds, the quiet beauty and inviting serenity of it all, and didn't know how to phrase her answer. For once, reality outshone the brochure. The house was stunning but not intimidating, the grounds ruthlessly maintained, yet lush and inviting. She felt less the science experiment and more spa vacationer for the first time since leaving home. Maybe this wouldn't be so horrific an experience after all.

"Not exactly what you expected?"

"Honestly, I didn't know what to expect. I saw the brochure, knew about the old Victorian house, but ..." Her gaze drifted back to the women.

"But you understand now why they don't have their pictures on the website or in the brochure, huh? Not the traditional fairy godmother types, are they?"

She smiled. "That pretty much pegs what I was thinking."

"You'll do fine, you know."

She took a deep breath, then let it out slowly. "I guess it won't kill me to try, anyway." Then she smiled. "But I've already made up my mind that my sister is going to spend some serious time in the barn, come the next foaling season."

Shane grinned. "Paybacks are supposed to be hell, after all."

"Exactly." She turned to face the house, trying to absorb the peaceful vibe of her surroundings, and accept what lay ahead for her beyond those gorgeous stained-glass double doors. Anxiety curled in her stomach. "And we all have our own definitions of that, don't we?"

Again he traced a finger down her spine, only this time it was as reassuring as it was tantalizing.

"Thank you," she said, quite seriously, but careful to keep her gaze on the house and grounds.

"For?"

She turned. "The distraction. The camaraderie." Her lips twitched. "For reminding me that I need to be kissed like that more often."

"Ah, so you've been kissed like that before, then." His blue eyes lit with devilment. "I must be losing my edge in my old age. You hit thirty and it all goes to hell, I guess."

"With age comes experience. Which does improve some things."

He glanced over at Mercedes and company, then stepped in close. Real close. "It's certainly improved my appreciation for some things." He leaned in and took her mouth in a searing power punch of a kiss. She was actually dizzy when he ended it. Jet lag, she tried to tell herself. But she wasn't buying it. Neither, from the look on his face, was he.

"It's only fair, you know," he said, steadying her with his hands on her shoulders. "Because you, Darby Landon of the East Coast Landons, have my full attention, too." He glanced past her at the house, maybe at something only he could see. "And in a far better way than it's about to be had, that's for sure."

He'd made it clear he had no more love for the power players of the Washington elite than she did. Apparently his grandmother had been an integral part of that high-stakes circle. Judging from the reactions of the three older women, it had been a long time since he'd been around. Which meant he probably faced a bit more than putting a house up for sale and sorting through a few personal belongings. She discovered she was dying to know more. Which proved the real shame. Because the women were heading back their way. And their time together was officially up. "I'd offer to swap places with you," she said, "but I'm not sure I don't have the better end of the deal. If there is such a thing."

His smile was tinged with resignation. "We're both going to be sucked into a world of ridiculous rules, obligations we didn't ask for, and expectations we never set out to fulfill in the first place. And worse."

She made a face. "What could possibly be worse?"

He laughed. "I like you, Darby Landon. I owe you thanks, too."

"What for?"

"Distraction, camaraderie. And proving to me that kisses like that actually exist."

Her mouth opened, then shut again, surprised into silence.

"Just follow their rules, Cinderella," he told her, tracing a quick caress along her lower lip. "They're good at what they do. You'll be a Washington Power Princess in no time."

"That is not a reassuring thought," she called out as he walked away, out of her life, and got one last wink for the effort. Then he ducked around the side of the house, with Vivian and Mercedes in tow.

And yet it was reassuring. Or he was, anyway. She'd never thought of herself as the deliverer of a once-in-a-lifetime kiss. And though there was a good chance he said outrageous things like that to every woman he met, she chose to believe that he meant it with her.

Believing gave her the strength to turn and face the phalanx of Glass Slipper employees with a bit of dignity, a shred of confidence ... and maybe just a fraction of her mother's ranch-hand-born élan.

"Good-bye ugly stepsister," she murmured. *And thank you, Shane Morgan, for making me feel, even for a few moments, that there is a little bit of Cinderella inside every woman. Even me.*

"Darling," Aurora said, taking Darby's hands in hers once again. "I'd like to introduce you to Beverly. She'll be your personal planner during your stay here." She leaned in and whispered, "Trust me, she's one of the best. If anyone can whip you into shape in such a limited time, it's her. She's fabulous."

Darby didn't quite know what to say to that, but Aurora was already motioning Beverly forward. She gave Darby a reassuring little wave, then turned away to speak to several other employees.

The young woman in a cheery lemon blazer stepped forward and extended her mannequin-smooth, perfectly manicured hand. "I'm Beverly. It'll be a pleasure working with you." She let her gaze skim over Darby's face and hair, her smile very carefully maintained. "Perhaps we should set up your salon appointments first?"

Her Cinderella confidence deteriorating rapidly, Darby started getting that petri dish feeling in the pit of her stomach again. For a split second she contemplated diving back into the limo, but, as if on cue, it pulled slowly down the drive. Stranding her with the Stepford Staffers.

Darby forced a smile at Beverly and the small gathering behind her. "Whatever you think is best."

Beverly exchanged a brief but telling look with her assembled assistants, who immediately leaped to attention, scribbling on clipboards, making calls on their little headsets, before scurrying off toward the house in what could only be described as a beehive of activity.

Beverly beamed at Darby and gently took her arm, steering her down the pebbled path toward the wide steps leading to the veranda. She patted Darby's arm reassuringly. "Since you only have a few days here, we're going to put you into our high focus, intensive program."

Oh, goody, Darby muttered silently. She was already being tagged a makeover emergency.

"We'll spend the rest of today and a good part of tomorrow working on the easier elements of your transformation. Namely appearance." Her smile never flickered. "Then we'll move into the more intangible elements: grace, style, et cetera. All of which will be interspersed with etiquette lessons and the like. Each meal will double as a chance to further your education on everything from place settings to dinner-party strategies." She gestured for Darby to precede her through the stained-glass doors.

"Alice through the looking glass," Darby murmured. Though it was fair to say that she felt more like Lurch next to Beverly's cute, blonde Alice.

"I beg your pardon?" Beverly asked brightly.

"Beautiful stained glass," she improvised, figuring it wasn't politic to alienate the person in charge of arranging her torture sessions.

"Yes, it's an original part of the house, dating back to the eighteen hundreds. If we have time, I'd be more than glad to give you the full tour."

"Lovely," Darby managed, then forced a smile when Beverly looked up at her quizzically. Most of their guests probably approached their makeover with a tad more enthusiasm, as opposed to Darby, who acted like a person facing an appointment with the guillotine. "Perhaps later. I'd really like to freshen up, if that's possible."

Beverly beamed once again as she enthusiastically tucked her arm through Darby's, patting her forearm. "Oh, we're going to do far more than freshen you up. Trust me, by the time we have our first session on dinner-party etiquette this evening, you already won't recognize yourself."

Darby's stomach pitched and rolled as Beverly opened a door to a small, beautifully appointed office. "I really don't think—"

"We're going to have fun," Beverly assured her, patting her hand.

Darby pulled her arm free and curled her fingers inward before she gave in to the temptation to pat-pat little Beverly here right through the nearest window.

Oblivious to her client's rebellious thoughts, she motioned for Darby to sit in a tightly upholstered Victorian chair. "It'll be like playing dress-up, only better."

Darby's lips quirked, thinking of Shane's comments to her in the car. This whole day was taking on a totally surreal vibe. Only she liked the one back in the limo much better. She sighed.

"Is something the matter?"

Darby regretfully let thoughts of Shane fade away as she took a deep, fortifying breath. She looked at her Perpetually Perky, Depressingly Diminutive personal planner and felt every inch her Incredible Hulklike self. Whatever Cinderella vibe she had left, vanished. In fact, she couldn't believe she'd really thought she could pull this off. Just who were they kidding? Even Bubbly Bev here was worried.

Darby's lips quirked again in a wry smile. "Just that it's not easy being green." At least she'd made Bev frown. Score one for the Hulk. "You wouldn't understand." She sighed a little and resigned herself to her immediate fate. Seriously, just how bad could it be to have her hair done and some makeup caked on, right? "So, where do we begin?"

Beverly flipped open a leather notebook, pen poised over what looked like a lengthy checklist. "We've already set up hair and facial appointments." She flashed a confident smile, then said, "When was the last time you waxed?"

Darby's newly formed bravado slipped badly. "My brows are fine."

She could have sworn Beverly's smile took on a demonic glow. "I don't mean your brows. We'll take care of that with electrolysis." She sent a meaningful look lower.

Darby carefully crossed her legs, barely refraining from putting a protective hand over her crotch. "Shaving is fine, really."

"Trust me," Beverly assured her. "You're going to thank me when this is all over."

The only thing Darby trusted at the moment was that for every moment of "fun" she had at Glass Slipper, Pepper was going to have an equally fun moment on the ranch. In fact, she was going to spend every waking moment of this nightmare devising her own little checklist for her baby sister.

Starting off with bicep-high rubber gloves as her first foaling fashion statement.

With a grin that actually made Beverly shift back a little in her seat, Darby said, "Oh, I'm sure the payoff will be worth the effort."

Cinderella Rule #4

*N*ever underestimate the power of fashion as a business tool. Unfair as it may seem, a well-tailored skirt matched with the right pair of heels often influences people more than the corporate presentation you spent weeks slaving over. Embrace that reality ... and accessorize ruthlessly.

—VIVIAN

*C*hapter 4

f you'll excuse me for just a moment."

The three men sitting across from his desk nodded, and Shane stood and ducked through one of the three doors leading from Alexandra's office. The first one led to the hall, the second one led to a smaller, private office. He took the third, which led to her private bathroom.

He felt like his head was going to explode, and it probably would if he had to listen to one more person say things like "expedite revenue velocity" or "solidify the manpower infrastructure." Didn't anyone just say what they meant anymore? He needed a minute, or fifty. He stuck a finger in the neckband of his shirt, trying and failing to loosen the noose around his neck. And along with common English usage, the aggregate corporate mentality had also lost its sense of humor. If they'd ever had one.

He huffed out a sigh, popped a few aspirin, then smoothed his retro Rocky-and-Bullwinkle tie before turning to leave. The tinny echo of voices floated through the vent screen, making him pause.

"Can you believe this shit? What the hell was she thinking, letting everything rest on this guy's shoulders?"

"They're actually kind of nice shoulders—"

"Down, boy," came another voice. "And wake up, Frank. Who did you think she'd leave it to? She all but printed it at the top of the corporate manifesto. Morgan Industries was, is, and always will be a privately held Morgan family business."

" 'Ding Dong! The Witch is dead,' but a Morgan still sits on the throne."

Shane wondered if Alexandra had ventilated the room specifically to pick up the acoustics of her outer office, and then figured she'd be just the type to think of something like that. He wondered how many times she'd stood in this exact spot and listened to people screw themselves right out of a job or deal. And since that visual made him feel more than a little creepy, he stepped back into the office. "Thank you, gentlemen." He walked to the door leading to reception, finding some joy in the way they all but fell over themselves to look sharp, in control, but with that all-important willing-to-kiss-ass-if-it-will-get-me-a-new-Lexus air about them.

He opened the door. "If you'll leave a copy of your proposal with my assistant, I'll give it due attention before making my final decision."

Even as they hustled out with their "Yes, sir; thank you, sir," Cuthbert was motioning another pair to enter. *Jesus*, Shane thought, head still pounding. Did it never end?

The two took their seats, and for the next thirty minutes he did his best to smile and nod in all the right places. But, honestly, he was with Frank. Or maybe it was Steve. What the fuck was he doing here?

"If you're considering going through with the Celentrex buyout, Mr. Morgan," the woman was saying as she mercifully wrapped up her presentation, "I think you can clearly see that my team would be in the best position to ensure a smooth transition." She smiled, but Shane wasn't fooled. He was pretty sure that if you scraped the surface of her ruthlessly tailored power suit, shark skin would gleam through.

"I was involved with your grandmother during the initial development phase, and I don't believe anyone is more qualified."

Shane said nothing, just continued to tap his steepled fingers against his chin. After a few moments, the woman shifted slightly on her sensible pumps and took a seat. Shane shifted his attention to the man who'd come in with her—one of the research guys, if he recalled correctly. He'd tried, he really had, to commit names to memory, but had given up some two dozen department heads ago. "Did you have anything to add?"

The man dabbed at his shiny forehead with a handkerchief. "No, sir. I concur with everything presented here. The technology is in place, and we have developed a strong relationship with the Celentrex team, which would guarantee a successful launch."

He *concurred.* Shane resisted the urge to sigh. Just barely. He slapped his hands on the desk, startling them both, and stood. "Well, then, I guess that's all. I'll get back in touch with you after I've seen the other presentations."

The woman was sharp, but even so, she took a moment to regroup. Clearly she hadn't expected to be dismissed so quickly. "Sir, if I may add something?"

Shane remained standing and met her gaze directly. "Certainly. But please keep it brief. I have another appointment waiting."

He saw the flicker of surprise, the reassessing look. Did they all really think he was a total idiot? Just because his master's degree had been earned in the college of global experience, didn't mean his mind wasn't sharp. They'd soon learn that, despite the fact that he could give a flying flip about the Celentrex buyout or any of the other business that Morgan Industries conducted on any given day, that didn't mean he wasn't going to at least attempt to make the most informed decisions possible.

God, three days and he was already being sucked into the whole corporate mentality. *Thanks, Alexandra.* He hated thinking she might have been right about him. Not that he had any intentions of staying, much less running the joint, or even pretending to try, but if she'd assumed he'd be unable to look at the faces of the various employees whose livelihoods might be on the line, and not at least try to do right by them ... well, she might have been a little right about him.

"Go ahead," he said, trying not to let the overwhelming nature of this whole ordeal send him back to the rest room. This time to vomit. How did these people live with this kind of stress every day? He'd been in meetings into the early morning hours both of the past two nights. In fact, he'd been told that was status quo. Who the hell worked that hard? And for what? The brass ring? Just what did one do with a brass ring, anyway? Show it off? Must get awfully tiring, having to find a new ring after everyone has seen your old one.

"I'm not sure where you are in the evaluation process," she began, smoothing the skirt of her power suit. Her smile was direct, her fin erect and slicing the turbulent waters of corporate power struggles once again. In any other situation, he might have admired her confidence. At the moment, however, she just struck him as another ring-grabber. "Forgive me if I'm reiterating something you are already aware of, but with the untimely passing of your grandmother, the Celentrex buyout immediately became a hotly debated property. We can't afford to drop the ball here. I assure you, we're ready to hit the ground running."

Shane was well aware of the concerns surrounding the buyout. How could he not? It was all anyone wanted to talk about. On the surface, it looked like a good thing. Celentrex was a small British engineering company that had developed a new technology to extract fossil fuels. An environmental boon and possible future solution to America's overseas oil dependence. Never a tree hugger or political activist, Shane assumed Alexandra's interest was more closely related to the boon it would bring to her bottom line in the corporate asset column.

Shane looked from the woman to the R&D guy, then back again. And smiled. "So, what you're saying is, the world will still get the benefit of the technology, no matter what. We just risk losing out on the money if we don't jump now."

"It's a great deal of money," the researcher blurted out. "The rumor mill is already grinding that—that you might not go through with it. Our window of opportunity is shrinking."

The woman smiled and rose to her feet, shifting smoothly in front of the older man who was dabbing at his forehead again. "Your grandmother was very determined to see this through. It meant a great deal to her."

Shane's smile grew. If she thought that playing the sentimental card was going to further her case, she was sadly mistaken. "Trust me, anything that would make her a boatload more cash, to add to the already obscene amount she was worth to begin with, was going to be vitally important to Alexandra. Me, on the other hand—" He shrugged. "I don't care all that much about money."

He motioned to the door. "Please leave your proposal with Mr. Cuthbert on your way out. Thank you for your time."

The woman stood there a moment longer, but Shane's gaze didn't waver and she apparently thought better of trying to plead her case any further. Smart shark. As the door closed behind the duo, he sat back down again, sighed, and massaged the now-permanent throb in his forehead. God, he wanted to get the hell out of there. He looked at the towering stack of folders in front of him, each representing yet another meeting on his docket. And that was just for today.

He hadn't had a moment to call his own since he'd left word with

Alexandra's corporate attorneys after checking into the Embassy Grand on Sunday. He'd opted not to go home after leaving Glass Slipper— mostly because any generic hotel room would be more welcoming— figuring he'd meet with the lawyers, sign a few papers, and resign what could only be a figurehead position at best. He wasn't interested in selling anything, or making any money off the whole ordeal. It wasn't his to take, even if he had wanted it, which he didn't. As far as he was concerned, whatever profit there was to be made, belonged to those who had, knowing his grandmother, sweat blood to make it in the first place.

That done, he'd planned to head out to Four Stones the following week. He also had to go over all the family and various nonbusiness holdings, but he'd optimistically thought he could wind things up in a few days, and be on the first flight to . . . wherever it possessed him to go.

Rarely had he ever been so wrong. He'd been correct in assuming that Alexandra hadn't built Morgan Industries into a global mega-lopolis by leaving things to others and hoping all went well. Oh, no, she'd made sure every last detail was overseen by a phalanx of per-sonal assistants, each of whom reported to her every other damn minute, each of whom knew the only answer to the command "jump" as an obedient "how high?"

It was just that all of them, very resentfully, now jumped for him. And only him. Shane sifted through the folders, absently wondering if, should he tell them all to head up to the top floor and jump off the roof, they would do so. Sure would make things a hell of a lot easier.

It was now Wednesday. He'd slept a total of nine hours since his first meeting Sunday night, which he'd been hard-pressed to avoid, as a raft of lawyers had shown up on his hotel-room doorstep within the hour of his phone call. Naively thinking that a jump-start on things might speed up his departure, he'd let them in.

His first in a long string of misjudgments. His eyes had crossed long before that first meeting was over. The bottom line was that, while Alexandra had a slew of pawns overseeing various independent elements of the business, there was no single individual geared to step into the top slot. Her lawyers had made it quite clear that what Frank and Steve had said was, in fact, quite true. She'd made it clear that a Morgan would always control Morgan Industries. Great way to make friends and influence the people whose lives he now controlled. They all resented the hell out of him and, frankly, he couldn't blame them.

She'd also tied him up in her innumerable assets, not the least of which was the family manse in Great Falls, along with various properties that had been in the Morgan family since right around the same time Washington had crossed the Potomac. He supposed Alexandra had thought that if she tangled him in her web tightly enough, he'd be smart enough not to struggle.

Well, Big Al had once again underestimated the last Morgan. It might take longer than a few days to sort it all out, but sort it out and divest of it—every fax machine, company jet, and polo pony of it—he would. He loosened his tie and popped the top button on his dress shirt. Just as soon as he figured out how.

He should have stuck around Glass Slipper longer. Hell, he should have checked himself in. He'd be having a damn sight more fun, anyway. "Fun," he said a bit wistfully, "now there's a concept."

Shane thought about what he'd been doing when he'd gotten word that a series of strokes had swiftly and shockingly claimed one of the most powerful people in Washington. He'd been pearl-diving in the South Pacific, where he'd been living for the past six months. The pay wasn't great, pretty much nonexistent as a matter-of-fact, but the locals were some of the happiest people he'd ever met. The food was basic but plentiful, and the location was truly paradise.

Big Al would never understand that kind of happiness, or that it could be so fulfilling. Of course, who the hell was he to tell anyone that the Holy Grail they endlessly chased after was nothing more than a worthless trinket? Just because he didn't down antacids like Tic Tacs, worship Xanax like it was a new religion, or think nothing of having a shrink on retainer, to keep the competitive edge sharp, didn't mean he was better equipped to measure true happiness than the next guy.

His gaze traveled to the bank of phones situated on the corner of Alexandra's mahogany desk. He thought about the last time he'd been truly happy. It had been in the backseat of a limo, what felt like an eternity ago. He wondered how Darby was holding up.

It was ridiculous, really. He was drowning here ... and he hadn't even broached the personal stuff yet. The mansion, its phalanx of employees, the other various and sundry accumulated bullshit. Cars, boats, a hockey team. But his eyes stayed on the phone. And the person he most wanted to talk to had nothing to do with solving any of his problems. Nor did she have anything to do with pearl-diving in Pulau, being a rodeo clown in Texas, guiding rafting tours in Patagonia, or giving ski instruction to the snow bunnies of the Austrian Alps. Or any of the other jobs he'd had, that he'd give his arm to be back doing again right at that moment. And yet, now that he'd allowed himself a spare second to think about her ... he couldn't seem to stop. Or didn't want to, anyway.

His smile spread to a grin. Right about now, she was probably ready to let Daddy cut her sister off without a cent. Interesting, he mused, how her rugged, take-no-shit exterior hid a pretty damn marshmallowy center. At least where her kid sister was concerned.

She was leaving Glass Slipper tomorrow, then picking up her Scandinavian guest, to begin her three-day whirlwind tour of the Washington social scene. A scene he could easily find a way to be part of if he wished to. Well, he wished to, he decided. He wanted to see her again. Of course, she might not have given him a single thought since she'd been swept into Glass Slipper. His fingers hovered over the now-buzzing intercom, signaling that his next appointment had arrived.

He yanked up the phone instead, imagining the pinched look on Linus Cuthbert's face when Shane didn't answer his latest summons. Alexandra's executive assistant could have given Torquemada a few bad nights, but Shane was immune to his little power trips. He smiled with sincerity for the first time that day ... and yanked the intercom cord out of the wall. Then he punched the button for the operator. "Get me Glass Slipper, Incorporated, please. Mercedes Browning—wait, no, Vivian dePalma." He paused while the young lady repeated his request. "Yes, that's right. Also, contact accounting." He flipped open a folder. "Have Sheldon Werner call my assistant and set up a meeting for tomorrow. Thanks." Before he made his decision on Celentrex, he wanted to know just how many jobs were going to be affected—one way or the other—and what kind of blow it would deliver to the company if someone else snagged the deal out from under him.

He looked upward, then rethought that and looked downward. "Thanks, Big A. You've done the impossible. I'm not only wearing a suit, putting in twenty-hour days, but I'm worrying about revenue velocity and upsetting the manpower infrastructure." He sighed. "May God strike me dead."

There was a tap on the double doors, then Linus's weasellike face peered around the corner. With as much disdain as he could muster and still look like he was kissing his boss's ass, he said, "Mr. Morgan, your next appointment has arrived." He sniffed. "And there appears to be a malfunction with the intercom system."

Ever the little lieutenant, Shane thought. He smiled. "I yanked it out of the wall."

Linus's mouth went slack, but he quickly regrouped. "But, sir, how will I—"

"Smoke signals for all I care, man. And cancel the appointment waiting out there. Give them my apologies. Then cancel everything after it for the next couple of hours. I'm heading out for a while."

"Out?" Linus actually spluttered.

"I know it's going to come as a shock to you, but there is actually a whole world outside these vaunted walls. A world filled with people who smile, and laugh, and don't give a shit about their job for whole hours at a time. You might want to look into it. Right after you cancel my appointments. Oh, and find out how to open the file drawers in Alexandra's private office." He hadn't gotten around to digging into that yet, but maybe there would be notes, something that would shed more light on this buyout. And God knew what else. He tried not to shudder.

"It's a private combination. Only your grandmother knew it."

"Then hire a locksmith. I want them open by the time I get back." Shane's private line buzzed. *Vivian.* Thank God. He leaned back in his chair as Linus flounced out. If he was in charge here, then it was time he started acting like it. And his first executive decision was to see Darby Landon. Today.

*S*he'd been plucked and painted, waxed and lowlighted. Exfoliated, lacquered, and buffed. Roadkill could be stuffed and presentably mounted with less work than had been done on her in the past four days. But she'd discovered that submitting herself to those degradations wasn't going to be the low point. Oh, no.

And this was including those idiotic sessions she'd gracefully—or so she'd thought—allowed them to run her through. Things like Intimate Place Settings for Forty, The Ten Worst Finger Food Faux Pas, or Working the Power Party (otherwise known as How to Close the Deal Without Actually Revealing You Have a Brain). Okay, so they'd called them something else, but who cared? It was all an endless wall of white noise to her. How in the hell did Pepper manage to care about all this crap?

Darby had begun to realize that her younger sister must have been a lot more on the ball than she let on. Anyone who could handle their father and remember all these endless rules had to be either an Oscar-caliber actress or a rocket scientist. Or both. Hell, table-seating alone apparently required the sort of strategic battle intelligence usually reserved for four-star generals.

And she could have handled that. Or faked it at least. Short-term anyway, for her sister's sake. Although, in all honesty, it was never going to freaking matter to Darby whether or not the escargot knife should be placed precisely at twelve o'clock. Or was it four o'clock?

But then the lovely folks at Glass Slipper had gone one step too far. They'd actually had the nerve to expect her to go clothes shopping. Voluntarily. At more than one store.

Somewhere around store number five her eyes glazed over. By store twelve, her feet, even in her own broken-in cowboy boots, had gone mercifully numb. She'd already tried to bribe Melanie, the dynamo Beverly had assigned to be Darby's "personal lifestyle consultant," but Merry Melanie couldn't be bought. Had she merely pointed to things and said, "Buy this, this, and that," Darby might have been able to hack it with little more than a snarl and the occasional peevish comment.

But nooo. She was supposed to put together her own wardrobe. Apparently the theory was that, this way, she'd develop her own fashion sense, her own "look," with an eye toward what enhanced her features and physique, so that on future shopping trips—that Melanie, such a comedian—she'd be able to zero right in on "her style" of clothing.

She really didn't want to tell Melanie that "her style" was usually found in the clothing aisles at Tractor Supply. And not always the women's section, either. Her "look" said "equine management," not "upper management."

"Lucky us," Melanie was saying as she led Darby into the women's department at Nordstrom. "Silks are on sale."

"Just kill me now," Darby muttered beneath her breath as she followed behind, barely resisting the juvenile urge to scuff her heels.

"You'll want to keep in mind your previous selections," Melanie continued, ever chipper and perky despite her protégée's death-row enthusiasm for the expedition. "That way you can maximize your wardrobe potential by mixing and matching."

"Mixing and matching what?" Darby asked, honestly confused. Maybe the piped in Muzak had finally seeped so deeply into her consciousness that she'd slipped over the edge into a catatonic state.

"Your apparel," Melanie said, just as perplexed.

Apparently the poor woman was unaware that, before today, Darby's wardrobe contained no two items that couldn't be worn together. Jeans went with everything, right? It was the only fashion rule Darby was certain of. And if she'd been wrong all these years, well, Tugger and the horses hadn't seemed to mind.

"As an example," Melanie said, perking right back up again, in the traditional Glass Slipper manner, "the black pants and jacket you bought this morning would go great with these silk tops." She led Darby to a rack of shimmering fabric in various jewel-tone colors.

Those were shirts? "But they're barely held together by more than a string over the shoulder. That's not a good investment. No durability."

"You're not going to clean horse stalls in them, Darby," Melanie said, not unkindly. "I'm sure that with the proper care, this blouse could last for several seasons, at least. Accessorized differently, of course."

"Of course." Darby didn't make the mistake of questioning her about seasons. She'd already learned that there were women who

willingly subjected themselves to this kind of hell, not merely annu-
ally, like she did, which was bad enough and done only out of neces-
sity. No, Washington doyennes overhauled their complete wardrobe
four times a year. Every year. Because God forbid they show up next
year in something they wore once, fourteen months earlier, to an
event attended by two-dozen people. She had apparently left too
young (or not young enough, depending on how you looked at it),
because she didn't remember her mother ever coming home with a
limo full of tissue-paper-lined boxes and glossy bags with little rope
handles that were, at times, fancier than what was packed inside.
Seemed like a monumental waste to her.

"I only need to get through the next three days," Darby muttered.
Of course, she could actually clean the barn wearing that blouse if
she so desired, then smiled dryly as she imagined Tugger's expression when she waltzed into the barn wearing jeans, chaps, boots . . .
and silk. And maybe the horses would like their feed delivered in little rope-handled bags, too.

"I know your budget doesn't extend to couture and some of the
name designers, but these will hold up." Melanie didn't add the
words "under scrutiny," but they were implied.

It would soon be no secret that Paul Landon III's eldest daughter
had once again waltzed into town. Fortunately, the focus had been
on Pepper during her last visit, so Darby had gratefully kept to the
background. She'd flown in early, hit Pepper's graduation, managed
to get a few minutes alone with her in the social whirl that followed,
then headed straight back to the airport by nightfall.

This time would be different. Grossly different. This time she'd be
examined, analyzed, discussed, and dissected from head to toe,
everywhere she went. If she didn't behave just the right way, wear just
the right things, make the appropriate small talk, why, her father's
reputation could be sullied. Or, heaven forfend, besmirched. Not
that Darby gave a flat fu—er, darn.

She sighed. The not swearing part was going to be the death of her, for sure. And she didn't care what her father thought of her performance, any more than she cared about the opinions of the uptight, pearl-throated society dragons who had nothing better to do than worry what designer label had been stitched into the butt seam of her dress. Like they weren't all made by teenage girls in the Honduras or something, anyway. And she gave even less of a damn about the supposed big deal her father was trying to close; a deal that obviously hinged on how thoroughly his business partner felt his lily-white Scandinavian ass had been kissed after three days of nonstop schmoozing with the *Town & Country* set.

Her concerns about her sister's welfare were beginning to stutter a bit. She had known for some time that Pepper had to start taking more responsibility for herself. Every hour that passed was making it easier and easier to cast her sister adrift on the sea of responsibility. And not having that trust fund life preserver might do her more good than harm.

She fingered one of the silk shirts. And had to admit it actually felt sort of . . . sexy. She swallowed a snort at the thought of making an actual effort to be sexy. If she tried something like this back home, everyone in Big Bend, population 1,356, would have a field day. She was pretty sure even the horses would roll their eyes.

Melanie, ever the sharp one, noticed her brief weak moment of femininity and leaped on the slight advantage. She slipped two blouses—one teal, one crimson—from the rack and pushed them in Darby's hands. "Why don't you go slip them on. See which is better with your coloring."

Darby eyed her suspiciously. "Is this supposed to be a test or something? Because I already had my . . . what do you guys call it?"

"Seasonal self-reflections analysis?"

"Right. And I know I'm supposed to wear cooler colors to play down my skin tone when I have a tan, which is pretty much all year.

So you might as well leave the red one there." She slipped an ice-blue one off the rack herself. "I'll take this one."

Melanie beamed. Darby gritted her teeth into a semblance of a smile, fully prepared to smack the woman if she patted any part of her body in approval. She wasn't a two-year-old being potty-trained, for God's sake. Although that was exactly how she felt.

"I'll wait out here."

"You do that," Darby murmured beneath her breath, privately wishing Melanie would get lost in the shoe department or ladies' handbags, allowing Darby to escape and go find a park to sit in and contemplate her navel for a couple of hours. At least until the Muzak mind-probe wore off.

Instead, like a good little Cinderella, Darby did as she'd been re-lentlessly trained to do for the past eleven stores and made at least a cursory look around for a dressing-room assistant. She knew all about department-store hierarchy now. Chosen for their eye for both clothing and wallet size, trained to be obsequious and ingratiating, it behooved the well-dressed woman to avail herself of their innumera-ble skills . . . not to mention take advantage of the fact that they would happily play gopher and bring endless other sizes and colors upon request. Darby wondered how they'd do mucking out stalls. Now *that* was the kind of dedicated assistance she could really use.

Mercifully, Darby didn't see one around. Possibly because she didn't look like she'd bring a decent commission. Despite the amaz-ing transformation that had already taken place from the neck up, from the neck down, she was still a fashion train wreck. Well, okay, there had been a few changes below the neck, too. None of them visi-ble to the public eye. She was still trying to forget about those.

Although she had to admit that even the heavy fabric of her jeans felt good on her smoothly waxed skin. She could only imagine how the silk was going to feel, and found herself eyeing the lingerie de-partment across the way.

Disturbed by the odd sensation that overcame her, one that felt a little too much like yearning, she poked her head in the dressing room area and called, "Yoo-hoo?" More to make sure none of the little fashionazis were around than because she wanted their help. Having been in the trenches for hours now, Darby was certain they were all trained in guerilla-ambush warfare. All while wearing sensible heels and trim, form-fitting skirts. The Army Rangers could take notes.

No answer. She breathed a sigh of relief. She would just let herself into one of the little rooms, and dress and undress herself. Like an actual grown-up. The dressing rooms in this store were completely private, with nice, thick paneled doors. A few moments completely alone. Heaven!

She headed to the far end and jiggled the doorknob on the last room. It was locked. Well, she was certainly not going to let that little guerilla technique deter her. She slipped her credit card from the purse Melanie had forced her to buy—apparently the back pocket of her jeans was never to be used to actually carry anything, especially her wallet. So why did they have them? she'd wanted to know. All she'd gotten was a silent stare and a small sigh.

She stuck the card between the door and the jamb and jiggled, swearing a little when the lock didn't pop right away. At this rate, she was going to chip her nail polish. *Jesus Christ, what have they done to me*, she silently swore. Worrying about nail polish, for crying out loud. Of course, it was only because she'd have to subject herself to having them done all over again if so much as one flake chipped off, and listen to yet another lecture on cuticle maintenance.

"Well, Blanca del Carmen #8 better damn well last me through the weekend," she groused, "because I'll die before I let one of those sadists come near me or my cuticles with another emery board or those vicious little cutters." She jiggled the card again, swore again as the silk shirts began to slide off their hangers. Juggling her items, she jumped and almost dropped everything when someone spoke directly behind her.

"Maybe I can be of some service?"

Apparently Nordstrom's was quite liberal, was all she could think. Because the guerilla ranger behind her was definitely not female. Perhaps the idea was that if a man fawned all over her selections, it would encourage her to buy more clothes. She was forced to admit that, if the voice was anything to go by, they might actually be onto something there.

She shut down that train of thought. It was embarrassing enough being caught breaking and entering—though she was pretty sure dressing rooms were exempt from that law—she would not be caught drooling over a male dressing-room attendant like the country-hick rube she obviously was. Her attitude kicked into automatic fallback mode. Which was always defense. "Do you really think these doors have to be kept locked?" she started, whipping around, silk shirts clasped to her exfoliated bosom. "Honest to God, it's not like your clientele is going to—Shane?"

"Hi."

That cocky grin she'd actually lost valuable sleep over was every bit as sexy as she'd recalled. Maybe more. "Nordstrom's sales would skyrocket if they let someone like you loose in the dressing rooms," she murmured to herself. Hell, one hour with him and half the departments would be nothing but empty swinging hangers. Starting with lingerie.

"I'm only here as your personal attendant." He picked up the corner of one of the shirts in her hands, and let the silk drift through his fingertips. "Nice choice. Need some help with trying this on?"

"I, uh—" The look in his eye, and the way that silk slid through his fingers, robbed her of every snappy comeback she could think of.

The very idea of both silk and those rough and rugged hands of his caressing her skin at the same time, left her speechless. Not to mention a bit breathless.

He plucked the credit card from her fingers, reached around her, and without taking his eyes off of hers, popped the lock.

"After you?" he asked, eyes full of mischief ... and a few other things.

Things that had her clearing her throat, suddenly desperate for a sip of water. Or him. "I, uh—"

"You know, I'd have thought Mercedes and crew would have worked on that speech problem you seem to be having, before cutting you loose in public." He lifted up a long strand of blonde hair, which now swung in a straight, shiny sheet, cut just below her shoulders.

It was the first time since she'd watched in horror as Andre, one of Glass Slipper's scissor wizards, lopped off eight inches of her hair without so much as batting one of his thick, lush eyelashes—much less asking her permission—that she'd wanted to do anything other than grieve.

"This is very nice." He let the hair slip through his fingers, much like he had the silk. "Though I liked it better all wild and sun-bleached."

"Lowlights," she managed.

His eyebrows quirked. Which somehow triggered her tongue to ON.

"One of the many forms of torture some women apparently willingly subject themselves to," she clarified. "They even pay for it."

"Lowlights," he murmured, running the ends of her hair through his fingers again. "It just looks darker."

Darby finally smiled. "Apparently you *can* be too blonde."

"Really?" he asked in mock surprise.

"That's what they tell me."

"Well, it's stunning. But it's not you."

It irritated her in some way, when it should have flattered her. After all, she agreed with him. Wholeheartedly. "Well, that's what I'm paying them for. To not look like me." Or act like me. Walk, talk, or think like me. She reined in the urge to huff.

And then somehow they were backing up into the dressing room, and the door was closing behind her.

"I know you are. I'm just saying that they're messing with perfection. So it's wasted on me." He stepped closer to her.

"Don't worry," she said, silk shirts hopelessly crushed against her chest. "The princess turns back into a pumpkin shortly."

"I'm pretty sure it wasn't the princess that turned into a pumpkin."

"One can hope," she said, regaining her footing. Something about his cocky smile and gleaming eyes stirred her tongue … amongst other body parts. "Whatever the case, I only have to suffer the indignity till Sunday."

"That's the part I really hate," he said, quite seriously. "And the main reason why I'm here instead of where I'm supposed to be."

Now her eyebrow arched. "You wanted to take advantage of the three-day silk sale at Nordstrom's?"

His grin went blistering hot. "No, I wanted to hear that sharp tongue of yours. And, if I got really lucky, take advantage of it."

Her pulse spiked. "Really."

He stepped closer. "Definitely."

"And were you going to wait for a formal invitation?"

"I don't believe in proper etiquette."

"Well, there's a happy coincidence," she said, tossing the shirts to the floral-print, stuffed chair in the corner, "because I've had it up to here with etiquette of any kind."

"God, I missed you," he said, tugging her hard up against him.

"Yeah, I know the feeling," she said, her voice just a bit shaky. "So shut up and kiss me already."

"You've got some of the princess rules down, I see."

She was dying to brush her lips against his. So close. "Which ones would those be?"

"Commanding your royal subjects to do as you wish."

Her pulse bumped up another notch. "Are you mine to command?"

He wove his fingers into her hair, tipped her mouth to his. "It's beginning to look that way. Let me know if this satisfies."

She pulled back just a fraction, though it cost her. "You know, I just might be able to get used to this Cinderella thing."

"Yeah," he said. "Me, too. Now shut up, Your Highness, and let me have my way with you."

Cinderella Rule #5

*T*here is a time and place for everything. However, it always pays to be aware of potential. Any situation can yield amazing opportunities for those who know how to capitalize on chance.

—MERCEDES

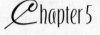

Chapter 5

Shane knew he was in deep trouble the moment his lips touched hers. But then, deep trouble was a place he'd landed in often enough. It didn't scare him.

Darby Landon, on the other hand, terrified him.

She tasted raw, undiluted. Real. And goddamn if that wasn't potent as hell. He wove his fingers through her hair. It felt like a silk waterfall. Erotic, tactile . . . but cool to the touch. He missed the heavy braided waves, made blonde by the heat of the sun. He had the sudden urge to drag her into the nearest shower and drench the straightness right out of her hair, until it sprang back to life beneath his fingers.

He sank his teeth softly into her lower lip, then pulled it into his mouth, so full and perfect, taunting him. "You taste like something decadent," he told her. "Forbidden, but too sinful to pass up."

She snorted and pulled away with a laugh.

Smiling, he framed her face with his hands. "You really don't take compliments well, do you?"

"I do when I've earned them. When it's about my horses, my work. But this?" She motioned to her face and body, then paused. "Okay, well, so this is no longer the real me. Maybe this me looks like some kind of dessert, but trust me on this, no one would typically think of me as being particularly sinful."

"I was talking about your mouth. And I say that exactly describes how you taste. No amount of face paint or hair dye changes that."

Her eyes widened, then darkened. And he found he liked that reaction. A lot. He grinned when she didn't find a fast retort.

"And, seeing as I've had a taste or two of you now—before and after, I might add—I feel qualified to make the judgment."

She rolled her eyes. "Fine, fine. Compliment accepted."

"Now there's a graceful acceptance speech." He chucked her lightly under the chin. "But I'm sure you'll get the hang of it."

"Yeah? I'm all aflutter now." She sounded breezy and unaffected, but the slight tinge of pink to her golden skin said otherwise.

And who knew that making Darby Landon blush could be so much fun? Actually, he was beginning to think there was no end to the kinds of fun they could have together. He walked her back so she bumped up against the green-and-white striped linen-papered walls of the dressing room. "You'll get plenty of practice. I tend to speak my mind. Who knows what else might pop out of my mouth?"

She surprised him by grabbing the front of his shirt and yanking him up against her. "I'm more interested in what I can pop into yours than in listening to ridiculous come-on lines."

He laughed against her lips as she crushed her mouth to his. His laughter quickly faded, however, as she slid her tongue into his mouth. He groaned, and accepted the invasion willingly. Damn if she didn't know how to kiss a man. And damn if he could explain why the thought that she might have done this with someone else riled him up a bit.

He was also startled to discover that her body aligned so perfectly with his. Knee-to-knee, hip-to-hip . . . and, most startlingly, pelvis-to-pelvis. A novel experience for someone his height.

She wove her fingers through his hair, making his skin tingle as her short nails raked his scalp, then angled her head and took the kiss deeper. He'd thought to taunt her a little, tease her a little, brighten up both of their days with a little harmless flirtation, just for the sheer fun of it. Fun being in such short supply these past couple of days.

But this . . . this hunger she'd spiked inside him . . . well, he hadn't counted on that. Much less that he'd react to it like a man just rescued from a long stay on a desert island. Which he supposed he was, actually. But she made him feel downright . . . barbaric.

He braced his hands on the wall beside her head and let his hips push more deeply into hers. She gasped at the feel of him, so perfectly fitted to her. And pushed back.

"Sweet Jesus," he murmured against her mouth, then let his lips drift down her chin, which she oh-so-helpfully tilted, allowing him full access to the tender skin of her throat. "It's insane how badly I want you."

"I know. Totally insane. Completely."

He parted the collar of her shirt with his teeth, his fingers curling inward as he kept his hands on the wall . . . and off of her. It was torture, but he was enjoying his exploration too much to compound it with any other sensation. Yet.

He popped a button free with his teeth, then used his tongue to trace a narrow line down the exposed skin. Then he popped another one. And when her hands came up to help him, he took them and pinned them to the wall.

"Awfully pushy," she managed, but did nothing to dissuade him further as he popped another button, then nudged aside the cotton shirt so he could lick his way along the edge of her pale blue cotton bra.

"I know it's not—" She broke off, squirming beneath the torturous feel of his tongue, now tracing the lower edge of one cup.

"I don't care what it's not," he said. Pale blue cotton was pretty damn arousing at the moment. "It's you. That's all that matters." He took the top edge of the bra between his teeth and pulled it down. It was tight and snug as it rubbed over her nipple, now hard and jutting out for him. He tucked the fabric beneath her breast, which plumped up and pushed forward. Right where he wanted it.

"There truly is a God," she murmured as he took her into his mouth and sucked, moving his tongue slowly, wetly around the engorged tip.

Like hot velvet, he thought. *Jesus.*

Her hips bucked wildly, and he wanted badly to feel them push up against his, where he was so hard and ready. But he couldn't press up against her and take her gorgeous, perfect nipple in his mouth at the same time. Decisions, decisions.

He slid their joined hands up over her head, which allowed him to straighten long enough to brush fully against her. They both gasped. Then he glanced at her face and thought he might drown in those eyes of hers. So bold, so honest . . . so full of want. For him.

He took her mouth in a fast, hard kiss, pushing his hips tight up against hers and rushing them both fast beyond control. She pushed back just as fiercely. He drew one hand slowly down between them, his hips still joined to hers . . . and their gazes locked on each other.

Neither said a word as he tugged the other cup beneath her breast, freeing it for his attentions. He watched her intently as he gently rolled her nipple between his fingers. Her pupils exploded, and her lips parted in a silent gasp. But her eyes remained open, and on him. Almost like a challenge. One he desperately wanted to be up to. Although *up* was not really an issue at the moment. He'd never been so *up* in his life.

"You like my touch," he murmured, dropping his mouth to hers. "Do you have any idea what that does to me?"

She thrust her hips out, making him jerk and twitch. "I have a general idea," she said, smiling against his lips. "You like my touch, too."

"Damn straight." He brushed her tongue with his, then made her watch as he slid one of his fingers in his mouth, then another . . . then gently rolled her nipple between his damp fingertips. She all but growled when he licked his fingers again. "Equal opportunity," he said.

"Take off your shirt," she demanded heatedly.

He lifted a brow.

"I want to feel your skin. On mine."

The command was too close to being exactly what he wanted to deny her. Or himself. He let go of her hands and yanked his shirttail from his pants. But before he could tug it over his head, she was shoving his hands away, a gleam in her eye. He liked that gleam. A lot.

"Fair is fair."

He smiled and lifted his arms.

She surprised him yet again by neatly maneuvering him against the wall as she tugged his shirt over his head. He was going to have to get used to playing with someone his own size.

His bare back bumped up against the cool linen wall. His entire body grew harder still as she casually tossed his shirt aside, then just as casually studied the half-naked man before her. With her shirt hanging open, her breasts pushed up and out of the cups of her bra, and her straight, silky hair cascading over all that tawny bare skin, she looked like some kind of Amazon warrior queen. And he wondered why in the hell anyone at Glass Slipper thought they could improve on that. Or why they'd want to.

"Nice," she said, stepping forward. He lifted his hands. She shook her head and lifted her chin toward the wall above his head.

He challenged her with a look.

"Don't make me make you," she taunted.

"It might almost be worth it."

"You doubt I can?"

"Right now, I don't doubt anything about you."

She grinned and sidled closer to him, until her nipples brushed oh-so-tantalizingly against his own.

He grabbed her hips and yanked her hard against him. His mouth was on hers at the exact instant her fingers fisted in his hair. He lifted her off the ground, surprising a grunt out of her, then spun her so her back was against the wall. She wrapped her mile-long legs around his waist and he thought he would come right there. He'd never wanted to be naked so badly in his entire life.

Their mouths remained mated and they battled for control of the kiss. He wrapped one arm tightly around her back so he could shove her shirt off altogether, then eyed the chair in the corner, wondering if they'd both fit. He was thinking he'd take her right up against the goddamn wall instead, when a knock came at the door.

They both froze, trying like hell to rein in their gasps.

"Darby?"

"Shit," Darby whispered shakily. At his questioning look, she added, "Melanie. Perky Personal Shopper From Hell."

Shane just grinned and pumped against her, making her catch her breath. She nipped at his lip in retribution, but he was grinning even as he nursed the sting with his tongue.

"Yes?" Darby finally managed. She tried to wiggle free, but that only served to enflame them both. Shane clamped her hard against him and pushed her tighter up against the wall. The action drove him up against her again, making them both bite back moans.

"Is everything fitting okay?" Melanie called out.

Darby's gaze met his, and it took a Herculean effort for them both not to burst out laughing. Shane wiggled just a little, prompting a fierce look from Darby. But, he noted, she didn't try to unfold herself from her current position, either.

"Fine," Darby finally gritted out.

"Are you sure? You sound ... Do you need me to help with ... anything? I can come in and help out."

Shane merely gave her a questioning look.

"That is *so* not funny," Darby whispered.

He shrugged. "I'm not really into threesomes anyway."

She puffed out a small snort. "Liar. All men are into threesomes."

"Did you say something?" Melanie called. "I know silk can be difficult to get off and on. Really, it's no problem if you need me—"

"That won't be necessary," Darby said rather abruptly, as Shane had started to kiss her neck again, tugging her earlobe between his teeth, nipping her just enough to make her twitch.

"How is the silk looking against your skin?"

Shane drew a tanned hand over her breast, trapping her nipple between two fingers. "Silk," he whispered. "Yum."

"F-fine," Darby stuttered, as he slowly licked his finger again, then drew circles around her nipple. "Stop it," she whispered fiercely.

"How can I when you like it so much?" Shane whispered back, the epitome of earnestness. "Unless you'd rather go back out there and shop some more."

"Well, when you put it that way ..."

"Exactly what I was thinking."

"I'm still—trying to decide," she called out to Melanie, swallowing a low groan when Shane wet his fingers again. "I am so going to pay you back for this," she threatened.

"Promise?"

She returned his wicked smile, and started to move against him.

"Stop now or we'll both need a wardrobe change," he warned her.

"Are you sure you're okay in there?"

The knob turned and they both went totally still. "Really, I'm fine," Darby called out, sounding only marginally panicked. They both breathed a sigh of relief when the handle went still again.

"I'm pretty sure it's locked," Shane said softly.

"Pretty sure?" She instantly unwrapped her legs, and they both sighed rather wistfully when she eased out from between his body and the wall. Both of them stood on shaky legs.

"I'm almost done. I'll be right out," she told Melanie hastily, eyeing the doorknob.

Shane pouted. Darby stuck her tongue out at him. He wiggled his eyebrows suggestively, and she bit back a laugh.

He shrugged. It was a gift, what could he say?

"Well, I did pick a few other things out for you," Melanie was saying. "I just thought they'd be perfect with your hair and skin tone. I hope you don't mind. Would you like to look at them?"

Shane nodded and pushed her to the door, even as she was refusing.

"I don't know," Darby was saying. "I really think—"

"Just give them a look. If you don't like them, don't try them on."

Shane ducked behind the door and opened it an inch before Darby could stop him. Her openmouthed shock was quickly replaced with a scowl and a leap toward the door, to keep Melanie from opening it farther. She stuck her hand out through the crack. "Okay." She all but yanked the hangers into the room and slammed the door in Melanie's face.

"The colors are slightly warmer, but flattering, I think," Melanie called out. "And the wider cut at the shoulder might be more your style."

"Thanks," Darby said.

"Take your time," Melanie trilled. "I'll be right outside if you want to show me anything."

Darby tossed the hangers onto the chair and began to fix her bra. "We can't stay in here," she told him quietly.

Shane's hand snaked out before she could cover herself up. "Wait." Some of the shirts clung to the chair, the rest slithered to the floor in a pool of silk. Shane couldn't help but picture Darby, naked and sprawled, hot skin splayed amongst all that cool, slippery fabric.

Apparently, his expression gave away his thoughts, and for a split second, he saw her look at the silk with a hint of longing. He took full advantage of the momentary edge ... and felt not a whit of shame for it. He took a step closer to the chair, pulling her with him.

She shook her head, but didn't fight him when he nudged her back until her boot heels hit the chair.

He pushed off her shirt. "Take off your bra," he commanded softly.

Her eyes widened at the tone, but even as her gaze met his, she lifted shaky hands to do as he asked. His body leaped in response. She was strong, willful, and every bit as capable of running this show as he was. That was what made the act all the more sexually charged.

She pushed her shirt off, then let her bra drop to the floor and simply stared at him. She wore faded jeans, cowboy boots ... and skin. And he'd never seen anything so damn erotic in his life. He motioned to the chair behind her. "Sit."

Her eyebrows shot up a fraction, but she slowly lowered herself into the thickly padded chair. Something about those long denim-covered legs, sprawled so carelessly amongst all that silk, was ten times more arousing than seeing her fully naked. Although he wasn't opposed to seeing her both ways in order to make a fair comparison.

He stepped between her negligently spread legs and knelt. Her body tensed, but she remained carefully watchful, not moving toward him or shifting away, as he lifted the peach tank top.

"What are you doing?" she asked, sucking in her breath a little as he draped the shirt across her naked upper torso.

"Seeing what you look like in silk."

She opened her mouth, then shut it again as he slowly drew the soft fabric down her body. "And?" she managed.

"I'm not sure. I'm thinking I like you better out of it." He slid the top back up over her stomach and breasts again, making them both shudder. "There is one thing I'm dying to know, though." Without giving her a chance to ask, he bent over and took her nipple into his mouth.

She jerked at the feel of him. "Shane," she whispered, "you'll ruin the shirt." But she moaned as he slowly moved to her other nipple.

"I'll gladly pay for it. And get hard every time I look at it."

She stared down at him, then let her eyes drift shut and her head tip back as he went back to tasting raw silk . . . and naked Darby.

"How does it look?" Melanie chirped through the door.

Darby jerked hard at the sudden intrusion, but didn't leap out of the chair. In fact, she grabbed Shane's head and kept his mouth right where it was. "Not sure," she managed. "Give me—dear God," she finished beneath her breath as Shane swirled his tongue around her nipple. "A few," she croaked out.

"O-okay. You need another size?"

"God, no," she breathed. "This one is perfect."

There was a pause. "Well. Okay. I'm glad you like it."

"I love it," she said, wholeheartedly.

Shane lifted his head. "Naughty girl."

She paused, listening to the retreating sound of Melanie's heeled shoes. "What can I say, I've been corrupted. It's not my fault."

"Something tells me I'm not much to blame in that department."

She eyed him over the damp shirt. "You think I carouse in limos and pricey department-store dressing rooms on a regular basis?"

"I sincerely hope not."

"Exactly right." Then she shot him a little impulsive smile. "Unless you're involved, of course."

"Oh, absolutely. Then it's entirely acceptable behavior. Encouraged, even." He drew the silk down over her skin. "I simply meant that you are a woman with no pretense. And that you pretty much take what you want, when you want, without apology."

She pondered the statement, then nodded and said, "Thank you."

He grinned in feigned shock. "Wow."

She grinned back, totally unconcerned with the fact that she was sprawled half-naked across a few hundred dollars worth of merchandise. "What can I say? I'm a fast learner."

Shane stood and pulled her to stand as well. "Then I guess I'd better try like hell to keep up."

"If you dare." She stepped around him and scooped up her shirt and bra. "I'm all done," she called out loudly, in a voice totally inappropriate for a pricey department-store dressing room, then looked over her shoulder at Shane. "But I'm hoping we're not?"

Shane scooped up the rest of the shirts. "Oh, not by a long shot."

"Good." She wriggled into her bra, slipped on her shirt, tucked it in, fluffed out her hair, then shrugged everything into place, without ever once looking in the mirror.

Shane wondered if she had a clue how incredible she looked. He doubted she much cared. Which made her all the sexier to him. Earthy, natural. Raw. Wild. *His*, he mentally tacked on. For now, anyway. If he was lucky. He planned to be very, very lucky. "Hey."

She paused, her hand on the doorknob.

Shane pulled the deep teal silk tank top from the pile in his arms and tossed it to her. "This one. Trust me."

She caught it one-handed. "That's the oddest thing of all," she responded. She sent one last glance his way. "Because I do." The door shut between them before he could utter a response.

Still wondering how in the hell she'd ended up with the last word, but smiling because of it, Shane put his shirt back on. And megamergers, inheritance headaches, and Scandinavian financiers be damned, he was going to see Darby Landon sprawled naked in silk again.

After waiting a full ten minutes, he waltzed out of the dressing room. And stumbled right into a matronly department assistant.

"I beg your pardon, sir," she said in her snootiest haute-couture tone. "But that is the ladies' dressing room."

"Great. As it happens, it's a lady I plan on dressing." *And undressing.* He flashed her his most charming smile and dumped the entire load of shirts in her arms. "I'll take all of these."

He pulled out his wallet. Another bonus for the day, he thought, as he bypassed his own cash and tossed his newly minted Morgan Industries corporate credit card on the counter. He'd finally found a worthwhile use for some of Big Al's money.

❧

*S*he didn't recognize herself.

Darby stood before the bathroom mirror as she packed up her array of "natural beauty enhancements" in preparation for checking out of Glass Slipper. The frosted glass bottles, stack of sleek compacts, canvas wrap stuffed with round brushes and vent brushes and blush brushes and every possible comb ever made—including one for her eyelashes, for God's sake—all lay ignored, while she stared at the stranger staring back at her.

"What have you done to yourself, Darby Landon?" she murmured. "Or should I call you Darmilla Beatrice?" She arched one perfectly plucked brow, amazed at the way it curved. "Why, how downright diabolical of you, D.B." She pursed her lips, and put her pinky finger to the corner of her mouth. "Dr. Evil, I presume?"

She tried out her newly acquired fake society laugh next, followed by the ever-so-sincere fake society smile. She swung her hair back over her shoulders—there was actually an art to that; she'd taken a class—then held out her perfectly manicured hand, ignoring tips she'd had redone twice already. If anyone came near her with another emery board, it was highly possible she might file someone to death.

She stared at her face. Botox injections my ass, she thought, wrinkling, then smoothing her forehead. She'd be boiled in oil first. She forced her facial muscles to relax, then worked on making her smile just wide enough, but not too wide. She had to speak without interrupting the perfect line of her lips, jaw, and chin. Too wide and those creases popped up at the corners of her mouth and her chin appeared to double.

The crinkles at the corners of her eyes had been carefully concealed with an amount of makeup normally reserved for circus clowns, but those deadly mouth brackets . . . She adjusted her smile until they faded. God forbid she look like she led any kind of a real life. Or at least one that a socially acceptable two-week, semiannual spa stay couldn't reverse.

"Yes, hello," she said, pretending to greet guests. "So wonderful to meet you, Mrs. Multiple Face-Lift, Mr. Stick-Up-Your-Ass. Please, won't you come in and make yourself at home. Our little twenty-room cottage is ever so nice and cozy, after all." She dropped her hand, and her game face. "If you like that down-home mausoleum feel."

In a few short hours she'd be returning to that very same cozy little mausoleum, where she would be forced to play hostess to a pretentious tightass, looking like . . . "Another pretentious tightass." *Dear Lord, have mercy on my plastic-coated, lacquered-up, foundation-covered soul.*

She grabbed a tiny rope-handled boutique bag and scraped all five hundred dollars' worth of clown goop into it. She'd give it all to Pepper. Who was going to need it to hide the strangle marks after Darby got done wringing her neck. Darby sure as hell wasn't planning on using it again. Surely she already had enough layers of crap on her face to last her through the weekend, as it was. She'd simply shower from the neck down and make sure she didn't sweat. "Excuse me," she said in cultured tones. "Glow. Become dewy." *Sounded like a condition requiring antibiotics.*

One thing was for sure, dewy or desert-dry, she wasn't touching her face. Or her hair. Because the chances of her re-creating the Country-Club-Snotty-Bitch look she currently sported was pretty much nil. Glass Slipper didn't employ an expert talented enough to teach her how to use a round brush or apply blended eye shadow. She was a woman who normally used Mane N' Tail shampoo, for God's sake.

Her mother had died before teaching her oldest daughter the fine art of makeup artifice. Not that she had used her expertise much. She had never spent an ounce more time on her appearance than absolutely necessitated by her position. Of course, Laurel Stockton Landon had been the kind of rare beauty who could come straight from the barn, toss on a floor-length beaded designer creation, run a brush through her shoulder-length hair, dab on a bit of lip gloss, and totally wow the Capitol Hill elite. Nope, that little strand of DNA had flipped right by Darby. Pepper, on the other hand, had gotten those little strands in triplicate. *And she's welcome to them.*

Darby resolutely turned away from the mirror. She did not, as instructed, check her "line": make sure everything was tucked smoothly, and that there was no VPL. Of course, that faux pas could have been avoided if Darby had agreed with Melanie's solution—the thong. Darby had informed her, quite plainly, that there was a better chance of getting her to agree to that Botox injection than there was of getting her to wear what amounted to a crotch stirrup.

Melanie gracefully lost that battle—it would have been completely unseemly to lose any other way—but didn't give up on winning the war. In fact, she'd gone on to navigate Darby through the selection of the icy peach raw-linen blazer, cream-toned light weave shell, and melon-toned cuffed trouser ensemble, with the kind of arbitration usually reserved for mediating the surrender of a small country. Darby had been assured the items were perfect for her coloring and sent just the right message. Which apparently meant that looking like orange sorbet was a good thing.

Flipping off the bathroom lights, she stalked back into the main room—as well as one could stalk in barely heeled flats—and shoved the boutique bag into the one piece of luggage Team Fairy Godmother had coerced her into buying. She'd argued that it was only three days and surely no one was going to know whether her clothes had traveled east in a set of matching Louis Vuitton or her grandfather's Army duffel.

Mercedes had pressed her point by tossing out one of the many little rules they were always hammering her with; in this case, the one about how "one had to be prepared for any contingency." *Like what?* Darby had wanted to know. Pepper was the one who flew to Europe for lunch on impulse. For Darby, an impulse action was buying strawberry jelly instead of grape. Which, as it turned out, didn't taste nearly as good with super crunchy peanut butter. So much for giving in to her impulses.

Which had her thoughts shooting directly to her most recent impulse ... making her skin grow dangerously dewy. What had happened in that dressing room yesterday already seemed like a dream sequence. Surely that hadn't been Darby Landon of the East Coast Landons, or the West Coast Stocktons, for that matter, ripping Shane Morgan's shirt off and yanking his half-naked body against hers ... in a public dressing room. The half dozen silk shirts that had been delivered to her room hours later assured it had indeed.

A discreet knock came at the door just as Darby was getting to the good part. "Ms. Landon?" came Beverly's perfectly modulated voice. "Your car is here."

Darby stiffened, all dangerously dewy recollections turning to damp, clammy dread, instead. She supposed she was just being delivered from one prison to another. But, all in all, Glass Slipper was preferable.

"Would you like assistance with your luggage?"

She looked around her room, making sure she had everything.

She knew she did, she just wasn't ready to give up her warmly decorated cell for the colder, austere one that awaited her at Landon Manor. One thing was for sure, she thought, as her gaze skimmed over the rich rose walls, deep pile rugs, and cloud-soft duvet that covered her sumptuous bed, Glass Slipper definitely delivered a lush nest to languish in while they did their best to hatch a swan from an ugly duckling's egg.

She smoothed her raw-linen feathers and walked to the door, telling herself it was ridiculous to feel nervous. She'd come this far, hadn't she? Still, her palm was damp on the carved-glass doorknob. "Hi," she said to Beverly. "I'm all packed and ready to go."

She beamed. "You look wonderful!" She looked her over. "Perfect ensemble."

"Melanie has great taste."

Beverly pursed her lips. "Now, now, you've taken an active role in this transformation. We talked about this yesterday."

Darby tried not to let her gritted teeth show. "Yes, we certainly did." She and Beverly had spent more than an hour on her "performance and objectives review" the previous evening. Darby's opinion was that they'd gone the extra mile and then some. She wasn't too sure how they felt about the results, though. She'd noticed that Bev had left a number of little check boxes blank. It had left her wondering what the makeover recidivism rate was here. Or if she'd become the first Glass Slipper guest recommended for remedial courses. Or, even more likely, if she would simply be asked not to mention to anyone that she'd been a guest in the first place. It might scare away potential clientele.

"Oh, good, I'd thought I'd missed you." Vivian bustled up. She beamed at Beverly. "I'll show our guest out, dear."

Beverly nodded and smiled at Darby. "Good luck."

She knows I'll need it, Darby couldn't help but think, as she nodded and said, "Thank you."

She took a deep breath and turned to face Vivian, who pursed her vividly painted lips and gave her a studied once-over, then shifted a very direct gaze back to Darby.

"So, do you feel what you learned here will help you with the tasks you're to undertake?"

The question caught her off guard. And the scary thing was, the answer was yes. Every bizarre thing she'd been put through would probably come in handy. She didn't want to ponder what that said about Washington society. "I don't think you left anything uncovered," she said judiciously.

"There's a diplomatic response," Vivian noted.

"I got what I came for."

"But not necessarily what you needed." Before Darby could question her on that—though what she'd have asked, she wasn't sure—Vivian followed up with, "Shane seemed quite taken with you."

Darby had no idea what to say to that, either. "He's an interesting man," she said at length. "Quite charming."

Vivian snorted. "He's a total hottie and everyone knows it, including Shane. He's led quite the storied life, you know. Lived everywhere, done just about everything. Quite the rogue," she said, with a faint smile curving her lips. She winked at Darby. "Will you two be seeing more of each other during your stay?"

Darby's first reaction was a jumble of panicked thoughts, ranging from *Dear God, she heard about the dressing room* to *Yes, I plan on seeing a great deal of him. Preferably naked and in private this time.*

Certain she had Dressing-Room Slut stamped in blazing neon on her forehead, she said, "I—I'm not sure. I suppose if time permits. I'm going to be rather busy during my stay."

"Would you mind overly much if I enquire what events you will be attending? We generally do follow up, if we can be of any help."

Darby's alarm must have shown on her face, because Vivian added, "It doesn't hurt to have an ace in the hole, honey. You never know when you'll need a quick refresher."

"Thank you. That's—that's very kind of you to offer." They'd reached the circular drive and Darby was never so grateful to see a stretch limo in her life. Her bags had apparently already been loaded, as the driver was waiting by the open rear door. She turned to Vivian. "I really do appreciate all you and your staff have done for me."

Vivian took her hand and squeezed it. "Our pleasure, dear."

Darby tried not to let her relief show too obviously as she climbed in the car and let the driver close the door.

Vivian had pulled out a long golden cigarette holder and used it to tap on the window, which Darby reluctantly lowered.

"Will you be attending the Belmont party at Four Stones over the weekend?" she asked quite casually.

Too casually, Darby thought, but what the hell did it matter. "As a matter-of-fact, yes, we will."

Vivian shifted the gold-stemmed holder and it struck Darby that she looked more like a siren out of an old forties movie than a fairy godmother. "We?" Vivian asked.

"I'm escorting one of my father's business associates. Stefan Bjornsen. I'm due to pick him up at the airport shortly."

"Ah," she said, her smile as bright as always. But it didn't quite reach her eyes. "Well, then, you'd best be on your way. With any luck, perhaps our paths will cross at Four Stones." She tapped the roof with her "wand" and the driver pulled away before Darby could do more than nod, smile, and wave good-bye.

"So," Darby murmured. "That was unsettling." She turned and discovered they'd put the bag containing her glass slipper on the backseat next to her. She lifted it out of the tissue paper and turned it around so it caught the sunlight. "Well, Cinderella, we're off to the ball."

Cinderella Rule #6

*D*on't ever underestimate the power of sex in the workplace. Not to suggest you seduce the boss or the client, but it would be ridiculous, not to mention a waste of killer legs, to leave the potential of natural attraction, or sexual influence, unrealized. Men and women are different for a reason. *Vive la différence!*

—VIVIAN

Chapter 6

Shane didn't know what he expected when he steered down the oak-lined drive of Four Stones for the first time in thirteen years, but it wasn't the buzz of activity he found. For a split second he thought the staff was loading up their stuff and heading out in some kind of mass exodus rather than face the new head of the household. Then he realized the numerous workers in white coveralls weren't taking stuff out of the house, they were hauling it in.

Oh, goody. Just what he needed. More shit to get rid of.

He got out of the shiny little Jag he'd rented—there had to be a few perks in the midst of all this crap—and raked his fingers through his hair as he stood and stared at the house he'd grown up in. Most of the time, at least. He'd been back in the D.C. area any number of times over the years, usually just passing through on his way to somewhere else, only stopping long enough to visit Mercedes and crew. He'd never once, despite Big Al's various threats and summonses over the years, come back to Four Stones.

The house sat high above the Potomac River on the Virginia side, just down from Great Falls. There was a fantastic view in the winter, when the leaves were off the trees. The name itself came from the four massive chunks of limestone that jutted out of the ground at the four corners of the property like nature's own boundary markers. Two were located just below the terraced levels at the rear of the estate, right before the land fell away completely in a steep drop, dotted with pine, ending in a huge tumble of other boulder-sized rocks at the river's edge. The other two flanked the front corners of the property, between which ran a low, stone wall, stacked by hand sometime between the Revolutionary and Civil Wars. Which was about as long as the Morgans had lived on this land.

He shaded his eyes and looked at the house itself. Only one of the stone chimneys was part of the original structure, which was one of the oldest buildings still standing in Virginia, or anywhere in the country for that matter. He supposed he should take some pride in being part of a history that was so firmly intertwined with the birth of an entire nation. And by a family that, in this generation alone, had endured battles that would put world wars to shame, he thought, but found himself smiling as he scanned the grounds around the house, which were still exquisitely maintained with dignity and grace. He took note of the one topiary that his mother had insisted on planting after a particularly inspiring trip to England. Maybe Big Al had more sentiment in her than Shane gave her credit for, because he noted that the dancing maiden had been scrupulously cared for. More than likely, Alexandra simply hadn't been able to do anything about it, as it was always featured in photo spreads of the house and grounds in various magazines, both modern and historical ... and removing it would have reflected poorly on her.

A lap pool ran along the south side of the house, one of two pools on the grounds, although Shane doubted this one had been used much since he'd been caught practicing belly flops in it as a twelve-year-old. "Definite waste of prime splash water," he murmured. It was the perfect width for sending a sheet of water out the other side like a tsunami, where it would crash over the edge of a sloping path, taking it directly across the tennis courts, the surface of which insisted on settling and cracking no matter how often they were torn up and resurfaced. Water in those cracks helped the weeds grow faster, and pissed the head gardener off good.

Other childhood memories came back to him. It surprised him that more than a few of them were actually okay. Playing hide-and-seek with the staffers' children in the many hidden servant passages, kissing some of those same girls years later on those same hidden stairwells. Of course, a goodly number of those incidents probably weren't viewed the same way by anyone else involved at the time. Except said girls.

His gaze shifted to the two-story building that sat to the east of the house. The garage, which had existed since the days when it was a carriage house, now had room for ten cars. Or nine cars and one motorcycle, he thought with a nostalgic smile. He was fairly certain, as his purchase of a beat-up old Kawasaki 450 had been pretty much the final straw between him and Big Al, that the garage housed nothing with fewer than four wheels these days. His gaze lifted to the rooms over the garage. Over the decades, they'd housed various house staff, grounds staff, garage maintenance staff and the like. But at the age of sixteen, from the day he'd been kicked out of his seventh and final boarding school, to the day ten months later when he'd torn out of here on that 450, with a hundred bucks and a backpack filled with clothes, that apartment had been his sanctuary.

He'd gotten drunk for the first time in those rooms. Lost his virginity there, as well. Looking back, he couldn't say which one had been the less fulfilling milestone. He'd certainly perfected the art of both over the years, although the former no longer held much allure. The latter however ... His thoughts drifted to a certain department-store dressing room. *Maybe you can go home again*, he thought with a grin, wondering if he could con Darby into coming over … then sneaking her up to those rooms and reliving a few old memories. Some of the better ones, anyway.

He turned back to the house, his smile fading as the glow of the few good times faded, and the weight of what he faced today bore down on him once again. "Should have stayed in the damn dressing room."

He set off across the front lawn, his attention once again on the hustle and bustle. On a good day, Four Stones was attended by a relatively large staff, both household and grounds. Today it looked like they had enough people to provide the extras on the set of *Braveheart*. Now *that* had been a great job, he mused. Paint your face blue, scream like a madman, and run at the other guys with big sticks. Easiest money he'd ever made.

He wound his way in and around the throngs, wondering just what in the hell any of them thought they had to do. He realized the house needed basic tending to, and he'd told the lawyers when they'd tracked him down not to let anyone go. He didn't want to be responsible for their livelihoods, but he also sure as hell didn't want to put a few dozen people out of work without even knowing what it was they did, or for how long they'd been doing it. He did know there were several families who'd had various offspring working for the Morgans for more than a few generations. He wasn't looking forward to figuring out who was going to stay and who was going to have to go. He'd do whatever he could to help them secure other jobs, if necessary.

He sighed, realizing just how much worse this was all going to get before it got remotely better. He searched the grounds for someone who looked like more than a worker drone, someone in charge. He was supposed to meet Big Al's personal lawyers here, but had hoped to beat them out by an hour or so. Have some time to get over whatever emotional impact seeing the old place might have on him. He hadn't been entirely certain what that impact would be, but he hadn't counted on it being so ... complicated.

He stepped into the grand foyer, stared up the sweeping split grand staircase, and actually felt his heart tighten inside his chest. He was one in a very long line of Morgans to stand in this very spot, to take in the magnificence of all that this family had created and built upon. "And just what is your contribution to this legacy going to be?" he murmured beneath his breath, as the real weight of the task set upon him began to fully sink in.

How was it he'd managed to make it all the way to this very spot and not realize how much more was at stake here than making a few massive, economy-altering corporate decisions and finding homes for a few million dollars' worth of personal belongings? In his mind, the Morgan legacy had been Alexandra's legacy. Not his. And not those who had come before them, either. *And never have I been more shortsighted*, he thought as he stared up at the portraits that lined the stairwell that rose a full two stories high.

But I've never been one of those people, he thought, heedless of the people bustling past him. Not that they were paying him much mind. He trailed a hand up the glossy banister as he slowly climbed one set of stairs, looking at the same portraits he'd seen hundreds of times before, but was only now really seeing for what they were. Maybe his sense of being an outsider stemmed from the fact that he'd lost his parents at such a young age, or because Alexandra wasn't the most maternal of people. Or because she'd tried so hard to conform him to her ruthlessly defined image of what a successful Morgan should be, that Shane had gotten her vision mixed up with what all Morgans thought success should mean.

"Shane? Is that you?"

Lost in thoughts far deeper than he was comfortable having, he gladly shoved them aside and turned at the landing, to find two older men coming toward him. Expensively dressed, leather briefcases in hand, they crossed the marble foyer. It was the first time he could ever remember being happy to see lawyers.

It wasn't until he reached the last step that he recognized the older of the two gentlemen. "Hal?" He grinned, as the man he'd once considered an uncle broke into a welcoming smile of his own. Shane tugged the hand Hal offered and pulled him—so much shorter than he recalled—into a quick hug. "It's been a long time," he said, once again surprised by the emotions pelting him.

"Too long," Hal said, patting his back before letting him go. His blue eyes had faded a bit but still looked sharp.

Hal Calloway had been Al's personal lawyer and erstwhile suitor for decades. He'd treated Shane with a sort of avuncular understanding when there had been little coming from other quarters, and even run long distance interference on the occasions when Shane had been in trouble at boarding school. His legal advice had rescued Shane from more than one scrape in his teen years. What little male influence he'd had in his formative years had come from this man. "I thought I'd heard you retired," he said, his throat surprisingly tight.

"I didn't think they kept you up on the latest in Bora Bora, or wherever you were."

Shane grinned. "Bora Bora was a few years back. And I do keep up on the important things."

A shadow of pain flickered across the older man's face and Shane was immediately contrite. Despite his affection for Shane, Hal had felt deeply for Alexandra for a long time, though she'd refused to acknowledge it, much less act on it. Her loss, Shane had always thought. Along with wishing Hal had found someone who could love him back. He'd asked him about it once—he'd been drunk at the time, upset after his first girlfriend of more than two weeks had dumped him—and Hal had simply shrugged and told him that you love who you love. You don't always get to pick.

Darby's face flickered into his mind, and he just as swiftly flickered it back out again. She was fun, she was here, and she understood family angst. More than that? Not that he planned on. She had a ranch to run.

And he had an empire to dismantle.

"I'm sorry," Shane told Hal, his first sincere condolence regarding his late grandmother's passing. "I know you always wished that she and I could work things out. Disappointing you is my only regret."

Hal shook his head, but the sadness didn't leave his eyes. "No need for that. And, to answer your earlier question, I did retire. But Alexandra still retained my old firm, and they asked me to step in and deal with this, seeing as it's going to get a bit tricky." His smile reached his eyes this time. "She was an old battle-ax, but I understood her motives and desires better than anyone. Who better to help you wade through this mess, eh?"

Shane squeezed his shoulder. "A mess it certainly is. And you couldn't talk her into leaving all this to someone who might have a clue in hell what to do with it?" He'd said it lightly, but Hal's smile evaporated, and his expression grew quite serious.

"You might have given up hope for reconciliation, but she never did. She certainly expected to have more time to make that happen, but she hadn't been idly waiting for you, either." He lifted a hand to stave off Shane's reply. "I won't sugarcoat it, she was furious over your continued defection. She wasn't used to being thwarted. Considering all she'd done for this family, to have you toss it in her face as if it meant nothing, you who were the last of the actual Morgan line, with Morgan blood running in your veins ..." He broke off, shook his head. His faded eyes were suspiciously bright when he looked back at Shane. "I'm sorry, I didn't mean to—I guess I haven't come to terms with this as well as I'd hoped. I just thought you should know that contrary to her occasionally vilified and, I'll admit, well-earned public persona, she was quite human, and quite capable of being hurt."

"Hurt?" Shane asked incredulously. "Did she ever stop to think about what she was doing to me? She asked for all this when she married my grandfather, and after his death she willingly took on the role of family matriarch, with a vengeance that was purely her own, I might add. I was never given that kind of choice. Did she ever once ask about my hopes, my dreams? We both know the answer to that. She and I didn't have conversations, Hal. She dictated, and I was supposed to prostrate myself at her feet in abject appreciation of all she had planned for me. It didn't matter if they weren't my plans, or if I'd be miserable carrying them out. It was always her way or the highway." He held Hal's gaze, but worked hard to soften his tone. "So I chose the only route I could. I don't regret that." He touched his arm. "I'm truly sorry if that hurts you. That's the last thing I want. But she's not the only one capable of being hurt."

Hal held his gaze for an interminable number of seconds, but said nothing else. Instead, he stepped back and gestured for the other man to come over. "Shane, this is William Baxter. He's been overseeing your grandmother's affairs since I stepped down."

Shane shook the man's hand, appreciating the no-nonsense grip. With Shane and Hal already on the verge of acting like overemotional fools, they'd both likely need someone with a little objectivity. "Nice to meet you. I appreciate all the hard work you're going to have to do to help me sort this out." He looked to Hal. "I do appreciate this. More than you can know."

Hal nodded. Shane forced his shoulders to relax, then smiled and motioned to the workers carrying in what looked like enough flowers to decorate a Rose Bowl float. "Now, would someone like to tell me what in the hell is going on around here?"

⁊

*D*arby wasn't sure what she'd expected while waiting for Stefan Bjornsen to disembark the plane at Reagan National. The Swedish version of her father, she supposed. An older man, probably blond gone to white, in that dashing Scandinavian way, with a cool smile and sharp blue eyes that didn't invite much in the way of bullshit. She'd already decided that, while she'd do her best to be civil and maintain her end of the conversation, she wasn't going to sweat it out much beyond that. She was here to be glorified arm candy, nothing more.

She had that charity event to escort him to this evening, which would keep them from having to make too much small talk. Of course, she was nervous about having to introduce him around to a bunch of people who were going to be more interested in sizing her up and gossiping about her surprise return the moment she turned her back. Well, screw them, she thought defiantly. Dad's big deal or no, she wasn't going to prostitute herself any more than she already had. Next time, her father could get on a goddamn plane in time and play host himself.

She'd be polite to Mr. Bjornsen, shepherd him around, then hustle him over to Four Stones as early tomorrow as possible. If she had to spend a couple of days in a family mausoleum, better someone else's than her own. Surely Stefan would migrate to his own kind, allowing her to hide somewhere and count the minutes until her father showed up to take over. Then she could head west. Home. To peace and solitude.

Shane flashed through her mind and she couldn't help but wonder if he'd be at the charity event tonight. Or at the Belmont party this weekend. He'd said they weren't done with each other yet. And if the amount of time she had spent thinking about what they had left to do with each other was any indication, she agreed with him. She wished she knew how to contact him, tell him where she'd be, finagle him an invitation to Four Stones or something. That would certainly give her something interesting to do while she waited for her exit cue.

The obvious route would be to contact Mercedes. "Botox to that," she said, straining to see if Bjornsen was in the crowd coming through the doors leading from Customs. The driver at her side held a tasteful sign so that Stefan would be able to find them, but Pepper had said that the one thing their father insisted upon was the personal touch, which meant showing up at the airport. Darby sighed and shifted her weight. Her flat shoes felt weird to someone used to boots. Her clothes didn't feel right, too slippery against her arms and legs. So different from cotton. And everything had to be all tucked in and pleated just so. Then there was the blazer with the lightly padded shoulders, making her feel like a defensive end for the Broncos.

And it only got worse. Tonight she actually had to wear a dress.

Just as she decided to retaliate by sleeping in ratty sweats and the oldest, baggiest T-shirt she owned, the crowds shifted in front of her. And a stunning, godlike creature of a man strolled through, parting people like Moses parted water. He was tall, easily topping her by a good couple of inches. His hair was the palest of blond, straighter and silkier than her own, although Darby was certain he hadn't had to pay to have his done. He wore it startlingly long, almost to his shoulders. The look made his face seem all the more angular and striking; his mouth as ruthlessly chiseled as his cheekbones and jawline.

He wore his suit with almost negligent elegance. He wasn't remotely rugged, but in his very refinement, the almost casual way his clothes hung on his lean, lanky body with effortless perfection, he seemed somehow all the more alpha male.

Darby tried to drag her gaze away from him, if for no other reason than to observe him with whoever it was he was here to meet. Probably a woman. She couldn't even imagine what he'd be like as a lover, although she couldn't deny, as her gaze drifted to his hands—long, elegant . . . and ringless—that she was imagining it all the same. Cold and distant, as his coloring would suggest? Or ruthlessly skilled and determined.

She shivered a little, deciding it had to be the latter. He looked far too self-assured to settle for less than explosively satisfactory sex.

And then he was stopping in a direct line right in front of her. *Oh, God, he'd caught her staring.* She quickly glanced away, at some oblivious point behind his shoulder, looking for the older gentleman she was expecting to appear. The older gentleman she wouldn't be fantasizing about as a lover. *Jesus.* First Shane in the dressing room and now she was having some Nordic God fantasy in an airport. Take her out of her element and she apparently became a raving slut. Or maybe she just needed to get out more back home.

Wait. Her gaze swung back to the man as it all clicked into place. Into horrible, can't-be-happening-to-me place. Nordic God. Nordic. As in Scandinavian. "Oh, shit," she murmured beneath her breath. Pepper said he was a business partner of Dad's. That meant sixties. Maybe late fifties. This … this … golden-maned, romance-cover model was, at best, mid-thirties. And he was looking her way.

Shit, shit, shit.

Apparently, she'd been blocking the sign bearing his name. Because he was headed right toward her.

It occurred to her that she should be rejoicing. If she was going to have to squire someone around, better Cover Model God than some old geezer, right? Not right. She was suddenly excruciatingly aware of every inch of satin and lace binding her body. And all the other non-Darbylike layers that covered them. She wasn't herself, and this whole charade would be a lot easier to pull off if she could just be an actor in costume. Genderless, for all intents and purposes. She didn't want to deal with being aware of herself as a woman, a sexual being. It was going to be hard enough to play this game. Hard. She forced a little swallow down her suddenly dry throat. Lord have mercy on her Cinderella slutty soul.

It flashed through her mind that she hadn't been all that concerned about sexual awareness with Shane. But then, she didn't have to impress Shane, did she? He'd liked her pasty and pale, wearing six-year-old jeans. She didn't have to fake anything to show her interest in him. And it wasn't that she planned to show any interest in Bjornsen, either. She'd just feel a hell of a lot more self-conscious now while she did her little hostess-gig thing.

She found herself wishing Shane was here, right now. He was the only one in this whole charade who understood how complicated and uncomfortable this was. On the other hand, she really didn't want to juggle two alpha males at the same time.

Bjornsen shifted his briefcase to his other hand and extended his free one. She refused to look at those long slender fingers again. Which wasn't exactly a problem since she was caught up in his surprisingly dark eyes. He was so blond that his hair was almost like white gold, and she'd expected bright blue eyes. Bjornsen's looked almost black. It was a very arresting combination. And a little ... well, she wasn't entirely sure. Unnerving, certainly.

He smiled broadly and she was surprised to see a pair of dimples winking on either side of those sculpted lips. He hadn't struck her as the dimply-cute type. But when he smiled ... well, maybe *cute* wasn't the right word. Boyishly charming, yet still predatory, was the definition that came to mind. She tried not to let her reaction show as he took her hand in his own. His wasn't soft, but it wasn't callused and rugged, either. Pampered, Darby thought, and let go as quickly as was acceptable.

"Welcome to the States, Mr. Bjornsen," she said. Hopefully all the noise and hustle of the airport masked the tight, squeaky element she heard, and subtly tried to clear her throat.

"Please, call me Stefan," he said, his accent strong, but his diction clear and sharp. He stepped back and gave her a clearly assessing once-over that was more than a little disconcerting. "Your father told me how lovely you were, but I had no idea. I was expecting someone ... shall we say, a bit more of a child? And yet, you are all woman."

She most certainly was, as the tight, tingly ache in her breasts would happily testify. Not to mention the twitchy feeling she was getting down below. Damn silk panties. This was all Melanie's fault. *I am woman, hear me moan*, she thought, disgusted at her lack of self-control.

"Penelope, is it?"

The tingly twitches vanished. *Oh, for God's sake, no one had told him.* She was going to kill Pepper. "Actually, I'm Penelope's older sister. She was unfortunately detained on some ... business." She mustered up her best fake sincere smile. "I hope you don't mind the last-minute substitution."

"Paul has another daughter?"

Darby didn't know why that stung. She was well aware that her father didn't speak of her any more than she made a habit of talking about him. "I'm Darby. Sorry for the confusion. Have you known my father long?"

It was as if his thoughts had drifted for a moment. His expression was remote, almost austere. Then he blinked those odd dark eyes of his, and his smile snapped right back into place.

It always amazed Darby when people could turn their emotions on and off like they had some sort of internal Clapper.

"For a short time only," Stefan said, dimples flashing once again. "I cannot believe he forgot to mention someone as lovely as you, or perhaps it's my own faulty memory."

He was being charming ... and lying through his teeth. He'd expected Pepper Landon and Darby suspected, Clapper control notwithstanding, he wasn't all that thrilled to find a pinch hitter in her place. What difference did it make? She might not be cute and adorable, but hell, she'd cleaned up all right. And arm candy was arm candy, right?

However, just in case he had any ideas about tasting that candy ... She planned on making a little international phone call to her sister as soon as she was alone. She didn't care what Pepper might have done in her place, but for the time being, Stefan could just Clap Off any ideas he might have about this sister being his personal lollipop.

"I spend most of my time managing my mother's family property out West," she said, putting her mind firmly back on the business-only track. She made the clutch call to stick as close to the truth as possible, yet still try to sound acceptable to a power player like Bjornsen. If he didn't go for it, well, tough shit. This was the best she could do without a script or knowing all the facts. She stepped back as the driver commandeered the luggage cart from the skycap. "We're slated to attend a charity function at the Kennedy Center tonight at nine," she told him. "Unless you're feeling jet-lagged, then we can always get you settled in at the house and—"

He waved away her concern. "I fly like most people drive a car. Jet lag does not affect me."

He didn't say it as a boast, but casually, like a man who spent an inordinate amount of time in the air probably would. And yet, she got the distinct impression that he was not the type who admitted to weakness. *Faulty memory, my ass,* Darby thought, all the while maintaining the fake society smile. "Good. Then we'll head out to the house. I can have something sent up to your room, as we won't be dining until late—"

He looked at her somewhat quizzically. "In Europe we dine a bit later than you Americans. Nine o'clock is quite acceptable."

And he assumed, as Paul's daughter, she'd be aware of such things. Jesus, she was screwing up already. "Of course," she replied, scrambling. "But with the long flight, I was just thinking you might be hungry. After all, we all know airline food is hardly haute cuisine. My father's chef is—"

"Wonderful, I'm certain. As is the one I employ on my private jet."

He owned a jet big enough to make transcontinental flights? How was she supposed to guess that? Again with the lack of information.

Pepper had only given her flight info and social itinerary. She'd said Darby was to keep him happy—but not *that* kind of happy. Well, she wasn't so sure about that. Pepper had some serious 'splaining to do.

Because while he'd made the comment kindly enough, there was undeniable curiosity in his eyes now. Curiosity like a cat staring at a mouse. Just before pouncing on it. Making her feel uncomfortably exposed, both as his Washington escort, and as a woman. Worse, she wasn't sure just which part he wished to exploit. Just what had his expectations been? Was he simply gauging her weak spots in hopes of finding a way to sweeten his end of the business deal with her father later? Or as a way to pass his downtime while waiting for her father to show up?

Well, years of observing animal behavior had taught her a great deal about reading character. Four-legged and two. And she'd bet the farm that the two-legged animal in front of her likely categorized women as the weaker sex. Meaning the cat-and-mouse game was all about him trying to figure out how to play her to his best advantage. He'd probably realized—quite rightly—that whatever game plan he'd devised for Pepper was not going to work on big sister.

What Mr. Bjornsen didn't yet know, but would soon find out, was that Darmilla Beatrice Landon didn't get played. Because she didn't give a rat's ass about the deal. Or putting in sack time with a guy just because he looked like God's gift to the female race.

Shane's image floated through her mind. That situation was completely different, of course. Comparing Stefan to Shane was like comparing a sleek racing car to a muscled-up hot rod. One was all about finesse and subtle performance. The other was all in-your-face confidence and knock-your-socks-off power. Well, well. Perhaps she'd been a power player all along.

She stifled a knowing smile as she turned with Stefan to follow their driver out of the terminal. And if there was a bit more swagger to her step than was advisable, well, so be it. If she was forced to play the princess, then she was going to be Cinderella with an attitude. *That* was her power.

If anyone thought they were going to use her because she represented the weakest link ... they were about to discover they were messing with the wrong woman.

Cinderella Rule #7

*O*n matters of importance, be aware that those closest to you may not possess the clarity of mind to provide an objective opinion. Don't be fooled into mistaking words of the heart for wise counsel. When in doubt ... get a second opinion from someone who doesn't love you.

—MERCEDES

Chapter 7

"We're having a what?" Shane paced the length of Alexandra's formal library. He'd never understood why it was called the formal library, since the one on the opposite side of the house wasn't exactly a warm and cozy little book nook, either.

Hal calmly placed his briefcase on the small sitting table, clicking open both locks simultaneously. "The Belmont. Third leg of the Triple Crown. You might have heard of it." A smile ghosted his thin lips. "Hell, for all I know, you've raced in it."

"I tried. I was too tall." Shane was joking, but didn't quite pull off the smile. He shoveled his fingers through his hair. By now it should be standing on end. "I guess I assumed that with Alexandra's death, the show, as they say, would not go on."

His grandmother, despite her off-with-his-head dowager duchess mien, was quite well-known as one of the more prodigious Washington hostesses. The parties always had well-coordinated themes that no one else would dare attempt, and the guest lists were renowned for their diversity. No one dared not attend, whether it was a spring luncheon featuring an Alice in Wonderland croquet tournament or a black tie and white teeth vampire ball.

Shane assumed it wasn't Alexandra's innovative themes that cinched the A-list attendance, but the purse strings she dangled in front of her guests' noses. Whether they hoped to secure a donation to a certain charity, or funding on a new wing for this hospital or that university, they were all marionettes and she the master puppeteer. Everyone seemed happy enough with their respective roles.

Shane pinched the bridge of his nose. "Who authorized this?"

William, Alexandra's current lawyer, cleared his throat. "It was stipulated in her will that any events or projects undertaken in her name at the time of her death were to be seen through to completion."

"Surely she didn't intend that to include a garden party?"

Both Hal and William looked at him in surprise.

"Garden party?" Hal chuckled. "It's hardly that simple."

"Those invited to attend generously donate to the Morgan Foundation. This event essentially gathers the working capital for the foundation for an entire year," William explained. "Not to mention that the guests likely anticipate being able to do a fair amount of wheeling and dealing for their own causes over the course of the weekend."

"Weekend? This shindig lasts *two days?*"

"Surely you've some experience with events like this?" William said.

Shane looked to Hal as if to say, "He's kidding, right?" He tried to summon the patience he'd lost somewhere during his umpteenth meeting two days ago. He should have grabbed Darby from that dressing room and taken off with her. He wondered what she'd think of Bali this time of year. He regretfully let that image go, and sighed. "I was kept in boarding schools during most of my formative years," he explained to William, "precisely so I wouldn't be here during Alexandra's many soirees. I don't think she trusted me to behave in a manner acceptable to the Morgan name." He looked to Hal. "Can you imagine?"

Hal didn't quite manage the hoped-for smile in fond reminiscence.

Since their little contretemps earlier, Hal had remained a bit tense. Shane wished he hadn't snapped the way he had. He'd been so relieved to finally have a possible ally, he'd discounted how deeply Hal was grieving. His mistake, and, he imagined, probably not his last one, before this was all over.

Shane took a calming breath, then said, "So, okay, two days. The race is run on Saturday, is it not? We party all night, shovel everyone out of here Sunday morning, and—"

"Actually," William broke in, "some guests will begin arriving tomorrow afternoon. A casino night is planned for the smaller ballroom tomorrow evening. All proceeds go to the foundation. Outside, we'll have a string quartet on the back terrace for those who might enjoy strolling the grounds. Saturday is race day, when the real event begins. The rest of the guests are scheduled to arrive by ten in the morning. The lawn party begins at one, with the catering staff in racing silks. This year's theme is 'Turn-of-the-Century Belmont, a Centennial Celebration,' with those attending encouraged to wear attire befitting that time period. The race itself will be projected on big-screen monitors both outside and indoors. There will be a sit-down dinner late that evening, around eight. Sunday will begin with a brunch. A round-robin tennis tourney is slated, then an afternoon supper." He waved his hand. "It's all taken care of by the staff, as is cleanup and the dismantling of the tents and ornamentation. It should all be over by three or so on Sunday."

The house was already a showcase, with numerous paintings, sculptures, carpets, and furnishings, all of which could be displayed in any number of museums. So why they felt they had to drag in life-sized racing horses, draped in flowers and stationed not only on the grounds but inside the house as well, Shane had no idea. Every room, from the sitting areas to the bathrooms, now reflected an early 1900's horse-racing theme.

Too much money seriously compromised a person's ability to exercise common sense, Shane thought, not for the first time. He dropped into a hard-as-stone Louis XIV chair. "Fine, fine. Maybe we should reschedule this for next week. I'll meet you both Monday. There are a few things I could be doing over the weekend myself." He had a stack of folders from Alexandra's private files out in the car. He'd only flipped through the three drawers full of folders, but a handful looked like they dealt with the Celentrex takeover, so he'd grabbed them for a closer look. Hopefully there'd be something to help him make the decision. Or, better yet, point him in the direction of who he might hand the decision-making over to.

But that wasn't where his thoughts went at the moment. Presented with the possibility of an open weekend, work was the last thing on his mind. Darby was the first. If only he could steal her away from her baby-sitting post. Maybe use the corporate jet to fly them both to Italy, show her the sunrise in Tuscany. It was the purest of golden light, and with her hair down and wild, and all that tawny, toned skin . . .

William cleared his throat. "Actually, you'll be expected to attend. You're the de facto host, as it were."

Shane wondered if Alexandra was somewhere in purgatory, having a great laugh over all this. "If what's already been done could happen without my overseeing any of it, then surely the party itself could go on without a host, de facto or otherwise."

"The planning was highly detailed, well in advance as always, and I've been overseeing the various crews, having power of approval on such things, pending your return."

"Well, you can continue approving, because if it was up to me, I'd just haul in a truckload of beer kegs, steam some Maryland blues, line a few tables with enough fried chicken and cole slaw to feed an army, and hire the best dance band I could find. Maybe dig a giant sandpit in the front yard and set up some beach volleyball. Run belly-flop contests in the lap pool. Hell, we could probably put together two fairly decent softball teams with a big enough guest list." He leaned back and crossed his ankles. "Now that's a party."

William looked properly horrified, but Hal surprised him by smiling. The honest warmth caught Shane off guard.

"Maybe if you'd stuck around all those years ago," he said, "things would have been different around here. Or at least more interesting."

Shane didn't know what to say to that. Hal's tone was teasing, but also gently chiding. Admonishing the young man he'd expected more from than he'd gotten. "You know I've always appreciated everything you did for me back then," Shane said sincerely. "But you of all people had to know I wasn't ever coming back. Not while Alexandra controlled things with her iron fist. I couldn't let her control me, too. And, while I respect your feelings for her, you have to admit that she wouldn't have been content with anything less than me jumping to her every command."

"You had more control here than you might have suspected. You were hardly a man when you left."

"I didn't want control here. I simply wanted to live my own life, be a regular guy."

Hal made a dignified snort. "Your life has hardly been patterned after that of a *regular guy*."

Shane's lips quirked. "True, but it's been mine to lead, to live. I didn't want the empire. I didn't ask for any of this." He lifted his arms to encompass the room and all the crushing enormity of what sprawled out beyond it.

"That's the odd nature of birth, isn't it?" Hal responded. "Some come into this world saddled with enormous debt, some with God-given talent, some with disabilities, and some with kingdoms. I doubt any of them asked for it, nor much wanted it. Yet it will be theirs." He gestured with his hand, much the same as Shane had. "Just as this is now yours. What I'm saying is, that if you'd stayed, perhaps you'd have had more say in what it has become."

Now it was Shane's turn to snort. "As if Alexandra would have allowed any vision other than her own to rule the day."

Hal shook his head. "You have no idea what enormous power you've wielded all along. Part of that is my fault, of course. But I was obliged to follow Alexandra's wishes." He glanced at William, who gave him a silent nod in return.

Shane looked between the two of them, then back at Hal. "What are you talking about?"

"You are the last Morgan. That was—is—your base of strength, and, I daresay, what would have put you on even ground with Alexandra." Shane laughed outright, but Hal waved him silent, his expression quite serious. "I well knew, as did anyone who spent any time with her, how important the family name was to her. She might have married into this family, but by the time her father-in-law passed the mantle to her, she'd well-earned her place. With his only blood heir—your mother—only a small child, Charles had no choice but to do his best to instill that fierce Morgan pride and loyalty in his daughter-in-law. He all but challenged her to do better with it than he had." Hal's own smile was somewhat fierce. "And *that* she most certainly did." He looked at Shane. "It was that intense pride and loyalty in the Morgan name, the importance of that heritage, that she wanted to pass on to you."

"I know you believe that, but more than anything, I think she was mostly interested in the importance of adding to the Morgan coffers."

Hal lifted a shoulder. "It was certainly a focus. She lived to one-up the old man. But she never forgot she wasn't a Morgan by blood. God knows, he never let her. And I think—no, I know—that it haunted her that she hadn't been able to instill the same pride and loyalty in the Morgan name in you, that Charles had in her. It was her one failure." His smile was affectionately amused. "And we all know how well she handled failure." Hal looked to Shane, but the wistfulness in his expression, the emotional sheen in his eyes, kept Shane from interrupting. "She was born with beauty, brains, and the kind of drive and determination that rightfully terrified those who weren't blessed with the same. But when it came to dealing with others . . ." Hal lifted a shoulder. "That was, perhaps, her real failure. She lacked patience, and, some would say, compassion." He sighed. "I tried to tell her that ordering you home, commanding you to make this or that appearance for the sake of the family name, was in direct opposition to your nature." His lips quirked again, though the grief was still clear in his eyes. "She didn't listen to me any more than she did anyone else. She was convinced you'd grow weary of trotting the globe eventually, and come to your senses. She simply couldn't understand why you'd wish not to."

"And yet you think she'd have listened to me if I had?"

"She wouldn't have had a choice." Hal paused, then glanced at William again before looking back at Shane. "This"—he gestured once again—"was always only going to be yours. Charles's will stipulated that all Morgan holdings would only pass to another Morgan. A blood Morgan."

Shane's mouth dropped open. "But Alexandra—"

William broke in. "She was, essentially, a trustee. Charles left her in charge of everything, as your mother was hardly more than a toddler when Alexandra's husband died. Your mother showed scant interest in the empire and, admittedly, Alexandra had grown quite fond of her role here and was more than happy to run it for her. Though she did try and rein Francine in from time to time. With your mother's untimely death, by the terms in her grandfather's will, all Morgan properties shifted to you."

Shane's gaze darted from one lawyer to the other. Still stunned speechless, he didn't know which question to ask first. "But Alexandra was the driving force—she pretty much single-handedly grew the Morgan holdings into an international empire."

Pride shone on Hal's face. "I think even the old man would have been impressed."

"But you're saying it was never really hers?"

"On paper? No," William said.

"But certainly emotionally, and in every other way it could be, yes, it was hers as much as it had ever been any blood Morgan's," Hal added. "Legally, once you were of age, she was bound to hand it over to you. Or at least begin the process of shifting it to your control."

"Why—" Shane broke off, then shook his head, unable to assimilate this latest bit of insanity. "I guess, given our history, I don't have to ask why she wasn't in any hurry to hand it over, but she never even told me."

Hal just gave him a look. "If and when she could track you down, she did try."

"I got orders to show up at this gala or that charity event. Never did I get so much as a postcard telling me that I was—"

Hal cut him off. "Those various summons home over the years were ostensibly for this function or that. She wasn't going to inform you of something that important via telegraph. By the terms of the will, you would have been bound to run the company and manage the holdings. Of course, you could have chosen to allow her to continue."

"Which she has to know I'd have gladly done. I still should have been told." He slumped back, still reeling.

"Yes, you should have. I argued with her many times over the years about that very subject. She kept insisting it wasn't time, that you needed to be older, more mature, before news of such importance was brought to bear on you." He lifted that negligent shoulder again. "Maybe you would have turned it over to her. But then again, maybe you wouldn't. Alexandra was no fool. Of course she doubted you'd have wanted it, but given the rocky nature of your relationship, she couldn't be sure you wouldn't have simply given it all away, just to spite her." Hal leveled a steady gaze at Shane, who felt his face warm at the silent accusation. "It was a risk she didn't take lightly. She had an obligation to Charles, and had you come home and decided you sincerely wanted to run things, she would have done whatever she had to do to prepare you for that role. But she hadn't worked herself to the bone, to let you waltz in and snatch it all away from her."

"You honestly believe that if I had come running when she'd snapped her fingers, she would have just handed me the keys?"

"Knowing Alexandra, she would have bent the rules to suit her needs. She did envision you taking over at some point. That was Charles's desire, and, as the last remaining heir, hers as well. But no, I doubt she'd have clued you in to the whole truth until she'd determined that you had the same Morgan pride and determination she'd come to have herself."

"I'm not so sure."

Hal didn't look insulted, but merely nodded. "As long as she maintained her place in the scheme of things, I believe she would have, yes."

"You mean, as long as I ran the empire the way she wanted it run."

Hal sighed. "Perhaps. Morgan Industries, along with all the family holdings, was everything to her. Her mark on its history was very important to her."

"Because of Charles?"

Hal smiled again. "In the beginning, maybe. You thought Alexandra was stubborn, you should have met your great-grandfather. The two of them made quite a pair. World Wars have been conducted and won with less strategy and combat skills than the two of them possessed."

Shane blew out a long sigh and let his chin drop to his chest. "I can't believe this," he said to no one in particular, although he knew Hal would take the remark personally. After all, he'd been her personal lawyer. He'd known all along, too. But his allegiance was clearly with Alexandra. Shane understood and didn't hold that against him.

"*Would* it have made a difference?" Hal asked, searching his eyes. "Had you known you held the keys all along, would you have come back?"

Hal wasn't asking lightly, and Shane didn't take his response lightly. But he didn't have to think about it much, either. He shook his head. "No. I didn't want it then, and despite understanding Alexandra's position a bit better, I can't honestly say I want it now, either." He held up his hand, stopping either man from responding. "You said she wasn't a fool, and I heartily agree. And though I know she wanted it to stay in the family as much as Charles did, obviously it had become her whole life. She wouldn't risk ruining all her hard work by handing it over to someone who might ruin everything. Why didn't she have someone in place to run it all? Did she honestly think that forcing me back home would suddenly turn me into some kind of industrial mogul? That it would instill in me the pride and loyalty that was so important to her?"

"Partly, yes, I think she did. She honestly didn't understand why anyone would willingly turn their back on such a rich heritage. She always felt that if she could only get you to come home, you'd see what you were missing." He sighed with obvious regret. "As to the rest of it, I think, to some degree, her innate arrogance prevented her from believing she would ever dare die before her time. She'd always pictured personally grooming you to eventually take the reins. She'd never allowed herself to imagine, well, this. Perhaps if she'd lived longer and the fences between you had remained unmended, she would have groomed someone to take her place. But, in all honesty, while all the many venues that comprise Morgan Industries are, in fact, run by a number of well-qualified people, she would never have trusted the business itself, or the family heritage, and everything she'd built on to both, to anyone but a Morgan."

Shane felt the weight of Hal's words press down on him. For the first time, he fully realized that what he faced here was a far more complex task than a list of assets to be disposed of and corporate divestitures to be dealt with. It wasn't just Alexandra, but several hundred years of Morgan history staring him down. Yet nothing else had changed. Unlike his forebears, he didn't have that same drive, dedication, and loyalty-above-all-else focused exclusively on the family name. Or, more accurately, the accumulated family wealth.

"So where does that leave me?" Shane finally asked, sounding as weary as he felt. "What are my legal obligations?"

William answered this. "Legally? You have none. Charles's will only stipulated his holdings be passed on to the next in line. That's been accomplished. What you do with it is up to you."

Shane leaned forward and rested his forehead on his steepled fingers. It was all up to him, huh? Dandy. Just dandy.

"You know," he said at length, "Alexandra was wrong. I don't feel like I'm missing out on anything." He looked up. "I've been in the Morgan Industries offices all week, pulling eighteen-to-twenty-hour days." He tried a wry smile, but only half-pulled it off. "Let's just say, the call of industrial imperialism isn't whispering my name." He stood, then paced to the window. "Maybe that's because I'm perfectly happy with my life the way it is. It may seem a bit bohemian to others, but it's provided me with an enduring sense of joy and fulfillment that has lasted thirteen years." He turned. "Not one day of which I've taken for granted. I've always felt that being a Morgan shouldn't be synonymous with being miserable." He looked to both men. "And I would be miserable trying to run all this. I know I was young when I made the decision to be true to myself rather than conform to the family mold, but I'm a man now, and my feelings on that haven't changed. Why should I have to conform? For the sake of ... what? Making my elders proud? Keeping the family account balance skyrocketing ever higher? Those are perfectly admirable goals for the person who wants them, the person who would gain some sense of accomplishment from achieving them. Alexandra was that person. My great-grandfather, his father before him, was that person." He sighed and stopped pacing. "I've never been that person. I could spend years here, doing my best to save all this, and it still won't make me that person."

The silence that met his declaration was palpable. Eventually Hal turned and slid a very thick file out of his briefcase. "Well," he said carefully, lifting a gaze that was unreadable, but into which Shane imagined a whole range of emotions, from deep disappointment to barely controlled anger. When he thumped the file onto the table, Shane amended that last part to barely restrained fury. "I'm sorry to have interrupted your extended holiday with such crass matters as settling the legacy it's taken a couple of centuries for your forebears to construct. But, like it or not, you're back in it now, aren't you?" He flipped open the top file as he withdrew spectacles from his vest pocket and jammed them on his nose. "We'll see if we can't hurry up and sell it all off, so you can get back to your South Seas clambake."

\~◦)

*W*hy didn't you tell me?" Darby burst out when Pepper finally came on the line. Someone who spoke very little English had answered the phone, a maid or something, and she'd been kept waiting for what felt like an eternity. She supposed she should count herself lucky that her sister was still there at all. Seven days under the same roof was probably a world record. Call Guinness.

"Darby? Is everything okay? Wait a minute, *you're* calling *me* long distance? You never call long distance, even when I'm in the States."

"And why would I?" Darby responded, struggling to bank her temper. "So I could get caught up in more of your harebrained ideas?"

"You sound upset. Wait a minute, what day is this?"

"Thursday."

"Oh!" she squealed. "That means you're all Cinderella'd up by now. Was it fabulous? Do you feel different? Oh, I wish I had one of those phone thingies with the monitor, because I am just dying to see how you look. And I know, I know, it all feels foreign to you, but trust me—"

"The only thing that's foreign is the Swede in Dad's guest wing," she broke in, talking with her jaw clenched. "Which is why I called."

There was a pause. "You're calling about Mr. Bjornsen? Did something happen? Is he okay?" She drew in a sudden gasp. "Oh, no. Don't tell me. He made a play and you decked him or something. And seeing as it's you, probably something worse. God, Darby, is he okay? Is he in the hospital or anything? Does anybody know? Because if something like that got out—" She sucked in her breath, then whispered, "Shit, does Dad know?"

"Actually," Darby said, surprised her molars weren't already ground to powder, "that's exactly what I want to know. *Does* Dad know?"

"What do you mean? How in the hell should I know if he— Oh. You don't mean that, you mean, did I tell him . . ." she trailed off.

"Yeah, that's exactly what I mean. And I take it the answer is no."

"Darby, it was really for the best that he didn't know, don't you see? He'd have never gone for this plan, and then where would we be?"

"Well, I know where *I'd* be. Anywhere the hell but here!"

Pepper talked right over her. "And by the time Dad got there on Sunday and found out it was you all along and not me, the deal would be sealed, right? Or would have been if you hadn't hurt Mr. Bjornsen—"

"I didn't hurt—" But she broke off on a long-suffering sigh as Pepper kept going. Once she was in a dither, there was no corking it until she was all dithered out.

"I was hoping that if it all worked out and Dad got the deal, he'd see what an asset you can be and it might even help the two of you to reconcile—"

"*Reconcile?*" She stifled the urge to scream. "You can't even keep your life straight, so now you're going to fuck up mine? I swear to God—"

"I know, I know, but I was just trying to help. To do something right for a change." She flipped the switch and the quavering kicked in, the sniffle of tears making her voice go all throaty. "I was only trying to reunite my family. You and Daddy are all I have in the world, and I—"

"Don't go there, Pepper. I'm not falling for the hurt tears."

"It's not an act," she wailed. "I really do think the reason I screw up so much is that—"

"It's because we let you get away with it! Or I do, anyway. And if Dad has a brain in his head, he'll cane me for being stupid enough to fall for this goddamn lunatic scheme in the first place."

"You really have to watch your language," she said in a small voice, with just a hint of the peeved, but poor, put-upon baby sister. "Things are bad enough without you making them worse by—"

"Shut up, Pepper. Just. Shut. Up."

The phone went silent. And Darby drew in a deep, hopefully control-enhancing breath. When she thought she could speak without banging the phone repeatedly against the nearest hard surface, she continued. "You don't have any idea what you've gotten me into," she said quietly.

Pepper wisely stayed silent.

"I don't know that I can pull this off. Mr. Bjornsen is not what you think he is. He's—"

"Is he okay?" she asked. "Because, and I know you know this, but DarDar, if he's hurt, even if it was his fault—and I totally believe your side of the story—it's probably going to screw the deal royally. And Daddy will never agree to—"

"Are you even listening to me?" Darby shook her head, tempted to just throw the phone out the third-story window, then leap out after it. With an exaggerated calm she was well beyond at the moment, she said, "I realize this might come as a shock to you, but I'm not really worried about you at the moment." Okay, so she might have shouted that last part.

There was a short pause, then a very small, "I'm sorry. It's just that—"

"Pepper."

"Right. It's your dime."

"Actually, it's Dad's dime."

"So you're ... home, then?" There was a quaver of uncertainty. Even she had to realize how difficult it was for Darby to be back in the house.

"No, I'm in the emergency ward with Bjornsen."

"Oh, my God, I knew it!"

It was probably small of her, but Darby enjoyed her sister's moment of abject panic. "Please. You put me through Charm School Hell and I get no more credit than this?"

She could hear her sister hyperventilating on the other end, seeing her entire trust fund, her entire future, coming to an end. Well, it was the least that she deserved. "Really, Darby, your sense of humor—"

"Was all used up sometime last Tuesday. Somewhere between the bikini wax—a ritual of the devil, by the way—and learning how to impress my peers by serving the right kind of mushroom torte."

"Ew. I'd never serve mushroom to—"

"Pepper," Darby warned.

"Right. Sorry. So if Bjornsen isn't in the hospital, then what's the problem with him? Does he not speak English or something?"

"No, he speaks just fine. He looks just fine, too. Really fine."

"What do you mean? He's—" She broke off, then hooted. "Bjornsen's a hottie?" Her laughter turned devilish. "All these years you've been giving me a hard time for the men I date being too old and—"

"He's not Dad's age, Pepper. He's my age. And he's not merely attractive. He's godlike. In a very disturbing kind of way."

"Godlike? Hmm."

Darby could hear the twinge of regret in her voice. "I thought Paolo was *the one*. How quickly they fade."

"Please ... godlike? For that we make exceptions." There was a pause, then, "I know how this sounds, coming from me and all, but you really shouldn't, you know, pursue him. In that way. Things are complicated enough—"

"I don't plan to. It's just that he's—" She stopped, unsure how to describe him. A sharklike demeanor, offset by boyish dimples that did odd things to her pulse? No. And it didn't help that she and her sister rarely shared this kind of conversation. Well, that wasn't exactly true. Pepper shared all the time. Darby listened.

"Earth to Darby. Have you heard one thing I've said?" She sounded concerned. "You know, if I didn't know better, I'd think you are thinking about him in exactly *that way*. Now I really wish I was able to fly in."

"No more than I, trust me." She huffed out a sigh. "It's just that he's one of those bigger-than-life types; a guy who's been used to getting his way for a very long time. Probably from the crib."

"Ah, so he's too much like you, then."

Darby's mouth dropped open in shock. "I beg your pardon? Princess Penelope?"

"Ha. Do you think Dad would have let me run off with Granddaddy like he let you?"

"You were barely in kindergarten!"

"I can't count the number of times you came in looking like the horse dragged you behind him. If I had so much as a curl out of place—"

"Ho, now, wait just one second, Miss Priss. You were the one who wailed if your clothes weren't just so, who had to have her shiny little patent leathers all buffed. So don't go telling me you were the persecuted one. If you recall, I got one lecture after the other and—"

"And he still let you go," Pepper said quietly.

The somberness in her tone made Darby pause. "He was probably happy to see me go," she mumbled when the pause grew uncomfortable.

"You know what I think?" Pepper asked, more serious than Darby had ever heard her. "I'm not sure he ever quite forgave Mom for dying on him. The great and powerful Paul Landon simply doesn't lose things that mean so much to him. And you reminded him of what he'd lost. You're just like her, Dar. You look like her; you have her love of animals. So maybe he was pushing you away because it was too painful for him to keep you close."

Stunned by Pepper's insight—as much that she had insight as to the actual viewpoint itself—Darby wasn't quite sure what to say. She knew what she should say. Something teasing, something that would firmly reestablish their proper roles. She was the one with the insight; Pepper was the one needing guidance. It went against the natural world order to switch things around like that. "You were so little when I left, I know this isn't coming from you. Does Dad? . . . " She couldn't make herself finish the question. Not in a million years did she think she'd be having this conversation with her baby sister. It was only because she was standing in the very library where she'd received so many of those lectures. And where not one picture of her mother remained. "Never mind," she said, her throat strangely tight.

"Darby, I—" And then it was Pepper's turn to fall silent. "I'm sorry that I put you in the middle of all this. I really thought—" She broke off, then said, "It doesn't matter. I guess you're right. If I stopped and thought things through, maybe I wouldn't get into half the jams I do. I know you think I'm self-centered and vacuum-headed, but I do think about you. And Dad. And I—"

"It's okay, Pepper," she broke in gently. "Just . . . it's done, okay? I'm here, and for better or worse, you and Dad are stuck with me as ambassador arm candy until he can get here to close this big deal."

"You want me to fly home? Dad doesn't ever have to know. I'll make sure Bjornsen doesn't say anything." She laughed a little. "I took a self-defense class, so you never know, I could make you proud and whup his ass myself if he won't toe the line." She giggled then. "His godlike ass."

Darby snorted, wondering how it was that Pepper always ended up making her laugh. And for the first time, she realized that just maybe their roles weren't so clearly defined as she'd always thought. "I'm here. I'll see it through. But if and when this blows up in our faces, you'll handle your share of the fallout from Dad."

"I have faith in you, Dar. I know you'll be great. Just let Bjornsen continue to think he walks on water, pamper his inflated ego, and before you know it, he'll be signing on the dotted line with Dad."

"Yeah. I'm so great at all that."

"You're great at anything you do. You're my hero."

Darby tried to laugh, but suddenly there were tears in her eyes. Pepper had been joking, of course, so it was silly, ridiculous even. "And you're not empty-headed," she said a bit roughly. "Anyone who's aced Dinner Party Warfare 101 deserves some kind of honorary degree."

"Yeah, I've got a master's in Martha Stewart."

"Don't sell yourself short. Having been in the trenches, I think you're shooting for a Ph.D."

"Oh, please. Then I'd be—"

Darby groaned even as she laughed. At the same time, they said, "Dr. Pepper," then burst out laughing.

"I love you, Darby," Pepper said as the laughter subsided.

"Back at ya," she said.

"Listen, I have to dash. There's a game this afternoon and I've been invited to sit in the W and G section." Once again she was bubbly, excited.

This was the sister Darby knew and tolerated. Hard as it was to admit, life was actually simpler when her sister was an airhead. "I know I shouldn't, but what is the W and G section?"

"Wives and girlfriends. I don't think any of them speak English, mostly Portuguese. I'll probably just smile and nod a lot."

"It's gotten you this far," Darby murmured, but with a grin.

"I'll try and check back in later tonight or sometime tomorrow. You can fill me in on what Bjornsen is doing. And I'll tell you how best to handle him." She giggled. "Now there's something I could have a Ph.D. in."

"Behave. And play nice with the other girls."

"Yes, Mother. Oh, yeah, what did you think of the costumes?"

"Costumes?"

"For the Belmont party at Four Stones. I thought the whole turn-of-the-century theme was so clever. Leave it to Alexandra Morgan to go out with a bang, huh? I've gotta dash. If I leave this conditioner in my hair a minute longer, it will be so soft I won't be able to do a thing with it. *Ciao!*"

"Yeah, I hate it when my hair is too soft," Darby said to the dial tone. She clicked the phone back on the receiver, not sure which bombshell to dwell on first. Not only was she expected to escort Sweden's answer to internal combustion, but apparently she was to do it in costume. She looked down at the clothes she wore. She had on a black pantsuit that could only be termed slinky, but was better than the shoulder-baring dress Melanie had helped her select for tonight's event. "Like this isn't costume enough?" she muttered. But even more unnerving was the news that the weekend-long shindig was being sponsored by Alexandra Morgan.

What were the chances that she was Shane Morgan's dear departed granny?

Cinderella Rule #8

*D*on't lead with your mouth. Lead with your legs. Or whatever feature best represents you. Offer information sparingly. Mystery is alluring, darling. And playing your cards close to the vest also tends to ensure that you're still in the game when the last card is played.

—AURORA

Chapter 8

*W*ant to take a hot dame out for a good time?"

Shane relaxed at the sound of the familiar voice on his cell phone. He leaned back in his chair and grinned for the first time in hours. Days. Eons. "Well, I don't know. I'm not sure I can keep up with a sexy young thing like you. Might wear me out."

"In your dreams, sugar," Vivian said with a laugh. "But I'm propositioning you anyway."

"Please do. It will be the best offer I've heard all day. By far."

"I have two tickets to a charity function at the Kennedy Center tonight. I bought the tickets as a donation and hadn't intended on going, as I had other plans. But those plans seem to have fallen through."

"Wore another guy out, did you?"

Vivian sighed. "Yes, well, they just don't make them like they used to, now, do they?"

Shane chuckled. "You mean, they used to make a model that could keep up with you?"

"God, we missed you around here," Vivian responded. "I knew you'd pick my spirits up. Why don't you go root through the closets in that old mausoleum, find a decent suit, and I'll send a car for you."

"What makes you think I'm staying at Four Stones?"

"Mercedes mentioned you were seeing Hal there, so I assumed . . ."

"That he'd guilt-trip me into staying? Well, you and Mercedes get the gold star." And all he would get were the nightmares.

"You'll have to forgive Hal, he's really grieving, sweetie."

Shane sighed. "Yes, I know he is."

"If it helps, we don't know what he saw in her, either, but love is nothing if not strange and unpredictable. I only regret that he mooned after her for so long and didn't check out greener pastures. He was quite a catch. Still is, actually, now that I think about it."

Shane had to smile as he all but heard the calculations begin spinning in Viv's brain. "Remember, he's grieving."

"Yes, yes, I know, dear. And what better time to go provide some . . . comfort. Who knows, maybe I can get him off of your back . . . and me onto mine. We'll both be happy!"

He'd been dealing with Vivian and company for most of his life and she could still make him blush.

"So, are we on for a good time? We haven't been able to catch up, and who knows if our paths will cross before you flit out of town."

"You just want to play girl detective so you can report back all the dirt to your cohorts. I know how this works."

"And all the better to get it over with while enjoying really fine champagne and contributing to a good cause, don't you think?"

Always shameless, Shane thought. He loved that about her most. "What is the benefit for?"

"Oh, heavens, honey, I have no idea. I bought the tickets ages ago. But I wouldn't have gotten them if I wasn't totally behind their cause."

Shane smiled and shook his head. "Now you sound like Aurora."

"Oh, and aren't you the catty one. Maybe I made the wrong phone call after all," she chided. But there was honest affection in her voice when she added, "Scamp."

He grinned. "Flatterer. What time should I expect my ride?"

"Two hours. Will that give you enough time?"

"Honey," he said, in a fair imitation, "I could get fitted for a suit, hit the barber, grab a shower, and still have time left to read a good book."

"Oh, to be a man," Vivian sighed.

"And destroy the hearts of half this town?"

"Only half? Dear me, I really have lost my touch."

"Not ever. I'll see you soon. And, Viv, thanks for the rescue." Which was exactly what this really was all about, if he knew her.

"What are fairy godmothers good for if they can't wave their magic wands once in a while?"

Shane was still smiling when he hung up the phone. But even the warm glow his trio of godmothers always seemed to cast about him dimmed, as he stared at the remainder of the giant stack of documents Hal and William had left for him to read through. Grief or no, he was still smarting from Hal's set-down, not to mention stunned by the enormity of the news they'd dropped on him. But he still hadn't changed his mind. Of course, after a week of hazing at Morgan Industries, he admitted he probably wasn't in the best frame of mind to make major decisions about property and the like.

He pushed back from the desk, stood and stretched. It didn't help. He still felt bone-weary. And, Vivian's dazzling company notwithstanding, he did not remotely want to hobnob with the Washington social set. But anything was better than staying here and dwelling on all the memories and emotions that Hal's comments had dredged up. Not the least of which was the point-blank challenge he'd issued as he and William had finally departed for a dinner meeting.

Shane had walked them down to the door, wishing he and Hal

could have reunited under any other circumstances. And yet despite everything that had transpired, he'd still been caught off guard by Hal's parting shot. He'd stopped Shane at the door and said, "If you're half the man I thought you'd become, you won't hightail it out of here and hide in your hotel room." He'd gestured to the grounds, then up to the house. "The very least you owe your forebears is to stay in this house, and consider very carefully how you intend to walk away from it. Because if you walk away this time, there will never be anything to return to. Not for you. Not for any offspring you might someday have. Close to three hundred years of Morgan history— All gone. Forever."

And he'd walked away without looking back.

Not wanting to think about it anymore, not tonight anyway, Shane punched a button on the house panel. "Is it possible to find a suit that fits me?" he asked the nameless, faceless voice that responded to his buzz. "Oh, and a pair of shoes, if you could."

"No problem, sir. Should we bring it to the office?"

Shane paused for a moment, then sighed heavily. "No. Take it to the guest wing."

There was a brief clearing of a throat. "Sir, would you prefer we take it to your suite? Your rooms have been prepared."

"My ... rooms?" Confused, his mind went to the rooms over the garage. Surely they didn't mean—

"In the east wing, sir. Ms. Morgan always kept a suite of rooms ready for you, in the event you should require a place to stay while in town."

The bombshells just kept blowing up in his face, didn't they?

"Begging your pardon sir, but I can have someone come up and direct you if you'd like."

Shane shook off the new set of emotions that pummeled at him. And here he'd thought he'd been put through all he could be in one day. "Yes," he said, then had to clear his throat. "That would be appreciated. Thank you." He clicked off and sat heavily in the desk chair. So Big Al had kept the home fires burning? If he had finally trotted home, as she'd apparently hoped he would, he could just picture the scene. She'd likely have waved to his waiting rooms and said something like, "I was wondering how long it would take you to figure out I was right all along."

He shook his head, swearing he could actually hear the echo of her voice in the air, and gratefully got up to answer a discreet knock at the door. A young Asian woman, dressed in the traditional black-and-white Morgan staff uniform, greeted him with a professional, competent smile and gestured for him to follow her.

"I should have stayed at the clambake," he said beneath his breath.

"I beg your pardon, sir? I don't know if the chef has clams, but—"

Shane smiled wearily and shook his head. "That's okay. Lead on." He fell into step behind her . . . and wondered if a guy could run away from home at the age of thirty.

❧

The limo from the airport hadn't felt this uncomfortably intimate, Darby thought, edging her pantsuited legs away from Bjornsen's. *Stefan*, she mentally corrected. He'd already assured her—twice— since they'd left the house fifteen minutes ago that he didn't stand on ceremony and would prefer them to be on a first-name basis.

Keeping her attention carefully averted out the tinted window, as if she'd sorely missed seeing this section of the Inner Loop during her long absence, she tried like hell not to imagine what other kind of "basis" he'd like them to be on. She thought about a very different limo ride in from the airport, what now seemed like a century ago.

She wondered what Shane was doing right now, and again found herself comparing the two men. Both were good-looking to a fault, both of them knew it, and both were confident bordering on arrogant.

Only, somehow, on Shane, it was sexy as hell and made her think about tousled bed linens, thrusting body parts, and multiple orgasms.

When she looked at Stefan, well, she couldn't put her finger on it exactly. Something about his eyes, so dark, so ... bottomless, made her think about sci-fi flicks where androids came to Earth disguised as perfect specimens of mankind and probed your brain—or worse— while you slept. The part she couldn't seem to ignore was the scene where he seduced his human victim first, then did unbelievable things to her in bed ... as a prelude to said mind-probe, of course. All of which should creep her out. And it did. Kind of. That last part kept hanging her up, though.

"Do you get to Washington often?" Stefan asked.

Darby gathered herself, and though he'd asked in a perfectly conversational tone, she'd already discovered in their limited time together that he didn't do anything casually. She prepared herself as she shifted her gaze away from the window and over to his. Yep. Android eyes. Riveting and emotionless, or at least unreadable. The smile curving his perfectly chiseled Nordic lips never quite seemed to reach his eyes. Which did nothing to explain the little tingle running through her, or why she had to fight the urge to shift in her seat, just a little.

Pressing her thighs together, she searched for an answer that was both truthful—much easier to keep straight—but not honest or open enough to leave her feeling vulnerable. She was supposed to be the urbane Washington hostess, not a hick from the wilds of Montana. He'd been surprised that she'd taken Pepper's place, and it was clear that he thought of her as some kind of enigma—like a specimen waiting to be probed. She resolutely shut out the whole Star Trek chain of thought. He was looking to set up a deal that, knowing her father, was probably worth more money than she'd see in a lifetime. With something like that at stake, she'd be wary, too.

"My business concerns out West generally prevent me from doing too much traveling," she answered finally, and prayed that he didn't ask too many questions about the ranch. For some reason, all of her protective sensors were on alert, and while she didn't mind sticking out her neck for Pepper, and by extension, her father . . . when it came to the ranch, all bets and favors were off. She wasn't going to offer that up for discussion. Or dissection, no matter how wary he was.

His gaze stayed on hers a tick too long, then he smiled and lifted a shoulder in that way Europeans had of shrugging. So negligent and elegant at the same time. "My business concerns create the exact opposite problem for me. I am rarely able to stay home for any length of time."

Darby seized on the opportunity to steer the conversation away from her. Bjornsen was probably the kind of guy who loved to talk about himself and his accomplishments. "Where, exactly, do you call home?"

He arched one brow. Another European thing. She wished they'd had that class at Glass Slipper. Oh, to be able to communicate volumes with nothing more than a shoulder and an eyebrow.

"Your father didn't mention much about me, I see. Well, that makes us even, I suppose. Göteborg is my place of birth, but I now reside in Stockholm. Have you traveled to Sweden?"

"My sister is the traveler," she answered. "I've never really overcome my aversion to flying."

His gaze sharpened. "Oh?"

Both eyebrows went up.

She'd piqued his curiosity further. Dammit.

"You don't enjoy flying?" His smile widened. "Oh, but then you simply haven't been introduced to it properly. I love to fly. I earned my own pilot's license years ago. I fly myself whenever possible."

"Quite the Renaissance man." Darby managed a smile—and prayed like hell that her father wasn't planning to contact Stefan at any point before he showed up on Sunday. She could only imagine how fun that conversation would be, when Stefan mentioned how surprised he was to meet Paul's other daughter. Of course, that might let her off the hook sooner, as her father would surely send her packing ... and what did she care if she pissed her dad off or blew his chance at this deal?

And that was when she realized that somehow, somewhere, she'd actually begun to feel more determined to see this through. Not for her father, certainly, but not entirely for Pepper, either. Maybe it was Stefan's smooth charm, or that way he had of looking into her. But she felt like it had somehow gotten personal. Now it was like some kind of internal measuring stick, a test to see what she was really made of. And, okay, maybe Pepper's belief that her older sister always got what she wanted had stuck in her craw just a little bit.

"Would you like to see the skies in a more friendly way, perhaps?"

Darby was pretty sure she understood what he was really proposing, but she definitely wasn't up for finding out if she was right. Tingle or no tingle. She'd be lucky to pull this off as it was, without courting that kind of danger. Apparently foreplay in Nordstrom's dressing room with a man she'd only known for a couple of days had maxed out her danger limit. She shifted a little, pasted on her best fake society smile. "I'm afraid we really don't have the time, but I do appreciate the offer. So, you're a pilot? What got you interested in flying? Is it a family hobby?"

Once again, he held her gaze a bit too long, making her wonder if she was being that obvious about playing out of her league. But then he smiled, and those dimples winked out at her, and she forgot about leagues and maxed-out danger limits.

"No, I'm afraid I'm the only daredevil in the family."

Yeah, I just bet you are. "Well, I'm sure they're proud of the achievement, though they probably worry about you."

He cocked his head slightly and continued to gaze at her in that singularly focused sort of way he had.

All she could think was, *Mind-probe, mind-probe.* Followed, of course, by indelible images of all the hot alien sex that came right after that. Christ. She wasn't playing out of her league, she was out of her galaxy. "I mean, it's a long flight over the Atlantic."

That one-shoulder shrug again. "We're not that close," he said. "But your father, he worries about you? You're close to him?"

Darby couldn't hold that gaze. God, she was mucking this up. She wasn't even entirely sure why all this mattered to him, but there was a vibe here that went beyond simple introductions and polite curiosity. It made her glad for the umpteen-millionth time that she wasn't in her father's line of work. She couldn't imagine living a life where everyone was suspect, and money, or the potential to make more of it, was a commodity that had to be guarded like the Holy Grail. "We're both fairly busy," she said at length. "We trust each other to take care of our own interests."

She could feel his gaze on her like a physical caress. And she had to admit the disturbing sensation wasn't entirely a turnoff. She could only pray the driver didn't hit any traffic snags through Rock Creek and arrived at the Kennedy Center as swiftly as possible. Before she did something really stupid. Like hooking up her sensors to his probes and to hell with danger signs and Pepper's trust fund.

She kept her gaze on the passing scenery as they wound their way along the parkway. Hours passed, or so it seemed. It was likely only a handful of minutes before the silence finally got to her. "Have you been to the Kennedy Center before?" she asked, trying to sound like there hadn't been an awkward—to her—lull in their conversation.

"Several times," he said easily enough. "The national symphony, I believe, and a ballet. But never for an event of this nature."

"Ah," she responded, ever the scintillating conversationalist. Mercedes and crew would be so proud. She dared a glance his way as she scrambled for something to say, on any topic other than her twitching, tingling self. "I just got into town myself, so I'm not entirely sure who's attending this evening, but I imagine they won't all be strangers to you."

He cocked his head again, considering her. "What makes you think that?"

She froze for a moment. Now what had she said? He hadn't somehow sensed she was having entirely inappropriate thoughts about her father's business partner, had he? What was it about her and limos lately anyway? Drawing a steadying breath, she gave the fake sincere society smile another shot, and even threw in the over-the-shoulder-hair-toss for good measure. As a confidence builder, it wasn't much, but she couldn't exactly afford to be picky. Her arsenal was quite limited. She'd kill for that European shoulder shrug. "Perhaps I was presumptuous," she began. That sounded snooty enough, didn't it? "I assumed, since you've spent time in Washington on past occasions, that you'd probably made at least a few connections. Most of the Hill's power players will likely be in attendance this evening."

He nodded, and for a moment, she swore he was going to give her a little golf clap for her less-than-sterling performance. Instead, he merely continued to smile at her as he leaned back in his seat, resting his hands on his thighs. She resolutely did *not* let her gaze drift to those hands ... or those thighs ... or, God forbid, what lay between them. But it didn't stop her from wondering if he wanted her to look. Or why, God help her, she kind of wanted to. *Note to self: get laid more often.* It was getting embarrassing.

"I've met a few, perhaps. In fact, it was under just such circumstances that your father and I initially made contact. Of course, he's probably mentioned that."

Now it was her turn to study him for perhaps a moment too long before looking away, but the way he kept circling back to what she did and didn't know about him, was making her feel a bit anxious. "I believe my sister mentioned something about it, but I'm afraid I don't recall the particulars." Well, well, she was getting better with the particulars and the affectations by the second. If this went on much longer, she'd be wearing matched pearls at her throat and calling everyone *darling*. "She was more in the loop, as they say, on this than I was. I do know that your business with each other originated in Europe, correct? Something about precious gems. Diamonds and emeralds, was it?" She tried the little shrug coupled with the vacuous laugh. Pepper could have pulled it off. She knew immediately that she hadn't.

His smile visibly tightened. Her gaze did drop to his hands then, and she noted his fingers had begun to curl inward. Almost the instant she glanced at them, he'd already smoothed them back out on his thighs. "She mentioned diamonds?" he asked, his tone perfectly casual. As was his smile. "Curious."

Darby thought back over that initial conversation with Pepper and wished she'd paid closer attention. Although, honestly, what could it possibly matter what she knew? The deal itself had nothing to do with her. She was only window dressing.

She tried not to dwell on just how repulsive that reality was, and focused instead on how to answer him. Maybe the truth, or as close a version to it as possible, was in order. There was a novel concept in Washington society. "To be honest, I'm not sure exactly what she said. She mentioned gemstones and I just guessed the rest, since my father is in Brussels at the moment."

Error number two. The flash of surprise had been microscopically brief, but seeing as she couldn't seem to not stare at the guy, she hadn't missed it. Or, this time, misinterpreted it. So, Bjornsen apparently didn't know the exact nature of the business holding her father up. Maybe Brussels meant something specific to him. Maybe her father was working two deals or something, and Stefan was worried he was being cut out. It would explain the tension.

And maybe she really shouldn't care about all this shit. No one had bothered to tell her what the hell was really going on, so if she said something inappropriate, it wasn't her problem, now, was it? Pepper hadn't said anything about not discussing certain topics. But then, she supposed Pepper might have assumed Darby wouldn't lead off with any information. She'd seen her sister "at work" on several occasions, and Pepper's modus operandi generally had a whole lot more to do with carefully placed nods and laughter, combined with carefully exposed sections of flesh, than it did any kind of cerebral interaction.

Darby let her hand flutter above her knee for a moment, in that indecisive, yet dismissive way women did. Ditzy women, anyway. She was a natural blonde, after all, so maybe along with her Inner Cinderella there was a little Inner Bimbo inside of her, just dying to get out.

It could happen.

"Or maybe it was Belgium," she said with a light laugh. "Honestly, my sister and I don't generally involve ourselves in our father's business dealings, other than from a social standpoint." She bluffed her way through a dismissive head-tilt-one-shoulder-shrug combo. "Pepper travels a great deal with her friends, and I'm wrapped up with the business back West." She noticed that they were approaching the Kennedy Center, and breathed an inward sigh of relief.

"What was it you said your family business venture dealt with?" he asked.

Feeling bolder now as they pulled around in front of the sleek white structure, she shot him a real smile, perhaps a bit more cocky than was strictly intended, and with one hand on the handle, said, "I don't believe I did mention it. Look, here we are."

Darby tugged on the handle the moment the car stopped, and at the precise moment the valet pulled the handle from the outside, which nearly caused her to fall out of the limo and almost into the gutter.

"Oh, dear. I had rather hoped we'd corrected that little problem you seem to have with making entrances."

Darby's head snapped up. "Vivian?"

Her Glass Slipper godmother smiled grimly at her as Darby untangled her legs from the limo, hopping a little bit on her heels until she steadied herself.

"Why, yes, darling." Then she leaned closer and said, "You didn't think we'd abandon you during your first outing, now, did you?"

Darby's mouth went slack. "Is that really why you're here?"

"Actually, it's a combination of things, as always. Never do one thing when you can be doing three." Her eyes widened a little as her gaze went beyond Darby's shoulder.

Darby knew that look. Any woman would know that look. Stefan must have emerged from the limo.

"My heavens." Vivian sighed. Darby wasn't sure, but she might have even purred. "Why do one thing, indeed," she murmured, then glanced back at Darby with a bright, conspiratorial smile on her face. "You will introduce me, darling, won't you?" She shifted a little, smoothed her hair, then her skirt. Her ensemble was as outrageous as ever—a black, sheer-sleeved top that bloused just perfectly over the pencil-straight skirt, that naturally ended well above her knee. All set off with a hat that only she, or maybe Joan Collins, could pull off with any real panache. "As a matter-of-fact, if you're not otherwise inclined, I might suggest we bend the rules and commit the social faux pas of swapping dates for the evening. He is just a business acquaintance of your father's, correct?"

Darby could only gape at the unexpected proposal.

"Press your lips together, dear," she said. "And use liner next time; you've all but chewed off the color. You did bring—"

Darby pulled back before Vivian could pull a Kleenex from her sleeve and dab at her mouth for her. "I can't possibly switch dates with you. I'm supposed to escort—"

"Honey, I don't think he'll mind. And the way you popped out of that limo made it seem as if you weren't exactly yearning for more alone time with him."

She was right about that. "But—"

"But nothing. Besides, I don't think my date will mind the switch at all. I brought him along for you, anyway."

Now Darby's mouth dropped fully open. "I beg your pardon?"

Just then, she felt a hand press warmly at the base of her spine. It didn't feel at all cold . . . or alienlike. Which meant—

She turned, and it was all she could do not to throw herself into Shane Morgan's very human arms, and beg him to take her away from all this. Far, far, away. Very uncharacteristic behavior for a woman used to pulling her own weight. But then, everyone else was behaving however the hell they wanted. Why not her?

"Hiya, sweetheart," he said into her ear.

Out of view of everyone, or so she hoped, he stroked a finger down her spine, stopping just above the curving slope of her buttocks.

He grinned. "Miss me?"

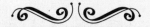

Cinderella Rule #9

*P*ublic displays are never encouraged. However, never underestimate the value of well-timed flirtation. For both professional gain . . . and personal advancement.

—Vivian

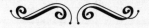

*S*hane glanced over at Vivian, who smiled innocently at the two of them. So, she'd done more than rescue him . . . she'd set him up. He'd make sure to reward her amply later. "Thank you," he mouthed.

Vivian nodded, then shot her gaze behind Darby and wiggled one eyebrow—a talent she was especially good at. Shane understood the signal. "So," he said conversationally as he stepped back to encompass Darby and her guest, "why don't you introduce us."

It was only when Darby moved that Shane got his first eyeful of the man she was in town to escort. Far from the stooped geezer he'd imagined—hoped for?—the man was the living embodiment of every Norse mythological god he'd had the misfortune to learn about during one of his Scandinavian boarding school pit stops.

"Vivian, Shane, may I introduce you to an associate of my father's, Stefan Bjornsen." She smoothly turned her smile on Bjornsen and said, "Stefan, this is Vivian dePalma and Shane Morgan."

Shane didn't miss the quick flicker in Bjornsen's eyes, though his smile never wavered as he extended a perfectly manicured hand. "A pleasure."

Shane gave his hand a quick, measuring shake. Strong, but smooth-skinned. No calluses. No character. His affable smile wasn't quite as sincere as he'd hoped for. "Likewise, I'm sure. So, how are you enjoying Washington? Is this your first visit?"

"No, I've enjoyed your fair city in the past." He paused for a brief second, as if he were about to say more, but smiled instead and placed a hand on the center of Darby's back. "Never with quite so lovely a hostess, though." He shifted his glowing goldenness to Darby, and there was no doubting the message he was telegraphing.

It wasn't that he was claiming Darby as much as tossing out a challenge of sorts. Not atypical when two alpha males find themselves in the presence of a desirable member of the opposite sex, but a challenge Shane would nonetheless do well to walk away from. He had quite enough on his plate at the moment. Better to be the bigger man, and concede the field of battle without firing a return volley. Darby had been one of the better distractions he'd ever come across, but pursuing a few more days with her wasn't worth this kind of trouble.

He decided to wind up the small talk ASAP and shuffle a sure-to-pout Vivian inside and lose them both in the crowd. He could always send a bouquet of "It was fun. If you're ever in Bali, look me up" flowers over to the Landon homestead later. In fact, he was already shifting back by Vivian's side when he made the mistake of glancing at Darby.

She'd subtly shifted away from Bjornsen's touch and was busily trying to mask her irritation behind a face he almost didn't recognize, for all the makeup and gloss. Then she shot him a quick "Can you believe his crap?" look that was pure Darby. He had to hide his bark of laughter behind a sudden cough. Then her face smoothed, her eyes warmed just the right number of degrees, her mouth curved in a smile that, if he hadn't met her before her Cinderella transformation, he'd have thought she'd perfected in the cradle. With a graciousness that had Vivian beaming in approval, she stepped in and said, "Why don't you both join us?" She tossed her hair over her shoulder in a silky wave and swung expertly back to Bjornsen. "You don't mind, do you, Stefan?"

Shane struggled not to shoot Bjornsen a smug smile of his own. She'd played him perfectly. Shane, too, as it turned out, since any ideas he'd had of bowing out now had been firmly pushed aside. What was one evening? If anyone could keep his mind off his worries for a few hours, it was this woman.

And although she'd made it perfectly clear that she didn't need a rescue, he was more than happy to play temporary White Knight. A slightly tarnished one, anyway.

Shane moved, expertly shifting Vivian into the midst of the fray. Right where she best loved to be. "Vivian, I wouldn't be surprised if you and Mr. Bjornsen share any number of acquaintances."

Vivian took her cue, as he had known she would. She gave his arm a little squeeze of thanks, then moved in for the kill. With a smile that would make a lesser man quail in his Gucci leathers, she expertly slid her arm through Bjornsen's. "Surely you've been out to Marrowood and met the Kingsleys?" she asked sweetly, already guiding him into the throng.

If Bjornsen was frustrated by the coup d'etat that had just been staged, he didn't show it. He smiled down at Vivian, whose teased updo barely brushed his bicep. "I don't believe I've ever had the pleasure."

"Well, we can certainly rectify that. They do a lot of import/export business in Northern Europe." She batted her perfectly placed false eyelashes. "Not a bad contact to have."

Shane and Darby exchanged a look as the five-foot-nothing Vivian steered the towering Bjornsen deeper into the crowd as expertly as she might lead a lapdog on a leash.

"My, you are a tall one" was the last thing they heard Vivian murmur before she and Bjornsen entered the soaring white building.

Darby turned to Shane. "I bow to the queen. A hundred years at Glass Slipper and I could never master that."

"She is something. But don't underestimate yourself. You played the field with the strategy of a four-star general."

She laughed. "Beginner's luck. Or maybe it was just desperation."

Shane stared at the back of Bjornsen's gilded head, easily spotted above most of the crowd, as he and Darby followed Stefan and Vivian into the building and started down the flag-draped Hall of Nations. "He's not what I was expecting."

"Me, neither."

"Is he giving you a difficult time?"

Darby smiled dryly. "Why, are you going to offer to beat him up after school for me if he is?"

Just like that, he had to touch her. Actually, he wanted to do a great deal more. If she was trouble, then he was already hip-deep in it. So what else was new? He slid her hand through his arm as he guided them through the fray. "What, you don't think I could take him?"

"It might be fun to watch you try. But we can't just go beating up guys because they're better-looking than you."

Shane was all ready with a rejoinder, but stopped with his mouth open. "Because what?"

She hooted, then quickly ducked her head when other heads turned in their direction. "You should have seen your face," she said, then quietly snickered. "Nothing wrong with your ego."

He pulled her closer and slid his fingers into the palm of her hand, stroking the soft center. He was rewarded with the slightest falter in her step, the tiniest catch of her breath. It was enough. "I thought we covered that in the limo." He pushed his fingers through hers. "And in the dressing room."

She gave him a look, then jerked her hand free, but he kept it trapped beneath his elbow. He leaned in close. "Maybe we should sneak off into a corner of the cloakroom," he whispered as they drew closer to the line queuing up to check their silk wraps and beaded jackets. "I could refresh your memory."

"You wish." She tried to snort, but the sound was seriously compromised by a slight gasp when he let his knuckles drift over the swell of her breasts.

"I know." He shifted back to an acceptable distance as they entered the red-carpeted grand foyer, lest people start to talk. Not that he gave a damn about himself, but it was clear that Darby had her hands full with Bjornsen, and didn't need the extra hassle of tongues wagging over the sight of her canoodling with the Morgan black sheep. So he'd make sure that when they did canoodle, it was in private. Which meant no more public teasing. Only it was so much damn fun with her. There he went again, thinking about having fun. Bad Morgan, bad.

They shuffled past the immense bust of J.F.K. as they drew closer to Eisenhower Theater, where the evening's program was to be held. "My God," Darby whispered, "there's enough jewelry on display right here in this foyer to make a sizable down payment on the national debt."

Shane bit back the urge to trace his fingers along her neck. "I think you look quite stunning without all that colored ice hanging off your ears."

"Yeah, but what about draped around my neck, halfway up both arms, and sewn into every stitch of my clothing?"

"Don't talk to me about stitches of clothing. I'm trying to be good."

She shot him a look. He shrugged and winked, then said, "So, your sister failed to fill you in on a few details, did she? Have you talked to her since meeting Stefan the Stupendous?"

She fought not to laugh. "You really have to stop that. Now I'll think of that every time I look at him, thanks."

"What, you weren't already?"

"Maybe. But your term was more accurate."

Shane shot her a look. "Gee, glad I could help."

"You're a regular Samaritan."

"I'll have you know that I have every intention of continuing my good deeds."

"I bet," she said, eyes dancing. "But I'm afraid you'll have to squeeze them all into the next hour or so. Mr. Stupendous and I are joined at the social-obligation hip for the next three days straight."

They paused at the rear of the crowd, close to the doors that led to the River Terrace, with its excellent view of the Potomac. He debated stealing outside with her and forgetting the event altogether. "Maybe you should give me a rundown of your schedule."

She looked at him as if he were out of his mind. "I'm having a hard enough time pulling this stunt off. For whatever reason, Bjornsen is already suspicious of me playing hostess rather than my sister, and you want to stalk the fringes of society so you can lure me into some sort of scandalous sexual fling." She paused a beat, then said, "You know, I'm kind of liking that scenario."

He'd started to ask her what she meant about Bjornsen being suspicious, but that last part tripped him up. "And I'm really liking how our minds work the same way. Tell me something, since you've been with me for the past ten minutes or so, have you thought once about your makeup, hair, or proper society etiquette?"

"No. Which is probably exactly why I shouldn't fall for your little schemes."

"*Little schemes*, is it now? What happened to *scandalous sexual fling*? I liked that much better."

"You're incorrigible. Which, of course, you know. With anyone else, I'd be completely and totally turned off by that, but somehow with you . . ."

Shane tugged on her hand as he pushed the door open, quickly ducking around the back side of one of the towering pillars that marched along the terrace front.

"What's wrong?" she said, darting a look back through the door to the foyer.

He didn't care if anyone had witnessed their sudden defection. "I don't want this to be the last time I see you."

Her mouth stayed open for a beat, then snapped shut.

He couldn't help himself. He suddenly had to take just one minute out of the swirl of social chaos to let her know that, while their teasing banter was fun and exciting, his attraction was more than sexual, more than finding another ship in the night that he could bump hulls with while they waited to set out to sea again. And the very thought that in three days he'd have no way to see her again, short of showing up at her spread in Montana, had, in the span of the last ten minutes, somehow become a completely unacceptable notion.

Of course, that would likely freak her out. Hell, it was freaking him out. So he told her the truth she could handle. That they could both handle. "And I want to kiss you so badly right now, I ache."

"I—I do, too," she managed, then forced a grin that didn't hide the concern in her eyes. "Why the sudden seriousness?"

"I'm not a complete scoundrel, you know."

She feigned a pout. "And here I was, so counting on that. Well, I guess this is good-bye, then." She pretended to pull away, then dropped the act when he didn't laugh and go along with her. "Okay, now you're beginning to worry me. I don't think I've seen you remain unsmiling or unteasing for more than two minutes since we met. I count on you for that, don't you know?"

"I could say something completely ridiculous right now, like I'd like to believe you could count on me for far more than that. Only I couldn't promise you that you could. And I'd hate like hell to ever disappoint you."

Her attempts to tease him out of this little moment disappeared completely. "Are you okay?" she asked quietly, and with such sincerity, that he felt a momentary pang for worrying her at all.

But the fact that she did care meant too much to him to shrug off. Other than the godmothers, he essentially had no one. And, until lately, that had been perfectly fine with him. But right now, he needed someone. Just for himself. Maybe he was the selfish bastard Hal accused him of being, after all, because just then, he couldn't seem to find the strength to put her needs ahead of his own.

"Has something happened?" she persisted. "Is dealing with your grandmother's estate a lot worse than you thought it would be?"

It wasn't until she'd asked, that he realized how badly he'd needed to talk all this out with someone. Someone who had no personal stake in it. He'd lived life on his own whims for so long, outside counsel was rarely, if ever, required. If he wanted something, he went after it. If he tired of something, he left it. Life, for him, was that simple. He wasn't sure what it said about him, that regardless of Hal's comments, or of his own confusion and doubts, much less the twist of emotions the woman standing in front of him had roiled up ... he still wanted to return to that life with a fervor that was almost frightening.

"You could say that," he said. And then she reached up and smoothed the hair that the wind coming off the river was ruffling. She stroked his face, her own filled with sincere concern. The need to drag her away, tuck them both in the nearest taxi, and find a quiet place to talk the night away and pour his heart out, was intensely strong. The need to pull her beneath him and work through the rest of his demons in a far more primal fashion was even stronger. But, as it turned out, not strong enough to push her to do it at the expense of her own goals and needs.

If only Hal could see him now.

"We'd better get inside," he said before his flash of chivalry dissolved. "The Stefanator will certainly be looking for you."

Darby searched his face, and Shane wanted to know what it was she found there, but when she smiled mischievously, he let it go. This was all that was meant for them. A pleasant, if highly sexually charged, diversion. One that he could certainly pursue through the weekend, but no longer. Because there could be nothing more.

He tried like hell not to let that thought depress him.

Darby's smile turned sly. "Unless, of course, Vivian has him naked and staked out in the back of that coat closet."

Now it was Shane's turn to muffle a sudden bark of laughter. "You ..." He drifted off as he shook his head. "Should never let Vivian hear you talk like that. The two of you might recognize a kindred spirit in each other and the world would never be the same."

Darby cocked her head. "I'm sure you didn't intend to, but that's probably the nicest compliment you've given me yet."

"We won't tell her that, either," he warned with a smile. "Or *I'll* never be the same."

Darby laughed, and suddenly Vivian and Stefan appeared in the crowd just ahead of them. Bjornsen was scanning the queue, probably looking for them. She shot Shane a look of resignation. "I guess we have to go play with the grown-ups now."

"Now where's the fun in that?"

Still smiling, she reached for his arm again and gave it a light squeeze as they slid back through the doors and into the throng. "Thank you."

"For?"

"Diversion, distraction. For making some micrometer of this evening fun and exciting."

"You're quite welcome, milady," he said with a courtly bow. And he allowed the crowd to bump them tightly together so that he could press his lips, ever so briefly, to the nape of her neck, and whisper, "See me again. Stefanless, if at all possible, but I'll take what I can get."

Bjornsen spotted them at that exact moment, and the crowds parted for him as he and Vivian reappeared at their sides.

Shane didn't want to move the respectable distance away from Darby that society dictated he should. He wanted to haul her into his arms, stake his claim for the world—and most especially Stefan—to see. Guys were like that. One glance at Stefan told him they both understood the score.

So it took a great deal more control than Darby could possibly know for Shane to remain where he stood as Bjornsen let a gleam of amused superiority seep into those damned soulless eyes of his.

He remembered then what she'd said about the blond Adonis's concerns over who played the role of hostess. Shane wondered why it mattered. And determined right then that he would find a way to see her again. Mostly because he wanted to be with her. But also because he wanted to know what was going on. And, admittedly, partly because it would stick in Bjornsen's craw.

An all-around good plan, then.

Vivian shot him a quick look of apology. Apparently, she'd finally met the man she couldn't overpower. Which wasn't at all comforting to him, either. But Shane had a brilliant idea. One that would guarantee Vivian another shot at it, and him more time with Darby. "You probably have a tight schedule," he began, "however, if you have the time, I'm throwing a big wingding this weekend for the Belmont race."

"*Wingding?*" Bjornsen questioned, and Vivian seized the moment to move in and explain it to him, temporarily allowing Darby and Shane to exchange another sentence or two alone.

But Darby was already smiling. "And you should check your own guest list. Except, and I'm afraid this is a deal-breaker for me, the next time you throw a weekend shindig, can you do it sans the costumes?"

"Heck, we can all strip down first thing if you'd prefer," he said, his entire mood elevating as he absorbed the news that Darby would be his guest. For an entire weekend. "Although I'm not sure *Town & Country* will do the feature spread they're planning. *Penthouse*, maybe. I'll have to look into that." It was ridiculous, but he felt almost giddy with relief.

Darby leaned closer. "Tell me honestly, does everyone dress up? Because I'm having a hard enough time in this getup."

"And I forgot to mention that for a woman who looked damn fine in jeans and boots, you do clean up nice."

She just gave him a look.

"What? I mean it. And I have no idea about the costume thing, but if you don't want to wear it—well, wait a minute, does your outfit include corsets and other interesting underthings, because—"

"You are such a guy."

"And I'm thinking that's what you like best about me."

"You'd be thinking right," she laughed, then quickly smoothed her grin into a cool smile as Vivian once again lost the battle to dominate every particle of Stefan's attention.

Shane wondered how much of their interplay he'd observed, and not knowing all the details about the man or why he was here, realized that he should make it a point to find out more about all that before he continued with Darby in any public way, for her sake more than his.

Hell, having power ought to be worth something, right?

Cinderella Rule #10

*Y*ou will deal with others who wear smiles on their faces but carry malice in their hearts. The difficulty is in deciding when your distrust is warranted. Just as you can make a bad first impression on others ... others may be simply making a bad first impression on you. Trust your instincts ... but wear a smile yourself. Just in case.

—MERCEDES

*C*hapter 10

*A*s it turned out, it did involve corsets. Darby scowled as she lifted the additional garments from the flat white box that sat open on the padded bench at the foot of her bed. All this went with the dress? She glanced at the flounced and flocked gown hanging from the back of her door ... to the contraption of crossed laces and skinny little stays that dangled from her fingers. "You have got to be kidding."

She laid the cream silk torture device on the bed and scooped up the pile of fluff that lay in the box next to it. Petticoats. Layers upon layers of them. She was so not a frilly person. She laid them aside and picked up the final piece of folded woven linen. It was filmy and soft. *What in the hell is it?* she thought as she shook it out. She turned it this way and that, noting the ties at the tops and bottoms and finally realized they were underdrawers, in the most traditional sense. Ones you tied at the waist ... and at the knee ... she lifted the fabric ... and which had no closure between the legs.

So ... it was the Spanish Inquisition from the waist up ... and *Playboy* centerfold from the waist down. Every man's fantasy. She tossed the pantaloons on the bed. "But it's definitely not mine." No way was she wearing this getup. She'd officially been on the job for twenty-four hours and already she'd been pushed well beyond the call of duty. Dealing with Stefan the Stupendous at the charity event last night had forced her to call upon every resource Glass Slipper had provided her, and then some.

Unfortunately, she'd been separated from Shane almost at the moment that they'd entered the main hall, as their seating had turned out to be as far apart as possible. Something Bjornsen hadn't minded in the least. At the time, even Darby had been a little relieved. Shane had an effect on her that got stronger with every meeting. She wasn't sure she would have been able to juggle the cavalcade of emotions he seemed to elicit within her so effortlessly, with, well, the response that the enigmatic Stefan managed to stir up a bit as well. A few more minutes fighting the Alpha Wars and she'd have likely cracked and told them both to take a hike.

Two men vying for her attention; two gorgeous, confident, wealthy men who stirred her blood, amongst other things. And she was whining. Pepper, on the other hand, would have been in hog heaven. "Well, then," she said, staring at the pile of whalebone stays and crotchless pantaloons on the bed, "she should be the one dressing up like a turn-of-the-century slutty governess."

Surely not everyone attending was playing dress-up for a horse race. She sighed, knowing she'd be expected to dress for the main event tomorrow and would have only herself to blame if she didn't try on the getup now, so she could have it altered if necessary. "I can alter it all right," she muttered, then sighed and slumped into the high-backed chair in front of the fireplace that dominated her room.

At least in a few hours she'd get to see Shane again. She wondered if he'd dress up for the party tomorrow. Most likely, he'd look dapper and dashing as an early twentieth-century racehorse owner, or some such. And she'd be excruciatingly aware, every second she spent in his company, that all he had to do was push her into the nearest alcove, lift her skirts and—

Swearing under her breath, she shoved herself out of the chair and stalked to the bathroom. Dammit, she was horny and frustrated, and pissed off at being saddled with playing baby-sitter to a Swedish studmuffin, when she'd rather be spending the weekend with the first man who'd truly intrigued her in, well, forever. With Shane, playing dress-up might even be fun. In fact, if anyone could make it interesting, it would be him.

She wondered if Stefan had tried on his outfit. The boxes had been delivered to their rooms while they'd been out the night before. She didn't want to think about what he'd look like in period clothing. Quite likely, the effect would be downright stunning. She could only hope some other belle of the ball would catch his eye, and give her a bit of a reprieve from the disconcerting way he watched over her every move and breath. Give her time to search out their host.

She frowned. She hadn't thought about that part. Even if she did manage to sneak away, there was little chance that Shane would find time for her. As host, he would be very busy, and missed if he were to disappear.

"Figures." All thoughts she had of having a very sexually satisfying weekend fled. Shane had to play cruise director to the Washington social scene. "And I have to do the arm-candy thing with the Stupendous One."

She'd rather do Shane.

There was a light tap on her door. "Miss, your breakfast is ready."

Okay, so there were one or two perks to the world of the rich and famous that she could get used to. Not crawling out of bed before dawn to make her own coffee and toast was definitely near the top of her list. She crossed the room and opened the door. "Thanks, Raj," she told the young room steward, who looked surprised that she'd remembered his name. She supposed it was years of dealing with ever-changing ranch hands, barn help, and horse owners, but she was pretty good at remembering names. She took the tray from him. "I can handle it."

The young man gave her a shy smile and nodded, then quietly stepped back. Darby went to kick the door shut with her heel, then stuck her head out in the hall. "Hey, Raj."

He spun around. "Yes, miss?"

"Is you-know-who up yet?"

His dark brows quirked for just a second, then a flash of a playful smile curved his lips. "Yes, miss. Several hours ago."

Darby thought that if she ever was forced to run a household like her father's, one that required a staff just to turn on the lights in the morning, she'd insist they all have a sense of humor. And use it. "Several hours?"

He nodded. "Yes. I believe he went out for a bit. A cab came for him just after seven."

Darby worked not to frown. After all, what difference did it make if Stefan wanted to wander around town alone? But something about it bothered her anyway. "Why didn't he take our car?"

Raj looked momentarily stricken. "I couldn't say. We would have offered, but he'd already placed the call before we—"

She waved a hand. "It's not important, really."

He looked relieved, then added, "He rang for coffee shortly after his return. He's in his rooms now, miss. Would you like me to—"

"No, no, that's quite all right." She lifted the tray in her hands. "Thanks for hauling this up here. I appreciate it."

He looked at her like she'd sprouted two heads, then glanced over his shoulder before shooting her a quick grin. "It comes up on the dumbwaiter. It's not that big a deal."

Darby grinned back at him. "Right. Well, it's appreciated no matter how it got here. Tell the cook that I said thanks for the extra pot of jam."

He looked surprised again, but quickly nodded and gave her a sincere smile. "Yes, miss. It was the morning kitchen maid, miss. But I'll be sure to tell her."

She thought about telling him to stop with all the formality, but figured she'd already pushed it far enough. If her father came home to find all his staff corrupted into actually behaving like human beings, well . . . the horror.

She kicked the door shut and crossed to the table in front of the fireplace, wishing for a moment that it was winter, so she could enjoy a low morning fire with her coffee and croissant. Memories that had been trying to force their way in since she'd returned to her rooms late last night pushed at the mental gates she'd locked them firmly behind. But as the sun rose higher, and filled her room with a beautiful golden light, they were getting harder and harder to keep at bay.

She needed to keep busy. Pack, get ready to leave. A few more hours and she would be out of here, never to return, and all those blasts from the past could stay safely tucked away for another decade or ten. She should be thankful that she hadn't been put up in the room she'd had as a child. Pepper had taken over her suite of rooms the day she'd finally emerged from the nursery. She was welcome to them, Darby thought, not at all upset at having her past here wiped clean.

But that hadn't stopped her from glancing toward her parents' wing, or what had been their wing, as the car had rolled up the drive last night. She'd spent the evening trying to be as inconspicuous as possible, and deflect Stefan's attention at the same time. Her hormones had been jacked around just a little too much for one night and she'd decided retreat was the better part of valor all the way around. But it hadn't been easily accomplished. Stefan was a suave, sophisticated, and very enigmatic man. People were drawn to him, as, admittedly, was she. To a point. But while her libido might have happily lambadaed the weekend away with him, the rest of her knew it would be far smarter to keep her distance. He was connected to her father, and that alone was reason enough to steer clear. She had no idea what Stefan's motives were. Nor did she really care to know.

She'd been relieved when he'd disappeared to make a phone call, mercifully giving her a bit of a reprieve. He'd come back fifteen minutes later to regretfully tell her he had several business calls to make and needed to end the night early. She'd begged off heading back to the house with him, pretending to be caught up in the orchestra. When in fact, the moment he'd left, she'd gone in search of Shane. If she was going to do the horizontal bop with anyone, well . . . she was keeping her dance card open for him alone.

Unfortunately, the intermission crowd had been too thick and stifling and she'd eventually opted to head home early herself. Her face ached from pasting on one fake smile after another as she'd worked her way through the throng, and her head pounded from fielding questions about her father, her sister, her escort, and, of course, her surprising sudden return to Washington society. She'd like to believe she simply wasn't that big a deal, but the number of appraising looks she'd felt directed at her back, not to mention the number of blatant stares she'd gotten face-to-face, told her otherwise.

Which made her less than enthusiastic about attending this horse-race shindig with more of the same crowd, and running the gauntlet all over again. Only this time they had two and a half days to wear her down. She shuddered just thinking about it, and went back to sipping her coffee.

Her thoughts went back to her arrival home the evening before. Stefan had retired for the night, and she'd been so relieved to be alone, she hadn't been prepared for having too much time on her hands . . . and not enough on her mind, in a place she'd just as soon have neither. She stood now and went to the tall, mullioned windows and looked out across the grounds at the rear of the house. From here she had a view of what had been her favorite spot in the world as a child: the stables. Her father had no interest in them. He'd only built them after falling in love with her mother. So she was surprised to see a number of horses, both in the field and the paddock, along with a fair amount of activity around the stables.

She tightened her grip on her mug, fighting the sudden yearning to go down there, wander the aisles of the barns, peek in the lofts, inhale the scents. She fought it, not because it made her miss the ranch, but because it wasn't Montana on her mind as she stared down at the grooms and exercise girls. Memories of her mother assaulted her, of the many times they'd snuck out to the stables just before sunrise, saddling up their own mounts and riding out for the trails in the woods beyond their property, trails only they knew about, because they'd been the ones to create them. Those times alone with her mother were the source of her most golden childhood memories. Ones she allowed herself to dwell on very, very rarely.

When her grandfather had been alive, he'd talk about his only daughter often, regale Darby with stories of her wild and woolly youth, growing up out West. Darby had yearned to hear them all, but had resisted talking about her mother herself for a long time. Slowly her grandfather had worn down her resistance. He'd understood enough to leave her memories alone and intact, allowing her to grieve in her own way. Instead, he'd wisely chosen to reveal the parts of her mother that she didn't know, poke at her natural curiosity, at that connection she'd felt went deeper than mother and daughter.

Darby wondered now if she'd ever truly shown him the depth of her appreciation for . . . well, for everything he'd given her. But most especially, new memories of her mother. From stories, to old photos, to the rare home movie. She'd come to cherish them all. She found herself staring at the copse of woods beyond the back fields and wondering if the trails were there. They were probably long overgrown.

And for the first time, she wished she could stay, just a little bit longer, and go find out.

She abruptly turned from the window, cursing under her breath. Damn Pepper for making her come back here. She didn't want this. Any of this. She should have been more prepared for the onslaught of emotions. She'd been so caught up in the battle of the hormones, and thoughts of clashing once again with her father, dredging up all the bad blood between them along with the memories of the fractious time spent here just before she'd left, that she hadn't stopped to think what coming home again would do to her in regards to memories of her mother.

And she wasn't thanking Pepper for that, either.

She set her mug down on the tray and crossed to the bed with renewed focus on packing up and getting the hell out of here.

There was a tap on her door. She sighed and dumped the petticoats in the box before quickly crossing the room. "Yes, Raj?" she said as she opened the door, only to find it wasn't Raj coming back for her breakfast tray. Her stomach dropped even as her pulse spiked. "Mr. Bjornsen."

For some reason, standing across from him in her father's huge house, with staff running around everywhere, felt a great deal more intimate than either time they'd shared a limo. Perhaps it was the fact that he was casually dressed, wearing black Dockers and a deep blue crewnecked pullover that only enhanced his shoulders, his chest, and, well, his overall goldenness ... while she was in her bathrobe, with a pale face and her damp hair pulled up in a messy knot on top of her head.

Or maybe it was the fact that his natural intensity made her heart race regardless that she didn't want it to ... and made her very aware that her bed was only one room away.

"Stefan, please," he said, holding her gaze. He waited a beat, and she realized he expected her to say it.

"Stefan," she managed, a little irked at his overt manipulation, but unable to ignore the muscles that twitched when he smiled in response.

"I'm sorry to intrude on your privacy," he said, sounding totally sincere, though she doubted he was remotely remorseful. "I wanted to make certain we were on schedule."

"No problem," she said, damning that hint of breathiness in her voice, all the while knowing perfectly well he could have checked with any of the staff, or contacted her on the house phone to get that information. She also knew that he expected her to step back and invite him into her rooms, rather than keep him standing in the hallway.

She hadn't considered her suite intimate. The sitting room alone was about half the size of the main floor of her ranch house. And yet, her feet remained where they were, one hand on the door, the other on the frame. "Everything is running smoothly. I'm just finishing up packing."

"Ah. Well, then, that is good." His gaze very casually dipped to the deep vee of her belted robe.

She fought the urge to take her hand off the door and pull the lapels closer. And thanked God the terry cloth was thick enough to disguise the fact that her traitorous nipples were now standing at full attention.

"I also wanted to apologize for abandoning you last night," he added.

"No apologies necessary. I'm well aware of how business opportunities have to be taken advantage of when they arise." She thought of her childhood, her father constantly leaving at all times of the day or night. She'd lost track early on as to how many times her mother had returned home alone from this function or that.

She thought of her run-ins with Shane, and decided that some personal opportunities were also best taken advantage of when the moment presented itself. She fought to keep the resulting smile from curving her lips. At least the tightening in her breasts felt more loyal now. Which was curious, since she didn't owe either man her loyalty.

See me again.

The echo of Shane's words from the night before, the seriousness of his declaration, played through her mind and made her wonder about that sense of loyalty. Odd how easily and naturally she'd fallen in with him, her fellow rogue black sheep. She forced herself to glance up at Stefan, and thought, conversely, how uneasy her reaction to this man made her feel.

"I imagined you would understand," Stefan murmured, drawing her attention to those chiseled lips. "Still, I felt badly for leaving you behind. Were you able to rejoin Mr. Morgan and Ms. dePalma?"

Darby blinked, breaking that almost hypnotic spell he seemed to so effortlessly weave around her, whether she wanted him to or not. Something about those bottomless eyes. His question caught her off guard, and she couldn't quite tell if he was merely being polite, or if there was something else going on behind the casual question. Of course, why would there be? Just because he and Shane had played their stupid little testosterone games last night, she didn't seriously believe he really cared who she saw or when she had gotten home. Sure, his arrogance and his inscrutable demeanor rubbed her the wrong way, but there was no denying a lot of the rest of him could seriously rub her the right way, if she let it. Let him. Not that she was going to. Not only was juggling two men and all of Washington society well beyond her limited resources, but he was way too intimidating to consider toying with, even if she wanted to. Which she didn't. Not really. With his privately owned jet and personal chefs, his secret morning meetings and enigmatic behavior, he was way out of her league, and she gladly admitted it.

"No, I didn't," she responded, relieved it was the truth. That hooded gaze saw far too much. "As it happens, I left after intermission.

It's been a hectic week and I thought it wise to get some rest before embarking on our weekend at Four Stones." That sounded cool and polite.

"Ah, yes, Mr. Morgan's ancestral home, I believe. Interesting that he didn't realize we are to be his guests."

It was as if he were purposely plucking at her nerves. Was he merely toying with her, or did he not have any clue just how hard it was for her to maintain her end of this little game? "He's just recently back in town, settling his late grandmother's estate," she told him. "I don't believe he has had the time to look over guest lists and the like." She hoped she wasn't speaking out of turn, revealing that bit of information, but she couldn't see how it would matter. After Shane's appearance last night, it was probably all over town that he was back. Surely Stefan would hear the whole story within minutes of getting out of the town car at Four Stones, anyway.

"You're old friends, then?" She must have looked surprised at the question, because he added, "You two seemed rather . . . chummy. Yet Ms. dePalma implied that you were recent acquaintances, so I was a bit confused." He waved his hand. "None of my business, of course."

It wasn't, and his interest could be just polite chitchat. Or simply one man sizing up his supposed opponent. She'd never considered herself that much of a prize. Unless this had something to do with her father . . . and their deal. That stopped her short. Did Stefan think Shane was a possible business opponent? That she was warming them both up for her father? *Ew.* But it would explain his little game of one-upmanship last night. "Speaking of Four Stones," she said, blatantly changing the subject and not caring how obvious she was. "Did you see your costume? Of course, you don't have to wear it if you're not comfortable with that, but—"

"Are you dressing for the event?" He glanced past her into the sitting room, his gaze probably taking in the pile of linen and silk, easily spotted through the open door to her bedroom. When he looked back at her, the corner of his mouth tilted just enough for one dimple to come out of hiding. "I believe I'd enjoy having you on my arm, in all your ruffles and lace." Now his gaze dipped downward again, his smile coming out in all its full glory. And damned if it didn't pack quite a punch. "Or out of them."

Ah. So now the cards were clearly on the table. Pepper would be able to handle this. Hell, she could handle Stefan, Shane, throw a dinner party for fifty, and be the belle of the ball at Four Stones without having to so much as reapply her mascara. Darby, on the other hand, felt fortunate if she got lucky once a solstice, and that with a guy who remembered to take his socks off first. And she'd forgive him that, if he remembered to wipe his boots before coming into the house.

What saved her was the stray thought that maybe he was only seducing her to get ahead in the duel he believed he might be engaged in with Shane, for her father's favor. Meaning that bedding her was merely a way to . . . close the deal. So instead of yanking the belt from her robe and begging him to take her, take her now, she smiled coolly and said, "I mentioned to the host that we'd had our costumes delivered, so he's expecting us to dress."

He held her gaze for a long moment, the amused smile remaining, even as that always surprising boyish charm of his flickered off. "Then dress we will. I'll look forward to it."

She resisted the urge to rub her arms as the hairs on them lifted. The energy coming off of him was definitely sexual, and also . . . something else. She wasn't sure which was more disconcerting. "Great," she said, her social polish slipping a little as he continued to keep his gaze locked with hers. She cleared her throat and did some serious regrouping. "Just ring the valet when you're ready, and he'll take everything out to the car. We should be able to get under way in an hour or so."

"Excellent." Yet he stood there, stared, waited . . .

She shifted instinctively back. "I should finish up my packing," she said, swearing silently when the words sounded a bit unsteady, even to her own ears. The man could really wear on a girl's reserves.

"Of course." He stepped back then, and Darby had to work not to visibly exhale in relief. "I'll see you out front."

"Yes. Right."

He paused, his eyebrow cocking just slightly.

It took her a moment to comprehend the meaning, and she was tempted to just shut the door in his face. Instead, she pasted on her very best fake society smile, certain he saw right through it, and for once, hoping he did. "Stefan."

He grinned, giving her the full double-dimple treatment and she hated herself immediately for wanting to forgive him almost anything because of it. It really was a very effective weapon. She'd just have to remember it was exactly that. A weapon.

"I'll be waiting for you. Darby."

She managed to hold on to her smile until she closed the door. Then she immediately leaned back against it and blew out a very long breath. "I really need to get back home. Where the air is clear and the men are uncomplicated."

Cinderella Rule #11

*S*ocial functions are really just business functions dressed up in fancy clothes. You can still enjoy yourself, and you should. All work and no play can make Cinderella a tedious young lady. However, never forget that your actions in the ballroom might reflect on your advancement in the board-room. In other words, be careful who you tango with, honey.

—VIVIAN

Chapter 11

*W*ell, now, Shane Morgan, as I live and breathe. I was hoping to talk to you today."

Shane stifled a sigh. This time the speaker was an older man with white muttonchops, and a protruding belly that even Shane wasn't fleet-footed enough to dance around.

"Hello, glad you could come. Sorry, can't talk business at the moment." He shot the man his best grin. Probably closer to a clenching of teeth by now, but he was certain the man was too caught up in his own intentions to notice. "A host's job is never done."

Proving Shane right, the man stayed right where he was and stuck out his hand. "Mort Jensen. Close friend of your grandmother."

Gee, where had he heard that before? Oh, right. From every other person who'd waylaid him since the first car had pulled up the drive a few hours earlier. Had one of them stopped to ask him how he was, what he'd been up to, how things were going? No, they'd tossed off a quick platitude about Alexandra, then launched into their business spiel, hoping he'd jump into this investment deal or that partnership plan. And that didn't even begin to cover the ones who'd bypassed the pleasantries and simply asked him outright to write a check. He'd been asked to financially support every cause from saving the endowment to the arts, to building a new community shelter for transients. In Guam.

"Her passing was such a shock to us all," Mort said, shading the avarice in his little piggy eyes and pretending it counted as sincerity.

Shane managed to keep his smile pasted in place as he gave Mort's beefy hand a quick pump. "Yes, it certainly was." *Your fellow investors probably still haven't recovered.* He feinted left, and felt no shame as he ducked around Mort's right when the man didn't catch on fast enough.

"I say, I wanted to discuss—"

"Have another mint julep, Mort," he called out over his shoulder. "Maybe we can catch up later." His smile slipped as he worked his way through the milling groups that dotted the grounds of Four Stones. "Like in my next life," he muttered. Was there not one person in all of Washington who could just come to a party to have a good time, and not work the crowd? Hell, he'd be happy if they'd just stop working the host.

He maneuvered through another cluster, nodding and smiling once again, but not slowing down enough to be pulled into yet another discussion. He was on a mission. Find Darby.

He hadn't spied Bjornsen's gilded mane floating above the crowd yet. His smile faltered briefly. Something about that guy still bugged him. Even Vivian had mentioned that, for all his charm, he seemed rather detached. Of course, Vivian wasn't used to any man resisting her charms, Shane thought with a brief grin. And he might have chalked it up to the very male response of wishing Darby was going home with him . . . and not the Blond One. Except Darby had seemed uncomfortable with him, too.

Well, the background report he'd ordered on Bjornsen might clear some of their suspicions right up. Of course, he was well aware that Darby might be pissed at his heavy-handedness, but she deserved to know exactly who she was tangling with, even if her father didn't seem too worried about it.

"Yeah, that's why I'm doing this," he muttered beneath his breath, jaws aching from smiling nonstop as he shook yet another hand, accepted another kiss on his cheek, and pretended to regretfully refuse to discuss how taking Morgan Industries public could boost his bottom line. He refrained from pointing out just whose bottom line the older woman was really concerned about. Jesus. How hard was it to disappear in a crowd this size, anyway?

It shouldn't take more than ten or fifteen minutes to skim over everything. Actually, Stefan had been a last minute add-on to some other reports he'd already ordered. He'd finally found time to sort through Alexandra's personal files, and some of the notes he'd found on the Celentrex takeover didn't add up with what the various teams of people, vying for top position on the deal, had been presenting to him ad nauseam all week. All that talk had been about the new fossil-fuel extraction technology. Only, in the sheaf of scientific data and engineering reports buried in her private files—which might as well have been in Greek for all he understood about matrixes and pegmatitic veins—the technology being discussed referred only to "mineral resource" extraction. And if the mining report from Brazil was any indication, the first projected "resource" to be extracted was emeralds. Which weren't a type of fossil fuel, the last Shane had heard.

So he'd gone on a little digging expedition of his own, the results of which were waiting for him upstairs on his Morgan-procured laptop. But he was like the main act in a freak show. And it wasn't just the business of doing business that was making him cranky. It seemed his bachelorhood was also the source of intense speculation.

He'd caught women of all ages openly scoping him out, for what variety of reasons he could only shudder to think about.

He'd almost made his way around the side of the house and to a lesser-used entrance into the sunroom that he prayed was unlocked. Still no sign of Darby and the Blond One. All he needed to do was duck behind a hedge, sneak inside, use the back stairs to the third floor and, voilà, he was alone. Until someone tracked him down, anyway. He'd be happy with fifteen minutes. Or however long it took to prove Alexandra was up to a whole lot more than helping resolve the world's reliance on the Middle East for oil ... and, while he was at it, whether it was simply the competitive Y chromosome that had him disliking Bjornsen, or whether the Blond One was a scheming player just like his grandmother. He didn't know quite yet what he was going to do about the first part, if there really had been some other side deal in the works, but if the latter proved true, he'd take great enjoyment in showing Darby the proof, then kicking Bjornsen out on his smug, predatory ass.

Of course, with the Swede out of the picture, Darby would probably hightail it back to Montana. Unless, of course, he could give her a reason to stick around.

"Why, there you are, darling. I might have known I'd catch you trying to sneak off. Don't tell me you've made an assignation with some pretty young thing already."

I wish, Shane thought. He allowed himself a moment of disappointment, both for being thwarted yet again and for the fact that it was a pile of reports waiting for him upstairs, and not Darby. But the smile on his face when he turned, was sincere. "Aurora, glad you could make it." Having a few more allies in the midst was reassuring. Although, even with Darby and the Glass Slipper triumvirate, it was still five against a hundred or so. And yet, he'd learned long ago to never underestimate the power of the godmothers.

Who knows, if they provided enough distraction, he might find time for some distraction of a far more diverting and entertaining sort. Vivian alone hadn't been enough for Stefan, but if Shane double-teamed her with Aurora, the man didn't stand a chance.

He hugged her, enjoyed the momentary comfort of being enveloped in all her softness and fluff, then allowed her to set him back and give him a thorough once-over. Best to get it out of the way up front.

"So," she said, eyeing him critically, "a week in, and you're already paling beneath the high-powered intensity of the corporate microscope." She picked at his polo shirt. "Losing weight, too." She *tsk*ed.

"I'm fine, Aurora, really. Sleep has been in short supply, that's all. But it won't drag on forever, so don't worry about me."

"So, you've decided, then, have you?" This came from behind him.

He turned to find a very stern-looking Mercedes. "Hello," he said, beaming his most impish smile at her. It didn't even make a dent.

He hugged her anyway, taking a little victory in the small sigh of resignation she let out before hugging him back. She didn't bother giving him the once-over, her battle strategy already fixed. Her gaze was unwavering, her displeasure absolute. "You've spoken with Hal?"

"Yesterday. And the answer to your question is no, I haven't decided yet. It's as complicated as you can imagine, maybe even more. I have a lot to look over, a lot to consider, and a lot of decisions to make. If it makes you feel any better, none of them are going to be easy."

Vivian bustled up just then, and after a quick squeeze and a firm butt-pinch, she immediately admonished Mercedes. "For heaven's sake, leave the poor boy alone. Isn't it bad enough he's been thrown to the wolves?" She glanced about. "Or perhaps *nest of vipers* is a better term. Did you see who Bootsy Farthington showed up with? A snake in Prada silk is still a snake in my book." She looked back at him, all saucy smiles and wafting sandalwood clouds of Black Cashmere perfume. "Either way, sweetie pie, you'll be lucky to escape with only that pinch on your fanny."

He grinned despite the scowl Mercedes shot at Vivian. "I'm glad you all could make it," he said, never more sincere. "Please help yourself to whatever you want. Food, wine, end table, sports car." He snapped his fingers. "Hey, that's an idea. A lawn party-slash-garage sale. Kill two birds with one stone. I won't have to worry about what to do with all this stuff, and the Morgan Foundation makes out like a bandit."

"They do well enough. The donation just to swing an invite this year was staggering." Aurora sniffed.

"Your grandmother would roll over in her grave," Mercedes stated sternly.

"Lord knows there's enough room in that elaborate casket she was buried in," Vivian murmured, fussing with her hair.

Mercedes shot them both a stern glare, then lifted her eyes skyward with a sigh when Aurora gasped and fluttered her hands.

"My dear Vivian, you should never speak ill of the dead."

"*You* just made a comment about the foundation!" she shot back.

"Yes, dear, but that's entirely different. It's a corporate entity, not a person."

"It was her corporate entity and—"

Aurora shushed her. "For heaven's sake," she whispered, "you're standing on the very spot where she walked this earth."

"Please, it's not like it's sacred ground. And I was only speaking the truth. You could have buried half of King Tut's treasure in that casket, which is likely what she had in mind. If anyone could take it with her, it would have been Alexandra."

Aurora looked scandalized, ringed hand clasped to her bosom. "Well," she huffed, when no one else jumped to her defense. "I simply think it's quite unbecoming to make snide comments at a time like—"

"Like what, Aurora? You know as well as I do that Alexandra would enjoy every last melodramatic moment of this circus," Mercedes broke in finally. "If I didn't know better, I'd think she planned it this way." She stopped, gathered herself. "I apologize, Shane. We're all behaving abominably."

"Grief does that to a body," Aurora said, slipping a lace-edged hanky from her voluminous sleeve and sniffing delicately. She pointedly ignored Vivian's eye roll.

"Don't be a hypocrite, Aurora," Mercedes chided. "You were no more sorry than anyone else. Not that any of us wished her gone, mind you."

"Can't you see he's overwhelmed enough as it is," Vivian cut in, all the while making shooing motions behind her back, where only Shane could see them. "He called us here for moral support, and injecting a little humor can do wonders for what has to be a horrendous ordeal for him. Besides, there's not a soul here who'd bat an eye at what we said. It's only the truth." She glanced out over the grounds, drawing Mercedes and Aurora's attention with her. "Not that too many of the fine citizens here would recognize the truth if it up and bit them on their fanny-lifted asses."

Aurora gasped.

Mercedes huffed.

And Shane used the moment to disappear behind the hedges. He sent a silent thank-you to Viv for rescuing him once again, and made a beeline for the sunroom doors. He slipped inside and took the back stairs three at a time. Judging by how things had gone so far, he'd be lucky to make it to his room without running into God knows who. He all but skidded to a halt in front of his rooms, hopped inside, and closed the door quickly behind him, shooting the lock into place for good measure.

"Bingo," he breathed as he booted up the laptop and spied a list of mail waiting in the private account he'd set up off-site. He hadn't dared have the reports faxed or messengered. Anyone could have gotten their hands on them that way. He smiled when he saw the E-mails he'd received from *wedigit.com*. He'd had them run checks on the engineer who'd put together the mining reports for Alexandra, on the Celentrex scientist whose name had been on some of the partial schematics of their prototype that he'd found in her files, and on the mining location itself in Brazil. His smile tightened when he skimmed down and found the last E-mail, which bore the subject line: Bjornsen, S.

Of course, he hadn't had the first idea of who to contact to run such a search. No doubt, Alexandra kept more than one discreet firm under her employ for just such a purpose. She'd been a great one for running background checks. In his experience alone, she'd had reports run on everyone from his second-grade summer math tutor to the man who delivered the *Post* seven days a week. She saw it as being careful and keeping herself informed. Shane knew the truth. She was the worst kind of nosy. And she liked the power that came with knowing everyone's business. He'd always thought she'd have made a hell of a blackmailer. Of course, considering how most deals were all about who held the power, in a sense, like any successful industry mogul, she was.

Shane, on the other hand, hadn't the faintest clue about what his neighbors or anyone else were doing, nor did he care. But he'd been put in charge of making some major decisions, and listening to Morgan employees was only giving him one side of the story. Ultimately, he didn't care which shark ruled the tank, but if there was one that wouldn't devour all of the little fishies along the way, then better to go with the shark you know.

For that, he needed complete objectivity. So he'd done the most logical thing. He'd Googled a search on the Internet and come up with We Dig It. Of all the myriad dirt-sifters, they'd had a pretty clever setup that appealed to his specific needs, and, more important, their irreverent wit had appealed to his sense of humor.

His finger hovered over the report on the engineer, but first things first. He clicked open the one on Bjornsen. He was barely through the first paragraph when a knock came at the door. Dammit! How in the hell had anyone found him so fast? He ignored it and returned his attention to the screen—after all, the party could certainly survive his absence for a few more minutes—when the tapping came again.

"Shane? Are you in there?"

He jerked his attention back to the door. "Darby?" He was there in two strides. He yanked the door open so fast that she actually jumped back a little. He grinned, happier to see her than he'd expected. And he'd expected a great deal. "Wow," he said, finally taking in the rest of her.

She smiled a bit nervously and glanced down at the crisp blue crop pants and starchy white boat shirt she wore. "I'm not sure this feels like any less of a costume than the getup I have to wear tomorrow, but I'm glad you like it."

"My vote still goes to the old boots and the wild hair, but if I have to put up with you all dolled up and slick-looking, I suppose I'll manage."

She relaxed and shot him a dry smile. "You say the sweetest things."

"Your legs still go on forever, and may I say I'm in definite favor of that polish on your tootsies."

"Well, get a good gander, because if anyone thinks I'm going to waste time polishing something nobody sees, they've got another think coming."

He reached for her then, unable to keep his hands to himself for another second. "Just because the horses don't care, doesn't mean someone else might not appreciate the effort."

"Then that someone else better be prepared to apply said polish."

Shane waggled his eyebrows. "I've been called a man of many talents, but that would be a new one. And yet, I find myself willing to stretch a little, dig deeper, reach higher. All in the name of self-improvement, of course."

She laughed. "You are so full of it."

"And yet, you're here anyway."

"Yeah, because you're the only one in this loony world that understands just how abnormal it all is." She smiled, brushed her fingertips over his hair. "Thank God I found you."

He didn't know if she meant here and now, or in general, but decided not to ask. It was enough that she was in his arms. "I'm pretty sure this is the only time I will ever be considered the normal one. But if it gets me more time with you, I'll try and act like it." He glanced down the empty hallway before tugging her inside his room. "Where's Lurch?"

She tried to give him a scolding look, but the little half-snort she hadn't been able to squelch sort of diluted the threat. "Downstairs playing ring-around-the-fairy-godmother. Vivian told me where you were."

"My debt to Vivian is growing by leaps and bounds. Now come here and let me muss you up a little."

"Awfully sure of yourself," she said, not remotely trying to free herself from his hold on her hips. In fact, it was her sandaled heel that kicked the door shut behind them.

"Just trying to do the thing any normal red-blooded male would do when confronted with the woman he's been fantasizing about every hour of the day and night."

She laughed, obviously assuming he was teasing her. If she only knew. "I don't think I've ever been the stuff of fantasies. I suppose I owe the godmothers a debt of thanks for the Cinderella moment, after all."

He could have told her that all the makeup, hair dye, and designer clothing were wasted on him. What made her his Cinderella was that fast smile, the dry laugh, the quick wit. The way her eyes lit up with that hint of rebel; the way she looked at him and wanted him just because. And it had nothing to do with his background, or his reputation. He'd been himself with her, and while she wasn't immune to the charm he'd used to get by in the world, she wasn't in thrall to it, either. She pushed him a little, poked at him, prodded him. Made him think, made him laugh, made him want her to want him. Made it important.

"What are you doing up here?" she asked.

"Waiting for you."

"Hiding out, more likely."

He debated telling her the real reason he was up here. Would it piss her off, or would she be flattered that he'd cared enough to check into Bjornsen? Probably some hybrid of the two. Better to kiss her now, while she'd still let him. "Hiding out definitely has its strong points. More important," he asked as he pulled her closer and slid his hands around her waist, "do you have more of that lipstick you're wearing?"

She smiled, bumped hips with him. It still shocked him a little that her body lined up so directly with his. Nice little zing, every time. He could get used to that zing.

"I don't think it's your color," she said, backing him up a few steps.

He let himself get backed up, only wishing, when his thighs hit the side of the desk, that they were in his bedroom and not the sitting room.

"But I'll be glad to share," she went on. "Just don't ask me to put it on. It's a miracle I stayed in the lines on my own lips."

"Now why would you want to go and do something like stay inside the lines," he said, his voice dropping to a murmur. He gripped her hips and spun them both toward the small, hard settee that fronted the fireplace. "When playing outside the lines is so much more rewarding."

He wasn't sure who tugged who down to the couch, but he certainly didn't thwart the motion. All he knew was that his back hit the back of the settee and she was straddling his lap. And he was fine with that.

"You're going to crinkle my linen."

He tugged at her blouse. "Then by all means, we should take it off."

He had the big clear buttons that marched down the front open, and her pale blue silk bra bared to him in less than a blink. "Okay, I take back what I said about plain jeans and T-shirts. Those are great, and you can ditch the rest of this wardrobe"—he glanced up into her eyes—"but can we keep the naughty little underthings?"

She looked down at the plain blue silk. "Naughty? There's no lace, nothing peek-a-boo." She looked back at him. "It's just shiny, is all."

"Well, you know how men are with bright, shiny objects."

She smiled. "I thought those usually came with four wheels and a ragtop."

He ran his hands up the sides of her thighs. "Your wheels are just fine." Then he dug his fingers into the silky waterfall of perfectly lowlighted blonde hair. "And this sunroof won't stay this way forever. Eventually it will be a ragtop again, all wild and sun-bleached. Begging me to dig my fingers into it."

She arched into him as his fingertips massaged her scalp, and moaned a little. "You're doing a pretty good job right now."

"It'll do. For now."

He slid his hands down her back, so she arched against them, freeing his mouth up to see how damp he could get that blue silk. "Definitely liking the interior."

She gasped as his mouth closed over a silk-covered nipple. "Any minute now, you're going to call me something like Your Little Deuce Coupe and I'm going to have to belt you one."

He chuckled against the smooth skin between her breasts, and dropped little kisses where the sun had scattered tiny freckles. "I promise to drop all car references." Then he dragged his mouth from the soft skin at the swell of her breasts, slid his fingers back into her hair, and tilted her head down to his. "About that lipstick, though . . . I'm going to mess it up a little."

Cinderella Rule #12

onfidence can come in many different forms. A raise, a promotion. A flattering hairstyle or a to-die-for pair of heels. From the important to the seemingly innocuous. However, the latter can be as powerful as the former. And what does it matter the cause, as long as the end result is the same?

—AURORA

Chapter 12

Darby had never considered herself a sexually adventurous person. And yet, apparently all Shane had to do was grin, and she was pulling her clothes off. Or letting him pull them off. With his teeth, no less. If she let herself think about it, she'd be scandalized at the fact that she was upstairs in Shane's rooms, a kiss and a grope away from a screaming orgasm, with a hundred people milling about not two stories below them.

So she didn't think about it.

His mouth ... Why even try to convince herself that his clever smile couldn't possibly seduce her again, that his kisses couldn't possibly be so intoxicating, that he was really just a charming rogue she had no business tangling with? Because here she was. Again. Right where she always seemed to end up within five minutes of seeing him. Half-naked and sprawled all over him.

She knew why. His kisses were more than intoxicating, they were addictive. His smile wasn't merely clever, it was full of promise, of fun.

Of hot sex, of a rollicking good time. And right there was the reason she hadn't ripped off her bathrobe earlier for Stefan. He definitely stirred her all up, but when she thought about sex with him, adjectives like *cool, controlled,* and *deliberate* came to mind. *Fun* and *rollicking* didn't even make the top ten.

Was she really so starved for fun? For a good time? She wasn't Pepper, out for the next thrill. She was the stable, steady one. Grounded. Reliable. She didn't have wild, chandelier-swinging sex.

Then again, she'd never had the opportunity, now, had she?

Admittedly, Shane was no Prince Charming, either. No White Knight. And so what? Every woman should experience at least one rogue in their lives, right? And not with a guy who unnerved her half the time. Besides, it wasn't like she was going to start globe-hopping after international soccer players or the royal prince of some small Mediterranean principality. Or smooth, calculated diamond-hunters with boyish dimples.

But one bad boy couldn't hurt. How else was she going to know the difference when her White Knight did appear?

Shane framed her face. She gave herself over to him when he moved her so he could take her mouth however he wanted. He skimmed his hands down her back, popped the hooks on her bra with little more than a flick of a fingertip, then continued until they slid down over her hips. She moaned, deep in her throat, and let her hips move with his when he cupped her tight against the full, hard length of him.

And my, my, what length. Prince Charming was going to have a lot to live up to.

The depth of the hunger he aroused in her was stunning. His kisses, his hands all over her, his body muscled and hard between her thighs, pressing up hot against her, proving just what lay in store for her ... and yet it wasn't enough. She wanted more. Now, now, now. It was raw. Intense. Overpowering.

He dragged his mouth from hers, leaving a trail of smeared lipstick. She didn't care. Nor did she care when he leaned forward, his hands bracing the small of her back, so he could again admire the silk of her bra, so up close and personal that he left icy peach smears across the pale blue.

"Who knew," she said with a gasp. "It is your color after all."

He glanced up, her lipstick smeared on that mouth of his . . . and didn't bother to wipe it off. "I'll replace it." He held her gaze quite directly, then proceeded to leave icy peach kisses down the center of her torso.

She moaned, almost arching down to the floor, reveling in the explosion of sensations rocketing through her. She bucked against him as he tugged the cups of her bra aside with his teeth. He groaned and gripped her hips tighter. His voice was a bit hoarse, a bit tense as she continued to ride him. "Did I mention that I really appreciate your equestrian background?"

"No," she managed, then gasped as his mouth finally closed over her bared nipple. "Glad I could be of some—Jesus, don't stop that. Ever."

She swore she could feel his grin against her breast. She gripped the back of the settee, mainly to keep herself from falling backward. Who knew she was so flexible?

"We've got way too many clothes on and we're way too close to an actual bed," he said.

"I was just thinking the same thing."

He tugged at the all-but-invisible zipper that slid down the center of the back of her pants. She didn't want to think about the state of her linen capris. They probably looked like she'd balled them up and shoved them underneath a cushion. Then jumped on the cushion a few dozen times. But Shane had slid his hands around to her thighs, then upward, with his thumbs riding right toward her—

"There is a God," she breathed as he pushed his thumbs higher, and closed his hot mouth over her other nipple. She jerked against him and would have gladly cut off every inch of the outrageously expensive clothing she wore. So what if her pants cost more than her entire winter, fall, and spring wardrobes back home? When there was a good—no make that life-altering—orgasm a mere brush of a fingertip away, certain things became relative.

"We really have to stop meeting like this," he breathed.

"It beats the hell out of not meeting at all," Darby said, then groaned in frustration when he stopped just shy of the goal and slid her back onto his lap.

"Hold on."

"Why?" She stilled. "Did you hear something?"

"No. I meant hold on." He tucked her legs behind his back.

She grabbed on as he stood up.

"Limos are nice," he said, dropping sexy little kisses along her neck and the curve of her shoulder. "And God knows I'm going to get a hard-on every time I pass by a dressing room from now to the end of time." He nipped at her earlobe, tucked his hand beneath her butt and snuggled her close around his body. "But you just can't beat a nice, huge bed."

"And you call yourself an adventurer? Mr. Rogue World-Traveler." Darby circled her arms around his neck and marveled at the novelty of a man who could actually tote her around like she weighed no more than a bale of hay.

"Exactly," he said, then nipped the side of her neck, surprising a very uncharacteristic girlish squeal out of her, which he enjoyed to no end. "That's how I know beds are better. Although there was this rope hammock once that—"

She nipped his bottom lip, then pulled it into her mouth, to soothe it. It was very effective in shutting him up.

He was kicking the door to another room shut, presumably his bedroom, though she didn't take her eyes off of him long enough to look around. He was probably always going to be the most interesting thing in any room anyway, so why waste time?

"What, you don't want to hear about the hammock?" He slid her down his body, his hands unerringly sliding her pants down over her hips.

She grabbed the front of his trousers and pulled him close. "Not unless it's a firsthand demonstration."

His eyebrows raised as she flicked open the hook and tugged down his zipper. His pants slid to the floor. His shirt followed in short order. "I think something could be arranged."

"Later." Then she pushed him back on his bed.

"Much." He grabbed the box of condoms he'd bought the night before, scattering them across the bed before he rolled her beneath him.

She rolled him right back, straddling his thighs and pinning his wrists to the bed. "I've always admired a man who plans ahead," she said, snagging a packet and tearing it open with her teeth.

Shane lifted his eyebrows, but didn't make any attempt to free himself. "Have I mentioned that wrestling around with tall, equestrian-trained women, top my all-time list of how to spend a summer afternoon?"

Her lips curved. "Make a habit of this, do you?"

His lips curved even deeper as he slowly shook his head. "But I'm going to." A long, low sound purred out of him as she slowly rolled the slick latex down over him.

She leaned down then, feeling bold and powerful, high on the leverage bestowed on her with nothing more than the desire she found in his eyes, in every twitch of the impressive male animal pinned between her strong thighs. She wanted to taste him, as he'd tasted her.

His chest was smooth, tan, and hard. She reveled in his swift intake of breath as she flicked her tongue over his nipple, twitched hard herself when he groaned and thrust upward as she nipped the other one. She pressed wet, tortuous kisses up the center of his chest, licked her way along the edge of his jaw, pulled that bottom lip that was the stuff of torrid fantasies between her teeth, then dove into a kiss that gave more of herself than she'd ever given to any man.

His wrists flexed and tightened in her grip as she took his mouth. Took it any way she wanted. Then took it again. He pushed up against the damp silk panel of her panties, pushing, prodding, seeking. She moaned deep in her throat as she pushed down on him, felt her muscles clench, felt herself climb closer, closer.

She ended the kiss with another soft bite of his lower lip, feeling almost drunk with power when she saw how dark his eyes had gotten, his lids hooded, his peach-smeared lips puffy from her kisses. "I'll warn you," she told him with a sly grin, too cheeky for her own good and not giving a damn. "Starting with me might ruin you for all those other tall, equestrian women out there."

Without warning, he hooked her ankle, rolled her over, and managed to snap the thin strap holding her panties together, all in one smooth move. He pushed between her legs, lowered that mouth to hers, and whispered, "Oh, sweetheart, you already have," right before he drove inside her.

She screamed. And it wasn't in pain. Before he could withdraw, she hooked her ankles behind him.

He slid one arm beneath the small of her back, angled her hips up and pushed deeper. One thrust. Then another. He growled. She climbed right to the edge. He climbed with her.

"Darby," he said, his voice a hoarse demand.

She opened her eyes, not quite aware of when she'd squeezed them shut. His expression, so atypically fierce and intent, instantly changed as he smiled, all dancing eyes and charming rogue. And yet something of that ferocity remained. She was sure it was the pending orgasm talking. And yet she couldn't look away, even if it meant losing hold on that elusive edge. "Yeah?" she managed, muscles clenching around the length of him. Damn, but he filled her up tight.

His smile grew to a grin. "Let me ruin you, too."

Now it was her turn to smile, even as she arched into him and pulled him in that sweet, impossible fraction deeper. "You already have." And she climaxed so hard it was like the Fourth of July and Christmas morning, all rolled into one.

Like waves, the sensations rolled over her and kept rolling. She was gasping, her eyes welling at the intensity of . . . all of it. She struggled to swim up from the depths of the pleasure still pulsing through her. She finally managed to blink her eyes open, only to find Shane watching her with something like awe.

"What?" she said, knowing she should feel self-conscious, but it was simply beyond her to care at the moment. "Did I scream too loud?"

He just shook his head. Slowly. As he continued to stare.

And then he moved, just a little, and she realized he was still hard inside of her when a little forgotten firework shot off. She was so sensitized, that if he so much as breathed, she was going to come again. Could a person die from overstimulation?

He twitched again, though it was obvious he was doing his best to stay extremely still. She gasped at the little shock waves of pleasure, and decided that everyone had to die sometime. At least she'd go with a look of delirious pleasure plastered all over her face. And really, you couldn't ask for much more than that.

"You're stunning," he said quite seriously. "Do you have any idea what you look like when you come?"

She laughed, then moaned as even that simple motion shot off another little rocket. "I generally don't look in the mirror while I come, so, no, I can't say that I have," she said, realizing how hard he was fighting to keep his control. "But I'd enjoy seeing what you look like." She shifted, willing to sacrifice death by extended multiple climax, if it meant giving him even a modicum of the same pleasure. She was selfless like that.

But he clamped down on her with his thighs. "Don't. Not yet."

"Is this some sort of test? Or a control thing?"

He shook his head, his gaze still unwavering. "I just don't want this specific moment to end."

And just like that, her heart swelled up.

"No one has ever—" He shook his head, smiled a little, despite how tightly clamped his jaw was. He lifted a hand, stroked her face, then leaned down to give her the sweetest, most gentle kiss she'd ever received.

Coming on the heels of such a rocking climax, it jumbled everything inside of her and she couldn't control her reaction. Tears sprang to her eyes when he lifted his head. Tender, so tender was all she could think. And yet his body was so taut, so hard, so demanding inside her. How was a person supposed to defend her heart against something like that?

And then he grinned. "Yep. Ruined for life. Hold on."

She was still absorbing that revelation as he drove inside her. And when he came two thrusts later, he did shout.

Darby had no idea how much time passed after that. She'd either drifted off or passed out; she wasn't quite sure. Not that it really mattered. She was still smiling when she began to regain consciousness. Shane had rolled off of her and she was half-sprawled across his chest. His heart thrummed beneath her ear in a steady *thumpa, thumpa*. She didn't open her eyes.

I just don't want this specific moment to end.

His words echoed through her mind, and all she could think was, *Amen.*

It took a few more moments and another level or two of consciousness to realize the *thumpa, thumpa* wasn't his heartbeat, but someone knocking on the door to the hallway, out in the sitting room.

"Master Morgan? Are you in residence, sir?"

Shane lifted his head as Darby pulled away from him. "Where are you going?" he said drowsily.

"You're being summoned."

The short rapping came again. "Master Morgan?"

Darby grinned. "Master Morgan," she said, mimicking the oh-so-polite tone. "I'm betting you love that."

She barely muffled her squeal as he suddenly yanked her across his body, then rolled them both right to the edge of the bed. "When *you* say it, I do."

She rolled her eyes, even as their bodies started to slide off the bed to the floor, in a heap of fine linen. "In your dreams."

He managed to shift so that he hit the floor first, tangling them both hopelessly in the sheet. "I'm thinking reality is much more fun."

She started to squirm. "Well, reality is about to get really embarrassing if we don't get up and get dressed." Where in the hell were her clothes, anyway? She freed one hand so she could shove her hair out of her eyes. It was as hopelessly tangled as the sheet. For all she knew, her clothes were all wrapped up right along with them.

"We can hide," Shane suggested. "Pretend we're not here."

"You forget, you're hosting this shindig. People might notice your absence. In fact, there's someone out there who's probably noticing mine right about now."

"Oh, yeah. Him."

"Oh, yeah," she said, not wanting to think about Stefan at the moment, either. "And the other hundred guests."

"I don't care about them. They're not going home with you."

Darby tucked her hair behind her ear and studied him. Was he teasing ... or could he seriously be a bit jealous? A man who could pretty much walk across the lawn and set up an hourly schedule with available women if he so desired. "He's not going home with me," she reminded him. "We're staying here for the weekend, remember?"

The rapping on the door had ceased, or maybe they simply were too caught up in one another to hear it. Shane pulled her head down to his. "Why don't you stay right here for the weekend?" He kept her from replying by keeping her mouth busy with his own.

When the kiss ended, she knew the sensible thing to do, the only thing to do, considering the reason she was here in the first place, was to toss out some smart-ass reply that would make him laugh, then wiggle free of his clutches before he could talk her into doing something else she had no business doing. Instead, she sighed in contentment and let her cheek drop to his chest. "Don't tempt me."

And they both knew it was far too late for that.

His hands slid under the sheet, and down her back. She'd expected him to keep going until he cupped her backside, do something obvious and try and seduce her. It might have even worked.

Instead he wrapped his arms around her, nudged at her chin with his nose until she looked at him. "Stay."

One word. But so sincerely spoken, no trace of cocky savoir faire, not a hint of arrogant self-assurance, that it undid her before she could throw up any defenses.

She kissed him, hoping it conveyed what she couldn't say. That she'd give anything to shut the world out and just stay and play with him, until they didn't want to play anymore. "I wish I could," she said against the curve of his shoulder, when the kiss finally ended.

The silence spun out a beat too long. Making her wonder if he was contemplating asking her to stay once the party and her obligation to her father and sister were over. She wondered what she'd say if he did. Suddenly Montana felt very, very far away. And it wasn't such a bad thing.

Then the rapping returned, only this time it was on a door some-where behind her. The bedroom must connect to the hallway as well.

How mortifying.

"Give me a minute," Shane called out, but didn't break their gaze.

Darby thought she'd need a whole lot more than a moment to get her act together. A week might do it.

"I'll go into the other room," he told her. "You can get dressed in here while I see what crisis only I can avert—which, when you think about the fact that I usually *am* the crisis, is pretty amusing," he added, his trademark grin surfacing again.

She grasped almost desperately at the thread he'd dangled. A path back to their easy banter, their casual acceptance of the blister-ing chemistry between them. Only now that they'd acted on that chemistry, she wasn't so sure she could pretend like nothing earth-shattering had happened. Before she could make the foolish mistake of wondering if he was thinking the same thing, she gathered the sheet around her and clambered off of him. "Sorry," she said when he sucked in his breath. "Equestrian training doesn't exactly equal grace and charm, I'm afraid."

He snaked a hand out and snagged the tail end of the sheet just as she managed to stand. One tug and she was instantly naked.

"I'm having no problems with your charms," he said, still sprawled on the floor, dark and muscular against the snowy linen.

Before she could give in to the urge to simply leap back on top of him, she gave him her very best over-the-shoulder-hair-toss, ignoring the fact that the snarled mess didn't exactly do the motion justice, sent him a saucy wink, then made herself walk away, every inch the studied, perfectly modulated Glass Slipper alumna. She only hoped the door through which she was making her grand exit led to a bath-room and not a closet . . . or worse, the hallway.

When she reached the door and flung it open with flair, giving thanks when she saw spotless, gleaming white tile, Shane clapped. Stifling the urge to laugh, she turned and executed a curtsy that would make the queen proud, and shot him a grin before closing the door between them.

"Oh, Darmilla Beatrice," she whispered as she leaned weakly back against it, knees suddenly shaky. "What have you gone and done?" Shane was entirely too good at . . . well, everything. She wasn't herself around him. Or maybe, just maybe, she was exactly herself. Not Darmilla, society-born daughter of Paul Landon III. Not Darby, escaped heiress turned ranch owner. Just . . . herself. She rolled her head and caught sight of herself in the full-length cheval mirror, positioned just inside the door. Her hair was wild from his hands, her skin was flushed from the heat of his body on hers . . . in hers.

She looked like female incarnate. And it had nothing to do with artificial enhancement. The woman staring back at her was one-hundred-percent real.

And that woman hungered for more. More time with Shane. More time simply being herself. If only she could live in a time out of time. With no obligations to her land, her horses . . . or to her sister and father.

And here she'd thought that doing Pepper's job was going to be the hard part of this little favor.

She should walk out there and tell Shane she couldn't keep playing around like this. She wasn't cut out for this kind of thing. It was hard enough dealing with Stefan, much less the fact that her father was due back in her life in less than forty-eight hours.

And yet, the very idea of not having Shane's smiling, joking, sexy self around . . . well, it simply didn't bear thinking about. Surely she'd be more rational once she'd had a chance to come down off the post-coital high.

Or not. Two days. That was all she could have. After that she went home, and Shane was nothing more than a memory. A really hot memory. So . . . just how much trouble could she get into, anyway?

She shook her head with a rueful smile as she pushed away from the door. "You are so screwed." But when she stepped into the shower, soaped her body, washed her hair, it was with a renewed sense of self. A new sense of empowerment. One she wouldn't be quick to discard, no matter what the next two days held.

Cinderella Rule #13

You'll always have enemies, no matter how you comport yourself. Success does breed contempt, after all. No sense in needlessly adding more names to that list. Therefore, treat everyone with respect, regardless of social station. It's not always the big fish who causes the most trouble. Or provides the most help. Allies—and enemies—come in all sizes, pedigrees, and estimated annual worths.

—MERCEDES

Chapter 13

"The caterer has run out of Chambolle-Musigny blanc?" Shane repeated, tightening the belt of his bathrobe. "My God, man, why didn't you come tell me sooner?"

The man immediately looked contrite and more than a little anxious. "I tried, sir. I've knocked several times."

Shane lifted his hands. "I was kidding."

"I beg your pardon, sir?"

Shane sighed. Was there no one who had worked for his late grandmother who had a sense of humor? "Let me ask you something."

"Yes, sir?"

"Was employment in your field so hard to come by when you accepted the position here that you had nowhere else to go?"

"I beg your pardon, sir?"

Shane clamped down on the urge to drop to his knees and beg the man to stop begging his pardon. And for Christ's sake, to stop calling him *sir*. But doing so would only confound him further. "Your job here, are you well compensated?"

The man looked truly worried now. "I've no complaints, sir. I promise, I'll try harder next time, I—"

"Jesus," Shane swore under his breath. "Just stop." He raked his hair off his forehead. "So, people are actually upset about the wine, huh? How many other kinds are we serving?"

"Seven, sir. But this one was selected especially to go with the foie gras canapés, sir."

"Ah." Shane scratched his chin. "Well, these people need to get a life, then. But that goes without saying." Despite just having had the very best sex of his entire life, he felt his week-long vise-grip headache return with a vengeance. "You can tell the caterer they can serve Kool-Aid, for all I care."

"Kool . . . Aid?" The young man looked truly perplexed.

"You've never heard of—?" He pinched the bridge of his nose. "Never mind. Just tell them to serve whatever else we have on hand that goes with the menu."

"From our own cellars?"

"Where else? Of course from our own cellars."

"Those are from Ms. Morgan's private collection, sir. The wine served today was specially ordered months ago for this event. We simply had no idea there would be such a run on the Musigny. We need your approval to call the supplier and order—"

"But we do have wine in the cellar? Perfectly good wine, right?"

"Yes, sir, the best, but—"

"Then please inform whoever is in charge of wine selection—"

"That would be Hayes, sir, the wine steward."

"Right. Tell Hayes he has my full permission to take from the cellar whatever he deems suitable. And as many as he deems necessary."

The young man's eyes widened. "Are you certain, sir? Ms. Morgan has always expressly forbidden—"

"Ms. Morgan is no longer with us. And I don't really see the need to keep a bunch of bottles moldering in some dark basement when they can see the light and be enjoyed. That is the purpose of having wine, is it not?"

The man's mouth dropped open, as if Shane had spoken some kind of sacrilege. But there was a light in his eyes now, and if Shane wasn't mistaken, it was a flicker of respect. Or maybe he was just looking forward to being the one to tell the wine steward, "Ding! Dong! The witch is dead," and it was party time. Whatever the case, the young man smiled for the first time. "Yes, sir."

"Is that it?" Shane asked, hearing the shower go on in the other room. He could go conserve water with Darby, to make up for the priceless wine he was about to squander.

"No wine is off-limits?" the young man clarified.

Shane cocked his head. "What would you say is the most expensive bottle down there?"

"Oh, I wouldn't know, sir. But I do know Ms. Morgan took immense pride in her collection. Some of them are considered quite rare."

"Great. Start with those."

His mouth dropped open, then snapped shut when Shane smiled and asked, "Was there anything else you needed to discuss with me?"

"N-no, sir." He stood there a moment longer, then seemed to realize that he could simply leave, that there were no further orders. "I'll get right on it, sir," he said, a wide grin on his face, then took off.

Just what had Alexandra done to these poor people to make them so jittery, anyway? He was backing up and closing the door, already visualizing steamy fun with Darby, when another staffer popped around the corner.

He waved his hand before Shane could duck away. "Sir, I say, sir!"

Shane groaned and let his forehead drop against the frame. He thought about banging it again. Repeatedly. The older man skidded to a halt in front of the door before Shane could shut it in his face.

"Thank goodness I located you, sir. We're having some difficulties with the setup for the musicians."

His British accent and gawky body movements reminded Shane of C3PO. He tried to look suitably concerned. "Musicians?"

"They're to set up by the fountains in the rear of the first terrace, but now they're claiming they were told they'd be set up indoors, when that certainly would never be the case."

Shane just stared at the man.

He cleared his throat, straightened his tie, then shifted his weight. "What do you wish us to do? We could release them from their contract, but then there would be no string quartet at sunset."

Shane clasped his hand to his chest. "Horrors."

The man nodded instantly, then paused as he realized that perhaps Shane wasn't being entirely sincere.

He liked the short guy better. At least there was still hope with that one. "I don't suppose we can just set up speakers, grab a few CDs and see if someone wants to play DJ?"

The staffer looked at him as if he was speaking a foreign language.

"Honestly—what is your name?"

The guy's Adam's apple bobbled as he swallowed. "Trasker, sir."

Shane smiled. "Trasker, nice to meet you. Listen, between you and me, I don't really care where they set up. If it's in writing, show it to them and tell them to set up where they agreed to or they can take off. If it's not in writing, then let them set up wherever the hell they want."

The man nodded anxiously. "Yes, sir, but—"

"No *buts*, Trasker." He leaned out the door to make sure no one else was going to harass him, then looked back at C3PO. "And if you can find a boom box and set it up by the lower terrace pool, there's a raise in it for you. Quartet at sunset and Led Zeppelin under the stars." He grinned. "Sounds like a smashing good time, eh, wot?"

"Uh, yes. Yes, sir, indeed it does." He took a small step back, looking as if he might be concerned for Shane's mental health.

With Shane's luck, a full medical team would be sent up shortly, ruining any chance he had to convince Darby to play party hooky a little longer. "Well, then, get on with it, man."

The man nodded and sketched a slight bow before retreating.

Shane was surprised that Alexandra didn't require them to click their polished heels together. Probably because she hadn't thought of it yet. He shook his head as he closed the door.

"What's this?"

Shane looked up to find Darby standing in his sitting room doorway, looking damp and delectable in a thick white towel, with a sheaf of papers in her hand and a frown creasing her freshly scrubbed face.

"I haven't a clue," he said as he crossed the room. "But may I say, you look every bit as devastating in terry cloth as you do in silk."

"My clothes are beyond help, not that it matters, since my hair and face are just as hopeless."

And here he was, thinking that for the first time since their initial limo ride, she looked like herself. "Depends on who you're asking, I guess."

She slapped the papers on his chest when he went to pull her into his arms. He lifted his arms out and stepped back. "If it helps, I did call down and ask for your bags to be delivered here. First," he added quickly. "I wasn't presuming anything except that you'd want a change of clothes."

"Thanks. But that's not my biggest concern right now." She waved the papers in his face.

He looked nonplussed. "I told you, I don't know. Where did you find them?"

"I was trying to shake the wrinkles out of my clothes. When I realized only a steamroller was going to help me with that, I came to find you, only I ended up in your sitting room by mistake. I was rubbing my hair dry and didn't see the papers on the floor and slid on them—"

"You fell? Are you okay?"

She looked surprised for a moment, then amused. "I routinely get thrown from horseback and you're worried that a slip might hurt me?"

He tugged her into his arms, paper fists and all. "I keep forgetting you're all rough and tough," he said, nipping at her chin. "I guess I forgot, because of all those soft and tender parts I got to see."

She didn't try to squirm free. "And I know where all your soft and tender parts are, as well," she said pointedly.

Shane raised his hands and stepped back. "Okay, I give up. What's up with the papers?" Then he realized what they were. When he'd heard that first knock at the door, he'd hit PRINT, thinking he could tuck the reports away to be read later. Darby had literally tripped over his report on Stefan. "Oh. Those papers."

Darby's smile faltered. "So, you do know what they refer to? Or should I say who? Why didn't you tell me?"

"You told me he made you feel uncomfortable, and frankly, I wasn't getting a good vibe from the guy, either."

"That was just from the testosterone poisoning."

"Ha, ha." At her look, he lifted a shoulder. "Okay, maybe just a little. And I know you don't want me or anyone else to worry about you, but I figured you should know more about who you're dealing with. What could it hurt, right? He'll never know."

"Was I ever going to know?"

His look of surprise was sincere. "Of course."

"Even if nothing popped on the reports?"

"Is that what they say? He's just a regular old Swedish businessman who only happens to look like a comic-book hero?"

"You didn't read them?"

He grinned then. "I was interrupted. Something more important came up."

Her lips twitched, then she gave up entirely and shook her head as she smiled. "You know, you're really just—"

He snagged her wrist, yanked her to his chest. "Amazing? Remarkable? Unforgettable?"

"I refuse to answer, on the grounds that your head may swell up larger than it already is."

He bumped hips with her and tugged at the belt of his robe. "Define more clearly, please, which head is in jeopardy."

She rolled her eyes, then sighed and let her head drop back as his hands snaked inside the towel and skated across her still-damp skin. "I had no business doing this the first time. I definitely can't do it again."

"You seriously underestimate yourself," he murmured, already nuzzling the side of her neck. "In fact, I would gladly make it my mission in life to prove otherwise."

She started to relax into him further, then snapped back to attention and shoved him away. "No, no, I can't. We've both been gone way too long as it is." She pushed at her hair and tucked in her towel.

He folded his arms, knowing he shouldn't enjoy seeing her flustered, but she so rarely was, he couldn't help himself. "But we're agreed that if it weren't for a hundred strangers outside, you'd be all over me."

She surprised him with a beautifully wicked grin. "Like white on rice."

He clapped his hands once, decisively. "That does it, party's over." He strode to the desk. "I'll just call down and have everyone pack up and leave."

"Very funny. And trust me, nothing would make me happier, but we both know—"

He turned then, and said, "You want to know what I know?" He'd intended to tease, but somehow the words had come out quite sincerely.

"Huh?"

He started to tell her what he'd really been about to say. That he knew she was different, that he'd known it before they'd had stupendous, life-altering sex. He'd known it in the limo. Known it before he'd touched her, tasted her. And what he didn't know, he wanted to find out. And he suspected that making her happy would be a satisfying endeavor. Which was a new one on him, since usually he only worried about his own happiness. Life was less complicated that way.

But life had managed to get complicated on him, despite his best efforts, and there was nothing he could do about it. So why not complicate it a little more?

Because now was not the time to put into words everything she made him feel. For them, that time was never going to come. Besides, she'd think it was about the sex; that he spouted lovesick nonsense to every woman he got into bed. When the truth was, he'd never been inspired to spout anything of the sort. Until right now.

"I know that I wish there were no party, no inheritance, no smooth Scandinavian mogul," he said, giving her—and himself—the part of the truth they could both handle. "I know that I'd have rather we met in an airport on our way to anywhere else but what we're dealing with here."

She smiled at that. "Like I'd willingly fly anywhere else."

"Darby—" Obviously she saw something in his expression he hadn't meant for her to see. Or maybe he had.

Her smile faded, and she crossed her arms at her waist. "You do realize that when the party is over, this is, too, right?"

He stepped closer. "Define this."

"Do I really have to?"

"Actually, I wish you didn't. I wish neither of us had to. I'm not good with boundaries."

"Because it's easier to just go with the flow, right?" she said. "Follow the path wherever it takes us."

"Exactly. Darby, listen, I—"

She raised her hand. "Which is exactly why this—whatever it is we're having—won't ... can't—go beyond the here and now." She tried to force a smile. "Black sheep we may be, but you're a wanderer by nature. I'm a settler."

"But—"

"I know you're in the middle of a really difficult time, with a lot of decisions to make. But can you honestly tell me that once this mess is sorted out, you plan on changing your life long-term? As soon as that last decision has been made, can you honestly tell me you won't be on the first plane, train, or automobile out of here and back to ... wherever it is you feel like going to next?"

He'd heard a variation on this theme from Hal. He hadn't liked it then, but this was somehow worse. Maybe because she wasn't accusing him of anything, or judging him. Not really. She was stating the facts as she saw them, as she knew them to be. As he'd always known them to be. But it was easier to be irritated with her than to face the reality that somewhere between seeing Hal's pain and hearing his disappointment, discovering there might be intrigue going on at Morgan Industries ... and losing himself between Darby's strong, tanned thighs ... those facts had started to morph, change, and drift. To what, however, he had no idea. And he didn't appreciate being made to defend himself again while he was still trying to figure it all out. "So, you fall on the side of those who want me to apologize for leading a life that makes me happy?"

"No, I'm not that person. In fact, I'm the last person who'll ever criticize anyone for escaping and finding their own personal happiness."

"You? Why?"

"Remember what I told you the day we met, about my sister? Well, the reason I feel responsible for her, the reason I end up doing stuff I have no business doing, is because of that sense of responsibility. I wasn't there for her when she needed someone. I wasn't there because I basically ran away from home. I was young when my mother died, but Pepper was barely more than a toddler. My father was—is—a tough man to deal with." She broke off, bit her lip, then squared her shoulders and continued. "Things went downhill rapidly between me and my father, so when my grandfather made me the offer to come live with him, I jumped at the chance. Even though I knew it meant leaving Pepper behind to fend for herself in a household full of hired help. So I could run off and—"

"Be happy," he finished. He walked up to her, took the papers from her hand, and tossed them on the nearest chair. "Come here."

"This is silly," she said, her lip trembling, her eyes dangerously glassy. "I came to terms with this a long time ago."

He pulled her tightly into his arms.

"Pepper knows why I left, she has no problems with it. In fact, she has quite happily enjoyed my father's lifestyle. But that doesn't mean she doesn't need someone to be there for her, in a way my father never could be. Then or now." She sniffed, rubbed her nose on the sleeve of his robe.

He nudged her head back, turned her face to his. "Maybe that's what this is, then."

"*This?*" She frowned as a tear trickled from the corner of her eye.

Oh, how she must hate losing control, he thought. She who'd had to keep such a tight control on everything since such an early age. He knew all about that, only he'd left it all behind. Because of her sister, she'd taken it with her. And yet, he couldn't help but think about how spectacularly she'd come apart for him, how willingly she'd relinquished her control. With him. For him. How could that be anything but a good thing?

He wasn't going to walk away from that. And if he had anything to say about it, neither was she.

"Yeah," he murmured, nipping at her lower lip, then pulling it gently between his teeth. "This," he said against her mouth, then pulled her into a deep kiss.

Her hands tightened on his arms and he thought she was going to push him away again, but then she sighed, her fingers loosened into a caress, and she gave herself over to that thing that happened between them every single time they came together. It was beyond a spark, beyond animal attraction. It was more like . . . a welcome home, a discovery of self, or of finding that indefinable thing in another person that you thought only you understood.

He shook his head and smiled as he lifted his mouth from hers. "It's not about me wandering and you settling. It's about us both hiding. We're both runaways, you and I. It's just that your hideout is a ranch in Montana. And mine is pretty much anywhere in the world but here." He caressed her cheeks with his thumbs. "Not so different. And maybe that's what this is all about. This . . . connection we feel."

She smiled then, made all the more potent because her eyes still sparkled with emotion. "And here I thought it was about incredible sex."

He brushed her lips with his fingertips. "That kind of incredible sex only happens when something else is going on."

"Is this more of that hammock philosophy of yours?"

He pressed one fingertip past her lips. "Nope, that one I just figured out today."

Her eyes widened a little, then drifted shut when he replaced his finger with his mouth and slid his tongue inside her, needing to take her somehow, claim her, make her understand.

She didn't pause this time, but accepted him fully. Her fingers raked through his hair and held him tight, so she could take him as fiercely as he wanted to take her, claim him in exactly the way he'd needed to claim her.

When they finally broke free of one another, both were breathing as if they'd just made love all over again. Oddly enough, he felt like maybe they just had.

He rested his forehead against hers. "Can we at least agree that you won't run off before we can talk more about this?"

She nodded. "Thank you," she said after a moment.

"For?"

"Caring. Enough to push me past my own defenses." She lifted her head, nodded in the direction of the chair. "Enough to run that report."

"It wasn't just a guy thing."

Darby sighed, and moved out of his arms as she scooped her drying hair back from her face. "I know."

"They found something on him?" Shane picked up the sheaf of papers and started sorting them back into order.

"Not really. But that's mostly because there wasn't much there for them to find."

Shane paused, then looked up. "What does that mean?"

"According to them, Stefan's name doesn't pop. Meaning, when they run him through their normal channels, they get an address and not much else. So they dug a little deeper."

"And?"

She shrugged. "I don't know, exactly. He appears to be what he claims, a wealthy businessman with numerous international interests—mostly technological in nature—and a number of Swiss accounts that indicate he might be good at it. Of course, they couldn't verify what kind of money he had in those accounts, but since I happen to know he flew his own jet over here, I'm guessing it's more than a few bucks. We Dig It did pick up on one clue about Stefan's most recent activity, however." She handed the printouts to Shane. "Some notes he received via E-mail just before leaving Europe." She gave Shane a look. "And I don't want to know just how illegal that might have been."

"Hey, the Internet can cough up some amazingly private details about the average citizen, I'm told." Shane glanced down at the print-out. "Maybe he's what he says he is. A businessman here to do a deal with your dad. Not so unusual to keep below the radar. Someone who moves in elite circles like that might make it his business to keep his business private." He flipped to the notes. "What is his deal with your father about, anyway, do you know?"

Darby said, "Something to do with gemstones, why?" at the exact same time that Shane's eyes landed on the last note. And two words came leaping out at him. Emeralds. And Brazil.

Cinderella Rule #14

*S*ometimes it's good to shake up the status quo. You just have to make sure that when you turn society on its ear, you don't end up on your couture-covered backside.

—VIVIAN

*C*hapter 14

*D*arby tucked her freshly blow-dried hair behind her ears and smoothed her peach silk trousers as she went over the story she'd come up with as to why she was wearing a whole new outfit less than an hour after arriving. Why anyone would give a damn was beyond her, but people would talk. She didn't care, but she also didn't want to draw unnecessary attention to herself. She was jittery enough about trying to figure out how to pump Stefan for more information on this deal he was setting up with her father. She paused in the downstairs hallway, catching her reflection in a small framed mirror.

Outfit: fine. Of course Melanie had helped her organize all her purchases into complete outfits, so she took no credit there. Hair: passable. It was dry; it was straight; it was tangle-free. Not much more she could do there. Makeup: ... well, two out of three wasn't bad, right? She smiled, remembering Shane's offer to help her out with her eyeliner. God knows maybe he'd have done a better job, she thought now, looking at the tiny little wobbly lines she'd managed on her upper eyelids. She'd given up outlining her lips. After her first try, she'd looked like a rodeo clown, so she'd gone for just a quick whip of color, blotted on tissue. Then she'd had to do that twice, because Shane had ended up kissing off the first attempt. Who knew makeup application could be construed as foreplay? Her smile turned decidedly content. She'd needed the practice anyway. With the lipstick, that is.

She pulled her gaze away from the mirror and forced away thoughts of Shane: the way he made her feel, the way he made her want him constantly, and the whole confusing tumble of emotions that went along with it. It was both exciting and terrifying. "And you don't have time to play dewy-eyed maiden." She had a job to do. Two of them now.

She knew all about Alexandra's apparent intent to dabble in private gemstone mining—or at least everything Shane knew so far. The other reports from We Dig It didn't reveal much by themselves, but had served to illuminate more of what Shane had found in Alexandra's private files. It appeared she'd been funding some kind of deal that would allow her to adapt the fossil-fuel extraction technology that Celentrex had developed—and that she'd been about to buy for Morgan Industries to produce and market—and put it to an entirely different use. It seemed she'd kept this little discovery out of the press, and from all appearances, out of the deal with Celentrex, too.

Shane had said that he wouldn't put it above Alexandra to let Morgan Industries reap the income—and the accompanying international goodwill—of mass-producing the technology for its original intended purpose . . . all the while using her own secret little adapted use to line her personal coffers. He planned to go over the rest of Alexandra's private files after the party and see what else he could find out.

In the meantime, they agreed that while they'd found no proof tying Stefan directly to Alexandra or her little side operation, one note of his they'd found was quite an interesting little coincidence. "Brazil site a go. Seams verified for tourmaline, rubellite, and emerald." So the question was: If Stefan was involved with Alexandra's private plan before her death, what was his involvement now? That note had only been sent days ago, weeks after Alexandra's funeral.

And, Darby thought, her stomach tightening, what role, if any, did her dad play in all this? She shivered a little, thinking about Stefan's reaction when she'd mentioned diamonds and emeralds. He'd focused on her comment about the diamonds ... but now she wondered. She'd naturally assumed Pepper had meant the kind of gemstones that were already cut and polished, but now ... She hated to admit it, but while some nefarious connection between Stefan and Alexandra's Celentrex deal sounded a bit too James Bond to her, as did her father's possible involvement, she simply couldn't discount that there might be more to the whole story, either.

Which was what her other job was all about.

Shane had put We Dig It back to work to see if they could find any concrete connection between Stefan and Alexandra, and Darby had tried to call Pepper to see if there was any additional information she might have that would illuminate their father's involvement in all this. But no one had answered at the villa. So she was going to keep her ears and eyes open for any potential business chatter Stefan might indulge in, and do her best to subtly pump him for more details about this deal he was here to make.

She hated that she even gave a damn. It wasn't her problem what Stefan or her father were really up to. But there was Pepper to consider. Not her inheritance. Darby had already come to the conclusion that the best thing for Pepper was to learn to take responsibility for her actions. And the only way that was going to happen was if Darby stopped stepping in front of every bullet meant for her.

But there was that other little bomb she'd dropped. Her surprising revelation about how desperately she wanted to reunite her family. Had Darby been so busy trying to mother her little sister that she'd missed the obvious? Darby still wasn't sure how she felt about all that. Her plan had been to bail out the moment her father stepped out of the limo on Sunday, keeping any interaction between the two of them as minimal as possible. But that was before she'd gone home, before all those memories of her past and the time spent with her mother had been wrenched to the surface again. Was her father's inability to deal with her somehow tied into her similarity to her mother, as Pepper had surmised? She shook her head, as much to negate that possibility as to shake herself free of the train of thought altogether. Like life wasn't complicated enough at the moment.

She steeled herself, taking a steadying breath before turning to face the gauntlet. She wasn't sure she was up to the challenge. Handling all the polite and not-so-polite inquiries about her return. Handling Stefan and the intense undercurrents that seemed to swirl between them every time he got close. Not to mention Shane, and what had just happened upstairs. She'd like to think she could be cavalier about it, think of it as nothing more than hot sex with a willing and very capable partner. But she was discovering that she wasn't a wild fling kind of girl. Not in the participation end of the deal ... but she was definitely struggling with keeping her emotions out of it.

"And if you start going down that path, you're never going to make it through the next couple of hours," she muttered beneath her breath.

She looked out across the rear lawn. There had only been small clusters of guests when she'd arrived, but the grounds were now clogged with people. She rubbed at her arms, certain that the itchy feeling was probably a bout of hives or something brought on by all the stress. "Pepper, you are definitely my barn slave after this."

A warm hand at the small of her back made her jump. Then she turned and discovered it was Shane. "Oh, dear God, you scared the—"

He kissed her gently, so as not to smear her attempt with the lipstick brush. "You're going to knock them all dead."

"If only," she said darkly, but the itchy feeling began to fade in the face of Shane's cocky, confidant smile.

"I can't believe you care what they think."

"I don't. I'm just not good at being the center of attention."

He moved in. "You didn't seem to mind being the center of mine."

She flashed him a look of impatience, but her body stirred at the promise in his eyes. "Which is entirely different." She put her hands up when he reached for her. "I'm not doing the makeup routine again. Not even for you." He laughed, but the promise in his gaze remained. And she got itchy all over again, but for entirely different reasons.

"I'd better get out there. And given the way Stefan and you circled each other last night, maybe it's best if we do our trolling separately," she said. It was only then that she really looked at him. All of him. "What on earth are you wearing?"

He held his hands out and looked down. "What I always wear to a pool party."

She stared in shock—and maybe a little admiration—at his white sleeveless T-shirt and the baggy wave-runner beach shorts, which were done in a startling Hawaiian blossom print, that rode low on his hips. "Funny, but the last time I saw you—"

"I believe I was naked. Now that's casual and all, but even I have a little modesty."

"While I believe that's debatable"—she smiled when he merely shrugged noncommittally—"I was referring to the trousers and polo shirt you were wearing when I first went into your rooms."

"Oh. Those." He smoothed his T-shirt, drawing her eyes to his flat abs—as no doubt he'd intended to—and nicely defined biceps, and said, "I changed my mind."

"So you don't care about the takeover deal and I can give up spying on Stefan?"

"No. My feelings on that haven't changed." His gaze shifted to the people clustered on the lawn. "I'm just done playing the game by their rules." He looked back to her. "Alexandra might have dragged me into this mess, but she can't stop me from being myself while I figure out what the hell I'm doing. I may be a Morgan, but I'm not one of them, Darby. Any more than you are. Or want to be."

She smiled. "I doubt anyone out there would have made that mistake, no matter what you wore. But you've gone beyond being yourself to thumbing your nose at them. And though I don't care about their precious social rules any more than you do, surely that's not going to make things easier on you."

He folded his arms, and she tried like hell not to stare at his arms . . . or his chest. Both of which she now had carnal knowledge of. "While you were in the shower, I dealt with not one, but two major crises that had the house staff in a total panic. Would you like to know what these all-important, life-threatening emergencies were about?"

She dragged her attention to his face. "Not really. But I can guess. The ice sculpture didn't glisten exactly right in the sunshine, or the water in the toilet bowls isn't at some predetermined temperature and a few of the guests' tight asses got an unexpected chill at the wrong moment."

Shane's jaw slowly relaxed, and his eyes danced. "Close. Actually, don't mention the water thing to any of the staff. It might give them ideas." His laugh held little humor. "I guess I just can't conceive of a world in which I'm ever going to care about that kind of shit, you know? I do care about people losing their jobs, people who need their paycheck to put food on the table." He blew out a sigh. "And I know that this house, and a great deal of the crap in it, has been here since the dawn of time. That it's important family history. My history. And if I had a drop of familial pride or integrity in my heart, I would find a way to preserve it." He looked up at her then, and she was amazed at the helpless—no, hopeless—look in his eyes. "I care about it all in the greater-good sense, in the do-what's-right-for-the-masses way. But in here?" He tapped his chest. "I can't relate it to me. Because it's not about me. This"—he gestured around them—"has never been about me. I'm the last guy who should be responsible for this. I didn't ask for it. I don't want it. But how in the hell do I just walk away from it?"

Darby stood silently, not knowing what to tell him. Not knowing how to deal with the honest, gut-wrenching crisis of conscience he'd revealed to her. It made those dangerous emotions she was trying to ignore all the harder to suppress. She thought about the things he'd said to her in bed. Or on the floor. In the shower she'd decided to chalk them up to the things a person says in the heat of the moment. And God knows, there'd been plenty of heat. Only they weren't in bed anymore. He wasn't saying emotional things because he was buried inside of her and wanted to make sure they could climb that peak of sexual intensity again. And again.

She folded her own arms now, not entirely sure if she was protecting herself from the growing impossibility of shoving her emotions out of this, or holding in the undeniable urge she felt to respond to them. *Digging yourself deeper every second*, her little inner voice warned.

"I don't know what to tell you. I can't imagine how I'd react if I were in your position. If you think this is the way to go—" She shrugged, but gave him an encouraging smile.

"What I think is that these people have way too much time and money on their hands if they're going to worry about what kind of wine is being served with the fish sticks, and whether the band plays outdoors, or up in a tree house. What I think—what I know—is that they all want a piece of me. Or, more specifically, a piece of the Morgan empire. And what I want *them* to know is that the game as they play it is over. If I have a prayer in hell of finding solutions to any of this, from making multimillion dollar corporate decisions to preserving my ancestral history, then I need an edge. And I finally figured out that my advantage, my edge, is that one basic difference between them and me."

"Loud surf shorts?"

He grinned. "Well, that, and the fact that I'm the only one who doesn't care what's in it for me. So, why not leverage my advantage? Make them dance to my tune instead of the other way around. Speaking of which, I put a call in for a disc jockey. He should be arriving shortly."

"Let me guess. He won't be playing Mozart's top ten."

"Hardly."

"Well, then." Her lips curved in a slow smile. This could actually prove quite entertaining. "Let the fireworks begin."

He bowed slightly. "Thank you for the vote of support. Can I count on you in the limbo contest I'm planning later? We need someone to teach these people how to cut loose."

She laughed now. "Oh, you've got the wrong girl for that. But I'm thinking there are a few fairy godmothers out there who might be game."

His eyes lit up. "You're brilliant."

Now she sketched a bow. "I have my moments." She nodded toward his outfit. "And I must say, those are definitely you."

He modeled briefly. "They're my lucky pair."

She gave him a look. "I don't even want to know what constitutes luck when it comes to Hawaiian flowery shorts."

"I could show you later."

"I'll bet you could."

"I'll take that bet. So, we have a deal, then?"

"As long as that deal involves me fading into the woodwork as the show out there unfolds, yes."

"Look at it this way. At least you won't have to worry about being the center of attention now."

She hadn't thought about that. Her smile was wide and quite sincere. "You know, for that, I just might be able to find a way to immortalize those lucky shorts of yours."

Shane's eyes darkened. "New rule. Party's over at sundown." He snagged her arm, dragged her behind a life-sized model of a racehorse, complete with a blanket of flowers, and kissed the lipstick right back off of her. He left her there, wavering on her feet, touching her lips, wondering how he did that every single time, as she watched him saunter outside. His grin came easily as heads turned with every step he took.

"You're something else, Shane Morgan," she murmured. And followed him out, bare-mouthed, probably flushed, and totally unconcerned. Like anyone was going to notice at this point. It wasn't exactly like wearing surfer shorts, or boots and jeans for that matter. But it was a show of support. "Black Sheep Unite," she said, snagging a glass of something sparkly from a passing waiter and raising it in tribute.

"There you are. We'd barely arrived and you vanished. I was becoming quite concerned about your well-being."

Darby almost gagged, but managed to force the chilled wine past the sudden tightness in her throat. Damn, she wasn't ready for this. But then, when would she ever be? She took a moment, then carefully engaged her well-rehearsed vapid-society-girl expression and turned to face Stefan. "I'm so sorry to have abandoned you like that. It was entirely unintentional." Which was the truth. She'd wanted to see Shane, to talk to him away from the crowd before he and Stefan did their little testosterone tango encore. But she'd only intended to be gone a few minutes.

"Nothing is wrong, I hope?" He skimmed his gaze over her before flicking those dark eyes back to hers. "You've changed."

She froze for a second, wondering if there were any obvious outward signs—beyond having her lipstick kissed off—of just why she'd changed. Somehow she knew, if there was even a trace of afterglow about her, Stefan would zero in on it. Which made her work doubly hard at accurately mimicking that disaffected society mien. "I'm afraid the outfit I selected this morning didn't travel well. I knew I'd feel better in something fresh. Then the staff couldn't locate where they'd put my bags—" She did the one-shoulder shrug. "You know how it is."

Stefan smiled, seeming to agree with her, but something about his expression still seemed too aware. Or a little too intent. She couldn't put her finger on it, but it didn't feel sexual this time. Just very . . . focused. Which was far more chilling in its own, emotionally detached kind of way.

She sipped her wine as she turned her attention to the extravagantly decorated grounds and the extravagantly decorated people tromping around on them. He came to stand next to her and she had to work at not shifting away from him.

"Quite the elaborate show," he murmured, nodding to the catering staff who were all decked out in racing silks. Not to mention the life-sized, flower-draped racing horses that dotted the grounds.

"Mmm," she responded, noncommittally sipping her wine, buying time to get her game plan in gear. Which she'd better do quickly. Using the bubbly as a means of avoiding direct conversation was effective, but continued application would leave her sloshed by sunset. And no good to the plan, or anything else for that matter. Her thoughts strayed to later tonight, after everyone stumbled off to bed. She and Shane hadn't made specific plans, but she didn't imagine she'd be spending the night alone. Not all of it, anyway. Would Shane come to her? Or would she go to him?

"My word, as I live and breathe. Little Darmilla Landon, all grown up. Turn around, darling, and let me get a look at you."

Darby stiffened at the sound of the society matron's grating voice. The gauntlet had officially begun. Amazingly, she was almost grateful for the interruption. Almost. She turned, society smile carefully in place. "Hello—?"

The woman's shrewd eyes flickered in disapproval. "Bitsy Henessy."

"Of course," Darby said, not remotely chastened.

"Well, you certainly have turned out rather nicely. The resemblance to your mother is amazing." Bitsy held her at arm's length. "And what a charming outfit you have on." Her polite society smile set firmly in place, she added, "Is this something you picked up back West?"

It almost killed her, but somehow Darby refrained from poking Bitsy's eyes out. "Let me introduce you to my guest. This is Stefan Bjornsen, an associate of my father's."

Stefan's smile was a shade too tight and Darby guessed he wasn't any happier with the intrusion than she'd been. "A pleasure," he said.

The older woman preened when Stefan bowed his lion's mane over her extended, heavily ringed hands. She rewarded him with a smile that stretched her unnaturally smooth complexion to its surgical limits. "How gallant. You've come for business, then?" She looked to Darby. "Is your father here, dear? I've been meaning to discuss a little proposal—"

"He'll be arriving Sunday," Darby answered.

The woman cast her gaze from Darby to Stefan. "How nice of you to fill in for him during his absence."

"The pleasure has been assuredly all mine," Stefan provided.

Bitsy beamed at him. "Well, well. I'll want to hear later about how you managed to lure her back to the family fold." She laughed, a shrill sound that had Darby fighting the urge to cover her glass, in case it shattered. "And don't think I won't hold you to it. Quite a coup, but then, I'm sure you're well aware of that. Oh, there's Pierpont. I do need to have a talk with him." She turned to Darby, took her hand without permission, and squeezed it. "Wonderful to see you back, my dear. I'm having a luncheon at the club next Tuesday. We're setting up our calendar for the fall charity events. Surely you'll make time to attend? And of course I'll make certain Margo sends you an invite to the embassy party she's organizing for the French ambassador." She leaned closer. "You've probably already heard the rumor that he's keeping a woman who isn't his wife in a little place in Adams Morgan. Tongues are wagging that she'll be at the ball." Her rings bit into Darby's hand. "You'll be thanking me for that invite, I assure you."

Darby was only sure that her fingers had lost all feeling. She was saved from making a response when Bitsy dropped her hand and turned one last stitch-popping smile on Stefan. "Until later."

He watched her retreat, then turned his gaze back to Darby. If anything, his focus was more intent. Oh, goody. "Your presence in town seems to have caused quite a sensation. Just how long has it been?"

She was supposed to be the one interrogating him. "Quite a while." She deliberately moved into the milling crowds, forcing him to follow. She needed a moment—okay, a few moments—to regroup and plot a strategy. She slowed beside the box hedges rimming part of the lawn, very aware of the stares aimed in her direction. She could only imagine the whispering conjectures being made. And Darby had no doubt that Bitsy was out there right now, stirring the speculation pot. Not that she gave a rat's ass what they thought, but her role was to fit in and keep him entertained. Not to make him feel uncomfortable, or the target of speculation.

Which meant keeping them out of the heavy traffic, and keeping the conversation focused on him. "So, your business with my father sounds intriguing." She took a sip of wine, careful to keep her expression smooth, her gaze on the crowd, as if she were only asking to be polite. "Of course, what woman isn't intrigued by diamonds?" She glanced at him with a smile, trying to gauge his reaction. "Are you involved directly with them? Or is this more of an investment opportunity?" She knew she risked encouraging his interest, and the lift of his brow only confirmed it. But how else was she supposed to find anything out? She didn't think she was asking anything too out of the ordinary. And hey, it was better for him to be on the defensive than her, right?

"I suppose you could consider it an investment opportunity."

Great. Now what? She sipped her wine, debating the wisdom of making another attempt. Her Mata Hari skills were apparently right up there with her mascara skills. "One of the staff mentioned you had to go out early this morning." She shifted her gaze to the crowds once more. "Another business meeting? That's one problem with modern technology, I suppose. You can be tracked down anywhere. Makes it that much more difficult to get away from it all."

Stefan shifted just enough that she was forced to look up at him. "And yet it seems you've managed to do just that. With your family business out West, that is."

She tensed and swore silently. She really sucked at this. "I'm sure your time is more in demand than mine. What exactly is it that you do?"

He looked into her eyes for a very long moment, but before he could answer, a house staffer appeared at his elbow.

"Mr. Bjornsen? There is a call for you."

"Thank you," he said, never taking his gaze from her. "I'll take it inside." Stefan took her wineglass, turned it, and putting his mouth where hers had been, drained the last sip. "Perhaps when I get back, we can discuss exactly what it is I'd like to be doing."

Her mouth dropped open.

He graced her with the full force of his smile, then tipped her chin with one elegant, tapered finger until her lips pressed together. "Who knows, by nightfall we might be able to really give Ms. Bitsy Henessy something to talk about."

By the time it occurred to Darby to follow him, perhaps eavesdrop on his side of the phone conversation, Stefan had disappeared into the house. She supposed his bold proposition shouldn't have caught her so badly off guard. He'd made it clear this morning that he was interested.

But while he still packed a wallop where her libido was concerned, she couldn't help but think that, this time, it had been more about getting her off her topic—him—than it had been about getting her into bed.

Cinderella Rule #15

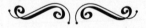

*O*bligations. Social. Business. Personal. Professional. Life is an unending parade of them. Balance is key. As is discovering how to succeed at fulfilling them without sacrificing your happiness in the process. So use one to enhance the other at every given opportunity.

—AURORA

Chapter 15

*W*ell, Shane had finally done the impossible. He'd discovered a group of people so tight-assed that even he couldn't shake them up.

He'd gotten quite a few stares, a couple of *Oh, my*'s, but apparently, when you had as much money as he now did, you could pretty much do anything you wanted, no matter how bizarre, and those around you simply smiled and accepted it as eccentricity. Because to do otherwise might mean they'd get left out of the deal, cut out of the will, or worse, crossed off the party A-list.

About the only positive thing he had to show for his grandstand play was that he was finally comfortable. No more ties or tasseled loafers for him. It was a start, anyway.

Smiling as the opening lick of *Mustang Sally* cut through the late afternoon air, he headed up the terrace steps, then spied Stefan heading into the house alone. He glanced out over the crowd and immediately spotted Darby. She looked a bit lost, but before he could decide whether to go to her or to duck inside and follow Stefan, she was set upon by two heavily pearled women who immediately pulled her into a conversation. She'd probably appreciate a rescue at the moment, he thought, wincing as she was subjected to yet another arm's-length inspection, but he knew she could hold her own. And the opportunity to check in on whatever Stefan was up to was too good to pass up.

He ducked into the hallway in time to spot one of the household staffers standing with Stefan at the far end of the corridor. Stefan took the cordless phone from the young man, then allowed him to usher him through the doors into the study for some privacy. Damn. No way was he going to hear anything through solid paneled oak. "Ah-ha," he said, snapping his fingers. He took one side of the split main staircase two steps at a time, then hustled down the second floor east wing corridor, through another small office used by the house manager. Ducking through the door at the rear of the room, he entered a narrow back stairwell used by the household help ... this one leading right to a faux panel at the rear of the study.

Once at the base of the stairs, he paused long enough so that he could hear something other than his heart pounding in his ears, then very, very carefully engaged the pressure latch, catching the bottom edge of the panel with his toe so it wouldn't swing wide-open. Allowing himself only a tiny sliver of an opening, he shifted slightly sideways. Stefan wasn't in his line of vision, so he kept his ear close to the crack, hoping to hear some of his conversation.

"No. From what I've observed, he knows nothing about it," Stefan was saying. There was a long pause. He could hear Stefan's shoes scuff across the century-old Persian carpet. He was pacing.

Shane held his breath and prayed that Stefan wouldn't tread too closely to the rear corner of the room.

"No," Stefan said abruptly, vehemently. "I won't risk that. No reason to jeopardize things now. I can take care of this my own way."

Another pause, then a short burst of Swedish epithets. "There is no need to do anything rash." His voice was closer to the panel now, and Shane instinctively shrank back. "Yes, I'm aware of that, but the buyout doesn't look good. I don't think it will go through. At least not soon. I have time."

Shane stiffened. Buyout? Was Stefan referring to the Celentrex deal? If so, then the coincidence wasn't a coincidence after all: Stefan was involved with Alexandra. And, apparently, if Shane was reading this conversation right, wasn't willing to let his and Big Al's profit-making little sideline die a premature death as well. Stefan walked away and Shane pressed closer to the open crack.

"It doesn't matter if it falls through. I told you, I can get it on my own. Funding won't be a problem. No. I've got that taken care of."

Funding. Was that what Paul Landon's role was? . . . And get what on his own?

"No!" Stefan barked suddenly, making Shane twitch. There was more than anger in his voice now. If Shane wasn't mistaken, what he'd heard had sounded a lot more like . . . fear. "Please," Stefan went on, quieter, but still sounding tense. "I just need a little more time, that is all. Surely you can trust me that far. I'll deliver. I promise.

"We're close. Very close. Just—please, don't—" He broke off, swore again, then slammed the phone down on the desk.

That was going to leave a mark, Shane thought, wincing. He shifted, trying to see through the crack, listening, waiting, in case Stefan picked the phone up again. But moments later he heard the doors to the hallway open, and sounds of the party and the bustle of the house staff filtering in. He waited another thirty seconds, then slipped into the study—just as the doors to the hall opened again.

He all but dove through the side set of French doors into the attached sunroom, barely making it past a potted palm before Stefan reentered the study. He couldn't close the doors behind him without being seen. He could only hope Stefan didn't notice the change. He held his breath, darted a look around. Not really much in the way of hiding spots out here. The doors to the study provided almost a full view, as did the wall of windows behind him. He risked a glance into the study just as Stefan slid a small cell phone out of his jacket pocket and punched in a number, his back angled toward Shane.

Stay or go, Shane thought. He wasn't sure he'd hear anything out here. The wall of windows didn't provide much of a barrier to all the party noises and the music. He spent a moment debating the merits of just strolling into the study and at least temporarily thwarting whatever Stefan's current plan was. He spent another considering just coming out and confronting the man. But Shane had spent too many years honing his survival instincts to go that route. No, he wanted more information before he decided the best way to play this out.

"Now where did that boy get off to? Honestly, Vivian, I can't imagine what he was thinking, putting on that outfit."

Shane froze as he heard the voices just beyond the louvered windows of the sunroom. Aurora. And, apparently, Vivian.

"Probably figured it would liven up this duller than dishwater party. I could have told him that even stripping naked wouldn't have done that for this bunch." She sighed deeply. "Although it would have made my day."

Aurora gasped. "Dear Lord, Vivi, the boy is almost like family."

"I can't appreciate his aesthetic beauty?"

"Honestly, I don't know why I bother. You're hopeless."

"Only when it comes to the opposite sex," Vivian assured her with absolutely zero remorse. "And if a girl has to have a hobby, well, it beats gardening or stamp-collecting, now doesn't it?"

Aurora sniffed. "I'm not even going to grace that with a reply. Come now, we must find Shane. He simply can't ignore his social obligations."

Shane shifted farther around the palm as the two women came

into view. The last thing he needed was the godmothers alerting Stefan to his presence.

"He most certainly could," Vivian tossed back. "In fact, he could be on a plane to Tahiti right now and, frankly, I wouldn't blame him."

"Well, then it's time both of you grew up a little," Aurora stated with surprisingly firm conviction. "He might not have asked for this inheritance, but the fact is—"

"The fact is, you chose to marry into your money—and you wear it quite fabulously, darling," Vivian said, not unkindly. "Alexandra did the same thing, although quite ruthlessly. And we both know she reveled in it. Shane made it quite clear to Alexandra that he didn't want the same things she did. She had no business burdening him this way."

"Like there was any chance of her letting someone else take over."

Shane shifted so he could see the two of them, and keep one eye on the open door to the study. Stefan's back was still to him, but as far as he could tell, he wasn't talking to anyone yet.

"I still say she should have never had him named in the will."

"Maybe she thought he'd come around if he had to," Aurora said.

"Well, then, that's possibly Alexandra's most critical mistake, thinking she could coerce him into it from beyond the grave."

"You have a point." Aurora sighed. "Still, Vivi, don't you think it's time he stopped gallivanting around the globe? The bohemian lifestyle is fine for a younger man, but he's thirty now. Surely he plans to slow down and settle at some point."

"I suppose he will, when he finds something worth settling for." Vivian lowered her voice. "Or someone."

"You say that as if you know something I don't."

Shane glanced back in time to see Vivian's smug smile.

Aurora swatted her gently on the forearm, but her expression was avidly curious. "Oh, come now, you have to tell. Does Mercy know? Am I the last one to know again? Why is it I'm always the—"

"Aurora, darling, you've met her."

"I have? Why, the only woman I've seen him with since his return is—" She broke off, covered her mouth. "No."

Vivian nodded. Smiled. "In fact, I've done my best to steer her in his direction every chance I've had. I think they're adorable to-gether."

"And I don't suppose the fact that you wanted a little time with that delectable gilded morsel she arrived with had anything to do with that."

"We all have to make our sacrifices for the happiness of others," Vivian said with a sigh.

Shane smiled despite his precarious situation. A shame Vivian wasn't a Morgan. Alexandra could have left the empire to her. The world would never have been the same. He glanced to the study. Stefan was talking, but he couldn't hear him now. Dammit. He wanted to get the hell out of here and find Darby, tell her what he'd overheard, put his head together with hers and see what she made of it.

It didn't look like Vivian and Aurora were ever going to leave. Sighing, he cautiously backed away from the French doors, staying in a crouch until he was right next to the opposite door, then slipped outside as quickly as possible, closing the door with a soft *click* be-hind him. "You two contemplating doing some laps?" he asked, mo-tioning to the pool fronting the sunroom.

Vivian and Aurora whirled around, smiles immediately beaming out of their expertly made-up faces. "There you are, darling!"

He quickly slid his hands beneath their elbows and steered them away from the sunroom. "Didn't you hear those Beach Boys tunes?" he said. "I thought you two would be in your bikinis and down by the pool by now."

Aurora flushed even as she swatted him. "Bikinis, my land's sake. I never wore one of those, even when I was fashionably figured."

Shane kissed her powdery cheek, even as he moved them closer to the other partygoers. "Your figure has always been fashionable and you know it."

Vivian leaned in for her kiss, then wiggled her perfectly penciled brows. "Well, I've never been figured for a bikini. But I'll have you know, I've got a leopard-print maillot that would turn your head, young man."

Shane grinned and looped their arms through his. "I don't doubt it for a second." He hadn't forgotten their conversation about him, nor did he pretend it hadn't given him a bit of a pause. He'd always known Vivian would approve of his decisions, no matter what. And Mercedes likely never would. But it surprised him to know how Aurora felt. Just as it surprised him to realize it stung a little.

"So," Vivian said, rubbing her heavily ringed hand up and down his forearm. "Did Darby manage to find her way to you earlier?"

"Why, yes, she did," Shane told her. He leaned down and kissed her soundly on the cheek. "I owe you one. More than one, I think."

Vivian laughed. "My, my, I'll have to remember to do you favors more often."

"So, you like this Landon girl, then?" Aurora asked, looking both interested and a bit concerned. "She seems quite nice, if a bit rough around the edges. I'm afraid we really didn't have as much time as we'd have liked with her. But we did the best we could with the time we had."

He gave her hand a squeeze, encouraging her to keep moving. "Your best is always top-notch, and I happen to know that Darby is very thankful for your help."

Aurora smiled and preened a bit, then looked worried again. "I believe she's only planning a brief visit. Have you two made plans? Will you be heading out West to see her when things are straightened out here? And my word, dear, how are things going here and at Alexandra's offices? I know it must be dreadfully overwhelming, but I'm certain you're up to the task." She patted him on the arm. "It's all a balancing act, to be certain. Juggling your social life with your other obligations. Why, I always used to tell Way he simply couldn't expect to put in all those hours at the office, then leave me sitting home all evening as well." She smiled brightly. "Balance is key."

Vivian sighed dramatically. She did that very well. "Could you be any less subtle? Let the poor boy come up for air. He smiles at a woman and you've got him locked into a three-piece-suit-white-picket-fence future. He's a grown man and certainly more than capable of setting his own boundaries and deciding what kind of balance he wants in life." She turned her gaze up to Shane. "So, have you two made plans?"

Aurora, to her credit, only rolled her eyes, then busied herself with primping the chiffon folds of her dress as they set out strolling along the terraced edge of the lawn.

Shane glanced back at the sunroom, then began scanning the throngs dotting the lawn for Darby. He wanted to get to her before Stefan reappeared. "We're just enjoying each other's company. It's not serious." Why did that sound like such a lie to his own ears? What *did* he want from her?

Vivian eyed him closely, but all she said was, "Hmm."

"We both have other obligations. Things are complicated."

"Perhaps she'd extend her stay, darling," Aurora put in.

"She has a ranch to run. She didn't exactly plan to take this trip in the first place." Although, this new wrinkle notwithstanding, he thanked God and Darby's baby sister for foisting it off on her. Her presence in his life might be short-lived, but not for all the hammocks in Bali would he have passed on the chance to share what little time they'd had. "Speaking of Darby, you don't happen to know where she is at the moment, do you?"

"No, dear, we haven't seen her in a while." Vivian leaned closer, eyes twinkling. "You know, there's no reason you can't go out West and see her as soon as you wrap things up here."

They were behind the house now. He scanned the milling crowds, but didn't spot Darby or Stefan. He turned his best smile on Vivian. "Maybe I will. Right after I sign the Morgan empire and this whole monstrosity of a heritage all over to you, sweetheart. God knows you'd do more with it than I ever could."

Aurora gasped, but Vivian merely hooted and cupped his face with her ringed hands. "You are such a scamp, you know that?"

Through squeezed cheeks, Shane said, "I might be serious."

"Seriously deluded if you think I want that hassle, honey," she said with a snort and released him with a cheek pinch.

He laughed, but eased out of her grasp. "Well, there is that. Listen, I have to scoot. You two enjoy yourselves, okay?" He was almost free when Aurora grasped his arm and tugged him around.

"Darling, all joking aside, you can't simply walk away from your ancestral home. Heritage means something, if not for you, then for your children and their children. It's quite one thing to sell off the business—"

"Aurora, I'm not selling anything off." *Yet.* "Please, don't worry about all this. I'll find a solution that satisfies everyone." *Right after I find a cure for cancer and come up with a solution for world peace.*

He dropped a quick kiss on her cheek. "I'll catch up with you two later, okay? Enjoy yourselves." He winked at Vivian. "And you behave."

"Now, why would I want to do that?" Vivian asked with a laugh.

Shane shot her a grin, then plunged into the fray, intent on tracking Darby down.

Shit.

She was on the far side of the yard, once again ensconced in conversation . . . with Stefan already back and smiling by her side.

Cinderella Rule #16

*S*tandards. Goals. Everyone has them. Or should. But before you judge yourself a success or failure, make certain the standards you're applying are your own. And that the goals you're trying to achieve aren't being pursued for the wrong reasons.

—MERCEDES

Chapter 16

It was hard to tell where the afternoon lawn party ended and the evening soiree began. Darby realized people were reappearing with dressier clothing, and that gradually everyone was moving indoors. She'd blown an extra outfit already today, so they'd just have to take her in the same clothes for a whole afternoon and evening. The horror.

She hadn't seen Shane since he'd plunged into the fray in his Hawaiian shorts. The few times she'd tried to wade through the human tide pool to find him, she'd gotten sucked into the undertow and missed him completely. It didn't help that since returning from his phone call, Stefan had stuck to her like fine sand on damp skin; a bit irritating and impossible to get rid of.

She'd intentionally kept the two of them involved in this group or that, all the while keeping an eye out for Shane. Of course, that meant subjecting herself to an endless stream of Bitsy-clones, which made grilling Stefan further almost impossible. Not that she was getting anywhere with that plan anyway. But it was a small price to pay if it kept him from pursuing his intention to push their arrangement in a more personal direction.

Over the past couple of hours, she'd gotten quite good at deflecting questions about herself, mostly by mercilessly shoving Stefan in the busybodies' faces every chance she got, and smiling until she thought her cheeks were going to be permanently stuck in that position.

"I understand they are setting up games of chance in the ballroom," one of the gentlemen in their current circle—Roger? Ralston?—announced. He sent a speculative look at Stefan and Darby, drawing the attention of everyone in their group. "Care to join us?"

"I don't know." Stefan turned to her, his dark eyes as intent as ever. "Are you a gambler, Darby?"

Her smile tightened. One thing she hadn't gotten better at was playing this cat-and-mouse game with Stefan. "The house always wins, doesn't it?" she managed. *Where in the hell was Shane when she needed him, anyway?* She liked his games better. Far better.

An amused smile curved Stefan's chiseled lips. "I believe that depends on who's running the house."

Two of the women tittered at Stefan's barely disguised innuendo. Great, just what she needed, more whispers and sideways glances. Like everyone wasn't already talking about the two of them.

"Would you prefer to go in and sample the buffet?" she suggested, refusing to play anymore. She'd already provided enough entertainment for the troops. What she really wanted to do was go in and sample the open bar. Heavily. Instead, she mustered up one more smile and looked to their little group. "I'm famished. Anyone care to join us?"

Several of the couples nodded, while two others demurred and headed off to gamble, instead. She sidled closer to two of the other women, thinking she'd corral them into hitting a bathroom to freshen up ... then slip away and find Shane.

But Stefan very smoothly slid her arm through his, keeping her close. "Enjoying yourself?" he asked, his gaze focused so intently on her that it was as if they were the only two people in the room.

Darby wasn't sure if he was sincere, or if it was his way of letting her know that he saw through her strategy. Every time she gained an edge, he'd do something as casual as focus that amazing gaze of his directly on her, and her throat would go dry, her pulse would speed up. And she'd realize that any notion that she was in control of things was merely an illusion. One he was allowing her to have. For now.

"I—well, it certainly looks like they've had a successful turnout."

He stroked her arm and all the hairs on her neck stood up. Other parts of her body had an entirely different reaction. How was it that the man could unnerve her and turn her on at the same time? Admittedly, Stefan was a devastatingly good-looking, larger-than-life male specimen. But he also made her very uncomfortable. Some women—okay, a lot of women—would probably enjoy being prey to his predator. She just felt like a mouse being toyed with, amusing the cat until he decided it was time to pounce.

"You didn't answer my question." With a little tug, he pulled her slightly to the side of the flow of people moving toward the ballroom. "You know, you handled yourself quite admirably today."

Right there, that was what bugged her. That slightly superior tone, with that amused undercurrent. She didn't care what league she was playing in, he was condescending as hell, and hostess job or not, she was done putting up with it. "What is that supposed to mean?"

The sharp edge to her voice obviously surprised him. Only she couldn't tell if it bothered him ... or encouraged him. Dammit. Then he pulled out the double-dimple whammy ... and she hated herself for it, but her knees did wobble a tiny bit. Okay, so maybe it did matter what league she was playing in. Just a little.

"It means that from everything I've gathered, you've been gone from this kind of ... lifestyle for some time. And I don't believe you're entirely happy to be back." His voice was velvety smooth, with that accent of his flavoring every word. And those dark eyes that missed nothing. "You must care for your father a great deal, to be willing to subject yourself to the kind of scrutiny you've been under since your arrival."

Well, shit. He'd seen through her charade right from the start. Lovely. All that time in makeover hell, and for what? So Bitchy Bitsy could make her feel like fashion roadkill? "It was more a favor to my sister," she said without thinking. Only when something flickered in his gaze did she realize that she might not have wanted to reveal so much.

"Ah. And your father ... does he realize you've chosen to stand in for your sister?"

Trapped. She was a cornered mouse with nowhere to hide. Something was going on here, something she didn't understand. He'd been suspicious of her since he'd found out she was taking Pepper's place. If she really was only here to play hostess until her father showed up, then it shouldn't have made any difference to him who escorted him around. She realized that not only did she not know the rules of the game they were playing ... she didn't even know what the damn game really was.

"Does it matter?" she finally said. She deliberately moved them back into the flow of people, smiling up at him as if he hadn't just called her bluff. "You know, you never did answer *my* question."

His smile didn't reach his eyes. "It seems we both have an aptitude for evasion."

She refused to take the bait. Maybe if she just pretended she wasn't the mouse, he'd pretend not to pounce. "You never did tell me what it was you did for a living. Are you a jeweler?"

He studied her for a moment, then said, "No, I leave that to the jewelers and appraisers. I'm afraid I'm in on the dirty end of things." His eyes darkened further and he stroked her arm, his lips quirking when he felt her shudder. "It's the raw element that excites me, the thrill of discovery. Unlike you, I enjoy risk."

She'd already figured that out. Now if she could just get him to stop touching her like that, she might actually be able to keep the conversation focused where she wanted it. "So ... you're an engineer? Of sorts?" She smiled, but no longer bothered with the hair swing over the shoulder or the Washington-ingénue eyelash flutter. She'd sucked at that, anyway. "I suppose it must be difficult determining where to dig." She glanced at him, irked to find that amused gleam still in his eyes.

"There's a science to it, but it also takes a bit of luck."

"And money, I'd imagine."

His gaze shuttered briefly and she felt a tiny surge of triumph. "Nothing in life is for free," he said finally, but his smooth smile and easy charm were no longer so apparent. "Nothing worth having, anyway."

"Money can't buy everything," she said, thinking about Shane, the joy he found in life just by living it. You couldn't put a price tag on that kind of fulfillment or happiness.

They'd come to the rear of the buffet line. A server handed each of them a chilled salad plate.

"I didn't say it could," Stefan said next to her ear. "What I said was that nothing worth having comes without a price. In order to get, you have to give." He drew a light finger along the back of her arm. "Payment, however, comes in many forms."

She shivered and knew damn well it wasn't because of the cold china clutched in her hand. He knew it, too. Jerking her arm forward and not caring what message she sent, she grabbed the salad tongs and tossed what looked like a pile of garden weeds onto her plate. When did regular lettuce go out of fashion, anyway?

She moved down the buffet line, filling her plate without much thought to what she was piling on it, more concerned with figuring out how in the hell she was going to deal with Stefan for the rest of the evening. Not to mention all day tomorrow. Jesus. While the carver at the end of the line sliced a piece of roast for her, she gazed around the room, which had been set with large round tables for group gatherings, as well as more intimate tables around the fringes. No sign of Shane, dammit. He was probably in the other ballroom, overseeing casino night.

"Shall we?" Stefan said right next to her ear.

She stiffened as he motioned to one of the smaller tables set up by the row of French doors that composed the entire wall, and which led to a long expanse of balcony. She really wasn't up for playing games any longer tonight. She seriously needed time to regroup.

"Why, darling, there you are. Over here!"

There is a God, Darby thought. Or godmothers, as the case might be. With her first genuine smile in hours, she turned to find Aurora waving at them to come and sit at their table.

She only hoped she didn't look too overly appreciative as she wound her way through the tables. It was all she could do not to fling her arms around each one of them.

Vivian patted the empty chair between her and Aurora. "Why, Stefan, darling, you look like you could use another glass of champagne." She motioned a waiter over immediately, before Stefan could demur.

To his credit, he gallantly accepted the champagne, and the offer of the seat. Darby moved quite thankfully to the other side of the table and sat near Mercedes. Vivian and Aurora immediately dominated every moment of Stefan's attention, for which Darby owed them a tremendous debt of gratitude. Until she realized that she was left alone in Mercedes' clutches.

"My dear. You've worked up quite an appetite." She didn't sound impressed.

Darby looked down at her plate. It was rather . . . moundlike. "It all looked so wonderful. I guess I didn't want to make an extra trip."

The look on Mercedes' face made it clear that a second trip to the buffet line was an etiquette faux pas on par with, well, apparently piling one of everything on a plate the first go-around. She sighed, but didn't otherwise comment. "So, how has the day progressed for you?"

Darby thought about the day she'd had and could find no suitable words to describe it. "I'm managing. Thanks to you and your staff," she added quickly.

Mercedes nodded, then leaned a bit closer. "May I make a suggestion, and please don't take it unkindly, dear."

Darby bravely kept her shoulders from drooping. "Certainly."

"It's expected that women will change for dinner. Men, too, although the rules are somewhat more relaxed for them." A small smile curved her tightly pressed lips as she cut her gaze to Stefan, who still managed to look crisp in his white linen shirt and pleated trousers, despite having worn them all day. "Unfair, but there you have it. I've always thought of the men as the fixtures and the women as the centerpieces."

"I'm really—"

Mercedes waved her silent. "Not to bother, dear. Today is more casual, as the guests are still arriving. However, traditionally, on a weekend gathering such as this one, tomorrow evening will be formal, so you will want to make certain you slip upstairs to your room, preferably between four and five, to make your change to evening wear."

Darby could only nod and mumble, "Yes, of course."

"One last item. While your makeup-free look is quite ... refreshing during daylight hours, evening light isn't so flattering, especially given your exposure to the sun."

Darby frowned.

"Oh, darling, and please, please, never frown like that. Smooth, relaxed." She smiled encouragingly and Darby did her best to get that Stepford-Wife look. "Much improved, dear." She snagged the artfully folded linen napkin Darby had shifted aside, flipped it open, and handed it to her. "Don't worry, you'll get the hang of things. And we're always just a phone call away, you know."

Darby took the napkin and spent a moment being tempted to tuck it into the collar of her shirt, just for grins, but decided it wasn't worth the lecture. She spread it over her lap, and Mercedes nodded in approval before turning her attention back to her salad and involving herself in the conversation Aurora and Vivian were having with Stefan.

Darby poked at her garden weeds ... and planned her escape.

Shane closed the heavy, leather-bound book and set it back on the small stack he'd made for himself on the floor next to the wing chair. He glanced at his watch and was startled to realize how much time slipped by. The buffet had already begun serving and casino night was probably gearing up. Which meant that while he'd been sitting here playing This Is Your Life, Darby was downstairs, still dealing with Stefan.

He got up and paged Chambers, the staff manager, on the house phone. He asked to speak with Trasker, who came on the line moments later and assured him that Miss Landon was eating dinner with her guest, Ms. dePalma, Ms. Favreaux, and Ms. Browning.

Shane sighed in relief. "And they've been together the whole time?"

"Since we last spoke, sir. In fact, they've been quite popular with your other guests."

And he bet Darby was just loving that. He promised himself he'd find a way to make it up to her. "Thanks. And listen, I really appreciate your help today. Could you do me one more favor and inform Ms. Landon she has a phone call, then send her to Alexandra's—I mean, my private office, please?"

"I'd be happy to, sir."

He'd wanted to send for her sooner, but he hadn't wanted to leave Stefan to his own devices until he had a chance to dig deeper into Alexandra's private files. Dinner would keep him stationary, at least for a little while. And he knew he could count on Vivian and company to keep him occupied well into the evening, if necessary.

For all the good it would likely do. There had been nothing more from We Dig It, and for all his digging on the home front, he still had nothing more substantial to show for it than he had before. Just a gut instinct and circumstantial evidence that Stefan had been in cahoots with his grandmother on some secret deal before she died. A deal he appeared still to be involved in. Somehow.

That phone call made it clear he was on a tight deadline with someone. Probably for money, which was the reason he was here in the first place. To meet with Paul Landon, his prospective investor. Nothing nefarious there. But the tone of that phone call hadn't been a business-as-usual deal. No, Stefan was in some kind of trouble. Shane would bank on it. And Pepper had mentioned that his proposed deal with Landon had to do with gemstones. Bringing him back to the possible connection to Alexandra's little side deal. But as far as he could tell, Alexandra had only funded the invention of an adaptation to the already existing Celentrex equipment. Even if Stefan was somehow in possession of the adaptation, it would be useless without the main piece of technology, the Celentrex-developed prototype.

Shane shook his head. His brain ached from playing and replaying that damned phone call. He wished like hell he knew who Stefan had called when he'd come back into the study. Shit, he wished like hell he didn't care. And frankly, if it weren't for the possible involvement of Darby's father, maybe he wouldn't. Maybe. A week ago he'd been a perfectly happy camper, digging life in the sunny South Pacific, had never heard of Celentrex, couldn't care less about corporate buyouts or industrial espionage. Amazing the difference a week could make.

Which brought his thoughts directly to Darby. He hadn't seen her, touched her, tasted her, in hours. And it made him ache. But more than that, he wanted—needed—to talk to her. Not just about what he'd overheard, or his suspicions, but about … well, everything. Shane Morgan, who never turned to anyone, had somehow found himself wanting to turn to her. For all kinds of things.

He pushed those thoughts away, too. Too much. Jesus, this was all too much. And he was mortally sick of dwelling on it. Stefan wasn't going anywhere. Darby was under his roof for the night. And tomorrow was another day.

He headed back over to the fireplace and sank down in the chair, wondering how long it would take for Darby to come to him. And what he was going to tell her when she did. Yes, he wanted to dump the whole thing on her and get her take on it. But this event already wasn't easy on her, and the mystery surrounding Stefan certainly wasn't helping matters any. He didn't want to waste the one night he knew he'd have with her dwelling on that crap. He knew how much she'd dreaded facing the speculation and open curiosity about her return to Washington. And the party today had only confirmed that she'd had good reason to. He'd overheard numerous guests buzzing about her, theorizing on why she'd come back and who that man was she was with and so on and so on. He'd wanted to march over, tell the busybodies to get a goddamn life, and drag her away from the whole mess. Had come quite close to doing exactly that, in fact. But he needed to put this other thing to rest, first.

Not that he'd abandoned her entirely. He'd tracked down Vivian and asked her to keep an eye on the two of them. She'd assumed Shane was just being a possessive, jealous male, which might have been partially true. But she'd gladly accepted her assignment. Then he'd tracked down Trasker and made it clear he wanted to know if Stefan received any more calls—before Stefan was told—or if he wandered off alone for any reason.

He'd headed straight to Alexandra's private office, thinking if she had secret files at work, then she probably had them at home. Unfortunately, unless she had some kind of secret panel behind one of the bookcases or something, he'd come up empty. He used the pass code Hal had provided to get into her computer, but nothing popped up there, either, except the startling discovery that his grandmother had apparently enjoyed playing the occasional blistering game of computer mah-jongg. He couldn't picture Alexandra spending time on anything so mindless. It shouldn't have mattered, but the image of her, sitting behind her desk, entertaining herself by clicking on little patterned tiles . . . well, it humanized her in a way that was a little disconcerting.

His snooping hadn't uncovered any other little secrets, espionage-related or not—but it had uncovered a treasure trove of an entirely different sort. He'd been poking through the glass-enclosed bookcases behind her desk when he'd stumbled across the family albums.

He'd looked through the most recent ones, covering Alexandra's tenure in the family, all professionally published with thick glossy pages and written by a carefully chosen family biographer. The last one ended shortly after his parents' death, so his existence was barely a footnote in Morgan history as yet. He'd been amused by that, thinking not much had changed since. The next volume must be in progress somewhere, and he wondered if he'd been included. He couldn't imagine what had been said about him—and was surprised to discover he might care.

He lifted the next volume and carefully opened the cracked leather binding. The family had already dwindled rather alarmingly by the time Alexandra had married into it. Her husband, Grayson, had been one of two sons borne to Edith and Charles Morgan. Grayson's brother, George, whom Shane had never even known existed, had died, fighting in the war. Her mother-in-law had also died young. Her father-in-law, however, had lived to the ripe old age of eighty-three and, as Hal had mentioned, been the man who'd groomed Alexandra to take on the mantle of the entire Morgan ancestry when his remaining son had died so suddenly.

Not much mention, however, was made of Alexandra's family. Probably because she and Grayson had eloped. It had been quite the scandal. Charles hadn't approved, seeing as Big Al's family, while moderately well-to-do, had made the fatal faux pas of only being able to trace their heritage back three generations before leaving American soil. Of course, once she'd married into the Morgan enclave and given Charles a grandchild, her family tree had likely become of lesser importance.

"Or, apparently, no importance," he thought, as he began to flip carefully through the yellowed pages. His father's family, the New England Lovelles, had been well-represented in the glossy printed pages of the newest albums. Their lineage dated back to the Mayflower.

He wondered if life would have been any different as a Lovelle, rather than a Morgan. They hadn't been as wrapped up in family heritage as the Morgans. In fact, Alexandra had dropped the hyphenated Lovelle from his name before he was old enough to write it down. He remembered vaguely his father's parents doting on him at holidays, but once he'd been shipped off to boarding school, that connection had dwindled to letters, which he'd dreaded receiving, as it meant writing letters back. Not exactly a favorite activity for any of the boys he'd boarded with. And writing those lengthy letters to Alexandra, with all the details that she demanded he include, had been painful enough.

His Lovelle grandparents had passed on when he was in his teens. If he had any Lovelle aunts, uncles, or cousins, he'd never met them, nor had he ever thought to ask after them. That sounded cold, but that was the truth of it. He'd felt closer to his boarding-school chums and some of the household staff at Four Stones than he had his own family. So it had seemed perfectly normal to be detached. Shit, maybe he was more like his ancestors than he realized. That was depressing.

He flipped through the current album, which detailed Charles's youth and rise to power, following in the footsteps of his parents—both of whom had lived to a ripe age and who had continued to build on the shipping interests begun by Charles's grandparents before them. Charles had had two sisters, both of whom had married late and been widowed during the war, neither of whom had married again or had children. That burden had fallen to Charles, who'd come through with two sons, but whose family legacy had ended up being continued by his daughter-in-law.

Shane thought about that, about the pressure that had likely been brought to bear on Alexandra, the enormous pressure given how proud the Morgan family was of their achievements, their place in history. He'd never really thought of it that way. Had seen her as a strong-willed woman who'd eagerly stepped in to fill her husband's shoes, enjoying the power her wealth and position in society afforded her. He still thought of her that way. But this definitely added another element to that picture.

He put the album aside and picked up the next one, which was decidedly more fragile. The pages were badly yellowed, and the book itself was more of an actual scrapbook, with real news clippings and photos adhered to the pages, along with carefully penned details and stories. He understood now why these volumes were stored in an air-tight, unlit case.

He began turning the pages, slowly becoming absorbed in the stories being told, the pictures so carefully included. Shane was well lost in the past when he heard the door crack open. "Whatever it is, just take care of it," he said, not taking his gaze from the page.

"I believe I was summoned."

Shane's head shot up, a smile instantly lighting his face at the sight of Darby standing in the doorway.

Funny how he'd spent the past several hours completely absorbed in reading about people he was related to by blood, sitting in the home they'd built with their own capable hands, and held on to with their nimble minds. And yet it wasn't until he'd lifted his gaze to hers, felt that instant punch of connection, that he felt even a remote sense of belonging.

Cinderella Rule #17

*T*he heart is a fickle thing. It doesn't always require extensive time or deep analysis to make up its mind on what it wants. It can happen in a blink. Be prepared. And don't be afraid to follow its dictates. It's only when you try to dissect its decisions that you get yourself into trouble. In other words, when it feels right, don't question it. Just go for it.

—VIVIAN

Chapter 17

*D*arby didn't move from the doorway. She was too struck by the picture he presented. He sat in front of a stone fireplace framed on both sides by floor-to-ceiling bookcases, a rich Aubusson carpet covering most of the inlaid wood flooring. He was ensconced in a deep leather chair, feet propped carelessly on an antique table, a portrait of casual wealth. His hair was a shade too long, his face too tanned, his smile too bold. The rakish lord of the manor.

"What?" he asked, as she continued her perusal.

She entered the room, smiling. "Nothing. You just have to-the-manor-born stamped all over you." His immediate frown made her laugh. "Don't worry, it's not fatal."

He slid his feet to the floor, closed an ancient-looking leather album he'd had propped in his lap, and set it aside. "I'm not too sure about that."

"The flowered shorts make their own statement," she added, noting the shadows in his eyes, despite the smile on his face. "A little light reading?" she asked, unabashedly curious despite knowing she had no right to pry. He'd smiled easily when she'd poked her head in, but she'd heard the distracted note in his voice when he'd thought she was household staff. And now that she was closer, she saw the lines of tension around his eyes, the corners of his mouth. Funny how quickly she'd learned his face, how easily she spotted even the tiniest difference.

She took the seat opposite from him. It was the first time she'd been alone with him since this afternoon, and just like that, the pressures and stresses of her day faded to the background. Replaced by a tangle of other emotions. She'd remembered the things he'd said to her, how it had felt to have him touching her, holding her, kissing her, thrusting inside her. And wondered if he'd called her here so they could do all that again.

Shane's attention had drifted back to the album. "Heavy reading, actually. The weight of centuries in fact." His smile was almost ... sad.

Concern immediately replaced lust. All thoughts of yanking him to the floor and having her way with him fled. Well, most of them, anyway. "What's wrong? Is it something about your inheritance?"

"In a manner of speaking." When he lifted his gaze back to hers, the only word she could come up with to describe his expression was ... lost.

"What is it about? Can you tell me?" She reached over, took his hand between hers. "I've wanted to see you all day, but I couldn't break free. Vivian dragged Stefan off to the roulette tables after I made my excuses that I needed to freshen up—which I intended to do with you, by the way—when one of your staff told me you wanted to see me. Great minds think alike, huh?" Her smile dimmed a little as she stroked her fingertips over the back of his hand, surprised at how deeply she felt the need to touch him, reach him. "But it looks like you've found something else you need to tend to first. You know,

I'll understand if you'd rather be alone. You can come up to my room later."

"No, I want you to stay. I've been thinking about you all day, too." He smiled then, and relaxed a little. "I was reading about my ancestors."

"Oh." She sat back. "And?"

He tugged her forward again, then kept on tugging until she stumbled to her feet and fell into his lap. "Shane, I'm too heavy—"

"You're just right," he insisted, easily arranging her sideways in his lap. He lifted her arms around his neck and settled her against him. "Now, this is the life of luxury."

She ran her fingers along the side of his face and he turned into her touch, pressed his lips into the palm of her hand, then cupped her face and pulled her into a kiss.

Considering his mood, she'd expected something needy, slow, exploratory. Instead it was fierce, hard, consuming. It took her breath away, and the rest of her conscious thoughts followed. And when she thought he couldn't take any more, he plundered deeper, demanded more. And she gave without question. His hands moved over her body. Her hands did some exploring of their own.

When he finally tore his mouth from hers, her shirt was half-undone and his hair was a tousled mess. He said nothing, just pressed his forehead to her cheek as he held her close while their breath steadied. She stroked his hair, his neck, his back, collected herself as well, even as her thoughts raced ahead.

Even in the short time they'd been together, she felt like she'd come to know him. Understand him. And yet this was a part of him she hadn't expected. Something deeper, more emotional, more ... complicated. "You don't have to tell me," she finally said into the stillness. "But I'm here to listen if you want to. Not sure how much help I'll be, but sometimes it feels better just to—"

"Holding you, kissing you, that's what feels better," he said with surprising emotion.

When she would have leaned back to look in his eyes, he held her in place, kept her tucked against him. He turned his face so he could nuzzle her hair. "I've always felt I only belonged to myself, to my own path, my own destiny," he said quietly.

She trailed her fingers up and down the back of his neck, teased the edges of his hair, letting him talk.

"I don't feel like I belong here, Darby. And I don't think time is going to change that." He pulled in a deep breath, then let it out slowly. "But maybe it doesn't matter how I feel. Obligations are obligations, right? You can't choose what family you get born into."

"Definitely not," she murmured, thinking of her father, his lifestyle, the things that were important to him. She would never have the same priorities he did. "I don't belong in my father's home, either. When my mother was alive, she and I kind of carved out a space that was ours, where I felt comfortable. She understood that I felt more at home in the stables than in my huge, perfectly decorated bedroom. I think she did, too. Only she adapted to the rest better than I did. Once she was gone ..." Darby lifted a shoulder. "That little space disappeared. Probably because what my father values most doesn't have anything to do with me or what I value. I don't expect that will ever change."

"You have obligations elsewhere now, though."

"Obligations I took on willingly," she said. "Important distinction. My grandfather would never have left me the ranch if he thought I didn't want it. But I was lucky. I found my space there." She did lean back now. "You know, Shane, you don't have to do anything here you don't want to. I know it's more complicated than that, but in the end, you can only do what you can do, what you can live with."

"I've thought about that a lot. And there are some things I want to see happen, specific things, mostly related to the business. But in looking through these books, reading about my ancestors, my family's history, I realize it's not the corporate entity that I feel burdened by. Not really. Morgan Industries is just an amalgamation of smaller corporations and groups and divisions that aren't really a family, or even about family. They're just about business. Life will go on for them, and they can continue to be successful and achieve whatever they decide is important to them. Not having a Morgan name on the masthead won't change that."

"That's a start, then. A step."

He sighed. "It's the rest of it that's kicking my butt. And I don't mean the other properties, or the boats, the cars, the hockey team—"

"You own a hockey team?"

His mouth kicked up a little. "You a fan? I'll make you a good deal."

She kissed him on the line of his jaw. "Thanks, but I only like sports where the guys wear tight pants."

"Why am I not surprised?"

She just grinned. "You know, I never really thought about all that other stuff. That's a lot to deal with."

"That *other stuff* doesn't really concern me. Those are just things. I can find loving homes for all of them." He smiled. "Even the forty or so odd guys missing a few front teeth." Then the smile faded, and she felt the tension return to his body. "It's the part we're sitting in that's giving me a hard time. Four Stones has been in this family since the seventeen-hundreds. Since Silas Morgan stepped off the boat onto Virginia soil. He came here to find a new life, to build a dynasty. He believed so strongly in that notion that he fought in the Revolutionary War, survived, and went on to build that empire. And begin a family who, even centuries later, still share his strength of conviction."

Darby didn't know what to say to that. For all she'd made the decision to walk away from a life of comfort and wealth, she'd never faced anything like what he was up against. Her father knew better than to leave anything to her. And the Landon holdings and interests had all been earned by her father. Hardly a dynasty in any shape or form.

"I think I've made peace with working toward dismantling the corporate empire. It's never going to be my calling. And if I do it right, the severed limbs won't die. They'll still go on to flourish or falter on their own merit. And the history books will still show that the foundation upon which they were built was initially constructed by a Morgan. And if a future Morgan comes along who wants to build another empire, let him."

"So, let the rest go, and hold on to the tangible part of your history. Hold on to the house."

He smiled, but there wasn't much humor in it. "With what? My good looks?"

"You don't have to sell everything off. Hire a manager and a good investment counselor—"

"I'm getting ulcers just hearing the words *investment counselor*." He shook his head. "And that's not really what I was getting at. After reading about how one Morgan built on what the Morgan before him started, in both personal and industrial growth, and so on and so on ... the question eating me is, how come I'm the only one who doesn't feel that burning desire to add on even more, make it bigger?"

She stroked his face, then lifted his chin until their eyes met. "Do you really think that every Morgan before you believed so strongly in capitalism and corporate growth? First off, every generation probably had a couple offspring from which to pick their successor. And I'm sure there were one or two in there who simply accepted the job because it was the path more easily taken. Alexandra wasn't even a Morgan by birth and she dragged Morgan Industries into the new millennium with an iron fist and a swelling bank account. You say strength of conviction; I say strength of greed. That, or merely bullied by a mountain of ancestral peer pressure. Or both." She leaned down and dropped a hard, fast kiss on his mouth. "But this go-around, there is only you," she said, pinching his chin. "The strong one, the first one with enough personal conviction to strike out on his own, to seek out and conquer his own world. Sort of like your great-great-however-many-greats-grandfather Silas did."

"And have what to show for it?"

"Something that can't be measured on a profit and loss statement. A concept admittedly forgotten somewhere up your family tree." She smiled. "You have happiness. The fulfillment of a life lived by your own terms. A life that's provided you with a wealth of experiences and the knowledge that you can do anything you want to do. I'd say that's not bad, and that latter part is, by your ancestor's definition, all Morgan."

He smiled then, only it was wistful, tender. He stroked her face, traced his fingers over her lips. "You're an amazing woman, Darmilla Landon."

She made a face. "Heard about that, did you? Well, that's the only amazing thing about me. The rest of it's just the same rationalization I've used for my own choices. Except for the world experiences, anyway. Mine are a tad more narrow in scope."

"I could change all that."

She grinned now. "Oh, honey, believe me, you already have."

He laughed and she decided it was time for a topic change. Partly to keep him from sliding back into the ancestral ennui he'd succumbed to, and partly to keep from begging him to take her with him whenever he'd finally had enough and struck out once again for parts unknown. Because, despite the sudden resurrection of his family consciousness, Shane Morgan was never going to let himself get turned into another tailored-suited, nine A.M.-tee-time, blue-bond-invested industry mogul.

"Besides, every family needs its wandering rogue," she teased him. "Keeps the family albums from becoming dry and boring. Gives the grandkids something to whisper and fantasize about. Maybe build their own dreams on." She framed his face, turned serious. "You'll figure out the business part. And because it's important to you, you'll find some way to preserve the family part. Then you'll get the hell out of Dodge and get on with the business of living your own life." She kissed him soundly on the lips. "And don't forget," she told him, grinning, "being last in the line does have its advantages. You can't do it wrong, because there's no one left to answer to."

Shane's gaze wandered to the stack of albums on the side table and floor. "I'm not so sure about that," he murmured, then turned back to her with a smile. "But enough whining from the poor little rich boy." He tugged her down, his kiss slow this time, and exploratory, but not at all moody. She relaxed against him, and wondered if she'd ever get tired of this, of him. She didn't think so. A shame they were so suited for each other this way, and not in any other way. If only they'd met under other circumstances . . .

That way lies insanity, Darby. And she couldn't deny that, given half a chance, she'd start trying to figure out some way to mesh his nomadic lifestyle with her deeply rooted one. Neither one of them fit here, in this world, but their real lives didn't fit with each other, either. She knew Shane wasn't her Mr. Right. Better for her if she embraced that reality right now. Shane was Mr. Right For The Weekend. In a lot of really wonderful ways that only began with the best sex she was ever likely to have. Better for her sanity to just shut up, and enjoy it while it lasted. Beats the hell out of never having it in the first place, right?

Shane ended the kiss on a sigh. "All this ancestral baggage got me sidetracked from the reason I called you up here in the first place."

"Judging from your expression, I'm guessing it didn't have anything to do with me ripping your clothes off."

His lips quirked. "No, but feel free to improvise."

Darby shifted in Shane's lap. "What happened?"

"Remember when Stefan got that call earlier?"

"Oh, that. I'm sorry I didn't get a chance to follow him, I—"

"I did."

She stilled. "And? Did you hear anything?"

He nodded. "He's in some kind of trouble. With who, I have no idea. But he's under a great deal of pressure to deliver something to someone, and soon. My guess is that that something is money."

"What, exactly, did he say?"

"He said *The buyout doesn't look good.*"

Her eyes widened. "So he *is* involved in this Celentrex thing."

"Looks that way."

"But . . . how?"

Shane shook his head. "Not sure yet. Whoever he was talking to wanted something from him, something big, and Stefan was all but begging for more time to get it done."

Darby quirked one brow. "Stefan—begging? That I'd have paid to see."

Shane gave her a look. "Is there something I should know?"

"Don't worry," she shot back, her grin saucy. "It wasn't a sexual fantasy. Although . . ." She laughed at the look on his face. "Did he say anything else?"

Shane stroked the tips of her hair. "One of the first things he said, was something like *From what I've observed, he knows nothing about it.*"

Darby put it together right off. "Meaning, he was telling whoever it was, that you don't know about your grandmother's little side deal? If they were partners, I guess when Alexandra died, the natural thing would have been to approach you and pick up where they left off."

"I think his phone pal was expecting him to do just that, but he knew if I said no, he'd be up shit's creek. I could also blow the whistle on the whole shebang."

"Which brings up another point. What is there to blow the whistle on? I mean, I know Alexandra didn't want to share her little prize with the company or the world at large. But, moral ambiguity notwith-standing, being greedy isn't illegal. Nor is emerald-mining."

"I have no idea, but there's something. The tension during that call today was palpable. He told the guy not to do anything rash."

Alarmed, Darby said, "Like?"

"Who knows what he's got invested in all this, or who he owes what to. He said he had it under control, and that it didn't matter if the Celentrex buyout didn't go through, that he had funding."

Darby swore. "Enter my fabulous father, I take it." She frowned. "But funding for what?"

He shrugged. "Maybe he's developing some connection directly to Celentrex, going direct to the source. And maybe that's going to cost big bucks. I don't know."

"There's a lot we don't know here."

"Exactly." Shane sighed, tugged her closer. "This is the way I see the whole thing so far: Alexandra is all set to buy out Celentrex, get-ting their new fossil-fuel technology in the deal. She's seen partial schematics for the technology, and somehow stumbles across the idea that there must be a way to adapt that equipment to enable it to extract an entirely different kind of fossil. She hooks up with Stefan, who has the expertise she needs, and on the sly, they work on devel-oping that adaptation. They begin to set up mining operations in South America. All that needs to happen now is the buyout. Then Alexandra will own the original technology and will have the plans, schematics, whatever, to build the whole thing. And voilà, they're in the emerald-mining business."

"Except Alexandra dies before the buyout goes through."

"Leaving Stefan holding the bag. A very expensive, useless bag."

"Unless..." Darby held his gaze. "Do you think Alexandra has the schematics, or whatever you called it, for the whole thing? Could he be here, trying to steal them back, maybe?"

"If he is, he's going to be shit out of luck. I've dug through every last file, pillaged her personal computer. Nada. All we have is that partial schematic from her private office files. Besides, if he thought he could get his hands on the plans for the whole thing, then what does he need the money for?"

"To build it? I don't know."

"Other than that phone call, he didn't wander off on his own today, did he?"

She shook her head. She thought over the conversations they'd had after his phone call. He was definitely more intense. She recalled thinking there was something more there than the sexual zing she'd felt before. Had he come on to her, hoping she might have some inside information? "No, he was with me all afternoon. I tried to get him to talk. I pressed him about his gemstone connection, asked him if he was a jeweler. He did say that he liked to be *on the dirty end of things*."

Shane snorted. "Yeah, it's sure as hell looking that way. Did he say anything else?"

Darby held his gaze again. "Just that he liked to take risks."

"Fuck. He came back in the study after the first call and made another one. I didn't get the chance to hear any of that one." He sighed. "There is more to this. A whole lot more. Dammit."

"So what do we do next, Sherlock?"

"My vote is that we wait for the We Dig It report tomorrow, see what else pops up. Right now, all we have is a great deal of speculation. Your father isn't due in till Sunday. I doubt Stefan is going anywhere until then."

Sounded like a good plan to her. She was heartily sick of this whole mess. She stroked a finger along his lower lip, deliberately drawing his attention down the path she wanted it to go. Right toward her. "And in the meantime?"

One thing about Shane, he wasn't slow on the uptake. He slid her around so she straddled his thighs, and a wickedly sexy grin curved his lips. "I say we do some further exploration of that other investigation we started today."

"Other . . . *investigation?*" she said, already weaving her fingers into his hair.

The phone buzzed on the desk.

He still nuzzled her neck, but she was already pushing at him. "Shouldn't you get that?"

"Nope." But when the buzzing started up again, Darby started to shift off his lap. Instead of letting her go, he merely wrapped her legs around his waist and said, "Hold on."

"Shane!" she squealed when he stood and carried her to the desk. He turned to lean back against it, keeping her wrapped around him, heedless of the papers and files that they were shoving to the floor as he reached out and punched the button for speakerphone. "Yes?"

"Hi, darling, hope I'm not interrupting things. You sound rather . . . intense."

Darby just wiggled her eyebrows and Shane delivered her a mock shushing warning. "You know I always love to hear from you, sweetheart. What's up?"

"Well, I did my level best, but my quarry has tired of my charms and gone to his room for the evening. I just thought you'd like to know."

"Are you certain he went to his room?"

Vivian's laugh was low and throaty. "My darling boy, she's with you now, so it hardly matters whose room he ends up in, does it?"

Darby lifted a questioning brow, but he simply tugged her hips so she snugged up tight against him, forcing her to stifle a little moan when she realized just how "with her" he was ready to be.

"True," he said, his own voice a bit tight. "Listen, I owe you a huge debt."

"My pleasure, I assure you. And you two can sleep in tomorrow morning. I overheard him put in a call for a car at seven A.M. Business meeting or some such. Ungodly hour, if you ask me. See you on the morrow, sweetheart. Sweet dreams, Darby," she added, before clicking off.

Darby didn't know whether to laugh or be mortified. "So what's all this about you owing her?"

Shane ran his hands up her back. "After the call, I tried to come find you right away, but I got waylaid by the godmother triumvirate and Stefan was already back by your side. I wanted to keep tabs on him."

"Just him?"

Shane smiled. "You can hold your own."

"I'd say thank you, but I'm not feeling all that cocky about my performance today."

He stood suddenly and spun around, pressing her all the way back onto the desk. "It's not today's performance I'm thinking about at the moment."

"Oh?" she said, barely able to keep her hips still beneath his. "Am I auditioning or something?"

"Hardly." He leaned in, took her bottom lip first, then the rest of her mouth. "You had me before I ever got in that limo."

She grinned even as her heart soared a little. She tried not to think about that. Too much. Her back arched up as he pressed more tightly between her thighs. "We've got way too many clothes on."

He nuzzled her neck. "Great minds."

"What about—" Her train of thought fled as he began working his mouth down the front of her shirt. But there was something else she was supposed to mention. Right. Stefan's morning appointment. "What are we going to do about ... ah ... oh. That feels ... Jesus." Screw the morning appointment. She had more important, more immediate concerns. Most of them dealing with helping Shane get her clothes off as soon as possible. Of course, he was already one step ahead of her. Her shirt was already open and her pants were close behind. "Are we going to do this here?"

His grin was downright wicked. "I'm recapturing the spirit of that proud, courageous Morgan who isn't afraid to go after what he wants." He slid down and tugged her zipper open. With his teeth. "And what he wants at the moment, is you."

Cinderella Rule #18

*T*he most lovely surprises happen when we least expect them. But do your best to be prepared anyway. Lipstick, mascara, and a compact should be carried at all times. And ... don't forget protection, darlings. Boy Scouts don't always come prepared.

—VIVIAN

Chapter 18

He had industrial espionage swirling about his head, not to mention a hundred or so people presently dining and gambling somewhere in his house ... and the only thing he gave a damn about was the taste of Darby Landon's mouth.

Her blouse and trousers alternately flew and dropped. He laughed when she dangled two condoms she'd tucked in her trouser pockets. His shirt and shorts followed in quick succession. And she laughed when he dangled the two he'd tucked in his. "Great minds, indeed," he said, and then she grabbed him and a second later his mind went blank. All he could do was feel. And taste. And touch.

"Door. Lock," she managed, which was more speech than he was capable of at the moment.

He took care of the problem in his own way. He pulled her to her feet, then backed her all the way up against the door, flipped the lock, and pulled her legs back up around his hips. And all the while he never left the luxury of her perfect lips. Her fingers dug into his scalp as he shifted her higher.

"This is total insanity," she moaned, then gasped as he pushed her up higher still, and slid his mouth lower. "Insanity is good."

Perfect lips. Perfect nipples. It was an embarrassment of riches. All that and a sharp mind, too. He might as well admit it, he was hopelessly lost in her. Any idea he'd had about keeping some semblance of perspective about this was more seriously compromised every time he touched her. Talked to, saw, or stood anywhere near her, too. And when he wasn't doing any of those things, he was thinking about when he could do them again.

She yanked his head back by the hair and took his mouth while sliding down the wall ... and directly onto him. Oh, yeah. This could definitely be love. Or close enough to it that he wasn't going to quibble. Now he just had to figure out what in the hell he was going to do about it.

Except right now, all the blood in his body had pooled south, leaving no brain cells left for critical thinking. Fortunately, there weren't enough left to make him care too much, either. Worry later. Pleasure now.

It had always worked for him before.

She locked her legs and rocked onto him, and he was pretty sure if she drove him any deeper, the top of his head was going to blow off. Hell, he didn't much need it anyway.

She sucked on his bottom lip, bit it almost hard enough to draw blood. He took her tight up against the wall, body pinning body as he drove faster, faster, her voice demanding it all the way.

He wasn't sure who growled through a climax first. They were so close that hearing her go there drove him over the edge. A first for him. Please, dear God, he hoped it wasn't the last.

His skin was so slick with sweat, and he was panting so hard, he couldn't even groan. Her legs slipped down his hips and he wrapped her up in his arms to keep them both from sliding to the floor. Their gazes clashed and he wasn't sure what it was she saw, but he guessed it was close to the same dazed look he'd found plastered all over her face. They both grinned, then began to laugh, in that giddy way people do when they hear they've won some ridiculous amount of money. Only this was better than money. And they both had the background to make a decent comparison.

Still laughing, Shane stumbled backward, landing them both in a tumbled heap on the rug. He was pretty sure he had brush burns on his ass. Small price to pay.

Darby rolled off of him and onto her back, splayed unselfconsciously as she stared up at the ceiling. Her laughter had faded, but the big grin was still plastered all over her face. "I'm sensing a pattern here," she said with mock seriousness.

Shane rolled to one side and dropped a kiss on a still-erect nipple, making her jump and gasp. "Pattern?"

She rolled her head to look at him. "Floors. We seem to end up on them a lot. And walls. Another pattern."

"Hm," he said, matching her tone. "Nudity within a short time of being alone together. An insatiable desire to taste you, touch you, kiss you. I begin to see your point." He grinned. "I've never been a fan of routine behavior, but I'm rethinking my whole philosophy on that."

"And here I was, thinking my whole life is about routine behavior. Get up, let horses out, clean stalls, feed horses, water horses. Training sessions. Groom horses. Feed, water, put in. Nuke dinner. Watch mindless television while doing books. Sleep. Start over." She smiled at him. "You can see why you're a bit of a shock to the system."

It should have sounded deadly dull. The very sort of stable, settled existence he'd run to the ends of the earth to avoid. So why did visions of pulling Darby back against him while they munched popcorn and watched an old John Wayne movie, before taking her off to bed ... or having her right there on the couch ... sound so good? Survival skills were apparently obliterated in a man who'd just experienced an orgasm of Armageddon-caliber strength. He found he wasn't anxious to recover.

"And yet," he said, striving to keep things light, because suddenly it all felt a bit too momentous and not a little terrifying, "you've managed to impose a certain pattern to it anyway. Now, me on the other hand—"

"Yeah, yeah, wild, swinging hammock sex. I know," she said with an airy wave of her hand. "I'm sure this was nothing to write home about. Which would be silly on my end since there's no one to write to, and of course, because we are in your home."

Shane realized she was babbling to cover up the huge, gaping opening she'd just created. He was very tempted to jump right into it, but his survival cells managed to kick into gear just fast enough to save him. "The Morgan family home," he corrected.

"Well, might I humbly suggest that I imagine it's never been put to quite as wonderful use as it was just now."

Shane grimaced.

"Oh, thanks," she said with a laugh. "My ego is dust now."

"No, that look was because of the visual that accompanied your statement. And might I beg you never to do anything like that ever again."

Darby snickered. "Yeah, well, for all you know a half-dozen of your ancestors were conceived right here."

He covered his eyes and shuddered. "Bad images, bad images."

She was still laughing as he rolled her body toward him, trapping her there with his leg over hers, then tipping her face up to his. "I know you weren't asking before. And you might not even want to hear it, but—"

"Shane, don't. I—"

He pressed his thumb against her mouth, then drew it softly over the contours of her lips. "You are like no one I've ever met. And the time I've spent with you defies description. Put plainly, you knock my socks off." He grinned when her gaze faltered, and wiggled his toes against her leg to ease the sudden tension of the moment. "Proof, see?"

She rolled her eyes. "You never wear socks."

"Technicality," he said, pulling her back when she went to roll away. "Okay, okay, enough mushy talk." He winced when his abraded backside brushed the floor. "Enough bristly carpet, too. Could I entice you back to my rooms and my big, soft bed?"

"Don't you have other guests you're supposed to be hosting?"

"I am hosting the guests. The only one I care about, anyway." He tugged her close before she could reach for her clothes. "Did you eat?"

She nodded. "I had the roast beef and etiquette lecture over rice."

"Yum."

"That's what I thought. But I'm fine, really." Her stomach rumbled then, as if to put the lie to her statement.

Shane laughed when she plastered her hands on the offending body part, looking momentarily horrified. It was a defining moment. Darby, blushing over a growling stomach, but completely unconcerned with her nudity. "Maybe we just work up an appetite when we're together."

She continued to gather her clothes. "What I think is that I won't have any clothes left to wear if I spend any more time with you," she said, examining her wrinkled blouse and trousers.

"And this is a problem?"

She shot him a dry look. "We're not all as Bohemian as you are."

"I'll have you know that almost all the jobs I've ever had required me to be fully clothed."

Darby held her clothes in her arms. "Almost?"

"Well, there was that modeling job for that art class in Thailand."

He grinned. "They'd never had a Caucasian model with blue eyes." He shrugged. "Not sure why that mattered, since they were working with charcoal."

Darby snapped her blouse out and caught him on the arm. "You're awful."

He snatched the sleeve and yanked her close. "That's what the art instructor told me."

"Yeah, right before she hit you up for some private remedial lessons."

"Oh, you know her, then?"

Darby tried to pry herself loose. "I begin to see how you make your way around the world without a nickel to your name."

"I'll have you know that there have been times when I've had plenty of nickels. It's just that money isn't what motivates me."

She stopped struggling. "So what does motivate you? I mean, how do you decide where to go next? What job to take?"

"Come," he said, pulling her across the room. "I'll tell you all my adventures in the shower."

"Your private office comes equipped with a shower?"

He moved to a panel in the wall that, when pressed, swung outward. "No, but Alexandra's adjoining rooms do."

"We're going to shower naked in your grandmother's suite?"

"Well, a) I think it's better to shower naked, but I'm open to new experiences. And b) I'm guessing she won't mind."

"Ha, ha. Very funny, hammock boy."

"You know, you're really hung up on that. Very bad pun there, sorry." He maneuvered them through the shadowed room and flipped on the lights in the elegantly appointed bath.

"Wow," she said, taking in the fabric-covered walls and gilt bath fixtures. "And I'm not hung up on it, I just—"

"You want me in a hammock, admit it." He reached into the smoked-glass-enclosed shower and flipped on the shower heads.

Darby smiled. "Oh, I want you all right." Then she shoved him under the still-cold spray.

He yelped, then pulled her right in with him. By the time she got done spluttering, the water was steamy and he had her pinned in the corner. "Where were we?"

"I'm pretty sure I don't care, as long as it involves hot water and your hands on me."

"Now who's incorrigible?" he said. "I like that about you, by the way." He reached for the bottle of liquid soap and pooled some in his palm. "Okay, deal time."

"Oh, you'll get your back washed."

"I was thinking more along the lines of show and tell."

"I'm not sure there's much more I could show you," she deadpanned.

"Yes, and that's to be commended. I meant tale-telling. I'll share one of mine, you share one of yours."

"Oh, yeah, that'll be fun. You tell me all about traversing some high Nepalese alp or something, and I'll tell you about the time Rookie threw me over the paddock fence and into the water trough. I'm thinking only one of us will be entertained."

Shane grinned. "Sounds like a fair trade to me. Only I've never been to Nepal."

"Well, then," she sniffed. "I guess the Rookie story stays with me."

He began to slide his soapy palms up and down her arms, then along her spine.

"Okay, drag it out of me, why don't you."

Shane found he wanted to drag lots of things out of her. Every detail of her life, in fact. Good, bad, and ugly. He turned her so her back was to him, then pulled her against him, rubbing their slick soapy bodies together before slipping his hands around her waist, and soaping her front. "I'm always entertained when I'm with you," he murmured, realizing the depth of truth in that statement.

"I'm thinking that's because I'm usually naked and—" She gasped as he slipped a hand between her legs. "Very ... oh, my God, you really can't think I'm going to—oh. Oh. Oh!"

He pressed his lips to her neck, trailed a water drop off the rim of her ear with his tongue, all the while never leaving the slickness between her legs. "Jesus, Darby," he said, swearing under his breath as she shuddered through a small climax, then another one.

"I can't help it," she managed, then gasped again. "You—it's your fault."

He chuckled at her aggrieved tone. "Don't expect me to apologize." Or stop anytime soon. God, how was he going to let her go? "Come here." He turned her around and pulled her into his arms. Water splashed off her shoulders and ricocheted against the walls as he slid his tongue into her mouth and took her. He wanted to possess her. In the way that would keep her from leaving him when their reasons for being here were done. For a man who'd done his best to not possess much, it was not a small revelation. And now was not the time to wonder about it. He didn't have to let her go yet. That was all that mattered.

"Meeting new people. Experiencing something different," he murmured against her mouth as he ended the kiss. "Learning new things. About the world. About me."

"Hmm?" she said drowsily.

"You asked what motivates me." Only, as she reached blindly for him and pulled his mouth back to hers, he couldn't help but think that he could have all of that and never leave the circle of her arms.

⟲

*D*arby winced as she bent over to pick up the shoes she was planning to wear with her stupid costume. Not only had she awakened a few long-dormant muscles, she was pretty sure she'd sent them into a full state of shock. Still, she smiled as she recalled the amazing night she'd spent with Shane. They'd tiptoed through Alexandra's wing, then crept, wet and quite bedraggled, into Shane's quarters. He'd snuck down to the kitchens at one point, returning with a tray loaded with enough food to feed an army, which they promptly devoured while swapping life stories.

She'd told her Rookie story after all, along with a number of others about the ranch, Tugger, her grandfather, her life there. Eventually even talking about her mom and her childhood, and her estrangement from her dad. That had led to telling him how surprised she was that her sister had secretly been hoping they'd reconcile. Any chance of which was all blown to shit after yesterday's revelations. Not that she'd held out any hope in the first place.

But she didn't want to think about that right now. She wanted to revel in the glow a bit longer. Shane's interest had been sincere, even though her life was mundane when compared to his. She still couldn't get over some of the things he'd done. She'd even told him he'd hooked up with the wrong Landon sister, and had regaled him with some of Pepper's more entertaining international disasters. He'd laughed, then pulled her close and told her quite seriously that there was only one Landon for him.

That was the moment her heart had tipped over the edge into free fall. She knew it was going to hurt a lot when it hit bottom. But for now she was going to concentrate on the lovely weightless feeling of the fall itself.

She'd snuck back up here at dawn, after they had decided Shane should try and follow Stefan on his early morning meeting. They'd tried to decide what they should do about the whole ordeal. Between Alexandra's personal files and Shane's overheard conversation, they did have some proof. But what in the hell were they supposed to do with it? Shane was determined to figure it out. Not just out of idle curiosity, either. He stunned her by telling her that he'd decided to go through with the buyout deal. His one and only executive decision before he stunned the rest of the world with his other decision ... dismantling Morgan Industries as soon as possible, breaking it down into individually held corporate entities. For those reasons alone, he had to dig to the bottom of the whole Celentrex-Stefan connection. If he was going to tear down an empire and split it into a fistful of self-supporting, nonfamily-held entities, then he wanted to make damn sure they had a fighting chance. The last thing he needed was the black cloud of possible scandal hanging over any aspect of it.

She didn't envy him any part of what he was about to face, but she was proud of him for doing what was right for him. And for the company. Because he was right. Being an industry mogul was not his destiny.

She sighed, reminding herself that she wasn't, either.

They hadn't talked about the rest of it, and she knew he was still struggling with the emotional part of his inheritance. Regardless of what he ended up doing with that, the industrial commitment alone would tie him down here for who knew how long. By then he'd be itching to fly off somewhere exotic and remote. And she'd have long since returned to her life on the ranch. Dammit.

Well, apparently the afterglow part wasn't going to sustain itself any longer. She reluctantly turned her attention to her mission for the day, which was more of what she'd done yesterday: keeping Stefan occupied and prying more information out of him if possible. Shane had already alerted the staff to let him know first if Mr. Bjornsen had any calls or messages.

Of course, her stomach twisted at the whole idea. Knowing Stefan, he'd take one look at her and know exactly what she'd been up to all night. And with whom. She didn't relish fending off his knowing gazes and veiled comments, all the while playing Mata Hari.

"So all of a sudden, I'm Darby Landon, Socialite Superspy," she muttered, staring in disdain at the costume she'd laid out on the bed.

Hell, she hadn't even pulled off the socialite gig all that well. She picked up the linen-and-whalebone corset. Whoever had thought up this stupid idea should be horsewhipped. Women had given up layer upon layer of froufrou lacy undergarments for a good reason. "They're a pain in the ass." She held up the white linen, authentic underdrawers, staring in disbelief at the little ties that held it together. "Literally, it seems." Not to mention that she wouldn't be able to use the bathroom all day. Not without major assistance, anyway.

"Darby?" someone said through her door in a whispered voice.

She grinned. Thank God. The one person who could actually make the torture of putting on this ridiculous costume more endurable. In fact, having Shane tie her up in her stays might be the most fun she'd have all day. She hurried to the door and popped the lock, knowing it was ridiculous to miss someone so badly when she'd just crawled out of his bed hours before. But there you had it. "I thought we weren't going to see each other until—" She broke off as the door swung wide, and stood there in openmouthed shock.

"Surprise! Now let me in before anyone sees me. I can't believe I made it all the way up here unnoticed. Except for the staff, of course, but then they have to be discreet. It's in their bible or something, right?"

Pepper pushed past her into the room, a whirlwind of blonde hair tied with an Hermès scarf, blindingly white leather Keds on her dainty feet, Liz Claiborne cuffed shorts showing off perfectly tanned and toned legs, leaving a black leather bag and a whiff of White Diamonds in her wake.

Cinderella Rule #19

*S*ometimes we see what we want to see. It's certainly easier to rationalize our decisions when they're based on what we want to believe about someone, rather than what might really be the truth. The problem comes when those we've categorized and neatly filed away under a convenient label no longer allow us that luxury. Life cannot be neatly filed, darling. And labels are never one-size-fits-all.

—AURORA

Chapter 19

Darby didn't know which part bothered her more, that she'd recognized the designers her sister was wearing, or that she wasn't as relieved to see her as she should have been. "Uh, hi. Why are you here?"

Pepper stopped in midskip and swirled—she was a big one for swirling—and propped her hands on her impossibly tiny waist. "What, you're not happy to see your only sister?"

Darby crossed the room, tugging the belt on her robe tighter, her Cinderella quotient dwindling by the second. "Of course I am. You just caught me off guard, I thought you were someone el—" She didn't catch herself until it was too late.

Pepper's eyes lit up. "Darmilla Beatrice, you didn't! I knew you had a little bit of slut inside you." She grinned and threw her arms around her sister and squeezed tight. "Feels good to let her out for a spin once in a while, doesn't it?" She stood back and looked her over, then yanked her robe open before Darby could read her thoughts.

"Hey!"

"Just checking for beard burn." She glanced down at her thighs, then looked up with a wink. "Good girl. You picked a hot one."

Darby snatched her robe from Pepper's perfectly manicured nails and wrapped it up tight. "Good God, Pepper."

"Oh, please. Just admit there are some things I know a lot more about than you, and deal, okay?" She swirled again and checked out her face in the mirror over the dresser. She wore bubble-gum-pink lipstick, and actually made it look good. Even Barbie would be jealous of her, Darby thought, then sighed, hating to admit she might be a little bit green-eyed herself. It was too early and she was too tired to deal with this.

Sure, Pepper was too perfectly beautiful for her own good, and realized her God-given glory to its fullest potential at all times, but generally that only made Darby worry about her more. Never once had she actually coveted any part of it.

She'd been totally unconcerned about her looks, her body, all of it, while she'd been with Shane. In fact, thinking about it now, it was really shocking just how little that part of it meant. Sure, he enjoyed her body. She sure as hell wasn't complaining about his. And yet, their lovemaking hadn't been about body worship, much less the rest of their conversation.

Yet, one look at Pepper and—*bam!*—she was transformed into the ugly stepsister. In last year's runway castoffs. With a hairstyle even Cyndi Lauper wouldn't be caught dead sporting.

"So," Pepper continued, having touched up her lips, reteased her fluffed bangs and straightened the impossibly tiny pink baby tee she wore. "Tell me about him." Then suddenly she gasped and spun around, hand pressed dramatically to her expansive, deeply tanned bosom. "Oh, no, wait a minute. You didn't—I mean, you're not knocking heels with—"

Darby realized what she thought and immediately shook her head. "No. Not Bjornsen."

Pepper's shoulders relaxed as she let out a whoosh of air. She seemed almost overly relieved, but then, drama queen was her middle name. "Good, good." Then, like someone had flicked a switch, she beamed again and bounced onto the bed. "So, tell me about him, then. Did you meet him here or at Glass Slipper?"

Darby just looked at her. "Glass Slipper? Like I had time to meet men there?" Then she thought about her little "shopping expedition" with Shane in the dressing room and turned away before Pepper could see the heat rise in her face. "Actually, I met him at the airport."

"Really?" Pepper crossed her legs and settled in. "I never figured you for a hangar banger."

"A what?" Darby asked, turning back around.

"Hangar banger. A layover pickup. Flight delay nooners?"

"You know, I really want to stop worrying about you . . . After all, you're a grown woman, but then you go and say something like that, and I swear you're making me gray before my time."

Pepper just rolled her eyes and laughed. "Stop worrying about me."

"Stop giving me reasons to worry," Darby shot back, like they hadn't had this conversation five million times. "Like, why did you think you had to sneak up here? Trust me, one more guest won't be noticed at the banquet tables." She grabbed the pantaloons off the bed. "Here, you can even have the costume. A belt and a few pins. And maybe some really, really high heels and it'll work, no problem. Okay, throw in a few more petticoats to make the skirt stick out farther, and voilà."

"So, you're totally going to avoid dishing on the airport hottie." She snapped her fingers, her eyes going wide. "Wait a minute! That skin is a bit tender for week-old beard burn. Is he here?" She darted a look toward the bathroom and hopped off the bed. "Oh, my God, Dar, did I interrupt something?" She didn't look all that upset at the prospect.

In fact, Darby couldn't remember her ever looking so interested in something having to do with someone else's life other than her own. Especially her older sibling's life.

"He's not in the room."

"Okay. But he *is* here. So? . . . Come on! You owe me."

"Just because you yearn to share every intimate detail about your life does not mean I want to share mine."

"I always figured it was because you didn't have any." She lifted her hands when Darby glared at her. "Totally kidding."

"Yeah. Right." She scowled, but mostly because Pepper was right. Well, she certainly had plenty to share now, didn't she? Only she didn't want to put it out there. It was still all hers—theirs—and she wanted to keep it that way a bit longer. She'd tell Pepper later. Years later. When her shattered heart had mended and their brief time together was nothing more than really good vibrator fodder.

"You still haven't told me why you're skulking around," Darby persisted instead. "If you're worried about Stefan seeing you, don't be. I'm sure he'd be relieved. I've been a horrible hostess and he's probably on the verge of canceling the whole deal." She put the pantaloons back on the bed. "Speaking of which, we need to talk." She pulled over the vanity bench and took a seat. "What exactly did Dad say to you about this deal?"

Pepper stilled, for just a brief second, but it was clear that Darby's question had caught her off guard. Something like alarm had flashed briefly across her face.

"Penelope Pernell Landon! What do you know that you didn't tell me? I swear to God, if you made me come all the way out here when you knew something wasn't right, without telling me—"

She lifted her hand to halt the lecture, then let it drop back in her lap, her mouth forming a perfect Pepper pout. "It's just another deal. How the hell should I know?"

"So why the look?"

Pepper didn't bother trying the "what look?" line of defense. It never worked and she knew it. Darby of all people knew her sister was a lot more on the ball than she liked to let on. But then, she wasn't trying to get into Darby's bed. Or her bank account.

She debated for a moment whether or not to tell Pepper what she and Shane had learned about Stefan ... and what they suspected about her father. She didn't want to worry her sister, but now that she was here, she was going to be right in the middle of it anyway. Besides, she'd be an extra set of eyes and ears. Hell, if nothing else, she could distract Stefan and allow Darby and Shane the time to do more digging. Or, screw the intrigue, they could just spend more time alone with each other.

Pepper waved her hands in front of her sister's face. "Earth to DarDar?" She grinned when Darby whipped her gaze over to hers. "Works every time."

"You're probably not going to want to taunt me anytime soon. Cowgirl."

Pepper blanched. Darby smiled.

"Okay, listen, I need to tell you some things Shane and I found out. About Dad. And this deal."

"Wait a minute. Shane? As in, Shane Morgan, heir apparent?" Pepper's eyes popped wide. "*That's* who you've been—"

"Yes, that Shane Morgan," Darby said, cutting her off before she could toss out another wink-wink euphemism.

"But you said you met him at the airport."

"I did. As it turns out, he's Mercedes Browning's godson. He saw the Glass Slipper limo and decided to hitch a ride in, to pay a visit."

She expected Pepper to explode with a barrage of questions, or, at the very least, a few inappropriate asides. Instead, she looked a bit stunned. And more than a little disconcerted.

Darby frowned. "Is it really so hard to imagine? I mean, I know I didn't get the girly genes in the family—"

Pepper absently waved her hand, her thoughts still obviously elsewhere. "No, no, that's not it. Though, I know I didn't say this before, but you really don't look like you at all with your hair like that."

"Thanks," Darby said dryly. "I think."

"It's just—" She shook her head. "Never mind. It's not about you. You could have anyone you wanted. You've always been the smart, self-sufficient, confident one."

Darby's mouth dropped open at the almost casual sincerity in her sister's tone.

Pepper smiled, but for the first time, Darby noted a hint of seriousness in her expression. "Hey, being labeled 'the pretty one' isn't always all it's cracked up to be. It's a lot to live down to, you know?"

"Pepper, you know I never—"

"Listen, we can hash this out later." Suddenly she was all business. In fact, Darby couldn't recall her sister ever looking so serious. It made her look like . . . a grown-up or something.

"What's wrong?" Darby asked. Then she sighed. "If it's about Stefan and Dad's shady deal, I know all about it. Well, some of it, anyway. And I wish you'd told me whatever you knew *before* I got here. It would've helped."

Pepper's gaze sharpened like a tack. To the point that Darby felt like she was suddenly sitting across from a complete stranger.

"You know what about the deal?" Pepper demanded. "Start at the beginning."

Darby frowned and studied the stranger sitting across from her. "Okay, now you're freaking me out. Who are you and what have you done with my lovable but kooky sister?"

She smiled then, a bit wistfully and totally un-Pepperlike. And Darby seriously wondered if she was looking at a stunt double.

"Who am I?" Pepper asked, then squeezed her eyes shut, shook her head, laughed a little before dropping her chin. There was a slight pause, and she huffed out a long sigh. Only it wasn't her typical it's-all-about-me sigh. This one sounded like it had a lot of years and a whole lot of pent-up emotion behind it. When she lifted her head again, the smile was back, but her eyes belonged to someone who looked a whole lot wiser than even she'd ever given Pepper credit for being.

"You wouldn't believe me if I told you," she said quietly. "But I guess maybe it's time I did."

༄

*S*hane shot the cuffs on his shirt and straightened his turn-of-the-century jacket. He'd boil to death in this thing the minute he stepped outside. But Darby was dressing up so she could hang on Stefan's arm, and he had enough ego to not want to look like a beach bum in comparison. Not that he was in competition with the Swede for Darby's attention or anything. Hell, he didn't compete period.

He rubbed his jaw and contemplated shaving. Again.

Okay, he was competing.

The question was, why? He knew she wouldn't go for Stefan, certainly not now, anyway. But what if the circumstances had been different? There was a clutch in his belly at even the briefest glimmer of imagining her with someone else. Which was ridiculous, since there was no commitment between them. She was free to do what she wanted, as was he. He could hardly demand otherwise, given that their . . . whatever it was they were having, couldn't go anywhere past this weekend.

His gut clenched even harder. Since he'd woken up with her in his arms this morning, he'd thought of little else. But, as yet, he hadn't come up with any answers on how to change things between them. She was supposed to be just another adventure in his life, right? One he could move on from. Conquer some new world, absorb some new experience.

Funny how he wasn't all that anxious to hit the road this time. Well, the road away from here, yes. But the one away from her? No.

He swore under his breath and turned away from the mirror. He snagged his top hat from the foot of the bed and strode to the door, not sure why he was so angry all of a sudden. He stalked out of his wing with the intention of heading directly outside. She'd come down eventually, hook up with Bjornsen. He'd wait for the We Dig It report to show up, and hope like hell that it helped clear things up. Because at the moment, he wasn't sure what in the hell to do about all this. And, if he was lucky—and he intended to be—he could sneak off with her for a few more hours of hot sex. Because that's all this could be, right? She was a diversion. A good time. Nothing more.

And goddammit, he was all about having a good time, wasn't he?

His temper grew with each step, his mind racing as fast as his pulse, until he somehow found himself striding down the hallway to her room. She could do whatever the hell she wanted, with whoever she wanted. Right after they were done with each other. That wasn't too much to expect, was it? And if she said no? Well, then that would take care of ending it right then and there. Because he wasn't sharing Darby. She was either his or—

He already had his fist lifted to bang on the door, but he decided the hell with it—it was his house, wasn't it?—and let himself in.

"Darby!" he called out, tossing his hat on the small desk in the sitting area. If he hadn't been so worked up, he'd have likely noticed she wasn't alone. Although he wasn't entirely sure that would have even slowed him down. He banged into her bedroom. "We have to talk. Right now."

Darby was seated on the vanity bench, facing a young blonde woman sitting cross-legged in the middle of her bed. The blonde looked up, smiled brightly, then shot a look of approval at Darby. "Dang, Dar, he's a hottie. And a bit hot under the collar, too, if I'm not mistaken." She stuck her hand out. "Hi, I'm Pepper, Darby's sister."

Startled, Darby swung around, then immediately leaped up. "Did something happen? Did you find out what Stefan was doing?" She gripped his arm, her expression full of something he couldn't quite place.

It was then he realized that he'd interrupted something. Something personal between Darby and her sister, from the looks of things. Well, from the look of Darby, anyway. He suddenly felt every inch the stupid, testosterone-charged idiot he'd been. Marching down here, slamming into her room, all set to deliver some kind of macho ultimatum that . . . He shoved it aside, all of it, and shook his head.

"No, no, I didn't. He was already gone before I got downstairs. Listen, I didn't mean to barge in here. I'm sorry. We can talk later." He turned to Pepper. "Pleasure to meet you." Then he covered Darby's hand, still clutching his sleeve, and smiled at her. "I'm an idiot, okay? With no class. Just . . ." He wanted to be casual, ask her to come find him later, before she went down to meet up with Stefan. Only he was looking in her eyes and all he could seem to think was that, after tomorrow, he'd never get a chance to do that again.

"Shane? Something is wrong, isn't it?"

He looked to Pepper. "I'm really sorry, but can I steal your sister for just a few minutes?"

Pepper just waved a hand. "Sure. Dar, I'm going to freshen up, change clothes." She sent Shane a beaming smile and a little pinky finger wave before slipping into the bathroom.

"I didn't know she was going to pop up," Darby said. "She's . . . I don't know. Something's going on, although—" She glanced back, then shook her head. "I don't know, maybe it's jet lag or something, but she's . . . not like she normally is."

"Did you tell her what's going on?"

"I started to, but then she told me she had to tell me something, and from the look of things, it's important."

Shane frowned. "You think she knows? About the deal?"

Darby lifted a shoulder. "I honestly don't know what to think. I have no idea what's going on with her. Maybe she's really fallen in love with Paolo—he's a soccer player," she added, as if that explained everything. Then she shook her head. "But when she falls in love, she's normally even more giddy and silly than she usually is. This time ... I don't know, it was like looking at an older, wiser Pepper."

Shane thought about the Gidget look-alike who had just bopped into the bathroom and figured Darby had to have seen something he hadn't. He shrugged. "Maybe he broke her heart."

"Oh, no, the whole house would be hearing about it then. She's not a quiet sufferer." She let go of his hand, paced the room. "She was just about to tell me whatever it was when you burst into the room."

"I really am sorry. I don't know what got into me." Which was a total lie. He knew exactly what had gotten into him. She was standing not ten feet away.

Darby moved to the window, her thoughts still obviously on her sister. "There she was, staring at me with this look in her eyes that was, well ... I can't even define it, but it was very un-Pepperlike. Then you bust in, and as if a switch was flipped, she instantly became regular Pepper. I looked at her and it was like that other person didn't even exist." She turned to face him. "Who knows, it's probably just me, but it was weird." Then she looked at him and truly focused. "So, what was the big whoop that sent you thundering in here? You missed Stefan totally? Did the report come in yet?"

"Yeah, I missed him totally. I do know he was gone less than an hour. He's back in his rooms. And no, no report yet."

"So, why the storm-trooper act?"

"Because I'm an idiot. Talk to your sister. Come find me later."

Frowning, she crossed the room. She turned his face to hers and he realized, not for the first time, how readily she was able to look past the surface with him. She smiled, despite the concern still coloring her gaze. "What kind of idiot were you being, anyway?"

He debated for a split second, then the words were just there. "The possessive kind that didn't want some big Swede pawing all over the woman he'd just spent the night with."

Her eyes widened in surprise, just before laughter bubbled to the surface. "You're jealous of me ... and Stefan? You can't be serious. Aside from the fact we think he's involved in some sleazy deal ... how could you question anything after last night? Hell, after that first limo ride, I was half in—" She broke off, snapped her mouth shut.

Shane's heart felt like it slipped ... and settled, right into the place it had always belonged. He grinned and tugged her into his arms. "I'm apparently also an egotistical bastard, because that admission just made me feel fantastic." He kissed her, mostly because he couldn't be this close and not. But also because he felt this need to seal things between them.

When he finally lifted his head, she lifted her hand to his face, traced it as she stared into his eyes. "It's weird, isn't it?"

Surprised, he gave a little half-laugh. "Weird?"

"How uncertain we can be, even when things are this amazing."

His smile faded and his pulse kicked up. This was as close as they'd come to stating how they felt. And now that the moment was between them, he realized it was both terrifying ... and tempting. Tempting in a way no adventure had ever lured him before. "I guess it's about trust. Trusting what you feel. Trusting the person who inspired those feelings with the weight of them and all they could mean."

Darby's breath caught. "Shane, I—"

He traced his fingertips over her lips, feeling her breath brush over them. "I don't want to burden you with that," he went on. "I know this isn't about that. It's about ... a place out of time, I guess." He looked at his fingers touching her, and felt an ache swell inside him as he shifted his gaze to hers. "But they keep growing. And I don't know what to do with them."

"What do you want to do with them?" she asked quietly.

"I tried ignoring them. Didn't work."

He felt her tremble. "So ... then what?"

"I honestly don't know. We—our lives—"

Now she was the one pressing his lips closed. "I know. I've thought about it, too. A lot."

The ache began to lift. "You have?"

She smiled then. "You look so relieved. Did you think this wasn't affecting me? I've never been with anyone the way I've been with you. And I'm not just speaking sexually." She looked away, the color in her face deepening. "Okay, I'm feeling naked here. Jump in anytime."

His smile was one of such fullness, he felt like his entire body was lifting it up. So this was what love felt like. It was worth the wait. He turned her face to his. "Just promise me one thing."

"What?"

"That you won't leave."

Her mouth opened, then shut. "But, I—you know I have to go back to Montana. I have—"

"I know. I meant that I don't want you to leave here tomorrow until we've talked. About ... all of this. Okay?"

She didn't look excited. She didn't look relieved. Or, for that matter, sad. Or disappointed. She looked ... worried.

He understood, because he was worried, too, and couldn't say anything that would take the worry away. So he did the one thing he could do. He kissed her, long and slow. Wishing he could be all that for her. Dependable. Enduring. Steady.

And knew he was probably the last man on earth who could be any of that for her.

Cinderella Rule # 20

No one wants to be under-estimated. However, while you are out there proving yourself, so is everyone else. It works both ways.

—MERCEDES

Chapter 20

"'m sorry. I guess I'm now the one barging in," came Pepper's voice from behind them.

Darby didn't break the kiss right away. Knowing Shane was experiencing the same wild fall had changed everything. And nothing. She wasn't sure anything could ever be settled between them. So she lingered, enjoyed the one thing she knew she could have. For now.

When he finally broke the kiss, he caught her gaze and she saw the message there. *It'll be okay.* She just wished like hell she believed it.

Then he shifted away and she got a look at her sister. Her mouth dropped open. The woman standing in front of them now, with her hair smoothed back into a sleek twist, her makeup very understated and decidedly nonglossy, wearing a trim pair of soft, black cotton pants with an elegant black sleeveless turtleneck, looked more like Hamptons Barbie than the Jet-Set Barbie she'd been minutes ago.

"I see what you mean about the split personality," Shane murmured next to her ear.

"Pepper?" she asked, feeling a little bewildered. "What's going on?"

Her sister's demeanor was calm and decidedly serious—All-Business Barbie—as she crossed the room. Only then did Darby notice the belt she wore, or more specifically, the stuff she wore on the belt. There was a small cell phone clipped to it, along with a few other hi-tech-looking gadgets.

"Can we sit down?" she asked, her tone smooth, very professional. "We need to talk." She looked at Shane. "I know you're hosting and need to head outside, but this involves you, too. I'd really appreciate it if you could give us a few minutes of your time."

Instead of demanding to know what the aliens had done with her sister, she asked, "How does this involve Shane?"

Pepper motioned to the settee and side chairs in the sitting area, then walked over and took a seat, waiting for Shane and Darby to settle on the love seat before continuing. "This is all going to sound somewhat surreal, but I assure you, it's all true." She looked at Darby, and for a moment, the old Pepper peeked through. "Dar, I want to say up front that I'm sorry for not telling you sooner. But I wasn't allowed to. And, honest, you were better off not knowing. Even now, they're not really comfortable with me revealing myself to you."

"*They?*" Darby asked, fighting to stay calm, despite feeling like she'd stepped into some kind of parallel universe. "Who's *they?*"

Pepper just kept talking. "But I was the one who dragged you into this, so it's only fair you understand what's really going on. I had to get special permission, and I can only tell you a little."

"What, because you're a spy, and if you tell us what you know, you'll have to kill us?"

Darby had spoken sarcastically, but Pepper merely smiled and said, "Pretty much. Except for that last part. I'm not licensed for that."

Darby looked around the room. "Okay, I give up. Where are they?"

"We're not bugged," Pepper said, quite sincerely.

She just looked at her. "*What?* No, really. The gig is up. End of charade. You were doing fine up to this point, though, so I have to give you props for that. You really had me going." She looked around again. "Where are the cameras? We *are* on *Candid Camera*, right? Or some twisted new reality show." She laughed. "Hell, they've probably been following me since I checked into Glass Slipper." She suddenly shot a look at Shane and turned beet-red.

"Now that's what I call reality programming," he said, choking on a laugh when she glared at him.

Pepper reached out and took Darby's hand. "It's not a joke."

Darby's gaze swung back to hers. "Oh, yes, it is. Because you're sitting there, actually expecting me to believe you're involved in some kind of ... of ... espionage ... or whatever. This is not you. This"— she tugged her hand free and waved it at Pepper, motioning to her whole look—"is not you. You're exasperating, free-spirited, funny, a little wild at times, and a lot irresponsible most of the time. What you are not is ..." She finally drifted off as Pepper calmly held her gaze. "Are you?"

"I am all those things. Well, I have been. I'm changing, or trying to. And what I've been involved in for the past ten months or so is really making the difference."

"Just who the hell is it you're working for? Wait. Did some guy you met on some godforsaken continent talk you into signing on with some whack political faction?" Her gaze narrowed. "Or some religious cult? Is that what this is?"

"Darby, Darby, stop. Just let me explain, okay?"

Shane laid his arm around Darby's shoulders, giving her a light, reassuring squeeze. She tried to shrug him off, still glaring at Pepper, but neither of them budged. "Fine. Go ahead. I'm dying to hear this."

Pepper sighed and said, "I am exactly who you described me as being. I still am, at least partly. But I'm growing up, Dar. And this job has been a huge part of my maturation."

Darby shook her head, obviously still struggling to even begin to comprehend any part of it. "What, exactly, is this *job*? Just tell me that. And who, exactly, you work for. Then we'll go from there."

"Well, I can't tell you for who exactly."

"So you found this job ... where, in the want ads? Under Secret Agent Man?"

"Come on, Darby," she said, a hint of a whine edging her tone. "This isn't exactly easy for me, either."

Darby spread her hands in frustration. "Okay, I'm sorry. It's just ... you gotta admit this is going to take some getting used to."

"I know," she said quietly. She paused, then said, "First I have to tell you something else that might shake you up a little, but it'll help explain how I got into doing this. I don't think Dad will mind."

"Dad? Dad knows about this and I don't?" There was a trace of hurt in her voice, along with continued disbelief.

"About three years ago, Interpol approached Dad with a request for his help. As a consultant on one of their cases."

Darby's mouth dropped open, then snapped right back shut again. "Okay, I'm officially hallucinating now."

"Just hear me out. It's not so fantastical as all that. They ask for civilian assistance all the time. And Dad does have some unique international business concerns. Some of which involve people whom Interpol is either actively investigating, or simply wishes to get information on."

"So, wait. You're saying *you* work for Interpol?" She looked to Shane. "Am I the only one here who's still in her right mind?"

Shane wisely chose not to respond and silently squeezed her shoulder.

"No, I don't work for Interpol. I was recruited by a private agency that accepts assignments from the government to help out from time to time. Anyway, when Interpol approached Dad a few years back, looking into a deal with a group of German investors, he agreed to help them out."

"What was in it for him?"

Pepper sighed in exasperation and rolled her eyes. "You really don't know him, Dar. And what I said before, about wanting you back here so the two of you could maybe mend a few fences, that was all real. I've been wanting that for a very long time. If you just gave him a chance—"

Darby waved her silent. "Just—let's get back to the part about you being Jane Bond. Did Dad actually get you into this? Because *that* I can believe, if it would help him out."

"Actually, he did, but not intentionally. I sort of stumbled into a thing he was doing, and, well ..." she broke off, beamed proudly, "I ended up being the one who got the guy to talk." She shrugged. "So, they sort of asked me to help them again. And that led to my being approached by another agency ... and the rest is history."

"And Dad's okay with all this?"

"No, not at all. In fact, it was my insistence on getting serious about my ... line of work that really led to our split last year."

"You told me he yanked your trust-fund access because you destroyed Sheik Al Khamal's sailboat."

She smiled a bit sheepishly. "Actually, I did do that. Although, technically, it was a yacht. But it was part of a case I was working on. And when Dad found out, he blew his lid." She sighed a bit petulantly. "He still sees me as his little girl. I think he just wants me to spend my life being his cute international hostess until I find a man who can 'handle me,' settle down, and start giving him grandbabies." She smiled dryly. "And you have me to thank for taking that pressure off of you."

Darby just sat there, blinking, as it all began to sink in. Pepper was actually serious. She was telling her the truth. Holy Spy Barbie, Batman. "You know, I see you sitting there; I see your mouth moving; I hear the words, and I know it's my baby sister saying them, but ..." She knocked her own forehead with her knuckles. "Not computing."

"If it's any consolation, it's been killing me to tell you. Even more than your estrangement with Dad, I hate you thinking I'm still this irresponsible baby. I'm not. Or, at least, I'm trying not to be." She sighed. "I'm not some super spy or anything, Darby. I just happen to be good at getting into places and talking to people who would never in a million years suspect that maybe, just maybe, I'm more than I appear to be." Pepper looked at her and the earnestness in her gaze made Darby's heart hurt.

"I want, more than anything, to make you and Dad proud of me," she said. "He's more scared than anything. Doesn't understand why someone with my background would want to do this. I think I finally get what you two have been going through all these years. But I'm making a difference, Dar. Maybe not a big one, not all by myself, but what I do allows the other real super spies to do their job a bit more easily." She grinned and the old Pepper finally peeked through. "Besides, the travel is great. And they cover my expenses. I'm still a bit big on expenses, I'm afraid. But I'm working on that," she added quickly. "Promise."

Darby just shook her head, then laughed and squinted at her sister. "Is that really my baby sister inside this grown-up woman I'm looking at?"

"Oh, Dar." Pepper launched herself off the chair and dragged Darby up off the love seat and into a tight bear hug. "Honest, I'm not in any real danger, no matter what Daddy will tell you. I just listen and report back." She set Darby back, her blue eyes sparkling with barely contained excitement. "I'm good at it, Darby. And I enjoy it. A lot."

Darby drew a deep breath, let it out slowly. "It's a lot to take in."

"If it helps, I can be in your corner now. With Dad. You know, the trick with him is to simply not back down. He's going to have to deal with this. With me doing this. He just won't have a choice." She looked at Darby with that odd mix of terribly-young-and-impossibly-wise eyes. "That's what you have to do. Talk to him. Make him deal with who you are. I want my family back together. We need to stick together, Darby. Because, when you get right down to it, family is all we've got."

Darby found herself glancing over at Shane, and sobered a little before looking back to her sister. "I've recently learned that maybe there is more to life than trudging along my own path alone, just for the sake of proving I could."

Pepper looked between her sister and Shane, and a slow smile curved her lips. She impulsively hugged Darby again, surprising a grunt out of her. "Oh, that's such good news! And I know that will help with our talk with Daddy." She took Darby's hands and squeezed them.

Darby frowned. "*Our* talk with him? He still doesn't know I'm here, does he?"

"No. But he'll be here tomorrow and we should go over what we'll say, how we'll approach this whole thing."

"What *whole thing?* Pepper?" she said warningly. "Oh. Right. The infamous 'deal.' So what else haven't you told me yet?"

"Oh, gosh," Pepper said, letting out a little laugh. "Here we are, talking about family, and I almost forgot about the real reason I'm here."

Darby looked at Shane. "Do you see what I've had to put up with all these years?"

Actually, Shane was beginning to see how Darby's little sister could be an effective operative. Naturally effervescent personality, too beautiful for her own good, and definitely a real people person. No one would have a clue. He shook his head in amazement, then shifted his attention back to Darby. What she'd said about not wanting to walk the path alone anymore still echoed in his mind. His heart had admittedly skipped a beat. Or two.

Shane grinned and found himself wondering if Darby knew how lucky she was. How lucky she and Pepper both were, to have each other. For the first time in, well, forever, he thought that maybe life's adventures would be a lot more interesting if he could share them with someone.

"Okay, what exactly is your 'mission,' " Darby asked, crooking her fingers in quotation marks around that last word.

Pepper pouted briefly. "This is serious, Darby." She looked from Darby to Shane. "Why don't you tell me what you two know."

Shane nodded for Darby to go ahead. "Okay, fine. Shane discovered some private files of his grandmother's—Alexandra Morgan, who was the CEO of—"

Pepper waved her hand. "I know who she is—was." She glanced to Shane. "I'm sorry," she said sincerely. "My condolences."

"Thank you. We weren't close." He glanced to Darby, who continued.

"Okay, then you know about the Celentrex buyout she had set up and the technology she was buying?"

Pepper nodded.

"Well, somewhere along the way, we think Alexandra hooked up with Stefan, and the two of them apparently developed some kind of adaptation to the Celentrex technology that would allow them to do something entirely different with it. Only she kept that part of the deal hush-hush. Even from Celentrex."

Pepper waved her hand again. "I got all that, too. Go on."

"So then I guess you also know they want to use it for illegal gemstone mining. Shane found documentation that they're targeting some sites in South America—" She broke off then, her eyes growing wide. "*That's* why you were down there?"

Pepper nodded.

"Jesus, Pepper. And Paolo?" Darby asked. "Was he ... what? A decoy? Was he even real?"

Her sister gave a little appreciative sigh and fanned her face. "Oh, he was real, all right. I met him at a party in Rio—I was there making contact with one of our operatives who was down there tracking Bjornsen's contacts—and we hit it right off. He was ... convenient, too, I'll admit. His house was just outside the city, which was a perfect base of operations for me, and certainly a lot nicer than the place the company wanted to set me up in." She lowered her voice. "They do take care of expenses and all, but they balk at some of the pricier places, and really, how believable would it be for me, Paul Landon's daughter, to stay at a Marriott? I mean, honestly—"

Darby held her hand up. "So you were there working on this deal, somehow, and? ..."

"I was keeping an eye on Bjornsen's contacts, trying to get close enough to any one of them, to see if I could get some information on exactly where they were setting up."

"We might be able to help you with that," Shane said. "If you haven't already figured it out."

Pepper swung her gaze to his. "You know where they're going to mine? Precise locations?"

"Alexandra had copies of some engineering reports in her private files that might be of some use. I can get them for you."

"Excellent," she said, beaming as she looked between him and Darby. "You know, you guys are amazing. I had no idea you'd be so good at this. In fact, I didn't think you'd get involved at all. But then, what were the chances you'd hit it off with Shane, or find out about the mining deal? Honest, I swear I'd never have put you into something like this if I had any idea you could get involved."

"Believe me, we didn't plan on it, either," Darby said. "But it's not like we've done all that much. We suspect that Stefan is involved in something shady, but we don't know what the hell he's really doing here, or, for that matter, what in the hell to do about it. So, given what we know now, I say we simply tell Dad what's really going on, he calls up his Interpol buddies, and they can deal with Stefan. And we're out of it."

Pepper looked at them both, switching back to Spy Barbie mode. "Tell me, exactly what has he been doing? Other than partying and waiting for Dad to show up? Anything suspicious?"

"Well, from what little you told me," Darby said, sending a pointed look her sister's way, "I knew he was here to talk to Dad about gemstones. At the same time, Shane's been taking meetings all week on the proposed buyout, and when he dug into Alexandra's private files, he realized something else was going on. So he hired a private firm to do some more digging. At the same time, he, uh, also had the firm do some digging on Stefan. I'd been feeling a bit weird about him and—"

"And I was being a typical guy with—what did you call it?" Shane asked Darby with a grin. "Testosterone poisoning?" Shane looked at Pepper. "We both felt something wasn't right about the guy, but we had no idea he was connected to Alexandra until the firm I used dug up some messages he'd recently received. One of which was about okaying a site in Brazil and mentioned the type of gemstones they found there. Both of which matched a little too closely to what I'd discovered in Alexandra's files. All circumstantial, but it was beginning to add up."

Darby picked up the explanation. "We were waiting on another report, but in the meantime, Shane managed to overhear a phone call Stefan got here, and he mentioned the buyout, amongst other things. So now we figure he has to be involved, and with Alexandra suddenly out of the picture before the buyout can go through, he's still trying to rig something up. Maybe he has the adaptation, but he needs to get his hands on the Celentrex technology, or at least something that will let him re-create it himself, to keep the operation going. Who knows. He's had several private meetings since he's gotten into town, and the phone conversation Shane overheard was pretty intense."

Shane picked up the thread. "From what I heard, it sounds like he's supposed to deliver something to the guy on the other end, and soon. He talked about not caring if the buyout went through, then said he had funding, which we figured was where your father comes in. What we didn't understand was why, when Alexandra died, he didn't just approach me directly. So we assume this deal is shady all the way around, which explains why my grandmother had this stuff buried in her private files to begin with."

Pepper sighed. "Well. You're right. It's definitely shady. I guess I should tell you that several agencies have been tracking Stefan for some time—" She lifted a hand to stop Darby's question. "He's been involved on the fringes of a number of deals that were less than kosher, but we've never been able to tie him directly to any of them. Then we got wind of the Celentrex deal and his private dealings with your grandmother." She looked to Shane. "When she died, we—well, we thought we might lose him again. But there was continued activity in Brazil, so we hoped he was still trying to make something happen. Only we didn't know who he was working with here, or how he planned to get the original research. Dad was called in, and he insinuated himself into position as his investor, to get close enough to be inside the deal itself." She gave Shane an apologetic look. "We initially suspected you might be involved, but our latest intel points in another direction. However, we decided to still have the meeting here, for simplicity's sake. I'm sorry."

"No offense taken," Shane said. "I think he realized I'm not money-motivated and not worth the risk that I'd blow the whistle."

"Did anything else happen yesterday?" Pepper asked. "Besides the phone call?"

"Not yesterday. We made sure he was with someone all day. He went to his room alone last night, but he did leave early this morning for a meeting." Shane didn't dare look at Darby. He was having a hard enough time keeping the color from creeping into his own cheeks. "Which I was going to try and follow, but I, uh, didn't get down there in time."

Pepper looked at Darby and Shane and a deep smile curved her lips. "Yes, well, totally understandable."

Darby shot them both a look, but couldn't quite keep the smile from curving her lips when her gaze met Shane's. They both looked at Pepper and shrugged, not as guiltily, perhaps, as they should have.

"That's pretty much all we know," Shane said. "Darby was going to keep Stefan busy today while we waited for the new report to come in. I wasn't sure what else to do. We were going to try and get to your dad when he arrived, feel him out, tell him what we'd discovered. We thought maybe we could get him to stall a little on the deal. I plan to publicly announce on Monday that Morgan Industries is going ahead with the buyout. Maybe that would end his scheme altogether." He leaned back on the couch and rubbed Darby's shoulder. "That's all we got."

Pepper just nodded. "Like I said, I'm really impressed."

Darby leaned forward. "So why don't you tell us what we don't know? I think we deserve that much, don't you?"

Pepper paused for a moment, then finally sighed and added, "I'm not authorized to tell you this, but when I asked permission, I had no idea you two were already as involved as you were." She looked earnestly at Darby. "I feel bad about that, but I had no way of knowing you'd get caught up in this. Things started to finally come together in Sao Tempre, right when Dad got hung up in Belgium. He was there tracking the people Stefan and Alexandra had planned to unload the raw mined material on. He asked me to fill in for him here, only I knew I couldn't leave just when things were finally happening." She looked to Darby. "Honest, I figured you'd take him to the party and just hang out. I would never have knowingly put you in danger."

Shane tensed, even as Darby said, "Danger?"

A guilty flush tinged Pepper's cheeks. "Okay, this is the part that I'm not cleared to tell, so you can't say anything. But seeing as you're involved, I think you have a need to know." She blew out a sigh, then scooted closer. "You wanted to know what was illegal about this setup. Well, Stefan has access to some sites in South America that aren't exactly legal to drill in, or do anything in, for that matter. Sacred grounds that are maintained by the government, like a national park would be here. Except some of these are deep in the jungle, ruins mostly, and not exactly tourist attractions. There are factions the government hires to patrol the land, keeping artifact-hunters from stealing anything, and—"

"Factions?" Shane asked. "I'm guessing these guys aren't national guardsmen or anything."

"Hardly," Pepper said. "More like drug-cartel thugs. But they keep the ruins safe from looting, and the government looks the other way as to what other business they might be conducting in the area. It can get a bit hairy at times, but they make it work. Most of the time."

"And you're telling me my grandmother decided to dig for gemstones right in the middle of all that?" Shane asked. The idea boggled him. His grandmother might have been focused on expanding the Morgan family coffers, and he could even buy the idea that she'd stretch the boundaries of moral ambiguity, if the payoff was big enough. But this? He shook his head. "This doesn't sound like something she'd do. She liked to be in control of things, down to the last detail. And I don't think she'd have risked the family reputation with something quite this far off the radar."

"Well, maybe she didn't know what she was getting into until it was too late."

Shane slumped back against the couch, not sure what to think, or how to feel. Alexandra ... vulnerable? It just didn't jibe.

"As for the selected sites ... we've long suspected Stefan has some kind of connection to Santoriaga. Drug lord," Pepper added when they both frowned. "As far as we can tell, the land controlled by Santoriaga is rich in gemstones. Regular technology would destroy the land in a way that would be hard to hide from government eyes, but this new adaptation would allow them to go in and drill in a way that leaves the surrounding area relatively undisturbed. We think Stefan worked a deal with Santoriaga, a percentage of the profits in exchange for drilling rights and protection. He's had a crew doing the preliminary site work for the past several months, only we haven't been able to get close enough to pinpoint the exact locations."

Shane blew out a heavy sigh. "Then Alexandra dies, and leaves him and his very nasty cohorts hanging. I'm guessing we now know just who he was talking to."

Pepper grew very serious. "Yeah. And it's gotten worse. We got word from one of our guys in the field down there that it looks like Santoriaga ran out of patience and took Stefan's men hostage. That's why I'm here early. If Stefan took that call yesterday, then he probably knows the stakes have been raised. And that's going to make him un-predictable. We don't know who he's in contact with here, or what his possible alternate deal is, to get his hands on the technology. We just didn't want him taking off when things looked to be heading south fast."

Shane raked his fingers through his hair. "I still can't believe Alexandra got involved in all this."

Darby looked worried and took his hand in hers. "Maybe Pepper is right, and your grandmother didn't know it wasn't on the up-and-up until it was too late."

Pepper nodded. "There's also the possibility she didn't have a choice. Someone steered her to the fact that the technology could be adapted in the first place. Maybe he had something on her. I wouldn't put it past him. Like I said, we've been tracking him for a long time."

Darby squeezed his hand when he swore under his breath. And here he'd thought his whole world had already been turned on its ass. Had Alexandra never intended to do anything wrong? Had she merely gotten herself in over her head? It was hard for him to fathom her getting herself in a position where she didn't have the upper hand at all times. Impossible really. "So now what do we do?"

"Does Dad know about all this?" Darby asked. "Wait a minute . . . if you never told him I was here, then that means he thinks you've been here all along. Not in Brazil." She smacked her palm on her thigh. "Shit, Pepper, does he even know you're working this case?"

She huffed out a sigh and looked a little defensive. "No, okay? He just thinks I'm here helping him out by playing hostess. I told you, he doesn't want me involved. When he asked me for help here, I could hardly tell him I was already involved, could I? He . . . he has no idea."

"Oh, great. And when he finds out you've dragged me into this, to cover for you, won't that make for a lovely family reunion. I swear, Pepper, what were you thinking?"

"I just needed someone here until I could get out of Rio. I didn't know this would happen! And . . . well, I wanted you and Dad to see each other. And, honestly, Darby, how was I to know you'd go and get all involved? Stefan isn't a threat—or he wasn't when I asked you to help."

Darby shuddered. "I don't know about that. Have you actually met the guy?"

"No. But he's not interested in you. Or me. He's just biding time until Dad gets here. You were just supposed to hang out with him. I knew I'd be here before anything important went down."

Darby shook her head in disgust and stood up. "Fine, then. Have at it. I'm done."

"No!" she said, alarmed. "First off, you're going to see Dad with me, Dar. I didn't get you all this close for that to blow up."

"Oh, it's going to blow up anyway! Do you honestly think he's going to be in a receptive mood when he finds out what we've been up to, hm?"

"Darby, come on," she said, wheedling. "Besides, you're in this now." She looked at Shane. "Both of you. We need you."

"Just who in the hell is *we?*" Darby demanded. "I think I have a right to know at this point."

"I can't tell you that."

"But it's not Interpol." Darby waved off her reply and scrubbed her hand over her face before sinking back onto the love seat next to Shane. "I cannot believe I'm even having this conversation."

Pepper perched on the edge of the chair. "It's going to be okay. I think I have a plan."

Darby laughed, sounding only semihysterical as she threw up her hands, then let them slap against her thighs. "Oh. Well, then. No need to worry. Your plan has been working out swimmingly thus far."

Shane pulled her resistant body against him. His gut was in a knot and a million thoughts were swimming through his brain. He had no idea what Alexandra's real involvement had been, and the only way he'd ever find out was to nail Stefan. Or help Pepper and company nail him. He wasn't even sure why it mattered to him so much. But the fact was, his grandmother had been in trouble, deep trouble from the sound of things. And though it made absolutely no sense, it burned his gut to know that she hadn't had anyone to turn to. "Why don't we give her a shot," he suggested quietly.

Pepper beamed at him. "Yes. Thank you."

"I'm sure she knows what she's doing," Shane added. "She is the professional, after all."

Darby glared at him. "At any other time I'd have been able to give you a list of everything that was so wrong with what you just said. But

I've got nothing left." She waved a limp hand at her sister. "Go, Go Power Rangers!"

Pepper smiled and clapped her hands together. "Okay, first thing, I'll need a costume. Since you're already in place here, I can be more effective undercover. And a wig! I'll need that, too. And, oh, yeah, I have a few wires we'll need to tape on both of you. And then we'll do something with your hair, Darby, to hide the mike thingie. And your makeup ... I thought they taught you how to put that on at Glass Slipper? Well, no worries, I can help you out."

"Oh, God," Darby muttered, burying her face in Shane's sleeve. "We're going undercover. I thought I was already here undercover. Now I'm going to be—"

"Cinderella Spy Barbie," Shane added helpfully, with a wink to Pepper. "She'll be fine, don't worry," he mouthed to her over Darby's head.

"I heard that," Darby said. "Shoot me now."

Cinderella Rule #21

*S*ometimes we're called upon to perform tasks that fall well outside our comfort zone. Just remember that nothing was ever gained by not trying. And that by succeeding, you ensure yourself a favor to be called in later, at your leisure.

—AURORA

$\mathscr{C}$hapter 21

$\mathscr{D}$arby hurried along the garden path toward the hubbub of the party, cursing when her gown caught for the umpteenth time on the hedges that lined the path.

"I heard that," came the little voice from the tiny earphone tucked in her hair, just behind her ear.

She startled. "Oh, yeah, this is going to work," she whispered, tugging at the goddamn corset that was cutting off her breath, before jerking her skirts free. "I jump three feet every time you say something."

"Sorry." Then came a soft chuckle. "But I sort of like being right next to you all the time. Even when I'm not."

Darby paused and sighed a little. She didn't want to tell him how good that made her feel, how comforting it was, knowing they were connected to each other as they set out to put this insane plan into motion. And to think she had believed that Glass Slipper was the worst thing Pepper had conned her into. Right now, that looked like a four-star vacation.

"Yeah," she finally whispered. "Me, too." She surveyed the milling groups, looking for Stefan's silver-blond mane. She was supposed to have met him at the base of the central staircase, but it had taken longer to get the stupid mike in place than expected. Then they'd had to wait for the local shop to deliver Pepper's costume, and well, it was a good thing national security didn't rest on their shoulders, was all she could say. Fortunately the butler informed her she'd only missed Stefan by minutes, but wouldn't it figure if she'd already missed him making or taking a call.

Her mission was to find Stefan and stick close to him. And, if he excused himself for any reason, to let him go, then check in with Shane and Pepper so they could follow him. Shane and Pepper were in full costume, too, with Pepper wearing a wig and carrying a fan to keep from being recognized. Anything said within earshot of their mikes was being recorded. They also had teeny little cameras. Darby wouldn't admit it to Pepper, but she sort of thought the little hi-tech gizmos were impressive. She still couldn't wrap her mind around the concept of her baby sister being involved in international intrigue— there would be time for that to sink in when this ordeal was over— though she'd readily admit that Pepper's number-one weapon was the fact that no one else on the planet would ever believe that about her either.

She sighed. Looking around to make sure no one was behind her, she whispered, "Any word from Inspector Gadget? Where is she?"

"You two do know I can hear everything you're saying, right?" came Pepper's whisper in her ear. "I did explain three times how these mikes work. And no mushy talk. If I had to leave Paolo the Wonderstud back in Brazil, the least you guys can do is not rub my forced abstinence in my face."

Shane chuckled. Darby just rolled her eyes.

"Okay," Pepper went on. "I'm right across the lawn, in front of Senator Howard," Pepper whispered. "Oh, my God, Dar, have you seen wife number three? Total trophy. And I don't know who recommended she wear a costume with a bustle, but someone needs to explain accentuating the positive to her, if you know what I mean."

Darby couldn't help it, she stifled a smile and shook her head. Pepper Landon, the Josie and the Pussycats version of modern-day counterintelligence.

"Hey, Crouching Cinderella, Hidden Barbie, our target is at three o'clock, using the lap pool as due north," Shane whispered.

Darby just shook her head. The entire time she'd been bitching and kvetching about the whole thing, Shane had been drooling over all the cool toys. He was loving this whole adventure, but then, why wouldn't he? Adventure was his middle name. "Okay, Bosley," she whispered. "That's a big ten-four."

"Bosley? Why do I have to play Bosley? I sort of pictured myself more as a Charlie type."

"No one ever sees Charlie," she whispered back. "And I plan on seeing a lot of you later."

"Well, there is that. Maybe I—"

"Enough, you two," Pepper whispered. "I just spotted him. Go get him, Dar. We'll be close by. Whatever you do, keep him in mike range."

Darby's stomach knotted, which, considering it was already being crushed by the corset, made it doubly discomforting. "Pepper, I'm not sure I'm cut out for this. I don't see why you can't—"

Pepper's sigh was audible. "We already went over this," she whispered. "You'll be fine."

"Look who's giving advice to whom."

"I've always believed you could do anything."

Darby glanced up then, and made eye contact with her sister, who was about thirty yards to her right, peering over the edge of the lace fan that blocked anyone else from noticing she was talking to herself.

"You won't let me down," Pepper said. "You never do."

Darby just stared into her sister's eyes, overwhelmed by the enormity of all that had happened in the past couple of hours. The whole concept of how she defined herself and her world had been stood on its ear. Actually, to be honest, that had all started happening during that limo ride with Shane. This was just the capper. She was worried for Pepper and proud of her all at the same time. It was that latter part that had her sucking in what was left of her gut and moving out from her hiding spot behind the hedgerow. "Here goes nothing," she murmured.

"You're stunning, Cinderella," came Shane's voice in her ear.

She glanced to her right and spotted him joining a small group of guests on the fringe of the crowd. She met his gaze for a split second above their heads. He flashed her a grin, nodded slightly. She smiled, gave him a brief nod, then turned and spotted Stefan, squared her shoulders, and entered the fray.

"There you are," Stefan said easily, moving away from the guests he'd been speaking with and smoothly turning her toward the rear of the lawn. "Difficult morning?"

Now that she was standing next to him, knowing the full extent of his involvement, and just what was at stake for him, her nerves balled up inside her like a tight fist, and it took all her willpower to smile up at him. "Problem with my costume. I had to have some last-minute alterations."

He took her elbow in his grasp, and again she realized just how large—and probably strong—his hands were. But then his whole body was quite intimidating. He held her at arm's length and let his gaze rove over her. She did her utmost not to react. Facing down a stallion in rut? No problem. But Stefan? Although, when she thought about it that way, she supposed it wasn't all that different.

"They appear to have been quite successful," he said, gaze locking on hers again after his thorough perusal was complete.

Darby absently wondered how eyes so cool and dark could transmit a look that was so inherently hot. "Thank you." She cleared her throat, forced herself to focus on her mission. Mission. Dear God, help them all. "Well," she said brightly, easing her elbow from his grasp. "You seem to have done fine without me. Did I miss anything interesting?" His gaze narrowed slightly and she rushed on. "I felt terrible about abandoning you. I was hoping you'd found some lively conversation to help pass the time or ... or something." *Lame, lame*, she scolded herself.

"Ask him if he's met anyone he knows," came Pepper's whisper in her ear.

Darby jumped a little and Stefan immediately looked concerned. "Is anything wrong?"

She nervously tucked her hair behind her ear. "No, no, just a stray pin the seamstress left."

"Do you need to go back inside and remove it?"

She tensed, waiting for him to pull out the dimple and offer his personal assistance. But he didn't. She glanced up at him and realized he was a bit distracted himself. His gaze was skimming the crowds as he moved them toward the house.

Wrong direction. She did not want to go into the main house alone with him. Sure, it was crawling with staff, but all the guests were out here. She felt better outside. Alone in a crowd with him was still intimidating, but it beat the hell out of being alone with him for real. "No, no, that's not necessary. It's fine, really."

"Actually, I think I'm going to step inside myself for a few moments." He did smile then, and the transformation struck her as it always did.

But, having noticed his distraction, the calculation was obvious this time. He'd switched it on as a means to an end ... and she didn't think that end was getting her naked. He wanted to get inside, and he wanted her to think his motives had to do with getting her alone. But it was something else he was after. Another phone call?

"Where I'm from, we're not used to all this heat." He fingered his suit. "And while I appreciate the theme, this is a bit warm."

She noticed his costume for the first time. He didn't cut quite the dashing figure Shane did in his. In fact, something about the waist-coat and vest, complete with watch fob, made him look autocratic and more than a little sinister. Of course, that could be her overactive imagination at work. Although even her imagination could never have conjured up anything as wild as the reality in which she was currently up to her petticoats in.

"I know what you mean," she said, unable to come out with a direct compliment, though she suspected he was waiting for one. "It's not my favorite thing, either, trust me." She laughed a little, wanting nothing more than to ease the steadily building tension. "I don't know how women managed all these layers. Between the rows of tiny little buttons and this corset—" She broke off, blanching a little. Not exactly the direction she wanted his attention wandering.

"Yes," he said, his lips curving in an amused smile. "I can see where that could be quite bothersome." He nodded toward the house. "Would you like to get out of the sun, or would you prefer to stay and mingle?"

"Don't let him go inside alone," Pepper whispered anxiously. "We're too far away to follow him."

Darby kept a firm grip on her composure. She smiled brightly. "Actually, it is quite warm." She knew that sounded like an invitation, and managed not to send a panicked look in either Shane's or Pepper's direction as Stefan smiled and smoothly took her elbow in his grip once again, and led her toward the sunroom on the far side of the house.

"It's quite the place," he commented as they left the crowd behind . . . and her protection with it.

Darby didn't dare look over her shoulder. She could only hope Shane and Pepper were somehow following them without being noticed.

"Yes," Darby said, forcing her attention back to him. "Quite."

"You mentioned before that you'd only just met Alexandra's grandson. How exactly did the two of you meet?" His tone was polite, casual. His grasp on her elbow was not.

His question took her by surprise. She worked to match his tone. "Why do you ask?"

His gaze touched her like a hot poker. "I see the way he looks at you. I can understand the fascination," he said, his low voice all but vibrating.

She kept her eyes focused in front of them, trying to figure out his ulterior motive. Did he suspect something? "What exactly are you asking?"

He slowed to a stop, pulled her around so he could look past her shoulder at the crowds they were leaving behind. "I'm asking if the two of you are . . . involved."

She looked up at him then, but instead of that hot probing look, she found him glancing past her shoulder. Was this more distraction? His gaze immediately moved back to her, and the hot punch of his dark eyes was surprisingly intense, confusing her all over again. She had no idea why he was really asking, so she didn't know whether to tell him the truth or not. When he looked at her like that, it was hard to think straight.

"I—I enjoy his company," she finally stammered. Then, in the acting job of the century, she smiled slowly and laid her hand on his arm and said, "Just as I enjoy yours."

"Hmm," he responded thoughtfully. But his eyes had flared for a moment. Only the result had been chilling, rather than inflaming. He moved them once again down the path to the sunroom.

Darby didn't dare press further, and wasn't sure where she'd found the balls to press this far. His initial question popped back in her mind and she realized he'd asked about Shane, not as Mr. Morgan, but as Alexandra's grandson. She blurted out the question that came to mind, as much in desperation to get the conversation shifted away from her and Shane as because she was really curious. "You knew Alexandra? You never mentioned it."

The pause seemed to stretch out to the screaming point. But when he finally answered, he sounded as casual as ever. "We'd never met. But of course I'd heard quite a bit about her. I was looking forward to the chance to meet her. It was one of the reasons I decided to accept your father's invitation to meet him here in Washington instead of extending my stay in Europe."

Stefan wove the truth so seamlessly with the lie that she'd never have suspected he wasn't completely on the up-and-up. "That must have been a disappointment, then. Will you be heading back to Europe once your business with my father is concluded?"

His attention seemed to shift as they reached the sunroom, and he barely made the attempt to cover his sudden distraction. Quite an obvious shift from just moments ago, but she wasn't sure how to capitalize on it.

"I'm not certain what my plans are," he said. He opened the French doors for her. "In fact, if you don't mind, I'd like to take the opportunity to make a few phone calls while you tend to that stray pin. Business," he said by way of explanation. "You understand."

Darby smiled and nodded, even as she scrambled to think what to do next. She needed to keep him in sight until Shane or Pepper could close in. "I suppose with all the projects you have going on that you're never truly off duty."

He smiled, but this time it didn't reach his eyes. "Not really, no."

"Just how many countries do you have mining interests in?" she asked as she gathered up her skirts to leave. "I suppose gemstones are mined all over. I really know nothing about the industry."

His gaze hardened then, and for the first time she realized how truly dangerous a man he might be. There was a lot more to him than probing gazes, sly innuendo, and killer dimples. She entered the sunroom in front of him and felt the impact of his gaze on her back ... only it felt a whole lot more deadly than sexual. Had she pushed too hard? Did he suspect she was on to him somehow?

Then another thought struck her. He couldn't possibly know about Pepper, could he? Had he spotted her out there? Or—shit!—maybe he'd known about Pepper all along. And her father. After all, he'd been staying one step ahead of them for a long time. It would explain his wariness from the beginning with her last-minute substitution. Did he think *she* was a spy? If so, that made her relationship with Shane look all the more suspect. Suspicions which would prove to be true, since, though she wasn't a spy, she and Shane had been investigating him. Holy Mission Impossible.

"It's a complex science," he said finally. "I currently have projects set up on several continents." He placed his hand on her lower back and she had to fight the urge to run screaming out of the house.

He steered her through the bright, plant-filled sunroom and into the dim coolness of the study. And all she could think was that she'd been a pretend spy for less than thirty minutes and she'd already allowed herself to get trapped alone with her quarry. Great job, Darby.

"Again, please accept my apologies for leaving you so soon after meeting up," he said, almost hurrying them into the house. "I shouldn't be long. Thirty minutes or so?"

"Yes, fine," Darby said, trying not to look vastly relieved when his focus shifted away from her. He wanted her out of here, and she was more than willing to comply if it meant she got to leave under her own power. Except that wasn't her mission.

She was really beginning to hate that word.

She glanced discreetly around to see if there was a way she could head out of the room, then retrace her steps and follow him. But the wide-open halls beyond the spacious study they'd stepped into didn't really afford her that luxury. Fortunately, he continued to guide her through the room and out into the hallway. "Can you find your way, or would you like me to accompany you to the main stairs?"

"No, that won't be necessary," she assured him. "They're just at the end of the hall. Will you be here in the study?" she asked, proud of herself for working in their location, hoping her mike was still transmitting. "Should I meet up with you here?"

"Why don't we meet at the base of the stairs," he said, barely glancing at her. His tone was smooth, but she could almost feel the tension rolling off of him. Something had changed, she just didn't know what in the hell it was.

She forced a smile and nodded. "Fine. Thirty minutes," she said, in case Shane or Pepper had missed that part. She began to ease her elbow free, assuming he'd nod gallantly and step back into the study to make his call. But, instead, his grip tightened. Just slightly, but his gaze shifted fully back to hers, and the slow intent that filled his gaze was enough to make the hairs on the back of her neck stand on end.

"I've enjoyed my time with you, Darby," he said.

"Thank you. I've enjoyed it as well," she said automatically.

His eyes flared. "Have you?" His fingers caressed the inside of her arm. "A shame we don't have more of it. As I said, you fascinate me. I believe I'd have rather enjoyed getting to know you better."

Darby's throat closed over when Stefan reached out a gloved hand and smoothed a stray hair behind her ear. She went completely still, terrified that his fingers would brush over the earphone and she'd be discovered. Hopefully, with this ridiculous updo Pepper had fashioned, he'd think it was a bobby pin or something.

His fingers paused when she froze, and his gaze narrowed, just slightly.

"Yes," she said, heart hammering, "it's a—a shame."

His gaze stayed focused on her for what felt like an eternity, then, like the sun bursting out from behind a cloud, he grinned. "Morgan is a luckier bastard than even he knows."

Darby was so relieved when he dropped his hand and stepped back, his words barely registered.

"By the stairs," he repeated, but made no move to go into the room. Instead, he bowed slightly and motioned for her to go on.

She had no choice but to turn around and walk down the wide marble hallway toward the main foyer and the split staircases that led to the upper wings of the house. Her legs felt like jelly after all that tension, and it didn't help that she could feel his eyes drilling into her back. But she didn't dare glance over her shoulder to see if he'd finally gone inside. She'd taken all of Stefan that she could for the moment. It wasn't until she was at the landing that she dared look back. She didn't know whether to be relieved or worried when there was no Stefan in sight.

"You okay?"

Shane's voice in her ears startled her, and was so welcome she could have sunk right to the floor as the rush of nervous tension left her body. "Yes," she whispered shakily, looking about to make sure none of the household staff was anywhere nearby. "He's in the side study on the south side of the house, off the sunroom. Supposedly making calls. I can sneak back and listen through the door." Although they were huge, heavy-paneled hardwood, and likely she wouldn't hear a thing above a murmur. "Or I guess I could duck out the front and go around to the sunroom we came in through."

"No," Shane said, "you need to be at the bottom of that staircase in case he gets done early. I'll head around to the sunroom. Pepper?"

There was no response, just the background noise of party chatter and glass clinking with ice. Pepper's mike was on her fan, so the party noise was minimized when she was speaking to them. Shane's was on his cuff link, so he could pretend to sip a drink and speak clearly to them both. Darby's was in her bodice. Lucky her.

"My, it's warm, isn't it?" came Pepper's voice suddenly, along with a whooshing sound that Darby realized was her fan being flicked back and forth. "I think I'll take a little stroll," she went on, obviously speaking to one of the guests. "That path over there looks enticing. A bit of shade, too, by the sunroom."

Darby paced the grand foyer. "Pepper? Shane, do you see her?"

"I'm already at the sunroom door. I'll let you know when—"

"Oh, thank God," came Pepper's rushed whisper. "I thought I would never get myself out of that little circle." Her breath was rapid, as if she were rushing. "My lord, you really can't run in this thing, can you?"

"The heels, or the corset?" Darby muttered, feeling the pinch in her toes, as well as her ribs.

"I was born in heels. But dammit, Dar, did you have to cinch me in so tight? I can barely breathe in this thing."

Darby just smiled, not feeling the least bit ashamed. "Fair's fair."

"Yes, but that was the only way we could get your buttons fastened. Besides, you have cleavage now, be thankful."

"Now, now," came Shane's voice. "I happened to adore her cleavage just the way it was."

"Okay, I'm almost there," Pepper said, huffing. "Dar, you stay in the foyer in case he comes out that way. Shane—"

"Dammit!" That from Shane.

"What?" both Darby and Pepper said at the same time.

"He's not in here."

"Are you sure?" Darby turned back to the hallway. He wasn't there, either. But then, she'd been pacing the foyer and not paying strict attention to the door all the way at the end of the hall. She hadn't thought he might sneak back out that way. The hallway led directly to the foyer, but there were other doors off to each side. She supposed he might have ducked into one of those, but that would have taken him long enough that she was certain she'd have spied him as she paced.

Fairly certain, anyway.

"Yes, I'm sure," Shane said. "Shit. He must have taken the back stairs, although how he'd know about them, I have no idea."

"Is there any other exit from the room?" Pepper asked Shane.

"No, just to the hallway."

"He might have ducked back out here and gone into one of the rooms in the hallway," Darby admitted. "My, uh, back was briefly to the hall." In fact, there was nothing to say he'd gone back into the study at all. "Do any of those rooms have other exits?"

Pepper hissed. "Dar! Weren't you watching him?"

"Dammit, I'm not trained for this, you know? I can barely breathe, my feet are numb, and gangrene probably is setting in from lack of circulation. And I wasn't—"

"Listen, there's no point in arguing," Shane interrupted. "I'm already heading upstairs. Pepper, you take the rooms in the hallway. Darby, you stay on the stairs. Other than this and the service stairs, if he's up here, it's his only way back down."

"You're good at this," Pepper said. "Okay, I'm through the study. Darby, I can see your skirts. Move up the stairs in case he comes out this way, so he won't know you're right there."

"What, you think I'm going to do a flying tackle in this dress?" She glanced back down the hall in time to see Pepper open the first door in the hallway. Her voice got louder and more airy as she said, "Why, I can never find my way around these big old—" She broke off the Southern belle routine as soon as she'd stepped inside. "Nope, clear."

She stepped back out again, shooed Darby up the stairs with her fan, then moved to the next door.

It was like playing Let's Make A Deal: the Nightmare Home Game. "Just . . . be careful," Darby hissed and resolutely climbed halfway up the staircase. Of course, it was a split staircase, so how she was supposed to cover both sides she had no idea.

"This room is empty, too," Pepper reported moments later. "Where the hell could he have gone? Shane? Any luck?"

"Goddammit!" Shane barked in her ear. "He's been in my rooms. And he wasn't too worried about being sneaky about it, either. Shit."

"What?" Darby whispered.

"I think he's figured out we're on to him. Maybe he spotted Pepper, or someone else tipped him off, who knows. But I think he's outta here."

"So what was he looking for?" Darby asked. "Alexandra's private files," she and Shane said simultaneously.

"I'm heading to Alexandra's private office," he said. "Get Pepper to check out his rooms. Be careful."

Torn between running up the stairs to help Shane, or down to get Pepper, she startled and turned around when a phalanx of guests in full historical costume came storming up both sides of the staircase behind her. "What the—" She grabbed hold of the banister as they rushed past. It was only when she caught site of the guns two of them were carrying tucked next to their thighs that she began to realize what was going on. "Shane," she whispered, wanting him to know the cavalry was on its way. At least she prayed it was the cavalry. Only the word got stuck in her throat as she turned and spied the man entering the foyer below, and froze.

He looked different with the silver graying his temples, she thought, but all the more dashing because of it. She'd wondered, a lot more often than she'd admit to, about what she'd think, or what she'd feel, if she ever saw him again. The last thing she'd expected was a wave of longing so strong that she found she had to grip the banister for support.

She must have made a sound, because he looked up. His eyes widened in shock and he stopped dead in his tracks. "Darmilla? Is that you?"

"Yeah, it's me," she said on a choked whisper. "Hi, Dad."

Cinderella Rule #22

You can't always wait for the
right time to do the right thing.

—VIVIAN

Chapter 22

"O h, shit," said Pepper, her voice sounding hollow in his ear.

But Shane didn't even pause. He ran to the door of Alexandra's private office, then swore himself when he found the room empty. He strode immediately behind the desk. The bottom drawer was closed. He tugged on it. Still locked. Only then did he smile. "Didn't find what you were looking for, after all. You bastard." He dug the key out of the pocket in his jacket lining. "He hasn't been in here yet," he said to both Darby and Pepper. "Any sign of him in his rooms?"

Which was when he heard Pepper rather breathlessly say, "Daddy, I can explain."

Daddy? Now Shane understood the *Oh, shit* remark. Because he was thinking the exact same thing. He fumbled with the key, needing to verify that the files were still in the drawer, but also wanting to get back to Darby before her father confronted her. He bent down and jammed the key into the lock.

"Step away from the desk," came a voice from the doorway. "Hands raised."

He straightened slowly and tossed the keys on the desk.

"Very good. Now turn around and move away from the desk."

"Daddy, honestly, I told you, he's on our side," Pepper said, bursting into the room behind him.

"You don't know what side he's on," he corrected, his tone one of strained patience. "He's a Morgan first."

Shane turned to find himself staring at Paul Landon III, international financier. And a whole lot more than an occasional consultant to Interpol, judging from the very lethal-looking gun in his hand.

"Please," Landon said, with a small wave of his gun barrel, "over there, if you will. Center of the room. Now."

"Dad," Darby said, striding into the room behind Pepper. "Will you put that thing away before you hurt somebody?" She looked to Pepper. "Consultant, huh? What else haven't the two of you been telling me?"

"Quite a lot, I imagine," her father said in very stilted tones, "given you have no contact with us."

Darby gaped at him, looked like she was going to argue, then glared at Pepper, instead. "Oh, yeah, this was all going to turn out peachy. *Just explain it to him*, you said." She waved her hands. "Now look what you've gotten us into."

"Darmilla, hush. You have no idea what your sister is involved in." He never once shifted his gaze, or his gun barrel, from Shane, who had done as he'd asked and moved to the center of the room. "We'll speak no more of this now. It's neither the time nor the place."

Darby snorted. "Oh, I'm sorry, I didn't realize we were breaching espionage etiquette. How gauche of me. But then, I was raised on a ranch, so what can you expect."

Shane noticed Landon's jaw tighten again. "I expect you both to let me do my job." He shifted his attention to Shane, keeping his gun level. "Now, then. Explain for me, if you will, exactly when you tipped off Mr. Bjornsen."

Shane's mouth dropped open. "Tipped him off? I haven't even spoken to the man since yesterday afternoon. I was up here trying to find him myself. He's already gone through my room, so I thought he'd come here next. Instead of standing here grilling me, you should be out there trying to find him."

"He seems to know an awful lot about the layout of this house. My daughter tells me he took some secret stairway to the second floor. How would he come to know of this?"

"I have no idea. When you track him down, ask him. In fact, I have one or two questions of my own I'd like to ask the man."

"Do you think yourself clever, Mr. Morgan? Bjornsen is no longer on the premises. But I'm sure you're well aware of that. Clever of you to keep my daughters entertained on some wild-goose chase, to allow him time to escape. I'm sorry to say, we have agents posted at both Dulles and BWI, so there will be no flight to Brazil this evening. Your little plan has failed."

Shane folded his arms. "I see. And what plan would that be, sir?"

"You'll be distressed to learn that you've been sold out, Mr. Morgan. Mr. Bjornsen made a deal with one of the scientists at Celentrex. He won't need you to procure the prototype for him."

"*What?*"

Landon apparently took his response for outrage. "You were planning to go ahead with the buyout, were you not?"

"Yes, but I'd only just decided that yester—"

"I'm afraid those plans might have to be put on hold temporarily. There will be a full investigation, of course. You'll be—"

"Wait just a goddamn minute. I had nothing to do with this. In fact, *I'm* the one who was trying to figure out what he was up to." It took him a moment to decipher the source of the real outrage that was coursing through him. It wasn't that he was being wrongly accused, although that did piss him off just a little. But he could take care of himself. It was the fact that Landon was threatening to topple Morgan Industries by starting a scandal of global proportions before finding out just what the fuck was really going on. "We'll talk," he stated, jaw clamped. "But I want your word that nothing leaves this room until I've explained everything. And until you've answered my questions as well."

And it hit him fully then, like the proverbial ton of bricks. First the revelation that there was a possibility that his grandmother might have been victimized, making her more vulnerable than he'd ever presumed the old battle-ax could be. Then there was the notion that he actually felt some kind of, well, sense of responsibility. To his late grandmother, and even more, to the people of Morgan Industries. They'd done nothing wrong in all this. It wasn't their fault Alexandra had died suddenly, that her only living heir didn't want to take over the empire. He still didn't. But if he was going to dismantle the company, sever the ties and break it down into independent corporations, then he wanted them to have every opportunity to go forward with the chance of succeeding, and not under the black cloud of corporate scandal. He owed them—and maybe his grandmother and all the other Morgans before her—that much. Didn't he?

Jesus, his head hurt. And maybe his heart. Just a little.

"Tell me one thing," he said, "then I'll answer all your questions. Did you stop him from getting the technology from his Celentrex contact?"

"I'm not at liberty to—"

"Yes," Pepper broke in. "We got to him first."

"Pepper, for God's—"

"Thank God," Shane sighed, then another thought occurred to him. "So, if he doesn't have the technology, and you're here, and not out there providing him with some ready capital ... how is he going to ransom his men? With his good looks? A promissory note, maybe?"

Landon sighed and darted a quick look at his youngest daughter. "Did you simply hand over the full dossier to him? This is why I worry. This is why I forbid you from signing up. I can't be expected to keep an eye on you every minute, and then the second I'm occupied, you turn around and hand the suspects classified information."

"I beg your pardon, but I had permission to bring them in on this. And if you'd only told me you were working for them, too, I could have communicated all this to you. But, no, you had to keep me in the dark and treat me like some little airhead with nothing better to do than file my nails and get my hair done. Well, I'm telling you, you're all wrong here. Shane isn't involved with Bjornsen. Never was. If you don't trust me, trust Darby. She sure as hell should know, and she'd never sleep with a guy who—"

"Pepper!" Darby glared at her sister, then turned her glare on her father. "She's right, though. And if you'd stop letting the same pig-headed stubbornness blind you with Pepper like you did with me after Mom died, you'd know she's good at her job. Sure, she has her own ... unique way of getting the job done, but she gets it done, or they wouldn't keep giving her work, now, would they?" She didn't wait for him to respond. She could see she'd gotten to him with the comment about her mother, but she couldn't think about that now. "Shane isn't involved in this. He was the one who figured out something was off about the whole Celentrex deal in the first place. He showed Pepper Alexandra's personal files, proving it. Why would he do that if he was involved? Hell, he doesn't even want Morgan Industries, much less Alexandra's money."

"Actually, that's not entirely true," Shane said, although now probably wasn't the best time to mention that, he added to himself, sneaking a glance at Landon's gun.

"*What?*" She turned to face him. "Since when do you care—"

"Since your father threatened to destroy what my ancestors spent the past couple of hundred years building. One wrong rumor, one wrong media story, and this will be the next Enron. I'm not letting my company take a hit when there was no wrongdoing on—"

"*Your* company? What does that mean? You're not going to dismantle it? You're going to stay and take over?"

He sighed. Why in the hell he'd opened his big mouth, he had no idea. Could he have timed this worse? "I don't know what it means. All I know is, I'm not walking away from this and letting the company implode on some big scandal. I want the buyout to go through. Because it's the right thing to do for a lot of people." He looked at Landon. "Not because of some under-the-table deal with Bjornsen." He looked to Darby. "But I also want to do what's right for those same people in the long haul. Alexandra may or may not have exactly been living up to the family name she touted so highly, but that doesn't mean all the people who sweat blood and tears to help her build onto the family empire deserve to get screwed. I'm not cut out to run the joint. I know that. But I can figure out who is. And you're right, the money means nothing to me." He looked back to Landon. "But my name does. Because I guess I *am* a Morgan first. And no one screws with what's mine."

He looked around him, seeing all that went beyond these walls … and felt the weight of responsibility settle on his shoulders once again … only this time, along with the terror, came a kind of excitement. Maybe even of entitlement. He might not have felt like a Morgan before, in anything beyond name. But by the time he left here, however long that might take, he would be a Morgan in deed. Of course, his version of Morgan might be a little different.

He grinned. "I guess I'm in for a different kind of adventure this go-around." He looked at Landon. "And with all due respect, I might as well warn you now that I'm going to do my damnedest to see that your oldest daughter enjoys as much of it as I can convince her into sharing with me. So why don't you and I have that little talk. Then maybe you can spend some time reuniting with your family."

Landon studied him for another endless moment, then lifted his free hand and spoke into what appeared to be a slim gold watch. "Move in." He looked at Shane. "Mr. Morgan, my agents will take a full statement from you."

"Dad, I think—"

Landon turned his head sharply toward Pepper. "Don't. I'll talk with both of you later, after we've sorted this out. If the two of you will please retire to your rooms, I'll send someone for you when I'm done."

Darby stepped in then. "Excuse me, and please, take this in the spirit it's intended, but go to hell, you arrogant ass."

"Darmilla—"

"No one calls me Darmilla. No one in the family ever did. Just you. It's Darby. Get used to it. Now, I believe that Pepper, as part of this team, needs to remain here, to see it through. And, as this is not your home, and I am a grown woman, you can no longer send me to my room when it isn't convenient for you to have me around. I might have spent most of my childhood there, but I'll be damned if—"

"Yes, you're quite good at hiding," he said flatly.

Pepper gasped and Darby looked like she'd been slapped. Shane took a step forward. Landon turned the gun his way.

"Stop it," Darby said, though it was unclear whom she was speaking to. "Actually, he's right." She shifted her attention to her father. "I was hiding when I ran to Montana. Hiding from a pile of grief, with no one to turn to, to help me make sense of it. But I found something that made sense to me there, something I felt connected to in a way I'd only ever felt connected when I was with Mom. Something that was important to her, and that I truly love. I'm sorry you can't be happy for me, or respect that." She paused, took a breath, then said,

"But I'm also sorry I didn't try and take the time to understand you. You were grieving, too. I don't know that I could have done much about that then, since I was only a child. But I've long since grown up. And I have no excuses now. I'm just as guilty as you are." The corner of her mouth kicked up in that dry smile of hers that Shane had fallen for that very first day. "Apparently, I come by my bullheaded stubbornness honestly."

Shane looked between father and daughter, and for a split second, he saw Landon's expression falter. *You idiot,* he wanted to shout, *don't you realize the gift that's staring you in the face?*

Darby nodded to the gun. "Obviously there's a lot more to you than I ever knew about. That's my loss. But there's a lot more to me than you know about. And that's your loss. Maybe Pepper was right, and all we needed to do was come together, sit down, and talk things out." She shot her sister a look, her expression as sober as he'd ever seen it. "Thank you for trying; I know this was important to you. But it doesn't look like it worked out the way you wanted. I'm sorry for that, too." She looked back to her father, but said nothing more.

When the silence spun out, Pepper took a step forward. "Dad?"

Landon finally cleared his throat. "As I said, this is neither the time nor the place to be having this discussion."

Darby sighed in defeat. "Right. You give me a call when it's the right time. You know where to find me." She met his gaze with a level one of her own. "Same place you found Mom."

A sharp knock came at the door. Darby stepped back to open it, and two men and one woman, all in full costume, filled the doorway. "Ah, it's the cavalry." She motioned them into the room. "Welcome to the party." She shot a look at Shane. "Come find me when this is all done, okay?"

"Remember your promise," Shane called out, afraid she was going to be on a plane to Montana before he could extract himself from this mess. Of course, he'd just be on the next plane out, scandal or no scandal. But she nodded, and he breathed a sigh of relief. She'd keep her word.

Darby tugged her earpiece off, pulled the mike and camera out of her bodice, then smiled and handed them both to the nearest agent. "The mike is probably a bit sticky from all the sweat and hairspray. Didn't take any pictures with the boob cam, though. A shame. I'll never have enough cleavage to hide one in ever again."

Then she was out the door.

"Darby, wait," Pepper said, trying to shift past the new agents, to the door. "Just hold on a minute—dammit," she swore when two more agents moved into the room and blocked her from reaching Darby in time. She looked at her father in exasperation. "Good God, you've got this many people on a case and not one of them saw Bjornsen leaving? Great work, Dad." Then she took off after her sister.

Landon's cheeks took on a deep flush even as he glared down those few agents whose lips had dared to quirk.

Shane grinned. "Quite the daughters you have there. If I were you, I'd be thinking about finding a way to hold on to them."

"Well, look here, Aurora! We found the party, after all." Vivian bustled into the room, holding on to an alarmingly elaborate head-dress that looked like it came directly from the set of *Moulin Rouge*. As did the rest of her bawdy outfit, he noted, as she spied him and pushed past the other agents. "There you are! Naughty boy, might have known you'd be having a private soiree inside where it's cool."

"I beg your pardon," Landon began, putting his hand out to stop her progress, "but this is private business; you'll have to wait outside."

Aurora gasped as she was pushed into Landon, knocking his arm and allowing Vivian to get past him. Aurora was laced and buttoned up to the hilt and breathing like she'd run a marathon. She'd been fanning her face with a wide lace fan, and she snapped it shut and slapped Landon on the arm. "Dear heavens, man, put that thing away," she said, waving her fan at his gun. "Realistic costumes are one thing, but you can't wave that around in polite company; it's not done." Then she stopped and squinted through the fancy opera glasses she was carrying in her other hand. She dropped them from her face and beamed. "Paul? Why, darling, when did you get in?"

Landon stood there, looking slightly stunned, as agents were busily moving into the room and pulling out various pieces of equipment, taking the key off the desk, and opening the file drawer.

Shane used the sudden commotion to duck around them and Paul. He leaned down and bussed Aurora on the cheek. "Excuse me, I have a damsel to hunt down." Then he turned to Vivian and said, "Darling, you look fabulous. Love the hat." He flicked at the two-foot pink ostrich feather as he ducked under it on his way to the door. "I'll be in Darby's suite," he called back to Landon.

"Morgan, see here—!"

"Paul!" Vivian crowed, blocking Landon from following him. "When did you get in? I can't tell you what a pleasure it was to meet your darling daughter Darby."

"You tell him, Vivi," Shane murmured under his breath. Then headed for the west wing at a run.

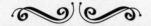

Cinderella Rule #23

You won't always have the luxury of a second chance. So be careful with your first one.

—MERCEDES

Chapter 23

"No, Pepper, I'm not hanging around to talk to Dad." Darby scrubbed at the makeup on her face, wadding up one tissue after another. "I appreciate that you tried, I really do, but I extended the olive branch. He can take it or leave it."

"Some olive branch. You all but defied him to ignore it. You missed some mascara under your right eye," she directed from her position in the doorway. "You know, leaving a little makeup on wouldn't kill you."

"Yes," Darby said, "it would. It's not me, Pepper. None of this is me. Why doesn't anyone want to see that?" She finished wiping her face clean, splashed water on it, and patted her skin dry. She tossed everything littering the counter into the rope-handled bag, then pushed it against Pepper's chest as she moved back into the bedroom.

"Hey!" Pepper said, grabbing the bag to keep it from falling to the floor.

"You'll get more use out of that stuff than I will."

"What are you so mad about, anyway?"

Darby paused. She'd peeled out of the costume, which she'd flung on the chair and which Pepper had picked up and carefully put back on the various hangers and zippered bags it had arrived in. She'd pulled on the jeans and T-shirt she'd worn on the plane ride that now seemed like a lifetime ago, and was in the process of packing—probably breaking some fashion-code ordinance as silk and cotton alike were getting shoved in her grandfather's Army-issue duffel with little care to things like folding or blocking.

Now she stared at the haphazard mess in front of her as she thought about Pepper's question. "I'm not sure." She finally huffed out a sigh and straightened, then looked at her sister. "Dad makes me nuts. But then, that's nothing new. I guess I'm having a hard time dealing with this whole other life you two have been leading without my knowledge. I guess . . . I don't know . . ." She trailed off, feeling stupid all of a sudden. It had been her choice, after all, to cut herself off from their lives. So she could hardly claim hurt feelings for being left out now. And yet, that's exactly what she was feeling. Hurt.

Pepper came over to her and hugged her. "I'm sorry. You know I didn't mean to hurt you. I just . . . I want you to be proud of me, Dar. Not mad."

Darby felt tears threaten again and frowned them into submission. "I'm not mad at you. And I am proud. I just wish . . . I guess I just wish you felt like this was something you could have told me about. That you could have trusted me with."

"I didn't exactly lie to you," Pepper said. "I called you when I needed you. And you were there for me. Even when I didn't deserve it. All of that was real. And it was true, even if my reasons for needing your help were a bit more complicated at times than I let on. Besides, it hasn't really been going on all that long."

Darby wiped at her eyes, sniffled once, then slumped down on the edge of the bed. Pepper sat down next to her and put her arm around Darby's shoulders.

"So . . . how long has Dad been doing the real spy stuff?"

Pepper shrugged. "I'm not sure. I didn't realize until today how fully involved he was. Apparently, keeping secrets is a Landon family trait."

Darby glanced at Pepper and a corner of her mouth quirked. "I can't believe you actually kept any of this quiet. You're terrible with secrets."

Pepper smiled. "I know. But this was important. And . . . I wanted so badly to succeed at it, to prove to both of you that I could do something important and not just be an irresponsible pain in the ass all the time."

"You're not a pain in the ass," Darby said, bumping her shoulder. "All the time."

Pepper swatted her and laughed a little. "Oh, thanks."

"Well, you have to admit, this whole thing wasn't exactly a picnic for me. I still can't believe I let you talk me into this. You know, you might just have a future in espionage. If you can get me involved in your schemes, you could probably talk anybody into anything."

Pepper's face lit up. "That's the nicest thing you've ever said to me."

Darby laughed, but returned the sudden exuberant hug from her sister. "Well, I mean it. And I am proud of you. I'm sorry Dad is hassling you about sticking with it, but if this is something you really want to do—for you, not to impress anyone, but because you believe in it—then do it. I'm a firm believer in that, if nothing else."

She stood and silently went back to tossing stuff in her bag. Pepper took each item back out and folded them before repacking them.

"Your support means a lot to me," Pepper told her. "I am going to stick with it. Although with Dad's current attitude, I might be spending my breaks with you instead of here at home."

Darby paused. "You know, you could think about getting your own place. In fact, I really think you should."

Pepper paused in the middle of folding another shirt. "You know, that's not a bad idea. I guess my trust fund is out of reach for life."

"Here's an idea," Darby said dryly, "you could save some of the money this super secret spy agency is paying you and buy one yourself."

"Oh, go ahead, make fun. But just maybe I will. And then I'll have a huge housewarming party and you'll have to come, since it was your idea. So there."

Darby smiled. "You buy yourself your own house, without any help from me or Dad, and I'll throw the damn party for you."

"Well, there's incentive right there. And you do owe me a thank-you, by the way," Pepper said.

Darby snorted. "What on earth for?"

"Shane Morgan. If I hadn't conned you into coming, you'd never have met him."

Darby's heart squeezed painfully. She didn't want to think about Shane right now. It was hard enough just dealing with all the family shit that had come down on her. She'd think about Shane again when they had their talk. No need to endure the heartache before she needed to. "I don't want to think about that right now." She impulsively leaned down and bussed her sister on the cheek. "But, yes," she said quickly, before she lost her nerve. "I do owe you for that one."

"He's yummy," Pepper said, beaming. "And he stood right up to Daddy, didn't he? Even with a gun on him. I think I'd have to hang on to a guy like that. What was it he said about not letting people screw around with what was his?" She hummed. "Did you see that look he sent you? Had 'you're mine' stamped all over it. Definitely a keeper."

Darby didn't know whether to laugh or burst out crying. Her heart competed with her stomach to see which could squeeze more tightly. She had to get out of here. She felt like she couldn't suck in even one more breath of this stuffy, rarified air—and she'd long since taken off that corset. She wanted to go home. "I'll be sure to keep that in mind."

"Can't you two work something out? I mean, I know Dad is being an ass as usual, but he'd probably be cool with you staying on at the house—" She broke off at the glare from Darby, lifting her hands in defense. "Okay, okay, just a suggestion. Shane has more than enough room here. And given that look I mentioned, I'm thinking he wouldn't mind you shacking up with him."

Darby went back to packing. With a vengeance. It was that or break down completely. "It's more complicated than that, Pep. He's got an enormous responsibility to sort out here and I've got a life of my own, a ranch to run, two thousand miles away. I don't want to leave it. And, except for Shane—and you, of course—I have no reason to be here. I don't like it here now any more than I did when I was a kid. I don't belong. And, no insult intended, I don't want to belong. What I want is to go home. And that, for me, will always be Montana."

"So, what about when he gets done sorting it out? You heard him say he wasn't cut out to run the company. He'll get this all worked out and then he can come to Montana."

Darby smiled, even as the ache inside her grew. The more Pepper tried to make it sound doable, the more she realized what a sucker bet it would be for her to buy into even one shred of it. "He's not any more cut out to sit on a ranch than he is to be CEO of Morgan Industries. He's a wanderer. I don't think that's going to change."

"I swear," Pepper said, shoving a carefully folded shirt in the duffel. "You jump all over me for not taking initiative, and here you are, just giving up on something that could be the best thing in your life. Maybe Dad was right about you running away."

Darby gasped, then turned her face away for a moment when Pepper looked stricken, lifting a hand to ward off her apology. "No," she said, struggling to get a grip on her emotions. "He was right, and I caught on to that downstairs." She looked back at Pepper. "But I'm not running anywhere now. I'm just going home."

"Without me?" came a voice from the doorway.

Darby and Pepper both swung around to find Shane filling the doorway. "I knocked this time, I swear. I guess you didn't hear me."

Pepper stood up, smoothed her hair and clothes in that instinctive way she had whenever a man was present. "I guess I'll leave the two of you alone."

Shane smiled at her. "Thanks. You might want to get back there. I passed a couple of agents in the hallway. Seems Bjornsen slipped past the authorities at the airport."

"Dammit!" Pepper scooted past him to the door, then paused and placed her hand on his arm. "Could you please talk some sense into her?" She jerked her chin toward Darby. "She's hardheaded as hell and she's in love with you, even if she won't admit it."

"Penelope Pernell Landon!"

Pepper just sent a little pinky wave back at her sister. "That would be me. But you know? I'm thinking it's time I lose the whole Pepper thing. I'm a woman of intrigue now. What would sound exotic, yet professional?" She tapped a French-dipped nail tip against a still perfectly painted and outlined bottom lip. "I'll have to think about that." Eyes twinkling with renewed excitement, she reached up and kissed Shane on the cheek. "I'll welcome you to the family, even if no one else will. And honestly, we don't always point guns at one another or act so melodramatically. Okay, so we do that last part. But I promise to keep the firearms out of Dad's reach whenever possible."

"That's reassuring," Shane said with a smile.

Pepper giggled and turned back to Darby and blew her a kiss. "Don't leave without saying good-bye, promise?"

"Promise," Darby said, already shaking her head as she watched her sister close the door behind her. *Look out world*, was all she could think.

And then she was alone with Shane.

He moved into the room, but didn't come directly to her. Instead, he leaned against the wall beside the bed. He nodded to what she was wearing. "I like you in that best, Cinderella."

Darby knew she had to be strong, be rational, not give in to silly emotions that would only make things harder down the line when the end inevitably came. And still, his words started a warm flush inside of her. *Might as well soak 'em up while I can*, she thought. It wasn't likely Tugger or the horses were going to be dispensing compliments anytime soon. "Thanks. I finally feel like me again for the first time in eons."

"I don't know, you felt a whole lot like you last night. And early this morning."

"Yeah, well." She paused in her packing. "Even that seems like eons ago."

Shane motioned to her activities. "Looks like it's going to be another eon or so before it happens again. Unless you're just planning on moving all this to my wing."

"Is that an invitation to stay?"

Shane pushed off from the wall, all his casual, laid-back charm disappearing in a blink. He took her by the arms, not entirely gently, and spun her to face him. "I guess I didn't think you'd need one," he said with a quiet calm that belied the storm in his eyes. "I thought I'd made it pretty damn clear that I don't want our time together to end."

"Until when? Until you get things done here? Until you get itchy feet and take off again to parts unknown? And then what do I do? Just forget about you? Wait around for the postcards?"

His anger dissipated in the face of hers. His hands stroked her arms, then he pulled her roughly against him, enveloped her against his chest. He buried his face in her hair and held on as if for dear life.

Darby's heart leaped foolishly in her chest, and yet she was simultaneously terrified. Because she wanted, more than anything, to hold on to him, too. She pushed his head back, framed his face with her hands, made herself look him in the eyes. Made herself say the words she didn't want to say. "I don't want to end this, either. But I don't see where it could go. Pepper's right. I'm falling for you. Hard. And the longer it goes on, the more devastated I'm going to be when it ends. I'm not used to caring about anything but my horses and my ranch. And occasionally, my sister." Her attempt at dry humor bombed. "I'm not used to relying on anyone, or counting on anyone other than myself. Until you. You make it damn easy to care. It scares the hell out of me."

"It scares me, too." He stroked her cheek, and looked at her with such tenderness that the tears that had been threatening before rose once again. "Yes, I wander, but mostly because I never had anything, or anyone, that made me want to stay. I know the timing is awful. That things here are too complicated to even begin to think about. But I know I have to see it done, and see it done right. If not for me, or for Alexandra, then maybe for the ones before her ... and the ones after me." He brushed his fingers over her hair, wiped the tears from the corners of her eyes with the pads of his thumbs. "I don't know what that means, or what it'll take to see it done, to make sure it stays right, after I'm done and gone."

"You know I can't just hang around here while you do that," she said, her voice trembling. "I have a life to run, too."

He pressed his forehead to hers and sighed heavily. "I know. I don't know what to say. Except wait for me. In Montana if you have to." He framed her face again, locked gazes with her. "Just ... wait. I know I have no right to expect that from you. But I'm asking anyway."

"It's not like I have anyone else I'm running back to. But I ..." She trailed off as her heart caught, cracked a little. She looked back at him. "I'm not sure I can just sit around, with hope in my heart, that one day you'll come riding across the horizon."

He tried to smile, but it didn't reach his eyes. Eyes that were filled with fear—and with something that looked a whole lot like what she was feeling ... and trying damn hard not to. "You know, they have this invention. It's called a telephone. And E-mail. You do have a computer, don't you? I don't plan to lock myself into seclusion here."

Darby tried to squash the little leap of hope. Dangerous things, those little leaps. "So we have a long-distance relationship. And then what? You're planning on moving to Montana?"

"Jesus, you make things hard."

She started to push out of his arms, but he held her tight. She didn't bother struggling. "I'm just trying to be logical."

"Well, what I feel isn't logical, okay?" he said, almost at a shout. "What I feel is huge. It's overwhelming. And it's not going away, god-dammit."

Darby couldn't help it. She smiled. "So ... what? I'm just supposed to cave to the greater power of your love for me?"

He looked poleaxed for a moment. And if she wasn't feeling the exact same thing, she might have called him on it.

"I do love you, Darby," he said, almost in awe. "I want a life with you. On whatever terms you'll have me. You want me to walk away from all this right now, pledge my life to you on that ranch of yours, sight unseen? Fine. I'll do it. Just tell me one thing. Do you love me? Could you love me? Like that? Enough to walk away from that ranch of yours and live with me here? Or anywhere?"

"I—I—" She couldn't answer that. Not about the love part, that part she knew. She was pretty damn sure the absolute joy and gut-wrenching pain that were blooming inside her was exactly what love felt like. But the rest ... he'd caught her off guard. And she believed him. He'd do it. For her.

"Okay," he said quietly, when time spun out and she just looked at him helplessly. "I guess that's my answer." He leaned down, kissed her once, hard, on the lips. Lingered over another one, until she began to sigh, and he began to deepen it. Then he pulled away. "You're one hell of a woman, Cinderella. And don't let anyone ever tell you otherwise." And then he turned and walked out of the room.

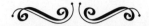

Cinderella Rule #24

*O*ccasionally, the right thing does happen at the right time. And you do get a second chance. For heaven's sake, don't screw it up!

—VIVIAN

$\mathscr{C}$hapter 24

$\mathscr{D}$arby sat on her back deck, feet propped up on the railing, and refolded Pepper's latest letter before tossing it on the table next to her. She smiled as she absorbed the beauty of the sun setting behind the distant snowy peaks. Fall was one of her favorite times of the year. It was only October and there was already a bite to the air. It was going to be a heavy winter, she predicted.

She sipped her beer and thought about what Pepper had said. Stefan's last-minute escape had haunted her sister these past months. She'd felt responsible, but helpless, and more than a little miffed that he'd gotten the best of her. The last they'd heard, he'd somehow managed to get his men out of Brazil, and was reported to be involved in some new deal in Russia. Which had been the final nudge Pepper had needed to take the plunge. Her sister was now in official training to be a real, bona fide agent. God help them all. But Darby smiled. "Go, Go Power Rangers!," she murmured.

Of course, other than promising her sister that this mysterious agency she worked for only took on "good guy" assignments, Pepper still couldn't tell Darby where she was training, or even the name of the agency itself. But it was clear she was having the time of her life. Even if the uniforms they made her wear made her butt look big.

Pepper had gone on to say that, while their father would still rather she marry wealthy and chair committees at the club, he'd grudgingly admitted that she was a grown woman who could make her own mistakes. Darby and Pepper both knew he was holding out hope that they'd flunk her from training and she'd have to give it up.

Darby also knew that was likely the one thing that would keep her sister from failing. She sighed and closed her eyes. At least their father was trying. In his own way. She recalled the day, a little over three months ago, about a month after she'd come back, when a long black car had pulled down the drive. And her father had shocked her by stepping out, hat in hand. It hadn't exactly been a heartwarming homecoming. He was clearly uncomfortable being there, and their conversation had been both stilted and heated at times. He'd only stayed one night, and that at a hotel. She'd met him in town the following morning for breakfast before he left. He'd refused to talk about his other life, other than to ask her to talk some sense into her sister. She'd made some smart-ass comment. And they'd parted, not really any closer than they'd been when he'd come.

Except . . . Darby had watched him, that one evening he'd been on the ranch, when he wasn't aware of it. She'd been upstairs in her room, changing into clean jeans, and she'd spied him from her window as he'd walked out back to the stables. She'd watched as he wandered in and out of the barn. He hadn't so much as glanced at the property, or asked anything about the place during their conversation down in the living room. So it had surprised her to see him back there. Until she'd remembered. Duh. That was probably where he'd met her mother. Right out in those stables. And it explained a great deal about why he'd kept the stables filled and running back home.

He was not a man to show emotion. Much less grief. She'd found herself wondering what he was thinking as he wandered the aisles. Was he remembering the good times, about how it had felt to fall in love? Or had he cursed her, like he'd done when Darby had been a child, for daring to leave him like she had? As if she'd died young just to make his life difficult. He'd been back in the living room when she'd come downstairs. He didn't mention his stroll, and she hadn't brought it up.

She sighed now and tilted her chair forward. She supposed she should be happy that he'd made any effort. Perhaps, over time, they'd figure out a way to communicate with each other. "Yeah," she muttered, "a century or two might do it."

She stood, finished off her beer, and scooped Pepper's letter off the table. Pepper had asked the same question she always asked: When was Darby going to stop "being as hard-assed as Dad" and fly back to see Shane? Somehow, despite being holed up in some super secret training facility, she'd managed to keep track of Washington society. Pepper was probably the only trainee who had convinced the brass to send in *Town & Country* and *People* magazine, she thought dryly.

Her smile faded as she let herself into the kitchen. She stared at the phone, then shook her head. Pepper made sure she kept up on how Shane was doing. And tortured Darby with every last detail.

He'd apparently made good on his promise to talk with her father and his team. Pepper had said that, in return for his complete cooperation, and because the Celentrex technology had remained secure, they'd made sure no scandal had ever surfaced. Darby knew he'd gone on to accomplish what he'd promised, which was to dismantle Morgan Industries into a number of successful, smaller companies, none of them with any ties to him.

Thanks to Pepper, she also knew he'd kept Four Stones in the family by turning it over to the Morgan Foundation, to use as their base of operations, with the clause that he, or any future family member could reclaim it for personal use whenever they saw fit. And God knew what contacts her sister had used, but she'd also found out that although he'd conceded to maintaining his obligatory position on the board of the foundation, which demanded he be directly involved in decisions about how the money was granted, he'd gotten a major concession of his own: His first order of business had been to insist the quarterly board meetings be held poolside at Four Stones, bathing suits mandatory. Thinking back to some of the foundation mucky-mucks she'd run into at the party, she shuddered at the visual that had accompanied that little revelation.

She also knew he'd auctioned off the other Morgan assets, funneling the money into a trust for the maintenance of the house. For a guy who didn't think he was cut out to run an empire, he'd sure done a bang-up job of preserving the best parts of the one he'd been given, she thought, rubbing at the nagging ache in her chest.

Darby never responded to her sister's comments or stories about Shane. She didn't want Pepper to know that she shamelessly clung to every tidbit. Or that, from the moment he'd walked out of that room in Four Stones, she hadn't heard from him. Not once. No phone calls. No E-mails. Not one telegram. Or a single smoke signal. Not that it mattered, of course. It was what she'd wanted. Right? A clean break. So her heart could mend.

Which was such a crock of shit. Her heart was as stupidly, foolishly caught up in Shane Morgan as it had been from the moment she'd laid eyes on him. She told herself time and time again she'd done the right thing. For both of them. She'd be miserable in D.C. He'd hate being stuck out here in the middle of nowhere. And yet, she couldn't seem to stop thinking about him. And wondering what if . . .

Apparently her malaise was more apparent than she'd thought. Tugger hadn't said anything at first, but he'd finally told her to either get over it, or get on a goddamn plane. Pepper had said much the same thing, not because she had a clue how her sister still felt, but because—as she'd just relayed in this very letter—Shane had wrapped everything up and would probably be leaving town soon. And she'd have no way of keeping track of him any longer. Darby had already thought about that. A lot. And it didn't take Dr. Phil to explain what that constant little clutch in her chest was trying to tell her.

She looked at the phone again. What would it solve? she asked herself for the millionth time. Nothing had changed. Sure, he was done in D.C. Had freed himself up to do anything he wanted. He'd be leaving town any moment now. If he hadn't set off already.

So. Did she want him to come here? Sweep her off her feet? Take her around the world with him? Was that it? Was that what she wanted? Adventure? Excitement? She stared unseeing out the back window. She didn't want to give up her ranch. But there was no denying that since her little stint in D.C., life here had seemed to lack a bit of . . . color. It was still rewarding, still fulfilling. But there was something missing now. And she suspected it was more than just the alone part. The part about not sharing it with anyone else. She wasn't cut out for Washington. But maybe, just maybe, she wasn't cut out for holing up in the middle of nowhere, alone with her horses for the rest of her life, either.

She snatched the phone off the hook and punched the number for the operator before she could question if she'd truly lost her mind. "Bozeman Airport," she said when the woman answered. "Yes, connect me please. Thanks." Her hands were shaking. Both in abject fear over what she was about to do . . . and the fact that she was willing to fly somewhere—anywhere—to do it. If that wasn't love, she didn't know what was.

"Yes," she said, voice shaky, when a young man answered the phone. "I want to book the first flight you have for Washington, D.C. I don't care which airport." She looked around blindly for a pen, then scribbled the information he gave her on the side of the box of Cheerios she'd left on the table. "Yes, yes, thank you." She dug out her credit card and rattled off the number, then thanked the man, hung up . . . and promptly buried her face in her arms. "Dear God in heaven, what the hell am I doing?"

She sat like that for too long, anxiety growing to almost paralyzing proportions as she tried to imagine herself striding into Four Stones and announcing to Shane that she'd been wrong, that she was, in fact, willing to give it all up for him. What if he was already gone? Or worse—

Her head shot up. What if he'd already found someone else? "Shit, shit, shit. Why didn't I think of that?" Of course he hadn't sat around like she had, pining like a pathetic, asinine, lovesick fool. The utter silence coming her way from Washington should have been her first clue.

She immediately grabbed the phone, started punching in the numbers for the airport. She'd been an idiot to think she could wait this long, then just stroll back into his life. She simply had to get over this. Over him. Get a new life. She'd take up square dancing or something. Smitty's wife gave lessons down at the hardware store in town after hours, she'd heard. She could find a hobby. Knitting, stamp-collecting. Something, anything. But she wasn't about to go chasing after some man and make a giant fool of herself. She had her pride, right?

She'd punched in the numbers three times and still hadn't gotten it right, and was swearing even as the tears trickled down her cheeks. Then she heard the dogs outside begin to bark and smacked the phone onto the table and shoved out of her chair to see what the ruckus was about.

"Great, just great." Who in the hell was showing up now? Probably just one of her boarders, wanting to spend time with their horse or go for an evening ride. She stood and looked out the back window, to see which boarder it was, hoping it was a long-timer, so she wouldn't have to go out.

But it wasn't a car that had pulled up, or a truck. It was someone already on horseback. The nearest ranch was a good ten-mile ride away, so it wasn't impossible that it was a neighbor, but it was unlikely. Besides, she didn't recognize the mount, or the rider. She pushed out the back screen door to her porch, absently wiping her face dry on her sleeve. "Excuse me, can I help you?" she called out.

The man was wearing a deep-brimmed cowboy hat that cast his face into shadow. He was a good-sized man, and Darby admitted he filled out his duster pretty nicely. Sat his mount pretty well, too.

"I came to see if you were looking to hire."

Darby froze. No way. She was hallucinating. Or she'd had more of a complete breakdown back in her kitchen than she'd thought. Because that voice sounded just like—

He doffed his hat then.

"Shane?" Her heart beat so fast she clutched her hand over it to keep it from busting through her shirt.

"Ah," he said, crossing his heart with his hat, "I see my name precedes me. Yes, I am Shane Morgan. At your service. Now, I know you probably heard I was something of an upstart. But I do have experience in ranching. Of course, it was llamas in Argentina. And then there was that emu farm in Tasmania. But horses can't be all that different, can they? I could get references." He grinned. "Probably."

Darby just stood there, balling her flannel shirt into a knot, trying to process that he was really and truly right there in front of her. Here. He was here. It was the grin that snapped her out of it. Oh, how she'd missing seeing that face.

"References, hm?" she said, not sure where in the hell she found the aplomb to pull it off. "Well, unfortunately, I'm not hiring at the moment. As it happens, I just scheduled a trip out of town. There's someone in D.C. I was hoping had waited for me. You see, I can be somewhat of an upstart myself. Not to mention a little hardheaded. Okay, a lot hardheaded," she amended when he arched one brow. She fought to keep it together. She had to get through this. She owed him that much, at the very least. "And when he gave me the chance to have everything I ever wanted, I blew him off, because I was afraid to take the chance. I was looking for the sure thing. But ... I guess I realized when I watched my dad wander helplessly around my barns a few weeks later that there is no sure thing. At any given moment, your whole world can be turned upside down. And I'd foolishly thought that if I didn't risk the danger of heartbreak, that it would never happen to me again." She wrapped an arm around her middle, fighting for the courage to finish. "Only it did. My whole world turned upside down during the space of one limo ride. Only I was too foolish to see it, to believe in it. So now I'm miserable. And my heart is breaking anyway. It doesn't seem to want to stop. So . . . I thought I'd go tell him that. Only . . . only I hadn't heard from him and I wasn't sure he'd waited for me. And I couldn't blame him if he didn't. But—but you see, I love him. With everything I have in me that's capable of it ... and if maybe, just maybe, we told the people we love that we love them, you know, more often, or even ever, then we'd all be a lot happier. No matter where we live. Or what we do. You know?" She fought to keep her legs from shaking. But it felt like her whole life had just opened up again ... in a giant yawning chasm of doubt and anticipation ... and she was scared to death she'd screw it up. Again. "Say something," she whispered.

He looked at her, his own eyes glassy with emotion. And said the only two words she needed to hear. "I waited." And then he was sliding off his horse and she was climbing over the porch railing.

She leaped, he caught her in midair. She wrapped her legs around him as he swung her around.

They were both laughing and a bit dizzy when he finally set her down. She touched his face, his lips. "You're really here."

"Well, I know how you hate to fly," he said wryly, but gazing at her so intently, and with such open adoration, she could feel it all the way to her toes. "I thought I'd save you the hassle."

"You saved me. You have. Oh, Shane." She couldn't wait. She pulled his mouth to hers, fell into his kiss, which was a thousand times more wonderful than she'd remembered, dreamed about, moped endlessly over ... and never thought she'd have again.

"I missed you, Cinderella," he said.

"Yeah, me, too," she said, reveling in his hands on her. "So," she said, sniffing a little as she tilted her head back. "Emu-ranching, huh?"

He shrugged. "It was a few years back, but I'm pretty sure it will all come back to me."

She grinned, but even knowing she wanted to take the next leap, she still had to take a little breath to steel herself to do it. "Well, I don't know. Maybe we need a refresher course."

"What, you thinking of expanding your operation here? I'm not sure emus like the northern climate."

"Actually," she said, holding his gaze steadily, finding her strength right there in his eyes. "I, uh, I was thinking about a firsthand refresher course. I've never been to Tasmania."

Shane stilled. "Darby, you don't have to—"

"I might not be cut out to be a Washington socialite," she said, far more steadily this time. "Or an undercover spy. But being with you ... well, I realized I had cut myself off from a lot of what life might have to offer me outside this ranch. So ... I propose a deal."

He leaned down and kissed her hard and fast. "Done."

She laughed, feeling giddier and more lighthearted than she could ever remember being in her whole life. "You haven't even heard it yet."

Shane just smiled. "Sweetheart, I have the whole deal. Right here." He squeezed her. "It's more than I could ever want. The rest is a bonus. I love you, Darby Landon of the East Coast Landons. I'm sure that my life will always be an adventure with you."

"You think?"

He tipped her chin up. "I know." He kissed her, only this time it was long and slow.

"I love you, too, Shane Morgan."

He sighed. "And my life is complete." He swung her around again, making her squeal. "Do we have to do this emu research right off?"

"Um, no. No, not at all," she said, reading quite accurately the look in his eyes. "It can wait."

"Good." He swung her up in his arms. "Because I can't. Four months without you was cruel and unusual punishment, and I'm telling you right now, I'm never going through that again."

"On that we're in total agreement."

He carried her toward the house, his stride determined.

"The tarnish on your armor is showing," she said, noting the gleam in his eye.

"And here I thought you wanted Prince Charming on a horse."

"Why would you think that? It's the tarnish that got me in the first place. Well, that and the way you kissed me in the back of that limo. Of course, if you promise to occasionally let the Dark Knight out, you can be as princely as you want. You do look awful cute in those chaps."

His grin did lethal things to her pulse. "You happen to have a hammock?"

"Very funny," but she was laughing, and planning on just where she'd hang one, as he pushed through the kitchen door.

"The bedroom is that way," she said with a nod of her head as he kicked the door shut behind them.

"We'll get there, Cinderella," he said, and sat her on the kitchen counter instead.

"Shane!" she said, smacking at his hands as he started peeling off her shirt.

"As it turns out, I'm not all that princely."

She started to laugh, then gasped as he pulled her bra down and ran his tongue immediately around one nipple, then the other. He started to lift his head, but she clamped her hands in his hair and kept him right where he was. "As it turns out, Cinderella doesn't really want a prince."

"Then I guess we're going to live happily ever after, after all."

"Oh, yes." She arched her back as he trailed his mouth lower, closed her eyes, and smiled. "Deliriously so."

Cinderella Rule #25

*L*ife is not a fairy tale. We're not all Cinderellas. And sometimes Prince Charming wears Hawaiian flowered shorts while riding his trusty steed. But there can be happy endings. You just need work at finding yours ... and then hang on to it. Even if it means you wear the pants in the family. Some of the time. (Those Hawaiian shorts are pretty comfortable.)

—DARBY LANDON MORGAN
GLASS SLIPPER GRADUATE

Epilogue

"o. Absolutely not." Darby smacked Shane's hand away from the phone. "No, I won't let you talk to Shane. He's as bad as you are."

"Oh, come on," Pepper wheedled. Or, Pen, as she liked to be called now that she'd finished training and had been unleashed on the world.

"You still owe me a foaling season," Darby reminded her. Again. "Convenient that you happen to be on a mission every time that rolls around, huh?"

Pepper ignored her. Again. "You have to admit that you guys had a good time on our last case."

"Good time?" Darby all but shrieked. "I was on my freaking honeymoon! And you had us racing around the desert on camel-back."

"Which you were really good at, remember? And tell Shane that trick he showed me, about distracting a charging bull, came in really handy in Spain last month."

Darby just sighed and flopped her head back on the pillow. Pressing the phone to her chest, she turned to her husband of six months. "She's hopeless. It's amazing the world still turns on its axis with her in charge of international safety. We should have never caved in to her that first time. I swear to God, when I said I wanted adventure—"

Shane snagged the phone from her. "Hey there, Pen. Listen, we've got to hang around here this time out. We're right in the middle of breeding season." He paused, then said, "Uh-huh, sure, anytime. They're just like most men, easily distracted by something flashy."

Darby elbowed him in the stomach.

He *oophed* a little, then said, "Right. Okay. Hey, any word on you know who?" He sighed. "Yeah. I know. You'll get him one of these days. Yep. I'll tell her. We love you, too." He hung up, then wrestled Darby under the covers, until they were both laughing.

Darby rolled him to his back when they finally came up for air. "How do you do that, anyway?"

"I thought it was pretty self-explanatory," he said, amused.

"Not that, Mr. Hammock Hockey. I mean, get my sister to back off without so much as a whimper. She never listens to me like that. She didn't pull her little sniffles on you, and you didn't have to yell, then cry all over me about how guilty she makes you feel when you don't give her what she wants."

He shrugged. "It's a gift, what can I say."

"And what was that about breeding season? It's not breeding season for another two months."

Shane rolled her to her back. "I wasn't talking about horses."

"Oh, well, because—" She broke off, her eyes going wide. "What? We haven't even celebrated our first wedding anniversary yet."

"Yeah, but it took me two years to get you to agree to marry me."

"And if I'd known you were going to let the godmothers do the wedding, I might have held off another three or four. Or ten."

"They loved doing it, and you know it meant a lot to them. Besides, we did eventually get all the costume stuff off the horses. Although Rookie still has a strong aversion to ostrich feathers."

Darby just rolled her eyes.

Shane chuckled. "Come on. We don't have to start now. But just start thinking about it, okay?"

"I'll think about it," she said grudgingly. "But you finally get me over my fear of flying, and now you want to trap me here with babies."

"Babies can travel."

She thought about that.

Shane pressed his advantage, and pulled her beneath him. "We'll just practice for now, okay?"

"Okay," she said, tucking her ankles behind his. "Just promise me one thing."

"Done."

She smacked him. "You always do that."

"I usually like your deals."

"No letting the godmothers plan any baby showers."

He thought about that. "Can they baby-sit for us when we want some travel time alone, just the two of us?"

"Absolutely."

"Done." He rolled to his back and pulled her on top of him. "See, I told you I was easy to live with."

Darby thought about the ranch outside. The one that had turned into a small zoo, with all kinds of exotic pets, some of which she still couldn't name. Then there were the wounded animals in the rehab shelter he'd built with the forestry guy he'd become buddies with. And the bunkhouses he was building for the camp he wanted to run that summer.

She didn't know why she'd worried about Shane needing to leave home for adventure. He'd just brought the adventure home to live with them. And she wouldn't have him, or her life, any other way.

"I'll show you easy," she said. And wrestled him back under the covers.

about the author

Once upon a time, Donna Kauffman was born in Washington, D.C. Alas, there were no glass slippers in her closet, but fate was kind, and a trustworthy (and totally hot) knight did cross her path. No fool she, Donna didn't need a fairy godmother to point out a good thing when she saw it. Their happily ever after is currently taking place in Virginia.

Did **THE BIG BAD WOLF TELLS ALL**
leave you howling for more?
Are you all brushed up on your
CINDERELLA RULES?

Then turn the page . . . and take
a sneak peek at what happens when
DONNA KAUFFMAN gets her
hands on a fairy tale.

Dear Prince Charming

Coming from Bantam in
Summer 2004

Donna Kauffman

Author of *The Cinderella Rules*

Dear Prince Charming

Dear Prince Charming

Coming in Summer 2004

Trust. A key element in successful relationships
is honesty. Namely, being able to detect when your
significant other isn't practicing it.

—Eric Jermaine, aka Dear Prince Charming

chapter 1

No. You can't be serious." Valerie Wagner put down her salad
fork and dabbed a linen napkin at the corners of her mouth, careful
not to smudge L'Oreal's #101 Beige Toscane lipstick. At nine dollars
a tube, she figured it should at least last through lunch. She was
worth it, but only up to a point.

"I'm sorry," she said weakly. "I must have misunderstood you.
Because I could have sworn you just told me that you're—"

"Gay."

No. This was not happening to her. She hadn't pissed anybody off,
stepped on any toes, or done anything wrong. This time, anyway. Her
karma was finally on an upswing. Mercury wasn't in retrograde. Life
was actually beginning to make sense. At thirty, she deserved to have
her life finally make some sense. Didn't she? Come on!

But, no. Eric Jermaine, the wildly popular Dear Prince Charming
advice columnist and bestselling author, known to women all over
the planet as proof positive that understanding, nurturing men did

indeed exist; the same gorgeous, suave man she'd wheeled and dealed into signing a seven-figure contract that guaranteed they'd both be making rent for the near and distant future, the man on whom her hard-won career now rested ... was the very same man presently sitting across from her, insisting he was more than just a guy deeply in touch with his feminine side.

His beautiful features were the picture of abject apology as he reached across the table to take her hand. Strong, comforting, sincere. "Yes, I did," he said, his blue eyes so heterosexually piercing, his deep voice so reassuringly masculine and calm. "I thought I could go through with this, Val. I thought this was the only way to get my life back. Hell, to get a life at all. But now that it's here, I can't do it. I can't screw you over like that."

"Except ... you are." The ruination of her finest moment, her one triumph, hit like the proverbial ton of bricks. Valerie slumped back in her chair. "Prince Charming ... is gay," she intoned. "The man who proved a guy exists who is actually interested in women as human beings first, and sex objects second ... is gay." She hung her head. "Like we shouldn't have seen that coming."

"Valerie—"

She held up a hand, staving off the inevitable for at least one more brief moment. Trying to digest both a tofu salad and the end of the world as she knew it was going to take her a little more time. "Gay," she said again. As if repeating it would somehow negate the absolute horror of the situation. Not that she didn't adore gay men. They were the ones she turned to for an honest answer to two of life's most burning questions: "Does this tight skirt make my ass look J. Lo curvy or like the rear end of a truck squeezed into spandex tubing?" And "What can I cook for my date that looks fabulous, tastes like heaven, guarantees me at least thirty minutes of foreplay ... and doesn't actually require, you know, cooking?"

Her gay acquaintances, however, weren't the ones who had signed a seven-figure contract, guaranteeing a successful magazine launch and sealing her career. They weren't the ones who'd agreed to take their infamously anonymous selves public for the very first time as cover boy and brand-new spokesperson for Glass Slipper, Inc. Eleven years spent dreaming of a job in the glamour industry, and another eight bouncing around fashion magazine publishing as everything from mail-room clerk to accessory stylist, she'd finally accomplished something worthy. Something to build a long-term career on. Fashion. If only she'd realized that was really a four-letter word early on, she could have saved herself decades of grief.

Eric sighed. "I know this comes as a shock to you."

"Shock? To me?" She let out a caustic laugh that Roseanne would have been proud of, one that, despite their discreet seating, had turned several heads. This wasn't L.A., where public scenes were looked upon as bonus entertainment. Nor was it Chicago, Boston, Dallas, or Miami. She knew. She'd worked at various magazines in all of them. National publications, trade publications. Fashion, gossip, and women's interest publications. She'd been in editorial departments, gophered for fashion executives, slaved for buyers. She'd tried marketing and even sales. None of them had been a good fit. Publicist was a new field. And, frankly, her last shot.

"I'd say this is more than a shock," she finally said. "This is a freaking disaster. With a capital freaking."

Just when she thought she'd finally found her calling, too. She remembered the day she'd gotten the call from Mercedes Browning, co-owner of Glass Slipper, Inc., the D.C.-based company renowned for performing what they called "life makeovers." She knew from the first day on the job that she'd finally found her niche in the fashion world she'd dreamed of being a part of since opening her first *Vogue* at age nine and thinking, "Hmm, spiky hair and raccoon eye makeup, there's an interesting trend."

Her fourth-grade teacher, Ms. Spagney, hadn't agreed. Valerie had been sent home with strict instructions to never scare the other students like that again. Privately, Valerie had always thought

Ms. Spagney herself could use spiky bangs. It would have done much to hide the deep grooves that came from too many years of frowning down at young, independent thinkers like herself.

But she'd been objective enough to see that maybe makeup artist and hairstylist weren't her strengths. So she'd stared down at her flat chest and thought … Hmm. Maybe she was runway bound. Valerie had been the only girl in her sixth-grade class secretly thrilled to not need a training bra. After all, she'd never walk the runways in Milan if she had boobies. Unfortunately, she'd forgotten about the height clause. By seventeen, even in wobbly four-inch heels and hair gelled to within an inch of its life, she barely flirted with the five-eight mark. Much less the five-ten she knew from her slavish devotion to *W* was the barest of industry standards.

Cruelly, the now-welcome boobies never had appeared.

Undeterred, she'd resolutely turned to design. If she wasn't made to model fashion, by damn she'd create it. Which would have been great, except that stick figures sporting triangle-shaped outfits weren't exactly going to win her any scholarships. And yet she'd hung in there, thinking she'd go for a degree in fashion merchandising and work for an upscale chain as a buyer. She envisioned trips to Paris, London, Milan. So what if the mere act of balancing her checkbook was·a struggle akin to formulating algebraic equations? It wasn't like she was going to be spending her own money.

Then, in her senior year of high school, the brokerage firm her father worked for transferred him to Chicago. She'd gotten a summer job with *Madame* magazine—for full-figured girls, not call-girl employers— though as switchboard operator she'd heard every hooker joke and pimp pun during the endless prank calls she'd fielded. She hadn't minded.

She'd found her people.

Obviously she'd just misinterpreted the gospel according to *Elle*. It wasn't what was on those glossy pages that mattered. It was the glossy pages themselves. Fashion magazines, the force that drove the

industry, decided what was hip and what was hopelessly last year. . . .
That was her true calling, her primary function, her niche.

Now, ten years, no degree, and dozens of primary—and
secondary—functions later, she was down to her last niche.

At the moment it was looking more like a gaping maw.

"Valerie? I wish you'd let me explain where I'm coming from. I'm
sure we can come to some acceptable agreement."

Agreement. She jerked out of her despondent reverie. They already
had an agreement. In fact, they had a signed contract.

She smiled. "You know, there is a little matter of possible contract
fraud here, Eric. Unless you're prepared to buy your way back out of this
deal." She leaned forward, propping her elbows on the table, enjoying
the way Eric blanched. Hey, it wasn't fair that she should be the only one
to suffer. "Your advance was, what, mid six figures? And that was what?
Five, almost six weeks ago? I hope you haven't been out shopping."

Looking deeply concerned now, Eric folded his arms on the table.
"I'm sure we can make this work if you'll only—"

"Are you saying you're still willing to be Glass Slipper's spokesperson? Willing to come out of hiding . . . without, you know, coming
all the way out? You've kept it a secret this long, after all. And trust
me, no woman alive will look at you and not be more than willing to
believe the fantasy."

He resolutely shook his head. "I can't live a lie any longer."

"Do you think your legions of readers will just accept that the man
of their collective dreams, the man who made them hope that one
day *their* prince would come riding up . . . the man they put up as the
example of all they wish their man to be, to their husbands and
boyfriends . . . is playing for the other team? You'd become a joke
overnight. Your credibility shot. It'd be one thing if you'd built your
reputation on your real self, but you didn't. Your whole appeal is
predicated on the fact that *you* know what women really want."

"But I *do* know what women want."

She gave him an arch look. "You just don't have any interest in actually delivering it to any of them."

"That doesn't mean my insights aren't dead-on. In fact, maybe they are precisely *because* of my sexual orientation."

"Then why didn't you just come out as our gay guidance counselor from the very beginning?"

Eric's broad shoulders slumped a little. "You have to understand how it started. I've always known I was gay. But I always had to hide it—I was captain of the football team in high school and college, for Chrissake! I had a lot of girlfriends, for show ... but I finally had to move across the country, to San Francisco, to meet anyone."

"Looking for your people," Val murmured, thinking of her own odyssey.

"Something like that," he said dryly. "And finally I started meeting men. And I hadn't the first clue how to react. You see, I'd spent so long with women as my closest companions, being their confidant, well, I knew all about what women wanted ... and not the first thing about what a man would."

Val just looked at him. He was really sincere. In fact, he seemed downright perplexed. It should have been funny, or at the very least ironic. That the man who'd successfully guided thousands of women to satisfying relationships with men couldn't guide himself into one. Instead it made her heart ache, just a little, for him. Dammit. "Don't you think, bottom-lining it, it's pretty much the same?"

"Maybe. I don't know. Before I could do anything about it, my mom's health went into serious decline and I came back home to take care of her. My dad died when I was in grade school. I was all she had. My mom's health had always been shaky, so I'd taken care of her pretty much all my life."

She liked him. Dammit. Even the whole momma's boy thing seemed somehow sexy on him. Really, really unfair. "Couldn't she have moved west with you?"

"Her friends were here. Her whole life had been spent here. It seemed cruel to take her away from all that. I knew she didn't have long. I got a job locally, nothing that really intrigued me, but it was a steady paycheck and allowed me time to care for her. I always figured I'd head back west, you know . . . after.

"Anyway, it was during that time that I got an email from a friend of mine from college, a woman friend. She was always talking about this group of women online that she chatted with regularly, they sort of all moaned about the dearth of good men, about meeting guys online, comparing notes, that kind of thing. This was five or six years ago, when online dating was still more scary than acceptable. But she got me to drop in, say hi. I know she was thinking she was going to hook me up with someone. She knew about my situation with my mom—"

"But not about your deep dark secret, I take it."

He shook his head. "That didn't matter to me. I was up for the friendship. And the great thing was, I didn't have to leave home to find stimulating conversation, laughter, fun. Even if it was all anonymous. In fact, it was the anonymity that I most loved. It was freeing, not demanding. It was exactly what I needed."

"And?"

"And that was where Dear Prince Charming evolved. Whitney knew me, but none of the other women did. She'd introduced me as the prince among men she'd let get away. As a joke, I initially signed on with the screen name Prince Charming, just to tweak her, but, I don't know, it caught on. I was just P.C. No one knew who I really was." He sighed a little, smiling now. "We talked a lot about male-female relationships and I ended up, as the default male, giving them advice. Who knows why, but my advice sort of caught on." He grinned. "Deflowering—so to speak—the accepted standards of various mating rituals. I think they liked my sense of humor, and I guess some of the things I said made sense to them. Someone joked about me doing an advice column for women. The Real Prince Charming. It was a joke, but after a while, I thought . . . why not?"

"So you started the online advice column as a joke?"

"No. No, I took it very seriously. But I don't think I ever saw it going anywhere. It was just, I don't know, fun. My life wasn't very fun at that time. I enjoyed the camaraderie. I had no idea it would take off like it did. I did some local radio call-in shows and I guess I sort of became a local celebrity. When the *Washington Post* offered a print column, I was shocked. Thrilled. Stunned. Fifteen months later, it was in syndication and I had a two-book deal with a major publishing house."

"And yet you remained anonymous that whole time. You're drop-dead good-looking and every woman in America and abroad is drooling over this secret prince—"

He gazed directly at her. "My mom passed away right around the time the *Post* picked up my column. I sold the house, bought a place in Adams Morgan, figured I'd keep the column anonymous, keep my name out of the public eye, in hopes I could finally get a private life."

Valerie tensed. "And did you? Are you telling me you have a boyfriend waiting in the wings I should know about?"

The self-deprecating laugh didn't erase the slightly haunted look in his eyes. "I wish. I became a victim of my own success. My anonymity had actually pushed my career further, faster. Speculation on who I was fueled talk, talk fueled book sales. It also fueled the tabloids. I was being hunted, or 'Prince Charming' was. I had recurring nightmares of the *Globe* sporting horribly lit photos of me taken at some gay leather bar on their front page." He shuddered. "I thought it would settle down at some point, that I could start going out socially. But then that meant either lying to the person I was seeing ... or risking telling the truth, which would've destroyed my career."

Valerie shoved her salad plate aside. "So, that brings us to now. Why did you take our offer to go public with your name and face?"

He hung his head now, then finally swore and lifted his gaze to hers. So damn earnest, those incredible blue eyes. "I decided late last year I couldn't do it any longer. It was eating me up. I had money, a fabulous lifestyle. I could do anything I wanted. And yet ..."

"You couldn't fall in love," she said quietly.

"Exactly. The trade wasn't worth it any longer. I was prepared to give it all up and just go quietly away."

"Instead you sign a deal for seven figures and agree to launch a national magazine by being its cover model. I'm sorry, but you'll have to tie the logic together for me."

His face colored, but to his credit, he didn't look away. "I've been making pretty decent money for a while. I won't lie. I've enjoyed it. Every penny. And then some."

Realization dawned. "You're in debt."

He held his thumb and forefinger close together, smiled sheepishly. "A little."

She mimicked his hand gesture. "A little?"

He moved his fingers farther apart. "Okay, a lot. I would've signed another book deal, but you came along with your offer instead. Book publishing is a long-drawn-out endeavor. This deal with you meant I could be done with all of this that much sooner. And, well, get paid sooner, frankly."

"You're contractually obligated to be our spokesperson for six months, with an option for a year extension. That's still a chunk of time."

"I figured those duties were going to dramatically decrease once I came out."

"And you'd be fodder for everyone from Jay Leno to Howard Stern for months."

He shrugged. "I didn't see any other way. Not really. And ... I guess, I don't know, I had some vague idea that by being up-front, giving my side of the story first, I might be like the famous actor who admits to drug use, or the athlete who admits to some wrongdoing and publicly repents his misdeeds."

She shook her head. She didn't want to smile, much less laugh.

"And here I thought it was my amazing people skills that won you over. You were my biggest coup, you know. It was like hitting the lottery first time out of the gate. My biggest fear was what I was going to do for an encore." The urge to smile faded. "Suddenly encores are the least of my problems." Val took a swig of white wine, wishing she'd gone for the Cosmopolitan after all. "Did you honestly think we'd keep to the monetary terms of the contract when you screwed us?"

His smile was fleeting. "I have very good lawyers. That contract is binding. As long as I hold up my end of the deal, which I was fully prepared to do. Technically, I wasn't in breach. My sexual orientation was never questioned. And any damage the magazine or Glass Slipper, Incorporated, might have incurred when it became public knowledge would not be my responsibility."

Valerie sank back in her seat. "You bitch."

He grinned then, wide and honest. "You know, it's the oddest thing, but I think that's the nicest thing anyone has ever said to me."

Valerie couldn't help it. She laughed. Gallows humor probably. "So." She lifted her hands, let them drop in her lap. "You had us cold. Why the sudden turnaround?"

The smile vanished. "As the time got closer and closer to actually doing the shoot and giving the interview, the guilt began to gnaw at me. I knew I couldn't go through with it. You've been nothing but fabulous to me. You and the Glass Slipper owners. I think what finally pushed me over the edge was finding out what this could mean to you careerwise—and what you had to lose if I was found out."

Valerie frowned. "How? I never talked to you about my career." Or lack thereof, she thought.

"I had a little chat with Aurora earlier this week. She called to see how things were going."

Aurora Favreaux was another of the three partners who owned and ran Glass Slipper. Along with Mercedes and Vivian dePalma, the three older women had played fairy godmother to countless women since beginning their business. While Mercedes was more Mother Superior and Vivian more ... well, Mae West came to mind, Aurora was Mother Earth. Swathed in her trademark chiffon, she was the understanding one, the nurturer.

"What did she say?" Valerie said. As far as she knew, all three women had been completely snowed by her presentation. And when she'd snagged Eric, she assumed they'd never guess she'd ever been anything but supremely confident about her abilities. And honest about her qualifications.

"It doesn't matter."

Valerie started to argue, but then realized he was right. It wasn't going to matter, since it was all going to come crashing down around her in very short order anyway.

"I've come to love all of you," he said. "I couldn't hurt you like that."

"You do realize it's too little, too late. You've already destroyed me. And God only knows what this will do to Mercedes, Aurora, and Vivian. They waffled for a long time on starting this whole project, but once they dealt with their various concerns, they've been totally gung ho. This magazine is their second child, their new dream."

"That's why I called you here. It's not too late."

"The shoot is fucking Monday, Eric," she said, finally, *finally* feeling the righteous anger flow through her. The denial stage was now officially over. "How in the hell do you expect me to salvage this … this flaming fiasco—emphasis on the *flaming*—in seventy-two goddamn hours?"

His smile this time was more tentative. Tremulous, some would say. Damn him. "I have a plan."

"A plan," Valerie intoned, not a little dubiously.

"Yes, a plan." He took a deep breath, squared his magnificent shoulders. "I may not be the Prince Charming you bargained for. But I know someone who is."

chapter 2

Jack Lambert was no Prince Charming. Just ask his ex-wife. Or, for that matter, any number of women dotting the globe. Charming, they might go for. Hell of a good time? Probably. But princely? That adjective wouldn't make anyone's list when it came to describing him.

"You sure you haven't been self-medicating?" Jack laughed and took a sip of beer. "I mean, it's been a long time, so nothing personal, it's just—"

"I'm dead serious," Eric responded. "I need your help. You know I wouldn't ask if there was any other way. Besides, this is going to be mutually beneficial. I have a solution to both of our problems."

Jack's current problem was unemployment. He was a sportswriter for an international newswire service, or had been until three days ago, when the service had been sold to the Reverend Yun Yun Yi, a right-wing religious zealot who made Reverend Moon come off looking like Mister Rogers. Jack had been stuck in Dubai at the time, writing about women's tennis. It had taken him two days and four flights to get back to his small apartment in Alexandria. Virginia, not Egypt. Although, since his divorce, it could have easily been either.

"What, exactly, could my sports background bring to the advice-for-the-lovelorn table?"

"My readers aren't lovelorn," Eric chided him. "They're intelligent, capable, caring women who are tired of being dicked around by the assholes of the world. That would be you, in case you were wondering."

"Hey, now. I never claimed to understand what women want. In fact, I willingly admit I have no idea what women want. And more to the point, I don't want to know. Frankly, the way women's minds work scares me."

"Well, when that woman was Shelby Morris, I agree. But not every woman's a psycho." Eric picked at the label on his bottle. "Did you ever stop to wonder why there's never been a steady woman—any woman, really—in my life?"

"Don't pull this lonely shit on me. You wrote a couple of touchy-feely books about understanding women's needs, and you and I both know they're crawling out of the woodwork, wanting nothing more than to spend some time with Mr. I'm In Touch With My Feminine Side. Hell, your motto since high school has always been 'Why Settle For One?' It's the greatest gig going, you're a fucking genius. I've told you that a thousand times."

"Yeah. I remember. But that was your assumption. I just never called you on it. It was easier to do what I've always done. Go along with people's assumptions. But—" He broke off, swore under his breath. "Okay, you know what? I can't find an easy way to tell you this. I've wanted to for years, but I was afraid it would, I don't know, ruin everything between us. But I'm in a jam, a really serious one, and so—well, maybe things happen the way they do for a reason . . . so I'm just going to say it straight out and trust you not to freak."

"What the hell are you talking about?"

Eric glanced at the bottles lining the edge of their table, then looked back at him and said, "The deal is, I need you to cover for me on a job I signed up for. Because . . . well, I'm outing myself."

"Fantastic, man! I never understood why you didn't do it years ago."

Eric's mouth dropped open, then he leaned forward. "You mean, you knew?" he asked, his tone almost hushed. "Why didn't you tell me?"

"What? Didn't I just get done telling you you've got nothing to worry about? I never understood the secrecy thing anyway." He laughed. "What, you're afraid you won't be able to handle them all when women can put a face with your name? Because if that's what you need help with, well, you've come to the right place."

Eric sighed. "There are no women, Jack. There won't *be* any women. Ever. I'm gay."

Jack was still laughing when Eric's words struck him. "I'm sorry, did you just say you were—"

"GAY!" Eric all but shouted. "Queer as the day is long. A raving homosexual. Why does everyone have to make this so goddamn hard?"

Jack looked around, but thankfully between the basketball game on the big screen and the guys shooting pool, no one was looking at them. Not that he cared really, he was just trying to buy some time, process information that was so totally foreign to any concept he could assign to his childhood buddy, that, well … Nope. More time wasn't helping. "What do you mean 'everyone,'" he said finally, latching on to the one piece of information he could process rationally. "Who have you told?"

Eric took a long sip, then propped his elbows on the table, bottle dangling between his hands. "You and Valerie. And I'm sorry I yelled. It's just, while this is a huge relief, it's also incredibly terrifying."

Still on rational processing time, Jack said, "Who the hell is Valerie?"

"She's the publicist for Glass Slipper, Incorporated. I just signed a contract to be the spokesperson for them in their new magazine. I don't know if you've heard of them, but they run a company that does makeovers—extreme, whole-life makeovers—mostly for women, but occasionally they handle—"

"Yeah, okay, got it." Jack massaged his suddenly throbbing forehead. "So …" He had nothing. His brain had locked up. Eric. The guy he'd known since they were both nine years old. Eric Jermaine. High school quarterback. Six-two, two hundred twenty pounds of manly man muscle. Jock of the Year. Total Chick Magnet from birth. A guy whose roof he'd lived under throughout high school. Gay.

Still not computing.

"Say something, man," Eric said quietly as the silence spun out.

"How … how long have you—you know? Known?"

"I did the denial thing through school, but I've probably known most of my life." His laugh was strained. "And if you're thinking about . . . you know, well, don't. You're not my type."

Jack plainly saw the strained tension beneath the attempt at humor. Guilt immediately replaced stunned disbelief. For Eric to carry such a huge burden for so many years and not feel he could trust him enough to tell him? Yes, that hurt. But more important, it made Jack feel like he'd failed the one person who meant more to him than anyone. "So," he said at length, struggling desperately not to let him down now. "I guess when we were up in your tree house reading *Playboy*, you really were reading the articles?"

Eric laughed and some of the tension lifted. "Pretty much."

"Why didn't you tell me sooner? And none of that bullshit about not trusting me. You know me better than anyone."

"Hell, Jack, I could barely admit it to myself. You—you are, for all intents and purposes, my brother. My only family. Bullshit aside, I care what you think. I—I didn't want you to think less of me."

"Jesus." Jack swore under his breath. "Do you think so little of me? Never mind. I'm pretty sure you're going to piss me off if we go any further there, so just shut up, okay? I know now, that's what matters. And, for the record, I'm not going anywhere."

Eric's sigh of relief was shaky. "Thank God. I know it might make things weird, but trust me, I'm still me. I just prefer—"

"Let's not go there, either," Jack said, not ashamed to admit it was going to take him a bit longer to deal with the visuals that accompanied this type of news flash. "Why are you telling me this now? Does it have something to do with this gig you took at a new magazine?"

"Yeah. I decided it was time to end the anonymous author thing, so I agreed to do a little PR for them, and write a monthly column as well. But I'm not willing to stay closeted anymore. I can't come *all* the way out without turning *Glass Slipper* into a national joke, not to mention ruining Valerie's career. So . . . I'm sort of hoping I can get you to stand in for me. Be a body double, so to speak."

"Excuse me? You want me to WHAT?"

"It's just one day of work. Someone has to show up at the cover shoot. It can't be me. Not the real me."

"When is this thing?"

"Uh . . . Monday."

Jack rubbed the back of his neck, not sure whether to laugh or curse a blue streak. He did a little of both. "If you aren't self-medicating, brother, you should be. Because only someone on massive quantities of drugs would even dream of asking me to do this. You're not a fucking genius, you're fucking insane. Even if I was willing—which I am not—we'd never pull off a stunt like this. You have to know that. Can't you just, you know, wait awhile longer? Until your contract is up?"

"No. I'm already well past that personal deadline. Besides, no matter when I do it, *Glass Slipper* will take a hit. And my career would be over. The genius of this plan is everybody gets what they want, and nobody gets hurt."

Unsure what to say, Jack finished off the rest of his beer.

"I know it's a lot to ask," Eric said quietly. "I know that."

"What were you thinking, agreeing to this? Never mind." Jack swore silently. He tried to put himself in Eric's shoes, but he honestly couldn't imagine it. He couldn't imagine living a life in denial, actively suppressing who he was. Yet Eric had done it for a lifetime. And in order to help him break free from that prison, all Jack had to do was help his best buddy out for a day or two. Put that way it didn't seem like all that much to ask.

Jack said nothing for several long moments, then blew out a long breath and said a silent prayer. "So, I don't actually have to dispense advice, or give interviews or anything."

Eric tried not to sound too excited when he responded. "We don't think so. You'll have to meet with Valerie, she's—"

"You don't *think* so? What do you mean you don't think so?"

"We can hammer out all the details tonight. We're having dinner at her place."

"Oh, we are, are we? Pretty sure of yourself there, Peter Pan."

Relaxed now, Eric smiled and leaned back. "Ah, so this is how it's going to be? I come out to my best friend and he makes gay jokes."

"You're making me prance around on a magazine cover as Prince Charming?" Jack stroked his chin, pretending to ponder, then grinned. "Pretty much, yeah."

Eric shrugged. "Deal. And you know I do intend to compensate you very well for your—"

"I don't want your money," Jack said flatly. There was no reason he couldn't look for a job while he did this thing for Eric. How long could a photo shoot take, anyway? "We both know how much I owe you."

"Hey, I never meant to pull that—"

"I know. Which is precisely why I'm not taking a red cent from you. You saved my life. The least I can do is give you back yours."

Eric was silent for a long moment.

Jack wasn't generally comfortable with emotional moments. Just ask Shelby. "Besides, if it's my face on the magazine, I'll get all the babes, right?"

"Like you need more. But yes, mercifully, you can have them all. And I am going to pay you. I have to, or I just won't feel—"

"I swear to God, if you mention money—"

"The contract was for seven figures. I can handle it, okay?"

Jack's mouth dropped open. No words would come out.

"I thought that would get you."

"Telling women what they want to hear is worth that many zeroes? Jesus, man. For that kind of smack, *I'll* tell them what they want to hear."

"Fine, except you'd have to know what that is," he joked. "Women actually *want* to hear what I have to say."

"Oh, so that's how it's going to be," he shot back, but Eric just grinned and downed the rest of his beer.

An hour later he was home, showering, in preparation for dinner with Valerie. The whole idea was totally insane. He'd known before leaving the bar they'd never pull something like this off. Which meant he had to come up with another solution to this mess. One that would keep Eric out of the press and out of court. And keep a certain publicist quiet.

And most important keep Jack off a freaking magazine cover.

As he soaped up beneath the hot spray, he wondered what this publicist of Eric's was like . . . and exactly what it was going to take for him to talk her out of suing his best friend for fraud. Jack might not understand women's minds, but he had a pretty clear understanding of their bodies.

Prince Charming Jack was not . . . but he definitely had other talents.